# THE EXILE AND THE SAVIOR

## Author's note:

*This book contains subject matter that might be difficult for some readers, including strong language, graphic sexual content, violence and gore, torture, colonial oppression, attempted sexual assault (not the main couple), domestic violence (off-page, not the main couple) depictions of mental illness, suicidal thoughts, animal death, loss of memory, and amnesia. Reader discretion is advised. The mental health of my readers is of utmost importance to me. If you feel that there is a trigger that is not mentioned above, please do not hesitate to contact me via the form on my website: kriskhainesbooks.com.*

For everyone who dares
to see the world the way they want to.
And is brave enough to fight for a better one.

# Pronunciation Guide

## *Characters*

Cassandra Fortin - kah-SAHN-drah FOR-tin

Tristan Saros - TRIS-tehn SAHR-ohs

Cael Zephyrus - kale ZEFF-russ

Xenia Cirillo - ZEE-nee-ah suh-RIH-loh

Alcander Pagonis - all-KAN-dehr pah-GOHN-iss

Alexei - ah-LECK-see

Aneka - ANN-ih-kah

Arran Zephyrus - AIR-ahn ZEFF-russ

August Lambros - [august] LAMB-brohs

Aurelie Lambros – OHR-ah-lee LAMB-brohs

Belen Erabis - BAY-lehn AIR-ah-biss

Borea (Mother Superior) - boh-RAY-ah

Byron - BUY-rihn

Cleo - KLEE-oh

Cora Aritia - KOR-ah ah-REE-tee-ah

Eamon Erabis - AY-mahn AIR-ah-biss

Hella - HELL-ah

Ione - eye-OH-nee

Isidora Pagonis - EES-uh-DOHR-ah pah-GOHN-iss

Laskaris - lahs-KAHR-ihs

Leonin Erabis - LEE-oh-nihn AIR-ah-biss

Maksym Rosopa - mack-SEEM roh-SOH-pah

Mila Erabis - MEE-lah AIR-ah-biss

Ohan Stolia - OH-hahn STOH-lee-ah

Psylbe - SIHL-beh
Reena - REE-nah
Richelle Pacha - rih-SHELL PAH-chah
Roeki - ROH-kee
Ronin Matakos - ROH-nihn mah-TAH-kohs
Sister Jorina - [sister] joh-REE-nah
Trophonios - truh-FOHN-ee-uhs
Varuna Lykan - vah-RUHN-ah LIE-kan
Zakariah -ZACK-ah-RYE-ah

*Places*

Akti - AHK-tee
Brachos - BROCK-ohs
Cernodas - SEHR-noh-dass
Delos - DEH-lohs
Diachre - dee-AHK-rah
Dordenne River - door-DEN [river]
Ethyrios - ih-THEE-ree-ohs
Icthian Mountains - ICK-thee-ahn [mountains]
Meridon - MARE-ih-dahn
Nephes - NEH-fehs
Primarvia - prih-MAR-vee-ah
Rhamnos - RAHM-nohs
Sea of Thetis - [sea of] THAY-tiss
Syvalle - see-VAHL-ay
Temple of Letha - [temple of] LEH-thuh
Thalenn - THAH-lehn
Typhon Mountain - TIE-fuhn [mountain]
Vaengya - VEHN-ghee-yah

## Terms

Adelphinae - ah-DELL-fee-nay

Aguaver - AAH-gwah-ver

Amatu - uh-MAH-too

Anaemos - ah-NAY-mohs

Aramaelish - ah-rah-MAY-lish

Arelinn - AIR-uh-lynn

Delirium - duh-LEER-ee-uhm

Dienses - DEE-ehn-sees

The Delphine - [the] dell-FEEN

*drachas* - DRAH-kahs

*Eurybia* - yoo-RIB-ee-ah

Faurana - fowh-RAHN-ah

*Inom Than* - ee-NOHM thahn

*lui ganeth, lui cathona* - lou-ee gah-NETH,
lou-ee kah-THO-nah

*Ma'anyu* - MAHN-yoo

*mei ganeth, mei cathona* - may-ee gah-NETH,
may-ee kah-THO-nah

Nemosyna - neh-moh-SEE-nah

Stygios - STIH-gee-ohs

Teles Chrysos - TEH-less KREE-sohs

Thakavi - thah-KAH-vee

Vasilikan - vah-SILL-ih-kan

Vestan - VEST-an

Vestian - VEST-ee-an

Vicereine - vie-sir-EEN

# Citizens of Ethyrios

## FAE

Nearly immortal, magical, humanoid beings. Descendants
of the High Gods.
Divided into three sub-species.

Windriders: Winged sub-species, both of feather and of
flesh. Ability to fly. Ability to manipulate air and control
wind. Descendants of Anaemos.

Beastrunners: Sub-species of mammalian bi-forms. Ability
to switch between beast and humanoid forms at will.
Descendants of Faurana.

Deathstalkers: Venomous sub-species. Ability to paralyze
another Fae with a bite from their three-inch fangs.
A full Deathstalker bite is instantly fatal for humans.
Descendants of Stygios.

## HUMANS

Mortal and non-magical. No sub-species.

# Gods of Ethyrios

## HIGH GODS

Anaemos: The Father, High God of Spirit and Sky

Faurana: The Mother, High Goddess of Land and Life

Stygios: The Reaper, High God of Death and Destruction

## GODS

Letha: The Stranger, Goddess of Oblivion

Nemosyna: The Chronicler, Goddess of Memory

Dienses: The Jester, God of Merriment

Amatu: The Lover, Goddess of Love

Vestan: The Warrior, God of War

Thakavi: The Scholar, God of Wisdom

Ker: The Killer, Goddess of Violence

The Fallen Goddess: Little is known about this Goddess, as her story has been stripped from Ethyrios's histories

# Territories of Ethyrios

## CONTINENTAL

Akti: Southern coastal region. Capital: Rhamnos.

Brachos: Northwest region. Capital: Diachre.

Cernodas: Western region. Capital: Aethalia.

Nephes: Central region and home to the Imperial Capital, Delos.

Northern Territories: Northeast region. Capital: Kheimos.

Syvalle: North central region. Capital: Thalestria.


## COLONIAL

Northern Colonies. Capital: Thalenn.

Northern Middle Colonies. Capital: Primarvia.

Southern Middle Colonies. Capital: Vaengya.

Southern Colonies. Capital: Meridon.

# CHAPTER ONE

A N EXPLOSIVE SILENCE HUMMED in Cassandra Fortin's ears, as if the Emperor's catastrophic greeting had blown her mind to pieces.

Tristan Saros was Emperor Erabis's brother.

Her rebellious, borderline treasonous friend—who had not only once caught her breaking the Empire's laws, but knew she'd committed many such crimes—was a member of the Imperial family.

Holy High Gods.

She'd kissed a member of the Imperial family.

Had done dangerously sexy things with a member of the Imperial family.

Was *living* with a member of the Imperial family.

She really needed to stop thinking the words *Imperial family* before she fainted.

Though the resemblance between the Emperor and the gorgeous, kind, funny warrior beside her was evidence enough, she found it hard to believe that Tristan was related to a male with such notorious disdain for humans.

The Emperor's only kindness towards her species in the scant two years of his reign had been his upholding of the Accords, the peace treaty that had forced the humans to abandon the continent and crowd together onto the colonies. A hefty price, but one they'd been all too relieved to pay, given the alternative—the decimation of their species due to unrestricted emotion feedings by the Fae.

Locked in some silent, psychological battle, neither Tristan nor the Emperor breathed or blinked as the tension thickened in Vicereine Lykan's stark, white office.

The Vicereine cleared her throat, gesturing to her leather chair. "Your Imperial Majesty, please have a seat. Take mine."

Emperor Erabis sniffed, breaking his brother's gaze and rustling his feathers—the gesture so reminiscent of Tristan that Cassandra's heart squeezed—then settled into the chair, intertwining his long fingers atop the glass desk.

Tristan refused to sit. "What the fuck are you doing here?"

Daggers shot from the Vicereine's ice-blue eyes.

"Oh, Tristan," the Emperor chuckled, stirring his short, unruly black waves. "Broadcasting your feelings as baldly as ever, I see."

"My hatred for you is not easily masked." Tristan's threatening grin exposed his sharp, snow-white canines.

"Sit *down.*" The Emperor summoned wind into the room, rattling the desk and blowing back Cassandra's hair. She toppled into her chair, and Tristan reluctantly followed.

The Vicereine remained standing, a portrait of unruffled calm. Already privy to Tristan's heritage, no doubt. She draped a hand on the Emperor's chair, behind his wings. A bold, familiar move that he did not correct.

"Why are you in the colonies?" The arms of Tristan's chair groaned as he clenched them.

"Is a ruler not allowed to visit his subjects?" The Emperor twirled an onyx ring on his finger, the one bearing the sigil of the Empire—a Typhon-steel broadsword bracketed by feathered wings and radiating lines.

Tristan scoffed. "You've been their *ruler* for two years and haven't deigned to set foot here."

"Maybe I just wanted to personally thank my dear brother for uncovering Councilor Rosopa's plot to overthrow me."

"I didn't do it for you." Tristan white-knuckled his fists into his thighs, refusing to meet Cassandra's questioning gaze. "Unfortunate side effect of saving several mortal women."

"Still harboring quite a fondness for them, aren't you?" The Emperor eyed Cassandra, his upper lip curling. She returned a blank look, unwilling to let him believe he'd insulted her. "Based on those doe-eyes she's aiming at me, she didn't have a clue who you were, did she?"

Cassandra bit her tongue, fighting the urge to lash out at him for speaking about her as if she weren't even there. But she didn't dare look to Tristan, didn't dare confirm that the Emperor had guessed correctly.

*The Emperor's fudging brother.*

Her heart hammered in her chest.

"What is she to you?" the Emperor asked.

"Not that it's any of your fucking business, but she's my partner. Mistress Fortin played an instrumental role in uncovering that plot you mentioned. Though, I'm sure the Vicereine has informed you that Maksym and Richelle Pacha have escaped with everything they need to fulfill their plans. So there's hope yet that Ethyrios could be rid of you."

"Watch it, Tristan," the Emperor whispered, his voice simmering with low menace. "Our shared blood will not spare you an execution."

Tristan finally, wisely, shut his mouth.

"And you misspoke, brother," the Emperor continued, leaning back and resting his hands on his stomach. The Vicereine followed his movements with hungry eyes; her tastes must run in the family. "They do not have *everything* they need to carry out their plans.

There is one piece still missing. And you are going to fetch it for me."

Tristan expelled a bitter laugh. "As if I'd willingly help you."

The Emperor ran his cool, hazel eyes down Cassandra's body, his lips pinched. "Maybe it *is* time I see what all the fuss is about. I've never taken a mortal lover. Rather gauche in Delos. "

Tristan flared his wings, his span so broad that the tips of his feathers touched the wall and opposite window. "You wouldn't fucking *dare*, Eamon."

The combined power of the two males stirred the room into a trembling frenzy, rattling the windows, bookcases, and glass tabletops.

The Emperor whispered into his palm, then opened it towards Tristan.

The message contained with the Emperor's gust stole Tristan's fight. His wings collapsed and his head bobbed onto his chest. "What would you have me do?"

A satisfied smile spread onto the Emperor's cruel, handsome face. "Surely you've already guessed. Varuna led me to understand it's the very reason you've come here today.

I want you to bring me that necklace."

*Cooperate or I will end your human. Don't forget what happened the last time.*

Tristan thanked the High Gods that Cassandra couldn't hear his brother's windwhisper.

He should have warned her, should have told her about his ties to the Emperor. But he was terrified she'd close herself off to him. Label him as just another terrible member of his terrible family.

This was certainly not how he wanted her to find out that he was an exiled Prince of the Empire.

Despite the anger coursing through him, his brother's words seeped through.

*I want you to bring me that necklace.*

"That's *not* why we're here. We've come to request additional resources to aid in the rescue of Sister Cirillo and Officer Zephyrus. Cael's father is one of the Empire's staunchest supporters. He'd be furious to learn you're not lifting a finger to find his son."

Eamon leaned forward, resting his forearms on the desk. "You underestimate me, Tristan. I've already spoken with High Councilor Zephyrus. A task force of warriors from Brachos is searching for his son as we speak."

Tristan exhaled a relieved sigh. He'd never met Cael's father, but the male's unflinching dedication to his sons was legendary. Arran Zephyrus would travel to the furthest reaches of Ethyrios to find Cael. Not to mention the Windrider and Beastrunner warriors of Brachos were the strongest trackers in the world. If anyone could find their friends, they could.

"Do they have any clue as to where Maksym might have taken them?" Tristan asked.

"They've narrowed the location to several regions on the *continent*," Eamon said with a sharp look. The message was clear; Tristan would not be permitted back there to assist with the rescue efforts. "You'll be of much more use to me here. We have no reason to believe the necklace has left the colonies."

Tristan had to agree. Sister Cora Aritia, Cassandra's fellow Shrouded Sister who'd hidden the real necklace wouldn't have had the time to journey to the continent and back before she'd been captured by Maksym's cronies.

Eamon continued, "I've doubled the security around the Thalassium seam along the Dordenne River. That necklace is the only means available for Maksym and Richelle to create their weaponized batch of Delirium. It's imperative we find it before they do."

The Vicereine fell to her knees beside Tristan's brother, bowing her head and dipping her golden wings. "Your Imperial Majesty, forgive me. I am ashamed this plot developed on my watch."

Eamon lifted her chin with a finger and ran a hand over her glistening blond hair. "I do not hold you accountable, Varuna. You've always been my most loyal subject." He pulled her from her knees and curled an arm around her waist.

What in the name of Stygios was going on here?

Tristan didn't really care. His brother hadn't yet taken a mate and was welcome to Tristan's sloppy seconds. But he couldn't help a shudder of disgust, envisioning Varuna as Empress. Luckily, the two heartless Windriders were too busy eye-fucking each other to notice.

"What about Makysm's lightning magic?" Tristan asked. He was surprised his brother hadn't yet brought it up. "Power like that hasn't been seen in Ethyrios for centuries. Do you have any idea how he acquired it?"

Eamon narrowed his hazel eyes. "Nothing you need concern yourself with at the moment. Just find me that necklace, or we will *all* suffer the consequences."

Cassandra cleared her throat and Tristan swiveled towards her.

The compassion in her blue-gray eyes nearly brought him to tears. But the underlying wariness made him want to howl, to tear the room apart.

"Your Imperial Majesty, Your Excellence, please allow me to assist Officer Saros." Her husky voice wrapped around him, soothing his rough edges.

Eamon sneered at her, and it was all Tristan could do to keep from smashing his brother's fucking head through the plate glass desk. "How could *you* possibly help, mortal?"

"I am a former Shrouded Sister," Cassandra answered, chin up, refusing to cower at Eamon's snideness. Her proud, calm tone heated Tristan's blood, made him ache for her even more desperately than he had been this past week.

He was adjusting, poorly, to the bittersweet torture of having her in his house while forbidden—by her own request—to touch her. A near-impossible concession, given he already knew how exquisite she tasted, thanks to their disappointingly brief trysts at the Temple.

"I'm in possession of a memory that, while scrambled, is said to reveal the necklace's location," Cassandra continued. "I am very close to interpreting it with my viewing powers, which I've temporarily retained despite having left the order."

Such careful phrasing.

If Eamon ever discovered the truth about Cassandra—Tristan couldn't even finish the thought.

"Show me your tattoo," Eamon demanded, snatching Cassandra's forearm and pitching her out of her chair.

A snarl ripped from Tristan's throat as he caught her around the waist before her chin smashed into the glass. He settled her onto her feet, smoothed her skirt, and ran a reassuring hand down her spine before reclaiming his seat.

He sensed her gathering retort and silently urged her to keep her mouth shut. He hated the thought of her stifling her snark—would love nothing more than to see her verbally flay his asshole brother. But to do so right now would be far too dangerous.

She pressed her lips together into a thin line, her body tense as Eamon examined her wrist.

"How long has it been since you left the order? Your tattoo has not faded at all." Eamon released her and she cradled her arm against her stomach.

"It's only been a week." Her voice was steady despite the insult, the audience, and the cautious lies she was weaving. High Gods, Tristan was in awe of her. "The tattoo will fade and my abilities will wane in another week or two without daily memory pulling. They'll have fully disappeared within the month."

"Best work quickly then," Eamon said.

"We leave for Meridon tomorrow to consult with the Artisan," Tristan chimed in.

The Artisan, a Turned Fae female and former Shrouded Sister with unique memory manipulation powers, had assisted Tristan and Cael in interpreting scrambled memories on a case they'd worked a few decades ago. He was certain she'd be able to help again.

Tristan couldn't stand to be in this room a moment longer. "Are we done here?"

"For now." Eamon waved a dismissive hand.

Tristan ushered Cassandra away from those monsters, dragging her through the door and along the hallway, down the spiral staircase, and out into the blinding sunshine.

"Tristan," she began, but he silenced her with a look before scooping her into his arms and flying them home.

He landed on the sidewalk outside his bungalow and pressed the key into her hand.

He needed time alone. Needed the wind to rip through him and numb his roaring emotions.

Eamon barreling back into his life after all these years had dredged up agonizing memories. Memories which, for the past two centuries, had lurked beneath his skin, ready to lacerate him at the slightest provocation. He was a fool to have ever imagined he'd moved past them.

Yet somehow, the concern on Cassandra's face as he launched into the sky cut even deeper.

# CHAPTER TWO

XENIA CIRILLO COULDN'T SLEEP.

Her insomnia hadn't been this bad in eight years.

Not since Cassandra's arrival at the Temple of Letha. Before then, Xenia had rarely enjoyed a full night of uninterrupted slumber.

Memories of the day she'd been ripped from her parents' arms would tear her from sleep, drenched and screaming. Her father's pleas would echo through her sleep-numbed brain, his wavering voice begging the red-jacketed Empire soldier to spare their only child.

Xenia could have asked one of her fellow Shrouded Sisters to remove the memory. But she couldn't bring herself to lose even those last, painful moments with her parents—no matter how much they tormented her.

As soon as Cassandra and Xenia had begun sharing a room, Cassandra's deep, measured breathing in the next bed chased Xenia's nightmare away.

On the nights Cassandra ran her missions, Xenia's sleep was long-coming and fitful—though she always pretended to be out cold upon Cassandra's return. Even threw in some dramatic snores.

But there was no one in this dungeon to perform for. No one's breath to lull Xenia to sleep.

So the nightmare came for her every night without fail.

Night, day, she wasn't sure of the time—there were no windows through which to track the sun.

Just filthy stone walls, an even filthier stone floor, and iron bars barely wide enough to poke her head through.

She'd tried when she first woke up here. And for a single, terrifying moment, thought she'd gotten stuck. She'd ripped her ears to shreds in a frantic attempt to free herself.

She hadn't tried that again.

If she pressed hard enough against the stone wall of her cell and angled her face just so, she could see a scarred wooden door at the end of the hallway.

The Deathstalker guards who came by twice a day to feed her entered and exited through it, so it must be the dungeon's only access point.

Based on the distance from her cell to the door, Xenia guessed there were other cells surrounding hers, but she could tell they were empty—she couldn't hear or smell anyone.

Torches lined the wall, providing just enough light to stave off absolute darkness. A blessing, since she was sure she would've gone mad by now without their quivering glow.

She was already going a little mad with only her own thoughts and feelings to keep her company: gratitude that Cassandra had escaped Maksym; hope that Tristan and Cass would come rescue her.

And gut-wrenching worry about Cael.

Xenia hadn't seen Cael since they'd been paralyzed together on Maksym's yacht. She didn't dare ask her Deathstalker captors about him. She doubted they would've told her anything anyway. The knot in her stomach tightened with each passing day.

And based on the number of meals she'd been served—the same thing every morning and evening: a bowl of lumpy oatmeal, a glass of water, and a hunk of stale bread—she'd been in this cell for a week.

Seven days wearing the same dirty clothes, sitting and sleeping on the thin straw mattress that scratched her skin and made her bones ache, offering little protection from the cold, hard floor.

Memories of her cherished books were the only things maintaining her sanity. Those stories she'd read and loved so fervently that she could recite every word.

Characters so alive, so familiar they felt like friends and family crafted from ink and paper.

To while away her dim, lonesome hours, she'd invent new adventures for them—a distracting pastime that bolstered her spirits when all she wanted to do was scream and scream into the indifferent shadows.

She was halfway through a newly imagined tale of her favorite fierce princess rescuing a handsome prince when the door at the end of the hallway opened. The Deathstalker with the scarred face—Alexei, the one whose sister Cass had killed—sauntered over to her cell.

Based on the grumbling in her stomach, she expected to see a food tray, but Alexei was empty-handed.

He wrapped his long, pale fingers around the cell bars, poking out his forked tongue, his serpentine eyes narrowed.

Xenia drew herself to standing and held her head high, mimicking both Cassandra and the fierce princess from her invented tale.

Alexei chuckled, a taunting hiss. "You can pretend to be brave all you want, little mouse, but we know you're scared. We smell it every time we open that door."

She wanted to ask where her food was, but didn't want to give him the satisfaction.

He opened her cell door with an iron key, then gestured for her to exit. "Maksym has requested your presence at dinner this evening."

Xenia couldn't help a shocked blink at the news. Nor the quick glance at her unwashed clothes and blood-stained hair.

"Yes, you look like shit," Alexei said. "That's why we've come to fetch you. You're to be cleaned up and delivered to him."

Horror churned hot and watery in her stomach.

*Delivered* to him?

In her books that typically only meant one thing.

Alexei scoffed, reading the terror on her face. "He doesn't tangle with human trash. He has a…*proposition* for you. Let's go, Sister." He popped his fangs to inspire her cooperation, then yanked her out of the cell, nearly dislocating her shoulder with his Fae strength.

"What…what kind of proposition?" Xenia asked.

Alexei's answering smile was cold, sharp, poisonous.

"The kind that will determine whether your gray-winged Windrider friend lives or dies."

# CHAPTER THREE

"I DON'T UNDERSTAND WHY HE never told me."

Cassandra pulled her mother's hand into her lap as a crisp breeze stirred the honeysuckles that climbed the trellises in the Temple courtyard. Their sweet familiar scent was as much a comfort to Cassandra as the warm hand she held.

After Tristan had dropped her off this morning, she'd intended to keep searching for clues within Cora's memory. But as soon as she'd plucked up the glowing vial, she'd been gripped by an unshakable, restless energy.

The thought of spending another day alone in that bungalow with nothing but silence and Cora's indecipherable visions had sent her careening through the streets of Thalenn, seeking solace in the one person, besides Xenia, who'd always been able to soothe her overactive mind.

And though Mama didn't react to Cassandra's lamentations, a peace settled over her as she recounted the details of this morning's disastrous meeting with the Emperor.

"I thought we had been growing closer during the investigation."

Mama turned her head, her blank gaze sweeping past Cassandra's face.

"Though I suppose everyone bears the burden of their own secrets." Cassandra pushed the fall of gray-streaked hair over her mother's shoulder.

Mama had also been keeping things from Cassandra.

Like the fact that she'd been a Shrouded Sister when she'd met and fallen in love with Cassandra's father. And that her blood had still been home to the Fae magic provided by the order when Cassandra had been conceived. The magic had fused with Cassandra's developing body in utero, and become as much a part of Cassandra as her pulse, her skin, her breath. Her memory pulling and viewing abilities would never fade.

A dangerous outcome, as a mortal child born with magic was viewed as a threat to the Empire's dominance. It was the very reason that the Empire's interspecies anti-procreation laws had been enacted. And why Shrouded Sisters were forced to take a vow of chastity upon entering the order.

Had Mama understood the risk of exposing Cassandra's abilities all along? Had she determined that the only safe place to hide her illegal child was with the Shrouded Sisters, a place where Cassandra's powers wouldn't be questioned? And had Mama sought obliviation—the mind-erasing result of excessive memory extractions—on purpose to ensure her secret died with her?

Useless speculations, really. Mama's mind was now as vacant as her once-lively dark eyes.

"I could have helped bear those burdens, though." A plea to both Tristan and her mother as Cassandra sucked in a shuddering breath and laid her head on Mama's shoulder. "He must not trust me as much as I thought he did."

The confession sliced through Cassandra's chest.

She'd opened up to Tristan in ways that she never had with anyone. And to learn so abruptly that he hadn't extended her the same courtesy had her rebuilding the freshly dismantled walls around her heart.

High Gods, she'd let herself believe that she was falling in *love* with him. A foolish notion that she chalked up to her inexperience, her impulsivity.

"Life outside these walls has been much more complicated than I anticipated. And the Emperor made it clear this morning that Tristan and I will not be able to aid in Xenia's rescue. I'm not sure what I should be doing with myself. My purpose was so *clear* while I was here as a Sister. Now, I feel…aimless."

A tear leaked onto Cassandra's cheek, staining her mother's cotton shift. She hastily brushed it away and sat up straight. "Enough blubbering. I should get back to the bungalow."

Cassandra stood and pulled her mother from the bench. "I'll take you back to your quarters."

She escorted Mama across the sun-dappled courtyard, puzzling at the unusually long line of supplicants outside the Temple. Most were dressed in drab denim and cotton, but a shard of guilt pierced Cassandra's stomach as she spied a few spots of silk and brocade within the queue.

Rare wealthy supplicants.

What treasures would she have found in their memories if she were still a Sister and they'd visited her extraction chair? Would their offerings have been the key to saving another family?

Yet another purpose of her previous life, unfulfilled this past week.

She guided her mother through the Temple doors and down into the obliviates' quarters, then hugged her tightly and promised to visit again soon.

As she wound back up the stairs and through the narrow stone halls, raised voices echoed from up ahead. She paused, eavesdropping on the conversation leaking through Mother Superior's office door.

"...Imperial decree. You do not have the authority to refuse it, Abbess." The rough male voice spat the title with none of the due respect.

"Does His Majesty not understand the burden this will place upon the Sisters? Not to mention the danger it will bring to the mortal citizens of the colonies." Mother Superior's soft, lilting voice rose with uncharacteristic viciousness. "This could decimate their species."

"That is none of your concern. You are a servant of the Empire. You will do as you are commanded. If you are in need of more Sisters to carry out this decree, more acolytes can be fetched for you."

"No!" Chair legs screeched across the floor. "No." Calm, steady footsteps walked towards the open door. "We will make due, as we always have. Now, if you'll excuse me, gentlemales, we *servants* have work to do. May the High Gods bless you on your journey." The blessing sounded more like a threat.

Cassandra tucked against the wall as three Empire soldiers in red jackets and golden helmets streamed out of the office and down the hallway.

She crept towards the door and poked her head in.

A hazy band of mid-afternoon sunlight fell across the abbess's hunched shoulders as she massaged her temples.

"Borea?" Cassandra whispered. "Is everything alright?"

The abbess's head snapped up. "Sister Fortin!" She touched her forehead. "Apologies, my dear. I should call you Cassandra now. Old habits die hard."

The abbess floated around her desk and folded Cassandra into a crushing hug. Warmth glowed in the abbess's black eyes, and Cassandra wondered how she'd never noticed it before. She'd been blinded by her own biases and suspicions of the abbess's motives during the search for the missing Sisters.

Mother Superior—Borea, as she'd asked Cassandra to call her—had only been trying to thwart the investigation in an effort to keep Cassandra safe. To keep the Vicereine and, by extension, the Emperor, from discovering the permanence of Cassandra's magic.

"What happened?" Cassandra asked. "What did those Empire soldiers want?"

The abbess gestured for Cassandra to take a seat, then plucked a document from her desk. Claws emerged from the abbess's knuckles—evidence of her polar bear form—and she tore through the thick paper, dusting the desktop with the shreds.

"The Emperor—" Borea's upper lip curled into a sneer "—has declared memory extractions mandatory. Every human in the colonies over the age of twenty-five must provide ten memories per week or risk imprisonment."

Cassandra blanched. Until now, humans could control how often they sold their memories, which were then turned into Delirium. The liquid elixir mimicked the euphoria a Fae experienced while feeding on human emotions. Not all Fae consumed the substance, but there were enough addicts on the continent to make it the biggest business in Ethyrios. One whose profits lined the Empire's pockets.

"Why would he do that?" Cassandra asked.

A dejected frown pulled at Borea's lips. "I don't know."

Fury burned through Cassandra's limbs. Despite this guise of freedom in the colonies, her fellow humans were nothing more than livestock to the Emperor.

"What can I do to help?" Cassandra asked.

"Nothing, I'm afraid. We Sisters will be as careful as we always have. But I'm afraid a catastrophic increase in obliviations will be unavoidable. And he has threatened that if we turn anyone away, we'll be replaced with more compliant Sisters. His soldiers have started perusing the slums for future acolytes. It has never been this bad." Borea cupped her forehead. "In my five centuries running this branch of the order, I have never seen the Empire display such blatant disregard for human life. The previous Emperor, despite his faults, would never have allowed this to happen."

Helplessness once again gripped Cassandra. When she'd belonged to the order, she'd risked her own safety to spare misfortunate human families from selling memories. This new squeeze by the Emperor meant those same families would be forced back to the Temple. All her small, petty mutinies had been for nothing.

Reading Cassandra's fraught expression, the abbess rounded her desk again and placed a comforting hand on Cassandra's shoulder.

"We will manage," the abbess reassured her. "You have more important things to worry about."

Cassandra didn't have the heart to tell the abbess that she'd been denied her request to assist in Xenia's rescue. That she was just as much the Emperor's pawn now as she'd ever been as a Sister.

"I'll visit again soon," Cassandra said, rising from her chair.

"You are most welcome at any time, my dear." Borea led her to the door.

As Cassandra turned to leave, the abbess grasped her hand. "Do not lose faith," Borea whispered. "Sparks of rebellion can catch fire, even in the darkest hour."

Cassandra desperately wanted to be the one to light the match.

# CHAPTER FOUR

"*A*S IT WAS, SO *shall it be.*"

*A rasping whisper uttered from dry, cracking lips.*

*Two wrinkled hands draping a glittering diamond necklace around a liver-spotted neck.*

*Dry leaves drifting along a pale stone avenue.*

*Nemosyna's ghostly marble visage twisting, eyes narrowed, lips moving. Uncanny. Terrifying.*

"*So shall it BE!*"

Cassandra ripped the glowing, golden vial from her wrist and replaced the cork. She settled the stoppered memory onto a low table, then flopped back against the plush, charcoal sofa in Tristan's living room.

One-hundred and twenty-seven.

That's how many times she'd watched Cora's scrambled memory.

And despite the confidence she'd displayed before the Emperor and the Vicereine, she was no closer to interpreting it. Especially not with her mind running an endless loop of all the potential terrible outcomes of the Emperor's new decree. He'd barely been in the colonies for a day and had already wreaked havoc.

She tried to focus on the scenes she'd just witnessed. The pale stone avenue seemed to signify an actual location, though it could be any number of towns or villages within the colonies.

For a split second, when Tristan had first viewed the memory last week, Cassandra swore recognition flared across his handsome features before becoming uncertainty. Another memory long forgotten, he'd confessed. This one pulled by time, not Letha. He'd told her to stop worrying, to stop watching the memory and await the Artisan's interpretation.

But Cassandra had never been comfortable just sitting around and doing *nothing*.

She padded to the bay window and peered down the sloping, moonlit lawn.

Still no sign of Tristan.

Though smaller than she'd expected—especially considering his newly revealed heritage—Tristan's bungalow was comfortably outfitted with the same magical energy and appliances that graced all Fae-owned dwellings within the colonies. And it was decorated with crumbs of his existence: a crumpled knit blanket on the couch; an abandoned coffee cup filled with a ladder of stains; an open cookbook folded over the arm of an over-stuffed chair.

During this first week of their experimental domesticity, Cassandra had been delighted to discover that Tristan devoured cookbooks in the same manner as others did fiction. He chuckled at some parts, raised his eyebrows at others, occasionally—and adorably—gasped at a plot twist. Cassandra, with her utter lack of cooking skills, couldn't imagine what a culinary plot twist might be—the use of a lime instead of a lemon, perhaps?

She ambled over to the chair and picked up the book, running her fingers along the oil stains and crusty bits dotting the well-worn pages.

The only room in the house that didn't bear the evidence of Tristan's casual approach towards tidiness was his state-of-the-art kitchen: a stainless-steel and marble shrine that gleamed despite the frequency of its use.

Abandoning her futile vigil, she stalked up the stairs to her room to get ready for bed and change out of her muslin dress. She cringed that she'd worn such plain attire in front of the Imperial leader of Ethyrios—considered burning the dang garment. Instead, she flung it into her closet and pulled out her nightshirt.

Well, Tristan's shirt.

He'd let her borrow it since she didn't own any pajamas other than that slinky white nightgown. And she certainly wasn't about to parade around in *that* in front of him.

Not anymore, anyway.

Even if that wicked thing within her, the wanton beast she'd finally wrangled under control, prodded her to do just that.

"He's the Emperor's brother, you idiot," she mumbled, slipping into the loose cotton shirt that fell to her knees and wafted enticing traces of Tristan's spicy, oaky scent. "Why would he ever choose to be with a penniless, homeless mortal?"

Penniless, homeless, and *useless*.

Needing a distraction from the restlessness itching through her, she padded over to a bookcase crammed with tomes of all shapes and sizes.

Last night, Cassandra had run her fingertips along the multi-hued leather spines, shocked to find a familiar title—the first book in Xenia's favorite series. The one about the outcast princess who overcame her fears and shortcomings, rounded up a band of like-minded rebels, and saved her long-lost kingdom from a tyrannical usurper. All while falling in love with a dashing, handsome prince, of course.

Cassandra had plucked the book from the shelves, nestled under the covers, and inhaled the story with a fervor she'd rarely experienced while reading. Journeying though the trials and tribulations of Princess Arelinn made her feel closer to Xenia, despite their separation.

She'd burst into tears at the cliffhanger ending, when the evil, usurper king took Arelinn's lover hostage.

Tristan must've heard her strangled cries through the wall they shared; he'd dashed into her room, a delicious, shirtless sight in low-slung cotton pants and sleep-mussed hair.

Her mouth had dried out and her tears evaporated at the sight of his broad, muscle-bound chest and sinfully carved abdominal muscles.

Once he'd realized she was unharmed, his tempting lips curved into a smug smile as he leaned against the door frame and rustled his feathers. "If you wanted to see me naked, Daredevil, all you had to do was ask. No need for such a dramatic ploy."

She'd huffed and the pillow she flung bounced off the door as he whipped it closed.

"Goodnight, *Cassandraaahhh*," he'd purred, returning to his own room.

A shudder had escaped her as warmth pooled low in her belly.

Stupid, horny, traitorous body.

Tonight, she plucked up the second book in the series, then climbed into bed and began flipping through the pages.

Princess Arelinn's adventures were not quite distracting enough this evening.

Every time she tried to start the first chapter, a vision of Tristan's anguished face as he'd blasted away this morning floated into her mind.

She still couldn't discern the reason for his exile, was unbearably curious about the exact cause. She refused to pry though. If he wanted to tell her, he'd tell her.

But she was determined to keep her guard up around him, and didn't know if she could stomach another blow like the one she'd been dealt this morning.

Friends, roommates, business partners—that's all they'd be from now on. All she felt capable of.

No matter how delectable he'd looked without his shirt on.

*Thunk.*

*Thunk.*

*Thunk.*

Cassandra's white cotton duvet pooled around her waist as she jolted upright, squinting at the undimmed sconces.

She rubbed the haze of sleep from her eyes as she swung her legs off the bed, jostling the open book nestled in her blankets.

*Thunk.*

She crouched below the window sill to avoid discovery by whatever...*thing* was making that noise outside. Pulling aside the diaphanous silver curtain, she peered into the backyard.

*Thunk.*

Tristan's wings glimmered in the moonlight as he drove his fist into the wooden fence.

*Thunk.*

As he cocked back for another blow, droplets flung from his hand and her stomach plummeted.

She didn't give a thought as to what she was wearing—or not wearing—as she dashed out of the bedroom, down the stairs, and into the chill night air.

"Tristan!"

He slumped his shoulders, his fists dribbling blood onto the lawn. But he didn't turn.

"Tristan," she murmured, maneuvering around his wings and placing a hand on his cheek.

"Don't," he begged, breathing raggedly, his bare, muscular torso glistening with a sheen of sweat. He shrugged her off. "Please...*don't.*"

She examined his torn knuckles. The tattered, bloodied pieces of fabric wrapped around his palm suggested he'd started this exercise with protection but had ripped it to shreds with the force of his punches.

How long had he been out here tearing himself apart before she'd woken up? Guilt tightened her chest.

"Why aren't these healing?" she asked, tapping a wound and drawing a wince from him.

He didn't answer, merely jutted his chin towards the wrought-iron patio table where a glowing, half-empty bottle of Delirium beckoned like a duplicitous lover.

"That shouldn't make a difference," she mumbled, more to herself than him.

Other than offering a feeling of euphoria—or deepening feelings of sadness and rage, in Tristan's case—Delirium couldn't alter a Fae's ability to heal.

"It does when you spike it with healing suppressant," he whispered, his voice splintering. Like he'd been screaming for hours.

She cradled his hands. "Why would you do that, Tristan?"

His weary, bloodshot eyes popped open, the lively golden-brown dulled with pain. "Because I needed to *feel* it."

"Come inside." She tugged him through the double-doors and into the kitchen, then sat him at the dining table and stepped to the sink to collect a towel and bowl of hot water.

His head drooped onto his chest as she settled into the chair next to him and laid his palms down on the table. She dipped the towel into the bowl, then pressed it against his battered knuckles.

He hissed in pain through gritted teeth, but didn't move away.

She flipped his hands over and sucked in a breath at the blood crusted into his left palm.

He'd sliced open his scar.

"Basket case, remember?" he said with a scowl. "Time for you to run away screaming."

"I'm far too dignified to scream." Tristan's lips twitched upwards. "And I'm not going anywhere. All the most interesting people have tortured pasts. Though I will admit, yours does have a few unexpected layers. I'm all ears when you're ready to tell me."

He dragged her into his lap and crushed his arms around her, trapping the dripping towel between them. It soaked her nightshirt as she let him hold her. She knew he needed the contact, knew the touch was a lifeline for him. She rested her head against his tense shoulder muscles.

"I'm a mess, Daredevil," he groaned. "You *should* run."

"Don't tell me what to do," she whispered. His breathy laugh stirred her hair. "Why didn't you tell me, Tristan?" She rubbed her cheek against his blazing skin.

"Because I'm a coward hiding beneath charm and swagger." His raw honesty bruised her heart. "And I didn't want to scare you away."

"Who else knows?"

"Most of the Fae who live here in the colonies. All the Vestian Guards, including Cael. Reena and Hadriel know too."

"Why did they never say anything?"

"They've moved past it, I guess. I thought *I'd* moved past it. I lost my title two hundred years ago. Many things have changed since then. They probably barely remember."

She pulled her head from his shoulder. "Or they care for you and don't want to dredge up past pain."

He snorted, attempting to look away. She wrenched her arm from between their bodies and brought her hand to his face, forcing him to look at her.

"You told me not to be afraid to talk to you. That there was nothing I could say to make you think any less of me. Well, I'm saying the same to you now. You are my *friend*, Tristan." She stroked her thumb along his cheek. "And I have precious few of them. I'm not about to let one go, even if they're a little damaged. Beggars can't be choosers."

His rumbling chuckle warmed her insides. He pinched her hip and she released a tiny squeak. She'd take the teasing, the flirting—as much as it tortured her—over the pain in his eyes any day.

"I *want* to tell you, Cassandra," he said, placing his hand over her own at his cheek. "I just…"

"Take all the time you need. I told you, I'm not going anywhere."

He blew a shuddering breath through pursed lips, then rose out of his chair and settled her on her feet.

The wet towel slapped to the floor, exposing her left breast through the now-transparent fabric of her night-shirt.

She did nothing to hide it.

"What is it with you and white fabric?" he murmured, transfixed. "You might as well just walk around here naked."

Incredulous, she gestured to his bare chest.

"You're the one who backed out of our agreement, *ex-playmate*. I never promised to make it easy for you."

Her chest loosened. *There* was her playful, irreverent friend.

How could she possibly convey the jumbled scope of her feelings for him? She wanted him more than reason would suggest was wise, but was terrified of the consequences. Consequences which had only grown more dire given his notoriety.

The agreement they'd made before she'd abandoned the order—to play together, explore together—seemed safer then. Like the limitations placed upon them by her chastity vow would keep her fragile heart protected.

And now, for the first time in her life, she had full control over her choices, had won the independence she'd so desperately longed for. She didn't yet know how to handle this glorious, terrifying new freedom.

She placed her hands on his chest, savoring the hard perfection beneath her fingertips, and he groaned softly.

She'd do everything in her power to ensure that light, that mischief, stayed in his eyes.

Without destroying herself in the process.

"You're definitely not making it easy. I must be a glutton for punishment, agreeing to come stay with you."

She stepped around him, intending to head back to her room despite her suspicion that sleep would be a long time coming.

He grabbed her wrist, halting her, and gazed from underneath his long, dark eyelashes. "Will you stay with me a little longer, Cass?"

His vulnerability awakened something primal within her—an urge to nurture, to soothe. Along with such a blinding wave of desire to wrap him in her arms, take him inside of her, and turn his grief into pleasure that she almost swooned.

She nodded, afraid of what she might say if she dared open her mouth.

He dragged her to the couch and plopped onto the cushions, angling his wings over the back before patting the space beside him.

She sat down and he curled an arm around her shoulder, nudging her to lay her head on the pillow he placed in his lap.

She stiffened, cocking a questioning eyebrow.

He grinned and shook his head. "No devious intentions. Can I just…rub your head?"

"After everything you've been through today, you want to give *me* a head massage? Shouldn't I be doing that for *you*?"

"It comforts me to touch you."

The sincerity in his voice triggered a dull ache in her chest.

She nestled her head onto the pillow, pushing her hands beneath and resting them on his rock-solid thighs. "You are too good to be true, Birdman."

"Don't you forget it, Daredevil." His strong, skilled fingers stroked her hair away from her forehead, tracing circles into her scalp.

She drowsily relished his touch, and after several minutes his fingers stilled and his breathing slowed.

Wrapping his other arm around her waist, she fell asleep more quickly than she would've thought possible in the pretend embrace.

A pleasant, dangerous fiction.

# CHAPTER FIVE

DUST-STAINED FLOORS COOLED XENIA'S bare feet as she followed Alexei down a breezeway of open arches. Through the crumbling stone, the watercolor sunset seemed too beautiful to be real—a kaleidoscope of dusty pinks and purples dotted with puddles of shining gold.

The ancient fortress that Alexei led her through was just as decrepit as the dungeon below. Some kind of abandoned structure that Maksym was using as a temporary headquarters.

She'd never seen anything like the foreign landscape outside, not even in the thousands of books she'd read. Tall, prickly plants cupped the sky, fingers clawing for the realm of Anaemos. Low bundles of dry grasses dotted rust-colored dirt that stretched for endless miles, nary a hill or mountain in sight—an alluring display of barren, deadly isolation.

She wouldn't last a day outside this fortress—if she could even escape in the first place. Not that she would risk it before finding out what she'd have to do to save Cael.

As they arrived at the end of the breezeway, Alexei opened a stone door into a circular room containing nothing but a free-standing tub that resembled a gigantic, hollowed-out pebble. Tendrils of steam curled up from the water's surface; she wondered how they'd warmed it.

Alexei shoved her inside, then pressed a towel and silken scrap of green fabric into her hands.

"Wash up and put this on," he hissed. "We'll be back to fetch you in twenty minutes." He locked the door behind him.

She peeled off her filthy training shirt and leggings, underwear as well, and slipped into the deliciously heated water.

She found an orange blossom-scented bar of soap sitting on the lip of the tub, then used it to wash her matted curls and scrub her skin raw.

Pink and glowing and smelling green, fresh and faintly of citrus, she was amazed at how human she felt with all the grime stripped away.

She rose from the bath and dried herself with the towel, then plucked the satiny green scrap from the floor, dangling the dress—if one could even call it that—from her fingertips.

She raised her arms and let the soft, silky material cascade down her lanky form.

The straps were thinner than a finger and the neckline dipped into a vee at her sternum. The fabric flowed down her torso, tightening over the flare of her hips before cascading to mid-shin.

Xenia barely had any chest to speak of, and had always been envious of Cassandra's lush curves. Though, she was grateful for her lack of endowment in the backless dress. She didn't bother putting her underwear back on since the dress scooped just above the swell of her ass.

She'd never in her life exposed this much skin.

The scandalous garment reminded her of that ridiculous nightgown Cassandra had worn to tease Tristan.

Xenia snickered at the memory before a pang of utter anguish gripped her. High Gods, she missed her friend.

Alexei didn't bother knocking before he yanked the door open and poked his head in.

"Let's go, little mouse," he growled. "Maksym doesn't like to be kept waiting."

She bent down to retrieve her clothes.

"Leave them," he bit out. "You won't be needing them anymore."

She obeyed, wondering if they'd offer her different clothes after dinner or if she was expected to wear this dress for the rest of her captivity. She padded out of the washroom, following Alexei back into the breezeway.

The black hilt of the dagger hanging at his hip looked familiar. She was almost positive it was the one Tristan had given Cass. Ker? Was that its name?

The sun had dipped lower during her bath, and spindly shadows speared towards the arches as Alexei turned down a long, empty hallway with two towering stone doors.

He hefted one open, gesturing for her to step inside. "Dinner awaits, *Sister* Cirillo."

Xenia sucked in a deep breath, a futile attempt to calm her pounding heart, and crossed the threshold.

Every inch of Cael Zephyrus's body ached.

He wasn't accustomed to such a state, given his Fae healing abilities.

Not to mention he prided himself on his pain tolerance, higher than any individual he knew, mortal or Fae. Higher than Tristan's even, and that fucker was a *beast*.

Cael had been offered plenty of opportunities to acquaint himself with pain during his boisterous childhood. Mostly while trying to prove himself to his two older brothers or be an example of bravery for his youngest. There'd been broken arms, pierced wings, black eyes, and knocked-out teeth every other week. If they hadn't been Fae, hadn't healed so quickly, his poor mother would've died a thousand deaths of worry.

His ailments had always come and gone so quickly, so unnoticeably, that he knew a healing suppressant was to blame for his current condition.

His hands were chained above his head, his shoulders throbbing from remaining in the same position for…days? Weeks? He'd lost all sense of time.

The toes of his boots dragged on the floor, his bent knees swaying listlessly.

Drooping behind him like two enormous, heavy sails, his wings pulled at his spine, threatening to tear away from his skin.

The door groaned open and he cracked his eyes, then sagged deeper with relief when he saw her alive and visibly unharmed.

Cael hadn't seen Xenia since he'd failed her so spectacularly on that yacht, getting them captured and allowing Maksym and his fuckwit cronies to do the High Gods-knew-what with her since then.

The anguish of imagining what she'd been suffering at their venomous, slithery hands was infinitely worse than any pain he'd felt since he'd been tied up here.

Her emerald eyes flashed with anger as she stepped into the room and caught his gaze. She opened her mouth, her brows furrowed, but he shook his head once, sharply. Discouraging her protest in front of the winged monster seated at the head of a substantial stone table lined with flickering candelabras.

"Sister," Maksym Rosopa crooned, rising and spreading his feathered, matte-green wings. "You're late."

Cael almost laughed out loud. Even in captivity, Xenia couldn't help being late.

She flinched as Maksym's booming voice filled the cavernous room, climbing the walls and sucking up all the air. But she didn't tear her gaze from Cael.

"He's fine," Maksym said with a wave of his hand. "Just a little tenderized."

Xenia pivoted to face Maksym and Cael finally noticed what she was wearing. The glistening green silk poured over her skin, leaving little to the imagination.

"He is most certainly *not* fine," she said, approaching Maksym and shoving her finger in his face. Cael chuckled internally at the memory of her flinging the same gesture at him in the Temple library on the day they'd met. "I don't know what kind of proposition you intend to make to me, but I sure as fuck am not going to agree to *anything* while you have him tied up there like a piece of meat."

The mouth on her never ceased to amaze him, to stir something in him. So obscene for a Shrouded Sister. An enticing contrast to the innocence she wore like a cloak.

Maksym wrapped his hand around Xenia's throat. "You squeak too loudly, little mouse."

Xenia raked her nails down his fingers, gasping as she tried to suck in a breath.

Cael's rage threatened to burst through his skin, but only a pathetic whimper came out. "Leave her alone."

Maksym's eyes darted to Cael, even as he refused to loosen his grip on Xenia. He laughed, a clicking, swallowed sound that didn't clear the back of his throat. "This is going to be even easier than I thought."

Maksym threw Xenia to the ground, and she wheezed, rubbing her neck. Her eyes remained glued to the floor, and tears shone on her cheeks.

Cael's rage boiled his veins as Maksym approached him slowly, warily. As if Cael were a chained predator, capable of violent savagery. He wished it were true.

"To ensure her cooperation, I'm going to unchain you," Maksym said. "If you do anything other than sit against the wall licking your wounds, I will end her right in front of you. Do you understand?"

Cael gave him the barest nod.

Maksym released Cael's chains, and he toppled to the floor in a heap, his arms, legs, and wings sparking with sharp, electric pain. He didn't dare try to push himself upright yet. Just hugged the cold, stone floor, sucking in deep breaths and trying not to pass out from the renewed agony.

Xenia's choked sob shredded through him.

Maksym yanked her to her feet and threw her into a chair. "Sit. Stay."

Cael let his fury dull his other senses so he could maneuver himself into a seated position, resting his aching, feverish wings against the cool wall. He pulled his knees up to his stomach, gritting his teeth against the pin-pricks running along his limbs as blood began to flow again. He removed the iron shackles digging into his wrists, and fresh wounds spilled trickles of blood into his palms before his skin knit back together. Whatever healing suppressant they'd given him was wearing off. He could feel his body mending.

He surveyed his surroundings, this once-grandiose chamber he'd been chained in for the entirety of his imprisonment.

The long stone table suggested the room had been a gathering hall. A human fortress, abandoned to disrepair after the war, perhaps? Piles of red sand dusted the corners and an overcast, starless night peered through several jagged holes in the soaring ceiling. A large canvas map of Ethyrios decorated the opposite wall, littered with red X's throughout the colonies' four islands.

Xenia slumped in her chair, massaging her neck.

Cael leaned back and angled his head towards her, determined to watch over her as her dinner with Maksym began.

Xenia's neck throbbed as she choked back tears. She didn't want to cry in front of this green-winged prick. Her tears were only half for herself anyway.

Wrath of Vestan, what had they *done* to Cael?

Seeing him chained to the wall had reminded her of the hogs her father raised for slaughter on their farm—though Cael was in worse shape.

She wished she knew how to fight like Cass, wished she had a weapon. She'd bring this entire complex to its knees.

Maksym took the seat to her left—the head of the table, naturally. There were only two place settings, so she guessed he wasn't expecting anyone else. He snapped his fingers, and a Deathstalker entered carrying a jug of wine and two covered platters.

It wasn't Alexei, but one of the other guards whom she recognized from dungeon meal-times. The lanky Deathstalker sported a pinched look with thin lips, a hooked nose, and long ash-blond hair that fell to his waist.

He set a plate in front of both Xenia and Maksym, then poured them each a glass of red wine before uncovering the plates with a flourish.

"Thank you, Zakariah, that will do," Maksym nodded. Zakariah placed the jug on the table and scurried out of the room.

Though Xenia didn't want to accept Maksym's *generosity*, her mouth watered at the meal's enticing scent. She couldn't help it after a week of eating nothing but cold, lumpy oatmeal and stale bread.

Fanned out over a bed of roast potatoes and asparagus spears, seared strips of beef oozed blood-red juices onto the plate.

Maksym sliced his meat, gazing sidelong at her. "It's not poisoned, Sister. I'm not in the habit of murdering my dinner guests. Not during the meal, at least."

She glared and crossed her arms, refusing to take the chance.

He snorted, then speared a piece of beef from her plate. He popped it in his mouth, chewing slowly before washing it down with a sip of her wine.

Her gnawing hunger won out in the end.

But fuck this asshole if he thought he was getting a dignified dinner companion.

Ignoring her utensils, she dug into the food with the frenzy of an animal denied sustenance for days. All five remaining pieces of beef fell prey to her clawing hands and ripping teeth. Chin coated with grease, she chewed the potatoes with an open mouth, peppering her plate with flecks of fluff, then crunched into an asparagus spear.

She gulped her wine, and the burgundy liquid trailed from the corners of her lips, flowing down her neck and staining her green silk dress.

Once she'd drained the glass, she wiped her chin with the back of her wrist, then flicked it, splattering chunks of potato, meat grease, and red wine droplets onto the floor.

Maksym remained utterly silent, wearing a suitably disgusted grimace.

*Victory.*

Her vision fractured, likely due to how quickly she'd downed the wine, and her head throbbed.

A choking, hissing noise floated over from the corner.

Cael huddled over his knees, his shoulders trembling. She almost stood from her chair to rush to him before his head reared back and he let loose the loudest, most booming guffaws she'd ever heard him make. Louder even than Tristan's thunderous laughter.

He struggled to breathe in the wake of his ferocious amusement. "I can't..." he winced. "That was... Frenzied Dienses, that was fucking hilarious. Thanks, Zee."

Xenia's lips quirked upwards, but her heart seized as she faced Maksym. His eyes were unblinking gems of glittering rage, his lips parted though no breath escaped, his body tense and still. Poised to strike.

He rose with supernatural swiftness, crossing the room in the split second before his chair clattered to the floor.

He punched Cael square in the face, and Xenia winced at the crack of Cael's skull slamming into the wall.

Maksym smoothed his white suit jacket and prowled back to the table.

"Worth it," Cael groaned, closing his eyes and propping his head against the stone slab.

As soon as Maksym regained his seat, he whipped a black cloth napkin at Xenia. "Clean yourself up."

She glared at him, stewing in her mess.

"There are worse things I could do to him, you know," Maksym crooned. "With all the healing suppressant in his system right now, he's extremely vulnerable. Shall we do a little experiment to see which parts grow back if I lop them off?"

Xenia blanched, then plucked up the napkin to clean herself.

"Better." Maksym poured her another glass of wine. And even though she shouldn't, she was already feeling the effects, she took a deep gulp. She'd rather be drunk before hearing whatever madness he was about to spew.

"As Alexei has already mentioned, I invited you to dine with me this evening because I have a proposition for you, little mouse," Maksym began, the wayward tufts of his silver hair limned in the candles' amber haze. "Well, not a proposition per se. That would imply you have a choice. You're going to help us fill our ingredient stores." His tongue poked out to catch a drop of blood-red wine running down his bottom lip.

"I don't understand what you're asking," Xenia said.

"Once I have the *real* necklace, I'll begin making my very special batch of Delirium. One that will be distributed across the continent to reignite faith in the Fallen Goddess and undermine the legitimacy of the Empire. I need the blood of active Shrouded Sisters to make it, and you will help me lure them."

Xenia almost laughed out loud at the absurdity. "You must be fucking insane if you think I'm going to help you capture any more of my Sisters."

"Not insane. Confident. Given my leverage." His gaze flicked towards Cael. Xenia pivoted to look at the broken Windrider.

Cael was listening to the conversation with rapt attention. As soon as she turned, his gray eyes bored into hers with a clear message. She could almost hear his deep, measured voice demanding she not do this, even to spare his life.

He was a fool if he thought she had a choice. She'd do everything in her power to keep him safe. Asshole or not, they were in this mess together.

"What, exactly, do you want me to do?" she asked.

"Xenia, no!" Cael pushed himself off the floor, and Maksym barked for Alexei.

The scar-faced Deathstalker strode in with a small vial of viscous purple liquid. Alexei straddled Cael, jamming his knees into Cael's shoulders before forcing his mouth open and pouring the liquid down his throat. He pinched Cael's nose and mouth shut so he was forced to swallow it, then pummeled Cael in the face and stomach.

"Stop!" Xenia cried, turning to Maksym. "I'll do whatever you want, just please stop hurting him."

The fleshy smack of a fist was followed by bones crunching and a pained groan. She couldn't bear to look.

"Please." She forced herself to hold Maksym's smug gaze through a terrifying crack and a muffled scream. "I will do whatever you ask."

"Alexei," Maksym grunted. "Enough."

Xenia dipped her head, the words *thank you* rising to her tongue on instinct before she realized she didn't owe this piece of shit an ounce of her gratitude. Two tears dripped onto her lap, staining perfect circles on the green silk.

"You will travel to the other three Temples of Letha throughout the colonies," Maksym intoned between bites of his meal. The whining scrape of his knife and fork against the plate grated Xenia's bones. "For obvious reasons, I will not be sending you back to the Temple in Thalenn. There's no reason the Sisters in the other Temples would recognize you, right?"

Her mouth pulled down at the corners.

"I'll take it from the look on your face that the answer is no," Maksym said, chuckling. She wanted to smash his lips into his teeth.

"And what, exactly, am I supposed to do once I'm there?"

"You'll be dressed as a Shrouded Sister, so you'll blend right in. I've had Richelle's robes tailored to fit you."

Xenia shuddered that they'd taken her measurements while she was unconscious—yet another violation. "Why can't she just help you herself?"

"She is far too important to our operation for such a dangerous task. You'll need to convince four Sisters at each Temple to drink a bottle of tainted Delirium, then lead them off the grounds to where our guards will be waiting to retrieve them."

Xenia scoffed. "How am I supposed to convince Shrouded Sisters to drink Delirium? We're not even allowed to drink wine."

Maksym shrugged. "You seem rather resourceful, Sister Cirillo. I'm sure you'll figure something out." He glanced sidelong at Alexei, who bent down and twisted Cael's wing, wringing a roar of such devastating anguish from the Windrider that Xenia nearly vomited.

"Stop," she whimpered. "I'll do it. I'll *do* it."

Maksym laughed again, that clicking, rattling sound that held not an ounce of warmth or true merriment. "I knew you'd eventually see reason. I hope you enjoyed the meal." He nodded towards Alexei. "Take them back to the cells."

Maksym flung his folded napkin onto his plate, then drained the last dregs of his wine. "We will fetch you when it's time for your first excursion." He turned on his heel and strode out the door, leaving Xenia alone with Alexei and Cael.

For a split second, she considered jamming her dinner knife into Alexei's throat.

But what good would that do?

Her lack of weaponry skills meant it was more likely she'd slice off her own hand. And Cael was so battered, he wouldn't be any help. His swollen right wing hung at an awkward angle.

Alexei yanked Cael from the ground and Xenia rushed over, shoving the Deathstalker out of the way. "Don't fucking touch him!" Alexei reared back, shock twisting his mangled features. "We'll come willingly, but *I* will help him back to the cells."

Alexei shrugged, then held open the door.

Xenia cupped Cael's face, and his stormy gray eyes popped open. "Can you get up?"

He moaned as she draped his arm over her shoulder and, using the wall for leverage, pushed them to stand. "Lean on me," she said. "It's okay. I've got you."

As they hobbled into the hall, Cael leaned down to whisper in her ear. "If you ever meet my brothers, promise me you'll eat like that. They'd love you."

# CHAPTER SIX

"THIS SHIP ONLY OFFERS single bed rooms."
Tristan held up his hands, trying not to show an ounce of delight as Cassandra narrowed her eyes. "And we were lucky to get the last two."

Though the trip to Meridon to see the Artisan would have only taken a few hours as a flight, Tristan couldn't carry Cassandra and both of their bags the entire way. Even with Hella, one of his fellow Vestian Guards, as back-up. So the trio had decided to book rooms on an overnight steamship instead.

"You could bunk up with Hella," he offered.

Cassandra let out a huff of annoyance as she pushed past him into the cramped berth. To the right of the door was a small bureau topped with a mirror—the only piece of furniture besides the bed. Through the room's sole, circular window, the setting sun cast a band of golden light over the sapphire waters of the Sea of Thetis.

"It's only for one night," she said, resigned. "You can keep your hands to yourself for one night, surely?"

"I don't make promises I can't keep, gorgeous."

Cassandra flung her satchel onto the bed and began unpacking her belongings, refolding each piece before tucking it into the bureau.

"Why are you unpacking?" he asked, leaning a shoulder against the wall and crossing his arms. "We're barely going to be on this ship for twelve hours."

"I don't know." She shrugged, a hint of shame flickering through her enchanting blue-gray eyes. "It feels strange to just leave everything in the bag. Too transient."

Tristan's heart clenched. Cassandra's life for the past week—for the past eight *years*—had probably felt transient. When was the last time she'd truly had a home?

"Let me help you," he said, squeezing in beside her and lifting up the black bathing suit he'd insisted she purchase during their shopping trip earlier. Since most of their time in the sunny city would be spent waiting for the Artisan to do her work, they might as well take advantage and wait on the beach.

His lips kicked up into a crooked smirk as he dangled the suit. "Sweet Amatu, I cannot fucking *wait* to see you in this."

She snatched it out of his grip and jammed it into the drawer. "And what will you be wearing on the beach? Trunks or briefs?"

"I prefer skinny-dipping." He waggled his eyebrows and she laughed heartily. "Hey, you didn't flinch at that curse. Should I be worried?"

She shrugged, bending over the bed to close her bag. "I must be getting used to your filthy mouth, Birdman."

He came up behind her and wrapped his arms around her waist, hauling her against his body and bringing his lips to the shell of her ear. "My filthy mouth would love to get used to you too, Daredevil."

She unwound his arms but he sensed the heat that coursed through her at his touch, his words.

"Friends and business partners only, remember?" she rounded on him, scolding. He wasn't deterred in the slightest. "Letha spare me, remind me why I agreed to help you?"

"Because you can't get enough of me," he winked, tossing her satchel into the corner. "Let's go, tiny human. Hella will drop kick me if we're late for dinner."

Tristan, Cassandra, and Hella gathered in the ship's dining hall for a simple but hearty dinner of chicken skewers, rice and flatbread from the food stall on board. Plus a bottle of red wine from the vineyards of Nephes, the continental territory surrounding Delos, that Tristan was pleasantly shocked they carried.

The ship's crowd was more mortal than Fae, but nearly every individual in the room spared a second glance for Hella. Her scarlet wings arced over the back of the chair she barely fit into. She was just as tall and hulking as Tristan, with tiny, golden braids that flowed to her waist and striking eyes of the same color.

Hella sliced her chicken, eating small, dainty bites as Cassandra stared at her. Cass seemed fascinated with Hella, not that Tristan could blame her. Hella often inspired such attention.

"So, Hella," Cassandra piped up between mouthfuls of chicken, "how long have you and Tristan worked together?"

"Little baby man?" Hella said in her robust, Northern Ethyrian accent. She clapped Tristan on the back and almost knocked him out of his chair. Wrath of Vestan, she was strong. "I am Guard two-hundred years before he come crying from continent, whining about—" Hella stopped herself, panic rounding her eyes, concerned she was about to reveal his deepest secret.

"It's okay, Hella," he said, popping a piece of chicken into his mouth. The spice mixture they used on board was delicious—savory, sweet and tangy. He made a mental note to ask the chef what was in the rub. "Cass knows all about my sordid history."

Cassandra shot him a withering look.

"Well, the big beats at least," he winked.

He wanted to tell her everything. Didn't know why he'd hesitated last night. She'd been so open with him, so caring. Cleaning his wounds, reasserting their friendship. He hoped she'd feel the same way once she learned the full truth. It was the only thing holding him back: the fear of losing her, despite what she'd said, despite the promises she'd made to stick by him.

"Do you live at the barracks, or do you have your own place in Thalenn like Tristan?" Cassandra asked Hella, spooning a pile of rice into her mouth and making those delectable noises she always made when she was enjoying her meal. He wondered how he could convince her to let him inspire those noises in the bed they'd be sharing tonight.

"Not all of us so... oh what is word... well-endowed as Tristan?" Hella said, and Cassandra burst into hysterics. "What? What I say?"

"I'm not sure that's the word you meant to use," Cassandra said, pressing a knuckle against her lower lashes.

"Oh that is *exactly* the word she meant to use, Daredevil, and you know it."

Heat simmered in Cassandra's eyes before she composed herself. "I think you meant well-*funded*."

Hella waved a gigantic hand. "Yes, yes, as you say. Well-funded, yes. What other word mean?"

Cassandra hesitated, struggling to explain such an idea to a relative stranger.

Tristan spread his wings as wide as they would go, twenty feet if they were an inch, blocking the paths of the other guests trying to get to and from their tables.

"It means I have an enormous...member," he quipped.

Hella snickered. "Not so big as Cael's."

Tristan roared with laughter, and Cassandra nearly spit out her wine. "Wh-what?" she sputtered, chuckling. "Have you done a side-by-side comparison, Hella?"

Tristan tucked his wings, tearing off a piece of flatbread and savoring the warm, chewy texture. "Showers at the barracks are co-ed. Vestians are not shy nor ashamed of their bodies. Cael is somewhat of a legend among the ranks."

Cassandra's face went slack, her eyes glazed and her cheeks reddening. Tristan was certainly no slouch in the endowment department, which Cassandra already well knew, so he could only imagine what she was picturing.

"I'm sure he'd be happy to show it to you," Tristan said around a mouthful of rice. The food stuck in his throat at the casual mention of his friend.

He knew better than to worry, knew Cael had been in similarly dangerous situations before, and had always gotten himself out. Tristan had utter faith in his friend's abilities to survive, no matter how dire the circumstances. Not to mention he had a cadre of Brachian warriors on their way to fetch him.

But Maksym was a new brand of crazy that neither Tristan nor Cael had yet dealt with. The Windrider's zealotry for the Fallen Goddess was unhinged and dangerous. Unpredictable. Tristan knew far too little about the Goddess's long-repressed dogma, a blindspot that would need to be remedied as soon as possible.

And Tristan had received no windwhispers from Cael at all, which suggested two possibilities. One, Cael's magic was being suppressed. Or two... Tristan didn't even want to consider it.

Cassandra's husky voice brought him out of his anxious thoughts. "So, Hella, what made you decide to come to the colonies and join the Vestians?"

Something flared in his chest at Cassandra's curiosity about his colleague. Maybe she was just making polite conversation, but he wanted her to get to know his world. Wanted her to be a much bigger part of it.

"Where I come, is honor to protect weak," Hella said before taking a precise bite of her chicken. She moved gracefully, economically for someone so large. It was what made her such a formidable foe—many enemies had fallen by underestimating her agility. "Every hundred years, is contest in my home, Syvalle. All warriors compete to serve as Vestian. I win first contest back four hundred years, after war. Bring great pride to family. Only females win contest since."

Tristan had very fond memories of his visits to Syvalle as a teenager. And of the territory's stunning warrior women who'd played a pivotal role in his pubescent dreams.

"By far the stronger sex." Tristan winked at Cassandra, and her answering smile stirred his feathers.

"And you?" Hella asked. "Why you leave order?"

Cassandra blew out a long exhale and laid her utensils down. Tristan refilled her wine glass, and she took a bolstering sip.

"I didn't want to be weak anymore." She echoed Hella's words, though Tristan suspected it wasn't to shame the female Vestian's assessment of her species.

"It take courage to make big change," Hella said, cradling Cassandra's hand. "You very strong, tiny human."

"Did Tristan tell you to call me that?"

Hella's broad, pink lips curved into a wry smile, her golden eyes twinkling. "Maybe so. But is true. You strong. You win contest in Syvalle."

"Against full-blooded Fae warriors? I know we just met, Hella, but you don't need to blow smoke up my ass."

Hella glanced down at her massive backside. "Smoke up ass? Is new sex game?"

All three burst into shrieking laughter, earning annoyed glances from the other diners in the crowded room.

As their hilarity subsided, Hella downed the rest of her wine and then rose from the table, a mountain of muscled flesh and sanguine wings. "Time to bed, friends. I see you in morning in Meridon, yes?"

Tristan nodded. "Goodnight, Hella. Thanks for the laughs." He tipped his wine glass at her.

"Goodnight," Cassandra echoed. "Sleep well."

"I not sleep well on boats," Hella groaned. "Too many rocking." She clutched her stomach.

"I have something that might help!" Cassandra chirped, reaching into her pocket and pulling out a tea sachet. "Ginger tea. It helps with nausea and motion sickness."

"Thank you, Cassandra. I will try." Hella took the sachet before striding through the room, angling her enormous body and wings through the crowded tables.

"Ginger tea, huh?" Tristan leaned across the table. "Who taught you about that?"

"Some smarmy, arrogant male who once helped me through a hangover."

"You planning on getting drunk with me, Daredevil? You were so snuggly last time. Might make it easier for us to both fit in that bed."

"I don't need to be drunk to snuggle with you, Tristan." The shocked look on her face as the words left her mouth suggested she might already be a little tipsy. She pushed her glass away. "But probably best if I don't finish this."

He drained her wine, then stood, offering her a hand. "Come on, Cass." She placed her palm in his, and he stroked his thumb across her knuckles, lowering his voice. "Let's go to bed."

She snickered, elbowing him in the stomach as she rose.

The tendril of earthy, musky scent that crawled up his nostrils as she walked away was encouraging.

# CHAPTER SEVEN

CASSANDRA BRUSHED OUT HER long, chocolate waves, struggling to avert her eyes from the panty-melting display of male perfection reflected in the mirror.

Tristan was sprawled across the tiny bed behind her. Shirtless, naturally. A compromise, since he'd informed her as they were changing for bed that he normally slept naked.

She'd blamed the heat crawling up her neck on the wine. He'd laughed, raised his hands and surrendered, agreeing to put on his low-slung black pants.

Not much better.

She'd closed her eyes and turned towards the wall while he changed, the sounds of popping zippers, creaking leather, and rustling wings doing nothing to tame her simmering blood. Then he'd pivoted, exposing the powerful muscles of his back and giving her a modicum of privacy as she shucked off her pants, bra and top.

She hadn't bothered buying any nightclothes during their shopping trip. Nothing could be as comfortable, nor smell as good, as the soft, worn cotton shirt he'd given her to sleep in.

Working on a particularly persistent knot, her eyes roamed over every detail of the mirror's magnetic spectacle. As if her subconscious wanted to etch the vision onto her brain.

His shimmering, iridescent wings draped over the bed. The ink-black strands of his shoulder-length hair nestled on the pillow. The arm tucked behind his head, showcasing his absurdly large biceps. The chiseled decadence of his torso, gilded by the amber glow of the matching oil-lamp sconces flanking the window.

"I'm beginning to feel a bit objectified." He closed his small, leather-bound book with a dull clap and laid it on his chest, snaring her in his caramel gaze. His lips formed an amused smile, exposing a hint of sharp canine and that lickable dimple. "But still happy to lose the pants if you've changed your mind."

She whipped her eyes to her own reflection, running the brush violently through the ends of her hair and wincing as it caught the snarl.

"Nope, I'm good!"

His dark chuckle slid over her skin like a silken promise.

"What are you reading?" she asked, an attempt to smother the blazing tension crackling to life between them.

"The memoir of a famous Fae chef from the continent." His unexpected answer coaxed a broad, involuntary smile from her. "Why? What did you think I'd be reading?"

She tugged at the brush. Bloody Stygios, this knot was stubborn. "Well, since it's too small to be a cookbook, I thought something like *How to Fell Your Enemies with a Single Blow* or *The Art of Seducing Females of Either Species?*"

"No need to read something I could've written myself." He re-opened the book. "This chef has got a restaurant in Delos that's supposed to be the best on the continent. It takes weeks to get a reservation and costs more *drachas* than most folks could earn in a month, but they say it's the best meal you'll ever have in your lifetime. And coming from the Fae, that's saying something."

"Have you ever been there?"

"I didn't get a chance before I was exiled." He peered at her over the sepia pages. "Not sure I ever will. Just a silly fantasy."

"You don't think your brother will commute your sentence and allow you back on the continent if you help him get what he's after?" She spun towards him, abandoning the knot and settling the brush onto the bureau.

He snapped the book closed, slamming it onto the narrow wood shelf that passed for a nightstand. "Eamon is… he's a monster. Probably why he and Varuna get along so well. Soulless-mates, those two." Cassandra flinched at the violence with which he'd said the Vicereine's name. She'd never heard him use it. "Now that he's sent Arran Zephyrus after Maksym, I can't imagine why he has us chasing down this necklace. Maybe he's just trying to tie up every loose end, but I can't help feeling like this is a fool's errand."

"Then why did we agree to it?"

A shadow of fear flickered across Tristan's face before he chased it away with a teasing grin. "Free trip to the beach?"

Cassandra burst into tears, and Tristan rushed over to cup her cheeks.

"I'm sorry, Cass." He wiped the wetness away with his thumbs. "That was a terrible joke."

"I'm so worried about Xenia," she said, her voice cracking. "It's been over a week, Tristan. What if she's suffering?"

"Listen to me," he gripped her chin, "Maksym is as good as dead now that he's in Eamon's crosshairs. And as soon as Arran's forces close in, Xenia will be safe."

Cassandra blew out a shaky breath. "Okay."

"Trust me. I've experienced first-hand the aftermath of Eamon's ruthlessness. And I wouldn't dare cross him. Especially now that you—" He glanced towards the ceiling and bit his lower lip. "It's in our best interest to do what he's asked."

"What do you mean?" she asked, leaning back against the bureau.

"Why bother coming to the colonies now, two years after his coronation? I don't buy that he's just *visiting his subjects*. He's up to something."

"Did you hear about his decree? That he's made weekly memory extractions mandatory?"

Tristan winced. "I had heard, yes."

"Why do you think he did it?"

"I'm not certain. But it can be nothing good. We need to stay on his good side. Figure out what he's truly after before too many innocent people suffer from his schemes."

He cupped her chin again and she almost sighed at the feel of his warm, rough hand on her skin, the stroke of his finger along her jaw, the sight of all that tanned, naked flesh mere inches from her fingertips.

"We're going to be playing a very dangerous game with a very dangerous person," he whispered. "One who has resented me for centuries."

"What are you talking about?"

"I'm older than Eamon," Tristan whispered and Cassandra's stomach plummeted. "*I* was the heir to the Empire before I was exiled." She didn't know if she was shuddering at his words or his touch, trying to ignore her rising anxiety that she was standing half-dressed in a cramped room with the once future Emperor of

Ethyrios. "But I would succumb to True Death before I let anything happen to you, Cassandra."

Exactly what she was afraid of.

"Turn around," he said. "Let me help you with that knot."

She blew out a shaky breath and handed him her hairbrush. She swiveled to face the mirror, the heat of his body a sinful temptation at her back. He gathered her heavy fall of hair and isolated the strand with the knot, then held it taut in the middle as he raked the brush over the tangled mess.

The same method Xenia—a master at untangling both physical and emotional knots—used to use. Another tear spilled down her cheek.

Tristan turned her to kiss it away. "I'm worried, too."

"You hide it well," she snapped. He didn't flinch, seeming to understand her anger wasn't for him.

"Falling apart won't help anyone. Keep the faith, tiny human."

She chuckled, wet and rattling; he sounded like Borea.

He pulled her closer, draping her wrists around his neck as he leaned down to murmur in her ear. "I can help you forget about everything for a while, *ex-playmate*."

Amatu spare her, she wanted him to.

But since she'd left the order, her life had been so unmoored. Was it wise to add her heart to the mix?

She vented an exasperated sigh. "The past week has been…complicated. Our whole situation is complicated. Won't this just make it even more confusing?"

"I'm not confused at all about how much I want you." Tristan wrapped his arms around her tighter, as if trying to fuse their bodies together.

"You say that now," she said, trying to ignore how good, how right it felt to be held by him. "What if you change your mind once you have me?"

"Only one way to find out." Tristan trailed gentle kisses across her freckled cheeks and nose. "Let me have you," he whispered, shuddering with need.

The evidence of his desire nudged against her stomach, sharpening her ache.

He pulled back to gaze into her eyes, his own clouded with lust and something deeper. Something that didn't seem to match the words that poured out of his luscious mouth. "Sex could be the one thing in our lives that's *not* complicated right now. Wouldn't you like a distraction from all the bullshit we're dealing with?"

Was sex all he wanted from her? Did she care?

"I…I'm not ready for that yet," she said, but made no attempt to untangle herself.

*I don't think my heart can take it.*

She swallowed that confession.

He ran his soft, plush lips down the side of her neck as he trailed a teasing hand up under the hem of her nightshirt, tracing his fingers along her spine and lighting up her breasts, her sex.

"I'm a patient male, Cass." He nipped at the pulsing vein in her throat. "Plenty of fun to be had until you *are* ready. Quit denying yourself and renew our agreement. I promise I can be extremely diverting."

Eight days. She'd lasted eight days.

Fu…dge it.

She ran her hands down the smooth, hard planes of his chest, then traced those muscles just inside his hips that she couldn't get enough of. She tucked her fingers inside his waistband, and her body rippled with aching desire at his responding groan. Arching her neck to give him better access, she whispered, "Prove it."

It was all the permission he needed.

He trailed his lips up over her jaw and claimed her mouth before hoisting her effortlessly onto the bureau, perching her at the edge. Nestling between her open thighs, he cupped his hand under her tailbone and hauled her hips against his.

Every painful, confusing, worrying thought scattered, chased away by his powerful hands roving over her body, his soft lips and probing tongue pillaging her mouth.

She threw her arms around his shoulders, needing him closer, and his responding growl bloomed wet heat between her legs.

Scenting her arousal, his fingers found the front of her panties, and she moaned into his mouth as he circled her clit.

"Your body isn't confused about what it wants." He pressed into the spot harder, and a strangled cry parted her lips. "You're fucking soaked for me."

He replaced his fingers with his cock, stroking her through his thin, cotton pants and over her panties. He snaked a hand up under her shirt and palmed her breast, running his thumb over her peaked nipple and squeezing tenderly in time with his thrusts.

"That's because it's a horny idiot who doesn't realize we're just friends," she whimpered, her statement losing its power as she ground against his erection.

A rumbling chuckle trickled out of him. "You really want me to correct that?" He drove against her harder. One hand massaged her breast as the other braced the base of her spine, holding her in place against him.

"Of course not," she breathed as her hips bucked.

"Didn't think so." He dipped a hand to the hem of her nightshirt. "Arms up," he commanded before dragging it up over her head.

"*Fuck* me," he exhaled at the sight of her exposed flesh, and she braced her arms behind her, arching her back and pushing her chest forward. She let him look his fill, drunk on his yearning.

"High Gods, I am dying to show you all the depraved things your delectable body was made for." He mapped her curves with gentle reverence, his fingertips caressing her breasts, her ribs, her stomach. As if she were a priceless piece of art.

He teased his knuckles along the waistband of her panties.

"I can tell you want me to take these off. But if I do, I won't be able to stop myself from burying my cock inside you."

She tilted her hips up, then almost sobbed with frustration as he removed his fingers from her panties and placed his hand at her jaw, pulling at her lower lip with his thumb.

"So better keep them on," he grinned wickedly. "Because right now, I think you'd let me."

She grabbed his thumb with her teeth and bit down. Hard. The flash of anger-tinged lust in his eyes tingled through her, stiffening her already painfully tight nipples.

"How badly do you want to fuck me right now, Daredevil? Grind harder and show me. It can't possibly be as badly as I want to fuck *you*."

She dug her heels into the firm muscles of his ass and pulled him as close as possible.

He laughed, then cupped her breast and dipped his head to swirl his tongue around the pebbled nub, nipping with his sharp canine. The sensation speared straight to her core, dragging a low, keening sound from her that she'd never made before.

He lavished the same attention on her other breast, flicking the tender peak with the tip of his tongue as he continued to thrust between her legs.

Her body alternated between tight and loose, her climax building. Despite the fabric barriers between them, his movements were precise, meticulous—a master at work. He studied her face, her breathing, her moans. Knew exactly when to pull back and tease or push in and increase the pressure, urging her towards an incendiary crescendo.

She couldn't begin to imagine how he'd feel inside her skin-on-skin, knew it would utterly ruin her for anyone else.

She curved her hand into his hair, fisting the silky strands and hauling his mouth to hers. She needed to taste him, needed his teeth on her lips, needed this moment, this transcendent distraction, to never, ever end.

With taunting swipes, she lured his tongue into her mouth, sucking hard as he teased the impressive length of his cock along the front of her drenched panties.

"Don't stop," she moaned into his mouth. "I'm close."

He grinned against her lips. "I know."

He placed his hand at her throat and pushed her against the mirror. "Look at me. I need to see your face when I make you come."

She was dangling at the edge of the precipice, a plateau of pleasure that was almost as good as the inevitable fall that awaited her.

He pinched her nipple and one final, powerful thrust against her clit had her screaming his name as every nerve ending in her body exploded with pulsing, liquid heat.

She'd experienced orgasms before, not only by her own hand, but inside the memories of numerous supplicants, scenes of shuddering cries and quivering limbs. But she had no idea that it could feel like this.

Like the ground had opened up to swallow her into the molten core of the world.

She crashed, limp and sated, against Tristan's chest, and he rubbed her back as she came to her senses. She panted against his shoulder, wondering what to say, what to do. Should she thank him? Return the favor? She hadn't planned for this to happen.

But his hands, his mouth, his body were all swiftly becoming addictions she couldn't deny herself.

He lowered his head and whispered against her hair. "Whatever you're thinking, stop." She huffed a laugh. "Thank you for letting me do that."

She pulled back and stared into his hooded eyes, choking back a cresting wave of dangerous emotion. He was so beautiful, so selfless.

He bent down to retrieve her crumpled nightshirt. "But you might want to apologize to our neighbors. You're awfully loud."

"You did accept that challenge." She cocked an eyebrow.

"So I did," he snickered, tapping her elbows. She lifted her arms, allowing him to drape her shirt down her torso. Once her head popped through, he sucked her lower lip between his teeth.

"I fucking love it. Next challenge is to make you scream even louder."

She wanted to tangle herself in his limbs again, gave a small sound of protest when he nudged her towards the bed.

"But now it's time for sleep."

"What about you?" She gestured to the darkened spot on the front of his pants. Too small to have been a release of his own.

"I owed you from your extraction room."

"What about the alley?"

"That was all business, remember?" His dimple-revealing half smile made an appearance. "Doesn't count. Though you arguing with me about getting me off is really fucking hot."

She glared at him and he sank onto the bed, angling his wings over the side and patting the space beside him.

"We don't need to keep score, Cass. What's an orgasm or three between roommates? Or should I say, playmates?"

She nodded. She was sick of fighting it. And with all the fear and grief and uncertainty in their lives right now, surely fate wouldn't begrudge them a few stolen moments of pleasure. Even if she wasn't quite ready to cross that final threshold.

He gifted her a dazzling smile, crooking a finger. "Come to bed, beautiful."

She crawled up the mattress as he turned down the oil lamps. The moon shining off the water bathed the room in silver-limned darkness.

He shifted her onto her side, then pushed an arm beneath her head before wrapping the other around her waist and tugging her back against him.

He sucked in a long breath, his nose poking through her hair. "Mmm, I could get used to sleeping like this."

"Goodnight, Birdman." She closed her eyes and nestled in closer.

"Goodnight, Daredevil." He squeezed her briefly.

And for the second night in a row, she swiftly tumbled into sleep wrapped in Tristan's arms.

She could indeed get used to this.

# CHAPTER EIGHT

XENIA'S KNEES NEARLY BUCKLED as she struggled to keep Cael's massive body upright. Thank the High Gods for the Sisters' mandatory training sessions, or she probably would've collapsed trying to help him down the narrow stone stairs that led to the dungeon.

Alexei clanged open her cell. "Get inside."

"Who?"

"Both of you."

Xenia's eyebrows flew to her hairline, but she didn't dare question it. Then her heart sank. Maksym would only let her and Cael stay together if he was confident they couldn't escape.

She dragged Cael into the small cell, then sat him against the wall.

Alexei slammed the door shut with a resounding clank, then pocketed the iron key, shifting Cass's dagger aside in the process. He must've grown quite attached to the weapon; he was keeping it on him at all times. A precaution against the hulking, muscled warrior wheezing in pain behind her?

Xenia approached the bars. "Dinner's over. Am I expected to wear this ridiculous dress all night? I'll freeze to death down here and your boss's plans for me will be ruined."

Alexei's impassive, serpentine eyes traveled up her body before he pivoted and strode out of the dungeon, his onyx hair glistening in the flickering torchlight.

Xenia snarled and threw her hands up then crouched next to Cael.

"Are you ok?" she whispered.

Despite the oozing cuts and purpling welts, his cynical expression was easily readable.

"Right, stupid question." She tucked her knees underneath her and flinched at the floor's cold, hard bite. "It seemed like the healing suppressant wore off there for a bit. Do you remember how long it had been since they last dosed you?"

He closed his eyes and inched his tongue out to worry at his split lip. "Few hours."

The wooden door creaked open, and clipped footsteps approached the cell.

Xenia jumped up and pressed herself against the bars. Before she could say a word, Alexei passed her a folded pile of midnight blue fabric topped with a round metal tin. "Dress robes for you and a salve for his wounds."

Xenia eyed the tin suspiciously as she lowered the pile to the floor. "Why would Maksym offer this?"

"You behave, the Windrider gets rewarded. You misbehave, he gets punished," Alexei said, his sinister smile curdling her relief.

She curled her fingers around the rough iron and lowered her voice. "What would I have to do to convince Maksym to stop administering the healing suppressant altogether?"

Cael grunted in protest. Damn his sensitive Fae hearing.

Alexei leaned in, darting his forked tongue in and out of his mouth and nearly brushing her lips. It took all her willpower not to recoil in disgust.

"Nothing." Alexei's black pupils dilated with renewed hostility. "Maksym would never agree to such a thing. The healing suppressant dulls elemental powers. Can't have the Windrider tearing this place down with a squall, now can we?"

She backed away, berating herself for even asking. But if she and Cael could figure out a way for him to stop taking the suppressant, it was good to know that both his healing *and* his wind magic would be restored.

Alexei banged his fist against the bars, laughing as Xenia jolted and bared her teeth. "See you tomorrow, little mouse and broken bat," he crooned as he sauntered away.

"He's not a bat, he's a pterodactyl," Xenia muttered under her breath, and swore she heard an amused snort behind her.

She stole a quick glance at Cael to ensure his eyes were closed before she turned her back on him to change into the dress robes.

Cael cracked his eyes open at the soft hiss of fabric coasting down skin. Thanked the High Gods that Xenia was facing away from him and didn't notice.

He watched her slip off the silky, green dress. Felt he'd earned the indulgence after the beating he'd taken earlier. Ignored the pang of guilt that she might not agree.

She slipped the straps off her slender shoulders, and her back was enticingly bare. The plunging neckline he'd spied in the dining room had already informed him she wasn't wearing a bra. Not that her small, perky breasts needed the support.

She bent at the waist as she lowered the green satin over the taut swells of her narrow, shapely backside, exposing long golden legs.

She wasn't wearing any underwear.

He let out a quivering breath, swallowing a wince, but didn't close his eyes. Kept them glued to those two dimples framing the base of her spine. Wondered what she'd do if he leaned forward and dipped his tongue into one.

He blinked away the flash of desire that pulsed through his veins, drawing his blood to the surface of his skin and making his bruises scream louder.

He closed his eyes, but the image of her naked back and stunning ass, haloed in the buttery glare of the torches, burned behind his eyelids.

Frenzied Dienses, this healing suppressant must be shredding his self-control. He'd never been this physically attracted to a human, ever. Sure, he'd had his fair share of trysts during his time in the colonies, but those were borne out of a combination of proximity, availability, and desperation.

His father was ruthless in his maintenance of the Empire's laws prohibiting relationships between Fae and humans, and Cael had never dared disobey him.

Had never even been *tempted* to disobey him.

Until now.

He buried his hands underneath his thighs to keep from reaching out. Touching her.

Bruised and battered and broken, he was desperate for any kind of healing touch. That's what he told himself to explain the craving roaring through his body. Well, that and he hadn't fucked anyone in weeks—not since he'd lost that Delos promotion and spiraled into one of his depressive moods.

The episodes came for him every few months. When he was younger, he would rage against the emptiness, determined to beat it into submission. Better to feel turbulent than nothing at all.

It never worked.

As he grew older, he coped by allowing the numbness to envelop him. He'd ride it out, hoping he didn't lose too many pieces of himself to the dark, yawning pit he'd plunge into for days, sometimes weeks, at a time.

The loss of the Delos position had hit him hard. The ensuing episode was one of the longest and blackest he'd experienced in decades. He wasn't sure he was going to make it out the other side, especially when the Vicereine had assigned him and Tristan to that ridiculous job at the Temple.

But the job hadn't been ridiculous at all. He'd found his way back to himself searching for those missing Sisters, researching ancient texts in the quiet library with a bouncy mess of blond curls twittering at him from across the table.

A ray of light coaxing him out of the murky recesses of his mood.

Best not get used to such a feeling, though. There was no way his father would accept him being with a *human*. Not to mention if Xenia ever discovered the true depth of the void inside him—

Gentle fingers grazed his cheek and he opened his eyes to two vibrant, green pools of worry.

"They gave me some salve for your wounds," she whispered. She wore those midnight blue dress robes again—her uniform for the job Maksym had assigned her.

The fucking *bastard*.

Cael hated that she was being forced into the task because of him. Would rather she let him die than debase herself and betray her Sisters. He worried it would break her, dull her shine.

He'd never forgive himself if that happened.

He groaned as he pushed himself upright, then stretched his legs out so she could straddle his lap. She knelt, hovering above his thighs so as not to put her full weight onto him. The consideration of the gesture almost made him wail. He closed his eyes, unable to look at her as she worked.

"Why are you being so nice to me?" he grumbled, flinching as her careful fingertips smoothed the cool, sticky substance over his split eyebrow. "It's disconcerting."

Her breathy chuckle tiptoed across his lips as she leaned in to inspect her work, bathing him in her fresh, floral scent. A hint of citrus hid behind the greenery—orange blossoms.

"Even *I* wouldn't be nasty to you when your face is so fucked up." Her slender fingers made another pass, wiping along his aching cheekbone. The salve was odorless, soothing on contact, imbued with some kind of topical healing agent that counteracted the suppressant.

His breath hitched as she applied the salve to his torn bottom lip, and his eyes popped open involuntarily. Light brown eyelashes rested on her pink cheeks as she stared at his mouth, engrossed in her ministrations.

"There." She pulled away with a mischievous grin and a swish of her curls. "You'll be pretty again in no time, and I can resume taunting you."

She had no idea how much she was already taunting him with her caring touch, her dark skirts draped over his lap, and his knowledge that there was not a scrap of fabric underneath.

Her face fell as she inspected his right wing, bent at an awkward angle behind his leather-clad shoulder. He could tell it was broken, and hoped there would be enough time between doses of healing suppressant for his body to repair it.

"Those fucking *monsters*," she seethed, crawling off his lap and sitting beside him.

He snatched her wrist as she reached for his wing. "Don't bother. The salve won't do anything for it."

"Won't it help with the pain?"

He cut his steel-gray eyes towards her. "I can handle it."

"Well, forgive me if I can't stomach the thought of you suffering unnecessarily." Her scowl was like looking in a mirror.

He must be rubbing off on her.

High Gods help her.

He gripped her wrist tighter. "I will not be your weakness, Xenia. Do whatever it takes to get out of here. When they take you to the Temple, run. Save yourself and forget about me."

She wrenched her wrist from his grip, her scowl deepening as she patted the salve onto his broken wing bone.

"I will do *no* such thing. You may not value your life, Cael, but I do. We escape together or not at all."

Her foolish words seized his reckless, hopeful heart. "Now unzip your jacket and lift your shirt so I can get to the rest of your bruises."

He was helpless to disobey her.

How could he even suggest it? As if she would leave him here to die.

Xenia ignored the sting in her eyes and the burning in her chest that Cael could give up on himself so easily.

He struggled with his zipper, but she was hesitant to offer help. Figured he'd want to do it himself, no matter how much pain it caused. In the weeks she'd spent getting to know him, she could tell he would rather suffer than appear weak or incapable.

He managed to peel down the zipper and as his leather jacket creaked open, she sighed in relief at his crisp, white shirt. No blood. But his soreness suggested unseen damage.

She placed her fingers at his waist. "May I?"

His head lolled against the damp wall, but he offered a subtle nod.

Whatever tingly, sparkling magic was in the salve worked quickly. Cael's torn lip and eyebrow had already threaded back together and the welts at his jaw and cheekbone were lightening.

She lifted his shirt up over his stomach and chest, momentarily distracted by the perfect symmetry of his muscles and that light dusting of ash-brown hair trailing from his belly button into his pants. In another world, at another time, she might bend down to put her mouth there. Use her teeth to playfully nip and tug at those hairs. The thought spread delicious warmth throughout her body.

Then she remembered Cael could scent such things.

Her head shot up, and she scrutinized his face. But other than a slight flaring of his nostrils, he kept perfectly still.

Right, he was probably used to this kind of reaction. Likely inspired it whenever he took his shirt off.

Other than a slight reddening along his left ribs, there didn't seem to be much damage. Which meant either there wasn't any, or that the bruises would take longer to develop.

She stroked her fingertips along the redness, and he jolted. "Sorry! Guess I found the spot."

"Don't touch it," he ground out, his stormy gray eyes narrowed.

She narrowed her own. "Why did you even let me look if you're not going to let me heal it?"

He flicked a wayward curl off his forehead. "Wanted to remind you how incredible I look without a shirt on."

"Please," she scoffed. "I've seen better."

An absolute lie.

Cael's body had been carved from her most wicked fantasies. Better even than how she'd pictured the brawny heroes in her books.

He chuckled softly, the hard knot of his throat bobbing as he dipped his head back against the wall. "Mmm-hmm." The low rumble of his voice crept up her thighs. "Nasty. My face must be healing."

Her lips quirked up, and she dipped her fingers into the cool balm. "I'm putting this on you whether you want me to or not. Not sure there's much you can do to stop me at the moment."

He clenched his teeth in anticipation. "You shouldn't have warned me. Do it quickly."

She settled the tin in her lap and clasped his hand with her clean one. "Try not to break my fingers, please."

She didn't hesitate another second, rubbing the salve in circles over his battered ribs. He roared in agony, then squeezed her hand so tightly she worried he'd fused her knuckles together.

"Done," she whispered. His chest quivered as he sucked in gulping breaths of air. She tried to remove her hand, but he kept hold of it as he descended from the apex of his pain.

He brought her throbbing hand to his mouth and brushed his lips across her knuckles. And damn if it didn't make them feel better. "I didn't mean to hurt you."

"It's okay," she said breathlessly, her heart racing at the touch of his plush, warm lips on her skin. "*I* can take it. Baby."

He smirked as he sat up straight and she tried not to be disappointed when he lowered his shirt. He seemed more lucid than he had all night. "Where are we?"

"Maksym's filthy sex dungeon?" she volunteered.

He laughed heartily, wincing and gripping his side. "Which is the filthy part—the sex or the dungeon? Must be the dungeon. Not nearly enough chains down here for the sex to be filthy. Or fun."

Heat crept across Xenia's cheeks.

Cael pushed his limp waves off his forehead, his face tightening with rage. "Have you been down here the whole time?"

"It wasn't so bad," she answered, pointedly dragging her gaze across his broken wing, his bruised ribs.

His expression turned anguished. "Xenia, I—"

"Stop. This is *not* your fault and I won't have you taking the blame. You've been punished enough. No more moping or self-flagellation. Focus on healing so we can get out of here."

"How am I going to heal when they keep dosing me with that suppressant?"

Her broad grin tugged at the edges of his lips. "I guess we have some experiments to run, pterodactyl."

# CHAPTER NINE

Cassandra's eyes dragged open, adjusting to the slice of murky moonlight swaying with the cabin. She'd only been asleep for a few hours, if the pitch-dark sky outside was any indication.

She attempted to sit up, but the hefty arm banded around her waist held her in place. Tristan's deep, plosive breathing tickled the back of her neck.

Something was scraping outside the door.

The unsettling, unnatural noise turned her thoughts to the sleeping souls on board, oblivious to the lurking danger.

She held her breath as it faded.

Tristan's peaceful face was cloaked in slumber, and she didn't have the heart to wake him. Didn't really want to wake him since she'd felt so utterly *useless* this past week. She was itching to *do* something. To prove she didn't need Tristan to fight all her battles. And if she could save some helpless passengers in the process, even better.

She strangled the small voice in her head begging her to take advantage of the muscled mass of killing power warming her bed. The ship wasn't that big, she assured the voice. She'd be able to run back and wake him if needed.

Slowly easing out from underneath Tristan's heavy arm, she scooted off the bed and tugged on her pants. She didn't put on her boots, wanted to be able to tip-toe as silently as possible. She grabbed Tristan's Typhon steel dagger from its holster on the floor—her weapon of choice. The black whorls on the blade swallowed the glinting light.

She pressed her ear against the cool door, listening for any lingering sounds. Nothing. She eased the door open and, with one final glance at the slumbering Fae warrior, crept across the threshold.

Darkness enveloped her and she paused, her heart ratcheting into a tumultuous beat as her overactive mind pictured the monsters awaiting her.

The corridor was empty.

Cassandra flipped the dagger and gripped her pendant. The warm, gold sphere was a familiar comfort in her palm, calling to mind her father's crinkled blue-gray eyes and emphatic instructions.

*Blade up, fear down.*

Bracing the weapon in front of her, she crept down the hall. Soft sighs and phlegmatic snores seeped through the thin doors along her route.

As she approached the end of the hallway, a silvery glow tinged the outer edges of her vision. She rounded a corner and peeked through a circular window set inside a swinging door.

The dining hall's wall of windows illuminated the vacant tabletops, and a rustling, metallic banging rang out from the food stall in the corner.

A dark form billowed up from behind the counter, and two wings unfurled in the darkness. Cassandra couldn't yet tell if they were flesh or feathers.

A kernel of fire bloomed to life in the Fae's palm, then flared into a flaming jet. The Fae burned an unfamiliar symbol into the wall—a circle bisected by a vertical line—then summoned the wind to spread the flames.

Adrenaline poured a frosty blaze through Cassandra's veins. As if Maksym's lightning magic weren't bad enough, now Fae had *fire* magic?

Visions of sleeping passengers burning alive in their beds unspooled far too realistically in Cassandra's mind.

So she steeled her spine, gripped the dagger tighter, and pushed through the swinging door.

*Gentle fingers walked down Tristan's torso, making his breath catch as they coasted across his ticklish spot, that muscled dip next to his hip bone.*

*A low, breathy chuckle caressed his neck before pillowy lips pressed soft kisses along his collarbone, and a hand closed around his rapidly hardening cock.*

He woke with a jolt, the scent of honey and rosewood coating his nostrils. He clenched his arm, intending to nuzzle into the very real woman who'd inspired his dream before realizing the bed next to him was empty.

Though still warm.

He scented smoke on the air, and fear prickled down his spine, stirring the downy feathers at his shoulder blades. He jumped out of bed, shrugged on his shirt, and reached for his belt.

His dagger was missing.

His fear froze into ice-cold shards that poked at his insides. Why would she take the dagger and not the stun pistol? Reckless little fool.

Though he wasn't surprised she'd dashed into the night on her own, bravely defending innocents against any perceived threat.

They'd be having a chat later.

Assuming he found her alive and unharmed.

He fastened his belt and it hung awkwardly over his thin black pants. Reaching down to ensure the pistol was secure at his hip, he ducked through the berth's flimsy door and into the darkened hallway. Though it wasn't dark for him; his Fae vision allowed him to see clearly in all levels of light.

The crashes of a struggle echoed from up ahead.

The dining hall.

He didn't spare a second thought for anyone in the rooms lining the corridor as he rushed forward, praying to the High Gods that he hadn't woken up too late.

Cassandra viewed the fight from outside her body.

It happened often when she tunneled deep into her mind, her senses as sharp as the patterned blade she wielded. She became a slashing, kicking, punching whirlwind, focused on her enemy with no room for doubts or fears of any kind.

A burning pain radiated from her forearm and thigh, and she dimly recalled bolts of fire arcing out and blistering her skin. Adrenaline must be holding the agony at bay.

The Fae—a fine-boned Windrider female with a long mane of unruly brown hair—screamed as Cassandra delivered a vicious slash to her right leg. The Fae lunged for Cassandra again, shooting another flaming stream.

Cassandra ducked just in time, the fire spewing over her head and singeing her hair. She pivoted and slammed a table into the Fae's side. The table exploded into ashes, consumed by a ball of fire as Cassandra darted out of reach to contemplate her next move.

The Sea of Thetis was a calm, inky expanse beyond the wall of windows. If she could lure the Windrider there, perhaps she could slash it and push it into the water to drown.

The Fae noted the direction of her gaze and, to Cassandra's shock, dashed for the windows herself.

The female spread her wings wide, the flesh a peachy-pink with golden undertones brought to life by the increasingly large blaze gobbling up the food stall.

Cassandra steadied herself, then hurled the dagger. The blade sunk between the Fae's wings with a satisfying thunk, inspiring a piercing cry. The Fae angled an arm behind her and plucked out the dagger, tossing it to the ground with a throaty growl. She shattered the glass with a blast of wind, then escaped through the broken window.

The extra oxygen fed the blaze, the flames enveloping the entire side wall of the hall.

The door to the dining hall crashed open, and Tristan barreled in, barefoot and clothed only in his shirt and sleep pants, pistol in hand. "What happened?"

Cassandra was pleased he asked for intel first, rather than scolding her for not waking him up. His eyes darted down, and a pained grimace twisted his lips at the burns on her forearm and thigh.

"A Windrider with *fire magic* happened," Cassandra coughed as the room filled with black, choking smoke.

Tristan surveyed the rapidly growing blaze, then turned back to Cassandra. "Go wake the passengers and lead them to the lifeboats at the back of the ship. Find Hella. I'll go after the Windrider."

Cassandra nodded before Tristan took several wide strides then pushed himself through the destroyed windows. He caught his bare foot on a shard of glass and a trickle of red crept down the wall. He didn't even notice, the wound closing up as soon as he blasted his wind outside and launched into the sky.

Cassandra bolted from the dining hall and into the corridor, encountering confused, terrified faces along the way. "Head to the lifeboats!" she shouted, shaking them out of their recently-roused state. "There's a fire in the dining hall. Hurry!"

She herded a young, mortal family along the darkened corridor, twin girls each wailing and clinging to a parent.

Behind her, the dining hall's remaining windows exploded in a tinkling crash as the fire raged. An orange glow crept down the hallway and her stomach dropped. How would she ever get everyone out in time?

Pounding on every door she passed, each room's inhabitants greeted her with the same blinking uncertainty. She had to scream at many folks who turned back to pack up their belongings.

The hallway spread before her like an endless abyss, and heat kissed her back as the fire rounded the corner and crawled along the walls, devouring the grass-cloth wallpaper. Panic shivered along her limbs as she realized she wouldn't have time to knock on every single door, wake every sleeping passenger.

A towering figure with blood-red wings ducked out of a room further down the hallway, and Cassandra almost collapsed with relief.

"Hella!"

The Windrider lumbered towards her, trying not to jostle the crowd of mortals and Fae rushing for the back of the ship.

"What happen? Where Tristan?" Hella asked, her face a portrait of calm determination.

"There's a fire in the dining hall. We need to wake the passengers and get them to the lifeboats *now*."

Hella nodded, then sucked in a deep breath and let out a high-pitched, keening shriek that rattled the doors. Cassandra clapped her hands over her ears.

Every remaining door in the hallway opened, and questioning faces beneath sleep-mussed hair peeked into the hallway.

"There is fire!" Hella bellowed. "Leave room, leave things, go to lifeboats!"

The crowd jolted into action, mortals and Fae pouring into the narrow hallway as a frenzy of frightened shouts ricocheted off the walls.

Cassandra and Hella stayed behind the stream of bodies, watching as the flames drew ever closer. The smoke burned Cassandra's lungs and eyes as the crowd moved at a glacial pace.

Coughing, tears streaming down her cheeks, Cassandra turned to Hella. "We're not going to make it," she choked out. "There's too many people and the fire is moving too fast."

Hella's burnished gold eyes darted from the crowd to the flames, assessing. She brought her fingers to her mouth and emitted a sharp whistle.

Every head in the hallway turned towards her. "Flames too fast, no time. Drop and cover!"

Cassandra had no idea what Hella intended, but she wasn't about to question the ancient female. She tumbled to the carpeted floor, then curled into a ball and shielded her head.

And tried not to scream in abject horror as Hella summoned the wind to tear the roof off the ship.

Tristan couldn't catch the Windrider, and tried not to let it bruise his tender pride.

His pounding wings shredded the clouds to ribbons of mist as he arrowed through the night sky, gritting his teeth against the exertion. The fluttering, pale pink wings that he'd finally located after a frantic, minutes-long search remained frustratingly out of reach, even after he summoned his power for a rocketing boost. The rushing wind ripped at his hair and pulled tears from his eyes.

And the bitch was agile too. On several occasions during the chase, he was sure he had her, only to clamp his hand around empty air as she dipped and pivoted, wringing frustrated growls from his raw throat.

He was only dimly aware of how far he'd flown. There was not a landmark in sight, and only simmering, inky water below. He could barely see the steamship, a faint orange aura staining the horizon behind him.

This chase was pointless. He should return to the ship, help Cass, Hella, and the other passengers.

The Windrider came to a halt. Her pale pink wings swished as she hovered in place, and a vicious cackle speared from her ghost-pale face.

"Catch me if you can." Her voice was high-pitched and hurried, the words tripping over each other as they escaped her mouth.

"Who are you?" Tristan barked, fanning his own wings to stay aloft as he aimed his stun pistol at her.

"A messenger from the New Ethyrios," she answered with a maniacal grin, her luminescent blue eyes glinting, daring him to shoot her. "She will rise to save us."

Just as he was about to pull the trigger, a deafening explosion boomed over the horizon. Chunks of debris shot through the air, then crashed into the sea with a hissing splash.

Tristan's stomach hollowed out and all the air rushed out of his lungs, his ears popping as though he'd launched into the sky too fast to adjust to the pressure.

*Cassandra.*

He didn't turn back to the Windrider. Didn't care about her cryptic words.

He barreled as fast as he could for the decimated ship, hoping it was the only thing he'd find in pieces.

The scene around Cassandra slowed and muddled, as if she were viewing it underwater. Hella towered over her, the Windrider's arms stretched to the starlit sky as she poured her power into the wind-shield surrounding herself, Cassandra, and the other passengers.

Jagged pieces of wall had replaced the cabins, and beyond them, the endless sea stretched for miles to the faint, obsidian horizon.

Behind Hella, surging flames crashed against the shield, momentarily abated in the pursuit of their prey.

Hella leaned down to urge Cassandra into motion. "Make passengers wait in water. I release lifeboats."

Hella dissolved the shield and the flames licking at the edges extinguished as cool night air rushed in.

In the wrecked hole that used to be the dining hall, the fire stalled, its ravenous consumption of the ship halted by Hella's destruction of its fuel.

Gusts of wind stirred Cassandra's loose waves as the other Windriders on board fled, gathering their families and belongings. Leaving flightless Fae and humans to fend for themselves.

Hella snarled, snapping her sharp canines. "Selfish." She tipped her head down, noticing Cassandra still crouched below her. "Go, tiny human!"

"Not sure how I feel about Tristan sharing that nickname," Cassandra sniped, rising slowly and awkwardly, trying not to pull at the burns on her leg.

"Fits too good," Hella smirked, then took off towards the back of the ship, her crimson wings streaming behind her.

Cassandra began a slow campaign down the ruined hallway, encouraging frightened humans to leap over the sides of the ship, splash into the night-dark waters, and float in place until Hella arrived with a lifeboat.

Hella put a Beastrunner in charge of the first boat. The newly appointed captain, a burly bear bi-form who even as a human was covered in dark brown hair, circled the wreckage, helping both humans and Fae into the boat—a welcome sight that eased the sting of those Windriders' self-centered abandonment.

As Cassandra was helping a young man and his wife over the side, a bolt of realization shot through her.

Cora's memory.

She'd left it in the cabin.

She watched the couple plummet into the water and then surveyed the mangled berths. She had no idea which was the one she'd shared with Tristan.

A vision of what they'd done in that cabin overtook her frazzled mind: his rough hand cupping her breast, his tongue flicking over her nipple, the hard ridge of his arousal pumping against her.

"Not the time for that, horny idiot," she scolded herself as she began a frantic search for their cabin.

Embers of the once-raging inferno smoldered along the ruined hallway as she checked each gutted room, trying to identify any remaining belongings.

She nearly collapsed with relief as she spied her leather satchel. Then jumped out of her skin as Tristan crashed onto the bed, splintering the frame and tearing through the mattress—finishing the devastation Hella had wrought.

He grabbed her shoulders, his mouth a slash of rage and worry, then turned her around to scan every inch of her body.

"Mighty Anaemos, babysitter, calm down! I'm fine."

He aimed a pointed look at the angry burns on her forearm and thigh, both blistered.

"Well, other than those two little nicks. Did you catch her?"

"No," Tristan ground out, his eyes boiling with murderous intent. "But I assume she was sent by Maksym. Probably to get rid of us."

Cassandra lifted up the flap of her satchel and let out a long string of non-curses.

Tristan grabbed her shoulders again. "What's wrong?"

She scowled, opening her satchel wide.

"Cora's memory is gone."

# CHAPTER TEN

XENIA WAS DETERMINED TO make it hurt this time. If only to wipe that smug half smile off Cael's face.

They'd been engrossed in experiments all day, testing how long it took the healing suppressant to wear off. A series of bite marks in various states of recovery ran along Cael's forearm. The bite she'd delivered this morning, soon after he'd swallowed his dose of suppressant, had scabbed over but still looked worse than the others. The four she'd administered since, at various intervals throughout the day, each looked increasingly less deep.

The wound she was about to deliver, moments before their evening meal and his second, final dose of the day, would hopefully heal instantly.

"Ready?" she said, gripping his forearm as her lips curled into a devilish smile.

"You are enjoying this far too much. I can't tell if it's the scientific nature of the experimentation that's turning you on or the fact that I'm willingly allowing you to inflict pain upon me."

"The pain," she grinned. "Definitely the pain."

"Sadist." His gray eyes gleamed with wicked delight. "Alright, Blondie. Bite me."

Xenia sank her teeth in hard and deep, right below the crook of his elbow.

Cael didn't so much as flinch.

She might be insulted if she wasn't so impressed by his pain tolerance. On any normal individual, she was sure her attack would've at least caused an uncomfortable hiss.

A few tiny beads of blood bubbled up from the red crescent she'd inflicted, then flowed into the bend of his elbow, catching in the tiny hairs dotting his forearm.

"Less uncomfortable than a bug bite," he teased.

She shushed him as she watched the wound fade, the tiny droplets of blood absorbing into his skin.

"That one healed right away," Xenia said. "Based on the size of the dose they're giving you, it seems like it takes about twelve hours to wear off. Assuming that's the amount of time between our meal deliveries. How does your wind feel?"

Cael opened his hand, and Xenia's curls swirled against her forehead as if she were standing at the edge of the sea on a sun-kissed morning. Gentle and pleasant and nowhere near the typhoon she knew he was capable of.

"I'd say it's at half capacity," Cael answered. "If I could skip the night dose, I'd bet my power would be fully replenished by morning."

The door to the dungeon opened—their evening meal.

Cael hastily rolled down his sleeve before Alexei stopped in front of the cell.

The Deathstalker said nothing as he slid the trays underneath the bars, aiming a pointed glance at the vial of suppressant—a silent command for Cael to consume it in front of him. Which Cael promptly did, licking his lips and smacking them together with a sarcastic exhale of satisfaction.

"Rest up, little mouse. We're taking you to the Temple in Meridon tomorrow," Alexei snarled before leaving the dungeon and slamming the door.

"What crawled up his ass?" Cael asked, before ripping into his bread, sending crumbs flying. If Cael had been biting into his own forearm, the wounds would've been much more gruesome—but far less amusing for Xenia.

"If you were second-in-command of an operation to take over the world, but your master assigned you to babysit an injured grump and a helpless Shrouded

Sister, you'd be pretty pissed too, no?" Xenia asked before breaking off a dainty piece of her own bread.

"Still," Cael said, "the service in this place is severely lacking."

Xenia snorted a laugh, even though the joke wasn't that funny. At least he was trying, and seemed to be in better spirits since they'd been in this cell together. She felt it too, had enjoyed her best night's sleep in days listening to his gentle breathing next to her.

"Are you worried about tomorrow?" Cael asked, sucking down a spoonful of oatmeal as if it were the most delicious food he'd ever been served.

Xenia couldn't help a disgusted frown. This oatmeal tasted like the chewed-up worms a mother bird might vomit into her baby's awaiting mouth. Or at least, what Xenia imagined such a substance would taste like. And she couldn't decide whether it was more revolting warm or cold.

"Yes," Xenia answered, choking down her nauseating dinner. "I'd be foolish not to be. I'm not sure I can go through with it."

*But I will, to keep you safe.*

"Then don't," he said, like it was the easiest decision in the world. "I already told you not to worry about me. If you see an opportunity to get free tomorrow, I want you to promise me you'll take it." He chucked his metal bowl onto the tray.

The oatmeal turned to ash in her mouth. "No."

"Xenia," Cael whispered, his use of her full name sending prickles down her spine. He rarely addressed her that way these days. It was either Zee or Blondie or some half-grunted syllable to get her attention. "I've lived nearly two full lifetimes. You've barely started one. If either of us is escaping this situation, it needs to be you."

Xenia scoffed and laid into him. "Two lifetimes, huh? And what do you have to show for it? No mate, no children, no home outside of that barracks room you share with Tristan? You may have *existed* for two centuries, Cael, but don't pretend you've been *living*."

Hurt scurried across his face.

Fuck.

She'd been too harsh. She only wanted him to agree that they were in this *together*. That they'd escape together or not at all. She didn't mean to hit a nerve. And based on the hardened look he now wore, she hadn't just hit it—she'd severed it.

"Do whatever you want." He turned his back to her and snapped out his wings.

"Cael." Her guilt-laden sigh bounced off the new barrier between them.

And Xenia questioned who was the true asshole in this cell.

Cael recognized he was acting childish. Putting a wall of flesh between himself and Xenia just because she'd bruised his tender feelings.

But he couldn't help it.

Was there a part of him that was flattered—and cautiously hopeful—that she refused to abandon him? Of course.

But it was buried beneath layers and layers of calcified hurt. Disagreements, slights, and full-blown rifts he'd refused to confront over the years, and instead had woven into an impenetrable skin that not even his closest friends and family could pierce.

And certainly not her.

Not when she, more so than anyone lately, had the power to pulverize his fragile insides.

High Gods, she'd made one slightly judgmental comment—a comment even *he* couldn't disagree with—and he'd recoiled like a turtle into its shell.

He'd pushed people away his whole life. And though he desperately didn't want to do it to her too, he didn't know how to change it. How to be less… *thorny*.

Only someone with extraordinarily high confidence, like Tristan, could weather the assault of Cael's barbs. Could wait around for Cael to emerge from the slump of his broody episodes.

Cael's harshness was the sharpest weapon in his arsenal.

He pulled his knees against his chest, folded his arms atop them, then hissed in pain when he tried to lay down his head. He rolled his sleeve back and winced as he noticed Xenia's most recent bite had begun to bleed again. The dose of healing suppressant must've undone the mending his body had performed on the wound.

He expelled a bitter laugh. It was almost too poetic—Xenia's teeth tearing him apart.

He wiped away the blood, then tugged down his sleeve, closed his eyes, and fell into a shallow sleep.

*"Stand down, in the name of his Imperial Majesty!"*

*A choked giggle burst from the freckle-faced boy, and the wooden sword he brandished shook with his laughter.*

*"Byron!" Cael whined, heat crawling up his neck as he spread his fledgling wings. "I'm supposed to be scary."*

*Byron collapsed in hysterics, rolling through the dewy grass behind Stoneridge, the Zephyrus family lodge. The sprawl of thick, sturdy logs accented by stone and glass dominated a windswept hill overlooking Diachre, capital of Cael's father's territory.*

*In the valley below, modernization was sweeping through what had once been a modest hunting village. Skeletal structures speared through the skyline, half-formed towers of glass and metal funded by an influx of capital that had flooded the territory during the war. Typhon Mountain—with its terrible, fire-breathing monster beneath—crested the eastern edge of Brachos, and its namesake steel had been a boon to both the territory's and Cael's family's wealth.*

*Arran Zephyrus may have spent his first three centuries as a warrior, but the continental conflict had transformed him into a shrewd businessman. He forged his wartime earnings into a new industry, replacing hunting and fishing* with weapons manufacturing, taking full advantage of the technological and scientific advancements traveling up the Dordenne from Delos.

Not that Cael understood much of industry at ten years old, but he'd gleaned what he could from overheard conversations between his father and his business partners.

Cael lifted his raven-head helmet, a replica of the one he'd seen the Vasilikans—the Emperor's personal guards—wearing on the Imperial couple's last visit to Stoneridge. Mother had helped him make it out of papier-mache earlier this week, trying to coax him out of the mood he'd fallen into.

As soon as the project was finished, Cael had begged his older brothers Tomas and Viktor to play pretend swords, but they'd dismissed him. They were too busy training with actual weapons to entertain their needy little brother.

And Cael wasn't about to ask his little brother Erik to play. The toddler would've been too busy chasing butterflies or eating dirt.

Pouting as he'd stomped away from his indifferent older brothers, Cael had found Byron, the ten-year-old son of one the lodge's human servants, stuffing his face with biscuits in the kitchen.

A consistently friendly and pliable last resort, Byron was always willing to go along with Cael's schemes. Besides, Cael wasn't about to traipse around the grounds alone in his magnificent new helmet. He needed a proper fake foe.

The younglings had snuck into the training yard and borrowed two wooden practice swords, then dashed into the meadows at the edge of the woods. Cael was careful to *keep them out of view of the large windows at the back of the lodge.*

*Especially the two-story one belonging to his father's office.*

*He'd been told time and again that it wasn't appropriate for the High Councilor's son to be cavorting with humans, but what was he supposed to do when no one else wanted to play with him?*

*Byron pushed himself up off the grass. "Okay, okay," he said with a slight lisp. "Let's go again. I won't laugh this time."*

*Byron squared his feet, the training sword wobbling in his chubby hands.*

*Cael shoved his helmet down and adjusted the eyeholes. He'd complained to Mother that she'd made it too big and she'd laughed, kissing him on the cheek and insisting he'd grow into it soon.*

*He gripped his own wooden sword, resting the tip on the ground, hands wrapped around the hilt like he'd seen the Vasilikans do.*

*He cleared his throat and said his line again. "Stand down, in the name of his Imperial Majesty!"*

*Byron didn't laugh this time, instead came charging at Cael with a squeaky war cry and a youthful approximation of fury on his soft face.*

*Cael's pretend weapon clacked against Byron's as he struck away the shaky blow.*

*The two young males laughed and shrieked as they chased each other through the grass, the afternoon sun warming Cael's wings despite the chilly winds.*

Byron made to rush him again, but froze in pure horror and promptly dropped the sword.

A strong, rough hand fisted the back of Cael's tunic, and the helmet tumbled from his head.

Arran Zephyrus's massive ashen wings were tucked, the black talons at their peaks winking over his broad shoulders with a promise of violence. The wind whipped at his braided copper hair and beard, his gray eyes honed to an edge as deadly as his territory's sought-after steel.

"What are you doing?" His voice was low and quiet, but ferociously sharp, slicing across Cael's skin and cutting to the bone.

"N-nothing, Father," he mumbled, shame heating his cheeks at both his choice of playmate and the fear quaking through his limbs. "We were just playing."

Arran threw Cael to the grass and stalked over to the trembling human boy.

Cael's father yanked Byron from the ground, and a sickening crack clapped across the meadow like a gunshot. Followed by the sharp tang of urine as the boy wet himself.

Byron's arm went limp and floppy in Arran's grip, and he wailed, a caterwaul of such deep agony that sympathetic tears blurred Cael's vision.

"How many times must I tell you that you are not to associate with humans," his father bellowed as Byron sniveled in his grip, pawing at his broken arm.

Arran dragged the boy over to Cael, waving Byron's floppy arm and nearly brushing Cael's face with the boy's purpling fingers. "You did this to him. Never forget it. And if I ever see you degrading yourself and our family by *playing with a human again, my punishment will not be as merciful as this."*

*"Yes, sir," Cael sniveled, staring at his feet.*

*"Look at me," Arran barked, and Cael slowly lifted his head.*

*His father's blow wasn't unexpected, though it still knocked Cael off his feet. He cowered, attempting to shield himself with his tiny wings as Arran loomed over him.*

*"Zephyrus males do not cry, boy. Wipe that pathetic look off your face and go clean yourself up for dinner."*

*Arran stomped towards the lodge, dragging a keening Byron behind him.*

*Once Cael was sure his father was out of earshot, he scrambled over to his discarded helmet and ripped it apart with his bare hands.*

*Cael's heaving, angry breaths mingled with the swift wind that scattered the black shreds across the meadow.*

*He never saw Byron again after that day.*

*And he—*

Cael shuddered out of his dream at the very intimate and lately unfamiliar feeling of a finger stroking his wing.

A rush of hot blood flooded his groin before a small voice whispered, "Are you awake?"

He jerked his wings, shaking off her touch.

"I...I'm so sorry about what I said earlier, Cael. It was cruel and untrue. I was..." She paused, calming her quivering voice. "I was upset that you didn't want us to stick together. And I lashed out at you. It was uncalled for."

His wings drooped slightly, but he remained silent.

"Can you please... I...I can't sleep... my nightmare... it's too quiet."

Curiosity piqued, he lowered a wing. The small crack in his defenses encouraged her to continue.

"I can only fall asleep when someone's breathing next to me. Your wings are blocking the sound."

He softened at her confession. He tucked in his wings and turned towards her, almost wishing he hadn't when he beheld her anguish.

Bloody Stygios, she looked exhausted. Purple half-moons lurked beneath her eyes, and he berated himself for causing her such discomfort when she'd need every ounce of energy to survive her task tomorrow.

But despite this realization, despite recognizing he was a selfish monster in the thrall of his own brittle ego, he couldn't bring himself to apologize. Not directly, at least.

"What nightmares?" he asked.

"Night*mare*," she whispered, head bowed. "The same one that's haunted me since I was ten. When I was stolen from my parents in Primarvia and forced into the order."

Rage smoldered beneath his skin at the shame lacing her words. As if, as a ten-year-old child, it had been *her* fault she'd been taken.

He'd never asked whether she'd joined the order willingly. If he were being honest, he'd never spared a thought for the mortal women who did Letha's bidding. Where they'd come from, what their lives were like before they'd become Shrouded Sisters. They were cogs in the Empire's grinding machinations—useful, disposable, replaceable.

He hadn't thought it possible to feel more disgusted with himself but he was wrong.

"You can wipe *that* fucking look right off your pretty face," she said and his heart leapt at the return of her sass. "I don't need your pity."

His laugh caught in his throat and he bit his lip to keep from smiling. "But you do need my *breathing*?" She'd told him an uncomfortable truth, exposed a bit of herself. The least he could do was risk the same. "I don't pity you, Blondie. You amaze me. You're always so…effortlessly positive."

She snorted, a fleeting glimpse of deep sorrow darkening her face. "That's the thing no one ever realizes. It's *not* effortless. It's a battle. Every High Gods-damned day. All you have to do is dare to see the world the way you want to."

He didn't know why he suddenly felt like crying, like breaking apart into a million tiny pieces and scattering away on the wind.

She made the most complicated things sound so simple.

Whatever world she saw through those kinetic green eyes, a soft world devoid of his father's hard cruelty, he desperately wanted to experience it.

He wasn't ready to admit that to her yet. He wasn't even sure he was ready to admit it to himself.

But he kept his wings tucked in. Laid down on the cool stone floor as Xenia settled herself onto the straw mattress next to him—close, but not touching.

Though sleep never reclaimed him, he controlled his breathing throughout the night, imitating the sounds as best he could.

For her.

And damn if he wasn't comforted by the peaceful silence of Xenia's nightmare-free slumber.

# CHAPTER ELEVEN

SEATED ON A SEA-WORN wooden bench and wrapped in a scratchy wool blanket, Cassandra marveled at the peach sunrise kissing the southern colonies' turquoise waters. She was only half aware of the flurry of activity around her on Meridon's concrete dock.

As soon as they'd arrived, Tristan and Hella had sprung into action. They'd summoned the Meridon branch of the Vestians to assist the survivors and search the off-shore wreckage for any unlucky souls who hadn't escaped.

Tristan had slipped into command mode, delivering orders to the sleep-weary Windriders who'd been torn from their beds, unaccustomed to early morning emergencies.

Cassandra watched him work and wondered how she'd never guessed at his lineage. He wore his authority like an invisible crown. Not a single Vestian on that dock, not even the captain of the Meridon branch, questioned his directives.

A few of them had even expressed sympathy for his exile, intimated that they'd have preferred it if *he* had become Emperor instead of Eamon. Tristan had shrugged them off, humble to a fault.

How much of his influence was due to his size and power and how much was due to his delivery? Gentle and compassionate, yet firm and unyielding.

Her heart swelled at the sight of her friend in his element. Sipping at cool water from a paper cup, she scanned the sun-warmed city.

Thalenn, that cramped metropolis of crooked rooftops, crumbling brick buildings, and twisty, narrow streets, couldn't have seemed more removed from this seaside paradise.

Meridon's breezy collection of candy-colored buildings meandered down palm-tree-lined avenues, through slate squares, and around burbling fountains. Steps from the dock in what Cassandra assumed was the city's main square, a statue of Faurana the Mother, High Goddess of Land and Life, perched atop a multi-tiered fountain, gloriously naked with water droplets misting her decadent curves and outstretched arms. Offering the full bounty of the land and sea to her worshipers.

The city roused slowly, yawning and stretching like a cat luxuriating in a beam of sunshine. Though she hadn't yet met one, Cassandra suspected the citizens of Meridon were a languid bunch. The relentless productivity that gripped Thalenn's citizenry would be difficult to sustain in these hot, humid conditions. Meridon was made for long afternoon naps and cold, slushy cocktails. No wonder the Artisan and her lover had decided to make their home here.

A broad shadow crept over Cassandra, and she shielded her gaze with her palm, squinting into a pair of concerned burnt-honey eyes.

She sighed, smiling up into Tristan's pinched face. "I'm *fine*. You're looking at me like I'm some kind of fragile, broken doll."

He offered her a hand, which she took not because she needed to, but because she wanted to touch him. Hoped his strength and calm would rub off on her.

Her pride would make it hard to admit, but she was still shaken by the incident on the ship. And was surprised Tristan hadn't yet scolded her for ditching him and rushing after the Fae arsonist.

"I'd feel a lot better if we could find someone to bandage your wounds before we head to see the Artisan." He pulled her closer.

Her pulse instantly quickened at their proximity. Would the electric energy between them ever run dry? And how much harder would it be to let him go if it didn't?

He inspected the burn on her forearm, beginning to peel at the edges but still bubbly and blistered in the center. The one on her thigh looked the same and she couldn't help limping as she stepped away from him.

She made it all of two paces before Tristan swept her into his arms. She yelped in protest, but not too forcefully.

Leaving Hella behind to assist the Meridon Vestians, Tristan carried Cassandra through the slowly waking streets. The smells of cinnamon, citrus, coffee and baking bread sent ravenous hunger clawing through her stomach. Though the simple dinner they'd shared on the ship had been satisfying, the exertions of the fight, not to mention the fire and subsequent rescue efforts, had burned through any lingering fuel in her system.

"We'll get breakfast *after* you're patched up," Tristan stated, in tune with her needs as always. Was it a Fae thing? A special ability bestowed upon him by his royal heritage? Though he didn't behave this way towards anyone else, and certainly no other humans. She tucked the information away, let it feed the foolish spark of hope she kept burning in her chest despite the obstacles between them.

Tristan turned down a wide avenue just beyond Faurana's square and they came upon a squat, whitewashed building with weathered wooden doors. The structure occupied an entire block.

Tristan answered her unasked question. "Meridon's Vestian outpost. They'll fix you up and give me a new uniform." He remained barefoot, and in his sleep pants.

She didn't need to ask about the rest of their belongings—an offering to the High Goddess behind them.

Thirty minutes later, the pair exited the utilitarian building, Tristan in a brand new leather uniform and Cassandra with two gauzy bandages wrapped around her forearm and thigh.

The Vestians had also offered her a pair of black boots in a size typically reserved for the Windrider children who participated in the Guards' summer training program. Tristan snickered when they'd handed her the tiny boots, and she nearly whacked him with them.

Despite her newly dressed wounds, she couldn't help a slight limp. She refused to let Tristan carry her, though. She might be wearing a child's boots, but that didn't mean she wanted to be toted around like one. He grumbled in protest, but respected her wishes.

She regretted the decision as they journeyed deeper into town. The streets sloped gently upwards the further they traveled from the water's edge.

Giving in to both her soreness and her hunger, Cassandra requested they stop for breakfast at a charming outdoor café with black and white rattan tables.

She ordered a flaky, sugar-dusted pastry from the polite waiter, then moaned in ecstasy as she tore into it. She ate three, washing them down with a cool, frothy drink flavored with chocolate and cinnamon. Tristan echoed her order.

"When in Meridon." He chomped down half a pastry in a single bite. "What?"

"You have…" she began, then leaned across the table and swiped her fingers across his lips to dust away the sugar. He grabbed her wrist and licked her fingertips with a mischievous twinkle in his eyes.

As it often did these days when she allowed herself a moment's joy, reality washed over her in a cold splash. "How many died?" she whispered, pulling her hand from his grasp and taking a bite of another pastry.

"Six. Four adults and two children." His voice cracked. "All humans."

Cassandra's sinuses burned, and the now-ashen lump of pastry caught in her thick throat. "Why didn't they help?"

"Who?"

"The other Windriders. They gathered up their families and flew away. Didn't spare a thought for any of the helpless humans on board."

Tristan's wings ruffled as he held her watery gaze. She could sense his churning thoughts, his conflicting desires to defend his species while not damning hers.

When he finally spoke, his face was a mask of cold fury. "They have been fed lies, for *centuries*, about what humans are worth. The most convincing from my awful brother and the rest of my terrible family." His face softened. "They don't know any better."

Cassandra wasn't feeling inclined towards forgiveness this morning. But perhaps she could, in time. Pushing her conflicting emotions aside, she refocused on their work.

"That Windrider. She had fire magic. Have you ever seen such a thing?"

Tristan stuffed an entire pastry into his mouth, spewing crumbs as he answered. "Not personally. Though other elemental powers besides wind magic did exist among the Fae centuries ago, long before the war."

"Like Maksym's lightning?" Cassandra shuddered as she recalled those flickering, electric charges. How they'd speared for Tristan during his airborne fight with Maksym.

Tristan nodded.

"So what are you saying?" she asked. "That Maksym and his minions have somehow found a way to activate long-dead magic?"

Tristan shrugged, nonchalant as ever. "It's possible."

"How?"

"I'm wondering if it has something to do with the Fallen Goddess."

"What makes you think that?"

"That Windrider said she was *a messenger from the New Ethyrios*. And that *she will rise to save us*. That certainly sounds like the nonsense Maksym was spewing at us a week ago. They must be working together."

"How would he have known where to find us? Who even knew we were coming here?"

"I'm sure Maksym has spies everywhere. Plenty of people saw us in the dining hall on the ship."

Cassandra flopped back in her chair, blowing out an anxious breath. "A group of crazed zealots wielding newly restored elemental magics seems like a far worse threat than a batch of tainted Delirium. Why do you think your brother told you to ignore it?"

"I'm not certain. But when have I ever done what I was told?" Cassandra huffed a laugh. "I told you this was a fool's errand. We need to stay a step ahead of him. Let's see what we can find in the Temple library after we meet with the Artisan."

"What's the point of the meeting, now that we've lost the memory?"

"You've viewed it enough times, I'm hoping she'll be able to pull it from you. And we'll have a few hours to kill while she's working. Might as well spend them doing something useful, now that our day at the beach is no longer in the cards."

She chuckled at his disheartened expression. "Sad that you won't get to see me in that bathing suit after all?"

"I'll take solace in the show you gave me last night." He pressed her fingertips to his lips, and her limbs went tingly. "And I'll buy you a new one when we get home. You can parade around the house in it for me, playmate."

She threw her head back and laughed, treasuring these small moments of levity among all the heavy things they were dealing with. She refused to feel guilty for them.

Tristan fished several *drachas* from his pocket, likely given to him by the Meridon Vestians, and left them on the table to pay for their breakfast. "Let's go, Daredevil. The Artisan is expecting us."

She winced as she pushed up out of her chair, her thigh throbbing in protest. "Where's her house?"

Tristan pointed towards a hill beyond the city where several buildings were nestled in the dense jungle. One dwelling in striking jewel tones of red, blue, green, and yellow perched on the crest like a tropical bird sunning its feathers. "It's a long walk. Will you please let me carry you?"

She waved him off. Her gait smoothed as she left the table and aimed for the rainbow-colored house on the hill.

"I'll manage."

# CHAPTER TWELVE

S HE COULDN'T MANAGE.

Cassandra's injured leg quivered with every step up the sloping avenue. She swore the house on the hill was retreating into the jungle. Beads of sweat dotted her brow, soaking the hair at her temples and trickling down her jawline.

She focused on Tristan's clomping footsteps, trying to hide how much she was struggling.

She'd been depending on herself and herself alone for the past eight years. And though he'd very willingly offered assistance, she didn't want to come to rely on him. Safer to cling to her independence.

On her next stride forward, her leg buckled. She'd barely laid her forehead against a rough, plaster wall before strong, warm hands curled around her and Tristan launched them into the sky.

The cool tug of the wind against her face was bliss, the relief she felt from being off her injured leg divine.

"Tiny *stubborn* human," he grumbled, aiming for the Artisan's house.

A few moments later, Tristan landed in the packed sand, his wings kicking up plumes of dust. He settled Cassandra on her feet, keeping an arm out for her to steady herself, but she swatted him away as her awed gaze roamed over the psychedelic dwelling.

A riotous explosion of color and sound greeted them. Wind-chimes of every imaginable shape and material hung from the eaves, translucent crystals and multi-hued shards of glass scattering prisms along the bright stucco walls. The crystals tinkled a tranquil melody in the lively, tropical breeze while metal tubes of silver, copper, and brass added harmonious bell-tones.

A willowy female clothed in a purple caftan floated through the front door with open arms.

"Welcome, welcome! May Nemosyna the Chronicler bless your memories," the Artisan sang in a serene, lilting voice. Her androgynous face was a striking contrast of strength and fragility, with a sharp nose, round cheeks, and supple lips. Short, pale hair in the same soft peach as her glowing skin crested above her forehead. Her piercing jade-green eyes sparkled merrily, framed by crinkling lines—remnants of her bygone mortality.

She grasped Tristan's hands and pressed a kiss to each side of his face. "Officer Saros, I was so pleased to receive your message. Lovely to see you again."

"And you, Psylbe" Tristan bowed slightly. "Just Tristan will do, though." He gestured towards Cassandra. "This is my partner Cassandra Fortin. She's a former Shrouded Sister as well."

"Praise Letha," the Artisan intoned, arching a wispy eyebrow.

"Praise Letha," Cassandra echoed, the greeting pulled from her mouth on instinct.

"Rare to meet another wayward member of the flock." The female turned back to Tristan. "Where is your other partner? Officer Zephyrus? He was here a little over a week ago."

Tristan's genial smile disappeared and the Artisan mirrored his grim expression, as if compelled by her boundless empathy.

"What's happened?" she whispered.

"Let's discuss it inside," Tristan said, inspecting the untamed greenery pressing in on the house. Plenty of shadowy pockets to hide an enemy or four. Not to mention the cacophonous blanket of sound from the chimes that would mask their approach.

The Artisan led them towards the home's ornately carved door, reminiscent of the Temple library entrance in Thalenn. This frieze honored Nemosyna, Goddess of Memory and ancient rival of Letha.

The Chronicler stared out from the door, naked from the waist up with a flowing skirt cascading from her hips and tangling in her feet. She cradled a candle in the upraised palm at her stomach, the flame's glow banishing curved, talon-like shadows creeping in around her. Despite the danger, Nemosyna's face was placid, confident. As if the Goddess had absolute faith that her light would keep the darkness at bay.

The Artisan stepped in front of Cassandra, breaking her mesmerized scrutiny of the door, and swung it into a wide room full of gentle curves. No interior walls divided the single-storied space, distinct areas instead delineated by silk-printed screens or gauzy curtains.

Psylbe led them to a row of screens across from the bed, behind which stood a waist-high, weathered wooden table. Several shelves were crammed with glass vials, both empty and glowingly full, and rows upon rows of stones and crystals in every size, sheen, and color imaginable.

Cassandra surveyed the Artisan's workshop with awe. "What are the crystals for?"

"They are God-touched stones, conduits of divine power. They influence the manipulated memories, alter the narratives to fit my client's needs." With a graceful hand, the Artisan plucked up a deep, ruby-colored crystal, flat on the bottom and jagged on top—like boiling blood. "This one channels Vestan the Warrior, adds conflict. An innocent comment or conversation can be tinted to be remembered as a fight. A declaration of war, even."

Psylbe replaced the blood-red crystal on the shelf and grabbed a shimmering violet cube. "Thakavi the

Scholar's crystal. It grants knowledge and understanding, can coax out even the deepest held secrets."

The Artisan glanced sidelong at Tristan, but he didn't acknowledge the look, and maintained his mask of aloof curiosity.

"But this cheeky little bugger is my favorite." The Artisan's jade eyes danced as she switched out the cube for a white, egg-shaped stone glistening with rainbow-colored flecks. "A fire opal bestows the influence of the Fallen Goddess. A memory will shatter into fragments, sowing chaos and confusion. Or it will coalesce into a narrative of such supreme balance that the viewer will swear they understand the meaning of all life in the universe. And I never know which outcome to expect. At full power, the stone is capable of manipulating time and space itself."

"Full power?" Cassandra asked.

"There are sites throughout the continent that have been blessed by the Gods. Pockets of their power in this world where the stones can be…recharged, shall we say," the Artisan answered with an enigmatic smile.

"What else do you know of the Fallen Goddess?" Tristan asked.

"Very little outside of the effects of the fire opal, unfortunately."

"We need to learn more about her history. Think we'll have any luck at the Temple library downtown?"

"Perhaps, though I wouldn't hope to find much. Most of her literature was destroyed after the war." The

Artisan settled the opal back on the shelf. "Her powers, the powers of all the Gods, are not to be taken lightly."

Cassandra couldn't help a spark of indignation. "And yet you sell your services to Maksym, the highest bidder?"

The Artisan eyed her coolly, an ineffable expression shuttering her features. She didn't balk at Maksym's name; Tristan must've told her about the client who'd been commissioning her services in the message he'd sent to arrange their visit.

"Is that what you think I did? I don't have to tell you that while his methods may be questionable, the seeds of doubt he intends to sow among the Fae will put Ethyrios on a path to true freedom. And I do nothing without Nemosyna's blessing. She has willed this."

"The Goddess wants *Maksym* to rule Ethyrios?" Cassandra sputtered.

"I did not quite say that, did I?" The ethereal female's coy grin stoked Cassandra's annoyance. "But we're getting off-track. I am sure this is not why you've come to see me?"

"No," Tristan answered. "Please forgive my companion's impertinence, Psylbe. We had a rough night and the information we seek is crucial. How much did Maksym's messengers tell you of his plans?"

"Only the barest details. As I mentioned, I confer with the Chronicler before taking on any job. I ask potential clients a single question before agreeing to take their commission. What do you seek through this work? I pass their answer along to Nemosyna, who either approves or denies the commission."

"And what was Maksym's answer to that question?" Tristan asked.

"An upheaval of power. Cleverly stated and vague enough to suggest the Goddess blesses an end to the Emperor, but not necessarily the installation of Maksym in his place." The Artisan aimed a knowing look at Tristan, and seemed inclined to say more but pressed her lips shut instead.

"Nemosyna would truly sanction a return to the days before the Accords? When the two species were at war with each other?" Cassandra asked.

"The Gods are neither fully benevolent, nor malevolent," the Artisan answered. "They would not sanction the destruction or subjugation of an entire species." She lowered her voice to a whisper. "You should ask yourself whether life since the Accords has really been so beneficial for our species."

Cassandra *had* been asking herself that question, for a while now. "You still consider yourself human?"

"I was human for the first forty-two years of my life and I consider it a great honor to have lived as both species," the Artisan answered, her voice as rich and sonorous as the Temple's grand bell. "When Cleo offered to turn me, I agonized over the decision for months. I was afraid of losing my mortal capacity for wonder. What surprises could the world possibly hold after centuries of existence?" The Artisan paused, blinking her green eyes several times slowly. "I needn't have worried. Each day truly can be a gift, if one remains grateful, humble, and purposeful."

Cassandra suppressed the urge to roll her eyes, but could tell by the female's expression that she'd meant every word. "Why don't you have wings? If you were turned by a Windrider, surely her ability to fly would've been passed to you?"

"Only the most powerful Windriders can bestow the ability to fly upon a Turned mortal. It's one of the few reasons, besides her family's influence, that Cleo was spared the death penalty after her crime. She's not powerful enough to have given me wings and therefore my Turning wasn't seen as an immediate threat to the royal family's power." Psylbe turned to face Tristan. "But surely, he has—"

Tristan cut her off with a sharp glance. "We're wasting time. Allow me to explain why we've come. I'm guessing neither Maksym nor his messengers shared with you how he plans to distribute the manipulated memory?" Psylbe shook her head. "He intends to add it to a large batch of Delirium which we assume he'll filter throughout the continent. He's working with Richelle Pacha, the daughter of a mortal Delirium exporter and former Sister herself. They need to add the blood of active Shrouded Sisters to the drink in order for the memory to affix within Fae minds."

"Horrific," the Artisan breathed out.

Cassandra fought the urge to call out Psylbe's hypocrisy. The Artisan had willingly participated in this scheme, and nothing the female had said today inclined Cassandra to let her fall back on the excuse that the Goddess of Memory had willed it.

"They also need Thalassium to stabilize the mixture," Tristan continued. "They'd intended to acquire it from a rock attached to a diamond necklace, which is now missing. Hidden somewhere by another brave Shrouded Sister who was working to thwart their plans the whole time." Cassandra's chest squeezed at the mention of Cora, her dear friend now lost to the mists of obliviation. "She buried the knowledge of the hidden necklace's location within a memory, which she scrambled by ingesting tainted Delirium. That memory was delivered to Cassandra last week. She's watched it hundreds of times, but can't make any sense of it. You've helped me unscramble Delirium-addled memories before. I thought you could do so again."

"And help, perhaps I can," Psylbe answered. "But I will need to confer with the Chronicler first. She must bless any use of my powers, even if it's just hunting through a discarded memory."

"There's another complication," Cassandra said. "The original memory is gone. It was stolen from us last night. But as Tristan said, I've viewed it hundreds of times, so was hoping you might be able to pull it from me to conduct the interpretation."

"It's possible, but the interpretation will take longer and I cannot guarantee the result will be accurate. Pulling a memory of a memory fades the details, like making a copy of a copy. Fortunately, the memory is only once removed. The more layers there are, the more difficult they are to decipher. Once I have the Goddess's blessing, we can get started. So I must ask Cassandra, what do you seek through this work?"

Cassandra didn't hesitate for a second. The answer had been prowling through her mind for days, a hungry, insatiable beast caged by her inability to rescue her friend. And if she couldn't deliver it, she hoped the High Gods would.

"Vengeance."

The Artisan spread her palms, a impish smile tugging at her lips. "The Chronicler's favorite answer."

And Cassandra nearly fainted at the sight of the faded red scar, similar to Tristan's, slashed across the Artisan's left palm.

# CHAPTER THIRTEEN

THE TEMPLE OF LETHA in Meridon was familiar, yet distorted. Like walking into one's childhood home to find the furniture rearranged and the walls freshly painted—a disorienting pang of nostalgia-tinged melancholy.

The structure exhibited the same pale stone walls and red-tiled roof as the Temple in Thalenn, though was only half the size given the small population in the southern colonies.

Which only increased the chances of someone noticing that Xenia was very much out of place.

She breathed through her rising panic as she peered through an iron gate into the atrium. Moss-covered sandstone arches ringed the two-storied courtyard and garden beds teeming with glossy leaves and fuschia flowers lined the brick walkways.

A crowd of supplicants languished on benches and leaned against the arches. Far more than Xenia would've expected for a Temple this size, at this time of the morning.

The statue of Letha stood sentry in the center, the spitting image of the one back home save a single detail—the Goddess's right arm was missing. The cleaved stump of her marble shoulder hovered above the water jug cradled in her sole remaining arm. Xenia wondered who had disfigured the statue: a disgruntled Sister, an angry supplicant, or something worse.

Xenia had no idea how she'd gotten here. She didn't even know how much time had passed. It was still morning, but could have been days later.

As soon as Xenia had awoken from a second blissfully nightmare-free sleep—after she and Cael had achieved their tentative peace—Alexei had barreled into their cell and tugged her out without so much as a word of warning.

She'd sent a panicked look in Cael's direction, but his face was stone cold, sharp. Not for her, she knew. For their enemies. He was showing her how to behave today. And she'd gratefully taken the lesson. Had put on an icy mask of neutrality as Alexei dragged her out of the dungeon and up into the breezeway. Alexei had pushed up her sleeve and sank a small needle into the crook of her elbow. Before she could even cry out, the world had gone dark, and the next thing she knew

Alexei was slapping her awake outside the Temple walls here in Meridon.

The bells chimed eight, a soft tinkling compared to the booming gongs in Thalenn. A line of midnight-blue-clad women spilled into the atrium, pushing through the crowd like a branching river.

Xenia creaked open the gate and scurried in among the flock, fixing the square of navy silk she'd ripped from the interior layer of her skirts to cover her curls. She couldn't risk rumors traveling the colonies about a blonde, bushy-haired kidnapper. Besides, the Sisters at the Temple in Thalenn must be aware by now that she was missing and if they heard such a description, they'd instantly know it was Xenia. She shuddered to think what Maksym would do to her—and Cael—if she could no longer be of use to him.

As she tucked in at the end of a line of four Sisters, she dipped her hands into her deep pockets, running her fingertips over the four tiny glass bottles of tainted Delirium. For her intended victims.

She scanned the heads in front of her. Two blonde, one silver, and one a deep chocolate braid so similar to Cassandra's that Xenia had to bite her tongue to keep from calling out her friend's name.

Which of these Sisters would Xenia damn to a cruel fate at Maksym's hands? She swallowed her rising nausea as the group scurried down a set of shallow stone steps and passed through an arched wooden door.

Stale, tomb-like air and cool, stone walls closed in on her, devouring the sounds of footsteps and lingering chatter.

Rounding a corner, the Sisters paused as they came upon a row of stone doors evenly spaced down a dim corridor. The women separated, each aiming for her own extraction room.

Heart ramming against her ribs, Xenia followed the dark-haired Sister to a door at the end of the hallway.

The Sister swiveled and her lips lifted into a tentative smile. She was a younger woman, in her mid-thirties if Xenia had to guess. "Can I help you?"

The woman's eyes were so kind and her expression so genuine that Xenia nearly confessed everything. Who she was. What she was doing here. Almost begged the woman to help her.

But she had no idea where Cael was being held. Couldn't stomach the thought of leaving him on his own to die.

She wracked her brain for an appropriate response to the query. Thought about the cunning heroines from her books, and asked herself what they would do in this situation.

"I...I'm..." Xenia's mind scrolled through an infinite number of story angles before it grasped a thread and the lie spooled smoothly from her lips. "I'm a novitiate from the Temple in Primarvia." She raised her wrist, exposing her tattoo. She prayed to the High Gods that this woman had never been to the Temple in the northern middle colonies. "I was sent here to shadow you today."

The Sister nodded. "Mother Superior did mention that we might have new Sisters showing up. Especially with the new extraction quotas delivered by the Empire."

Xenia had no clue what the Sister was talking about, but played along.

"Yes, just that. I arrived this morning. A bit late, unfortunately. The Abbess was rather curt with me. She directed me here then shooed me away."

The Sister huffed a knowing laugh. "Don't take it personally. Curt is her default setting. I'm Sister Jorina." The woman extended a creamy white hand, her tattoo peeking over her cuff.

Xenia blurted the first name that rose to mind: the fierce princess from her favorite series of books. "Sister Arelinn. Nice to meet you."

Xenia stared at the Sister before her, wanting to warn her of the danger. But lingering visions of Cael's battered face, his groans of pain, and his bent and twisted wing kept her mouth clamped shut.

"Welcome to Meridon." Sister Jorina inclined her head, the friendly smile never leaving her face. "You can view and classify the extracted memories after I pull them." Xenia nodded quickly, remaining quiet. She could hardly believe this ruse had worked.

Xenia wondered what Maksym's henchmen were doing while she was in here attempting to lure innocents into danger. They hadn't specified how much time she'd be given, merely instructed her to lead the four dosed Sisters around the back of the Temple where they'd be waiting. Had they seen her come into the extraction rooms?

A soft knock followed by a mellow female voice informed Sister Jorina that her first supplicant was ready. The Sister padded to the door, gesturing for Xenia to have a seat in the viewing chamber at the back of the room. The woman whispered a warning about the state the supplicant was in. Something about an accident she'd suffered the night prior.

Sister Jorina left the room, returning moments later with a disheveled young woman who was quaking like a leaf.

Sister Jorina guided the young woman to lie prone on the stone extraction chair. "Relax and close your eyes," she hummed, low and calming. "Take a deep breath and focus on the memory you wish to sacrifice to Letha the Stranger, Goddess of Oblivion."

She placed her fingers at the woman's temple and massaged in slow circles, chanting the words that would pull the memory from the woman's mind. "*Lui ganeth, lui cathona. Lui ganeth, lui cathona.*" Out of body, out of mind.

Pale gold light leaked from the woman's temples and into Sister Jorina's awaiting palms. Undulating her fingers, the Sister coaxed the memory into the still air of the extraction room.

The young woman exhaled a long, slow breath, signaling the end of the ritual. Sister Jorina guided the light into a small glass vial, then corked it to keep the memory intact.

Since Sister Jorina did not repeat the process, Xenia suspected payment was not this supplicant's motivation. She must have come to sacrifice a painful or frightening memory. The Sister left the young woman breathing deeply in the chair and walked the glowing, golden vial back to Xenia.

"You know what to do Sister, yes?" Sister Jorina whispered, handing Xenia the cool glass. "View the memory and determine if it's potent enough to flavor the Delirium. I will check your work once you've viewed it. Take your time. I'll need a few minutes to wake the supplicant and escort her to the waiting room." Sister Jorina's kind brown eyes swept over Xenia's face, misinterpreting her anxiety. She tenderly squeezed Xenia's hand. "Don't worry, Sister. You can do this. I'll return to help you soon."

Sister Jorina closed the door, leaving Xenia alone in the dim chamber. Xenia dipped her head into her hands, wondering what the fuck she was going to do?

What would Cass do? Stop sniveling, for starters. Play along, look for advantages. Perhaps she could sneak out of the chamber once Sister Jorina and the supplicant left? But that wouldn't get her any closer to the task that Maksym had set for her.

She took a deep, bracing breath, figured she might as well view the memory while waiting for Sister Jorina and the young woman to exit.

Xenia uncorked the vial and closed her eyes, then pressed the opening to her tattoo as she whispered the second half of the chant. "*Mei ganeth, mei cathona. Mei ganeth, mei cathona.*" Into my body, into my mind.

*She bolted upright in a hard bed to shouting and an acrid, choking smell that burned her lungs. An orange glow and tendrils of smoke crept into the small berth from underneath the door.*

*"Wake up, Theo." She gripped her new husband's shoulder, shaking him as icy fear sluiced through her veins.*

*Something had gone terribly wrong on this ship.*

*Not a great start to their blissful honeymoon week in Meridon.*

*The pair tumbled out of bed and threw on their traveling clothes.*

*She reached for the doorknob, but Theo shouted, grabbing her wrist to halt her. He tapped his palm against the brass knob, testing to ensure it wasn't skin-melting temperature before he whipped the door open into absolute chaos.*

*A crowd of mortals and Fae streamed down the cloudy hallway, bleary-eyed and panicked as they scrambled towards the back of the ship.*

*Theo tugged her into the rush of bodies, and an unnatural, blazing heat coated her back. She glanced over her shoulder just in time to see a pair of red wings widen across the hallway. A booming, accented voice shouted at everyone to take cover.*

*She crashed to the ground, Theo curling around her body, and a rumbling explosion nearly blew out her ears before the world went black.*

*She was re-awakened by a hand on her cheek, a voice shouting in her ear.*

*Theo.*

*Was she still alive? Her ears were ringing, her vision swimming.*

*Theo's hands were joined by another more delicate pair, and she was hauled to shaky feet as she gazed into steadfast, blue-gray eyes. The woman supporting her was beautiful, radiating a strength and confidence that calmed her frenzied fears.*

*"You're going to have to jump," the woman said, in a husky voice completely at odds with her small stature. "Can you tread water?"*

*She nodded, tried to open her mouth to answer that she could swim, but her lips refused to obey.*

*"Good," the woman answered. "Wait in the water for the lifeboats."*

*Without another word, the woman helped her over the wrecked remains of the cabin walls and she held Theo's hand as they plunged into the dark, churning waters of the Sea of Thetis.*

Xenia pulled the vial away from her wrist and re-corked it, reeling in both shock and excitement at the sight of Cassandra in the young woman's memory.

If the survivors of that shipwreck were here in Meridon, there was a good chance her friend was too.

Xenia poked her head out of the extraction room, tucking a few wayward curls into the silk fabric wrapped over her hair.

The hallway was empty and silent, no sign of Sister Jorina.

If she could escape the Temple unseen, perhaps she could find the other survivors. And Cassandra. Xenia had no doubt that Tristan would be with her. Where Cassandra went, Tristan was sure to follow. Like an over-sized, lovestruck puppy.

Xenia knew, without a shadow of a doubt, that the hulking Vestian was over the moon for her friend. But Cassandra could be willfully oblivious to that kind of attention.

Xenia stepped into the hallway and plastered herself against the cool stone wall. She crept around the corner and aimed for the wooden door to the atrium.

The door opened and Xenia dashed to hide behind it, grabbing the iron handle to hold it in place. Swift footsteps whispered down the hallway followed by Sister Jorina's soft voice.

Xenia ducked out from behind the door and rushed up the shallow steps into the atrium, startling two Sisters conversing on a stone bench.

"Praise Letha," Xenia muttered as she passed.

"Praise Letha," the two women echoed, inclining their heads and tracking Xenia's movements with suspicious eyes.

"Sister Arelinn!" Sister Jorina shouted.

Xenia bolted as the Sister rushed into the courtyard, her cries causing the two other Sisters to fly out of their seats.

Xenia didn't dare look behind her as she tore open the iron gate and rushed into the street, hiding among the flowing crowd. She ducked behind a wide marble lamp post.

The Sisters gathered inside the gate, scanning the street beyond but disinclined to leave the grounds, even to chase an intruder.

Xenia waited until the three Sisters had abandoned their perusal of the crowd, then scanned the street for the tell-tale serpent's eyes of Maksym's Deathstalker henchmen.

Spying none, Xenia pushed away from the lamp post and headed down the sloping avenue towards the concrete dock surrounded by glittering turquoise water. Surely that's where the survivors of the shipwreck would've come ashore.

Xenia approached the water's edge, sweat beginning to coat the back of her neck under her heavy fall of curls in the midmorning heat. She stepped up onto the concrete dock, raising a hand to shield her eyes from the light glinting off the rippling, crystal clear water.

She spied a frenzy of activity out on the horizon, several small vessels and winged forms bustling over the surface. Likely searching the wreckage of the ship. Xenia said a silent prayer to the High Gods that no one had perished.

The dock was crammed with tourists. Mostly Fae from the continent, based on their sleek, skin-baring outfits and the commstones tucked beneath their earlobes. A rare sight within the colonies, the violet stones allowed all sub-species of Fae to send the windwhispers that only Windriders were otherwise capable of.

Xenia turned back to survey the lovely city behind her. She wished she were visiting under different circumstances and that Cass was here with her.

A flapping pair of iridescent black wings thundered into the sky several blocks away and her stomach hollowed out.

Her eyes stung with overwhelming, relieved tears as Tristan landed at a colorful house on the hill abutting the city. She rushed across the wide avenue along the water's edge, pushing through the crowds.

Though the streets themselves were wide enough for two vehicles to traverse side-by-side, the narrow sidewalks held barely enough room for a couple to stroll down shoulder-to-shoulder, the stone worn slick and shiny by years of wandering tourists. She bobbed and weaved around the current crop, suppressing an urge to shout at the meanderers to walk faster or get the fuck out of her way.

Five blocks up, she turned onto a less crowded side street that flowed up to the hill. She rushed past several storefronts, then came upon a long expanse of sandstone wall topped with a red-tiled roof.

Shit.

She was back at the Temple.

Rushing past an old man sweeping the sidewalk in front of his well-kept storefront, she was about to cross to the next block when a bell jingled.

Someone leaving the old man's shop.

The back of her neck prickled and she turned, her lungs seizing at the sight of long black hair and glowing yellow eyes.

She'd barely lifted her leg to run when a pale, supernaturally strong hand encircled her wrist.

Alexei's scar pulled taut as his lips stretched wide and his fangs popped out.

He clenched something in his other hand. Streaks of glimmering rainbow light glowed between his pale fingers.

"We will so enjoy watching Maksym teach you this lesson the hard way," he sneered before bringing her hand to his mouth and raking a shallow gash across her wrist.

Cassandra's name was on the tip of Xenia's tongue before paralyzing pain seared through her veins and the world melted away in a haze of crimson mist.

# CHAPTER FOURTEEN

THE FADED RED SCAR on Tristan's palm was mocking Cassandra.

Each time he reached for a book, each time he turned a page, each time he tucked a strand of his onyx hair behind his ear, the scar filled her mind with destructive whispers.

*He Turned a human Fae.*

*He didn't offer to do it for you.*

*He has no desire to keep you in his life for any longer than a single mortal lifetime.*

If Tristan noticed her increased attention to his scar, he didn't bring it up.

She struggled to quiet the callous voice as they searched the Temple library in Meridon for texts referencing the Fallen Goddess.

Since the Meridon Temple of Letha was much smaller than the Temple in Thalenn, its library was more like a reading room. Only four parallel rows of stacks occupied the quiet, oak-paneled hall, with books organized not by title or author but by year of publication. The unique organizational system made searching for relevant texts rather difficult, even with a consultation from the lone, harried librarian.

Rushing along the stacks behind a clattering push-cart, the silver-haired Sister had snatched book after book from the over-stuffed shelves before depositing Tristan and Cassandra at a small table nestled in a hidden corner.

At the sole other table in view, an older balding gentleman with a ring of jet-black hair gnawed on the end of unlit pipe as he flicked through a leather-bound book.

"Come over here and take a look at this," Tristan whispered.

Cassandra closed her own book, then rounded the table and sank into the chair next to Tristan. He cupped his wing around her back and pressed his shoulder against hers, dragging his fingertip along a thin, crumbling page. "This is one of the oldest books in the stack. A transcription of an oral history detailing life in Ethyrios in the centuries before the war.

"Before the Accords, nearly the entire Fae and human population in Ethyrios worshiped a Creator Goddess named Adelphinae."

"Delphae," Cassandra murmured, recalling the bright star depicted in the mural that blanketed the ceiling of the Temple library in Thalenn. "It was named for her."

"Sounds like it," Tristan nodded.

"And your father renamed it Erabis after the Accords."

Tristan grimaced. "An attempt to suppress the Creator's influence, if this report is to be believed. It says here that Adelphinae is the Mother of all life on this planet—including both Fae and humans.

"The Goddess possesses not only the power of creation, but also the power of destruction. She can see into the past and future, occupies a plane of existence in which linear time does not exist. Ethyrios is her greatest experiment, an amalgamation of the sentient life she's observed on other planets throughout the cosmos. It says here that she modeled Ethyrios after one called Gaia, set in motion a similar process of evolution but with a few extra magical touches. And that she has created—and destroyed—entire worlds in her quest to achieve utopia."

A bone-deep shudder rocked through Cassandra. The destruction of an entire world? She suddenly—though only briefly—sympathized with the Empire's quest to suppress the Goddess's influence.

Tristan continued, "Adelphinae gifted elemental magics to the Fae upon their creation. The ability to manipulate wind, water, fire. Lightning."

"Maksym," Cassandra whispered. "What happened to the other powers?"

Tristan flipped to a new page. "Before the war, they had been fading for centuries. The last Fae to possess elemental magic besides wind—a fire-wielding Deathstalker—died nearly seven hundred years ago. A group of powerful Fae families—mine included—started chafing against the notion that humans were their equals, as Adelphinae's dogma suggested. They raised up their own deities, the High Gods, and Adelphinae's believers suspected that the disappearance of the other elemental powers was her punishment. Said the Goddess was angered that her creations would dare turn away from her."

Cassandra frowned. "If she created both species, what gifts did she bestow upon the humans?"

Tristan turned to the end of the book. "Here. Humans once believed that mortality itself was a gift. That the Creator had blessed them with heightened emotions due to their shortened lifespan. In Ethyrios's earliest days, that was why the Fae consumed human emotions—to commune with the Goddess, honor her gifts. It was a mutual act between the species, one of divine worship. And it only occurred on a few holy days throughout the year with willing human participants.

"But in the centuries before the war, as more and more Fae turned away from Adelphinae to worship the

High Gods, the justifications for the practice shifted. Emotion feedings became less of a religious act and more of a means for the Fae to assert their dominance over humans. Many Fae had become addicted to the euphoria they experienced during the ritual, and decided to take it whenever they wished. They were careless about the safety of their prey. Scores of humans perished, even before the war. The death rate only dropped after the Accords were put in place, when Trophonios invented Delirium and peace was once again restored."

Cassandra toyed with the end of her ponytail, a thought gnawing at her brain. "If the disappearance of elemental magic was Adelphinae's punishment for the Fae, why didn't she take away *all* of them? Why leave the wind magic intact?"

Tristan chewed his lip. "Those families claimed it was because Windriders were the superior Fae sub-species, and that they weren't beholden to the Goddess's influence. They used it as an excuse to divide the continent into the six territories and establish themselves as the leaders."

Cassandra's gaze swept over the delicate pages. Though she recognized the swooping Aramaelish letters, she'd never learned the language of the Fae. "Is that what Adelphinae's supporters believed?"

Tristan shook his head. "Her worshipers claim that a Windrider is the key to her return. There's an allusion here to a prophecy that foretells her restoration."

"Don't suppose the prophecy is outlined in there, is it?"

Tristan closed the book with a frustrated grumble. "That's the end of this text."

Cassandra crossed her arms and sat back against her chair. "None of this explains how the other elemental magics are starting to appear again. If the Fallen Goddess has something to do with it, how have Maksym and his minions regained her favor? They don't exactly share her beliefs that Fae and humans are equal."

Tristan dragged a hand down his face. "I don't know."

Cassandra plucked up the book she'd been perusing before Tristan's interruption. She turned a page, then gasped.

"What?" He leaned in closer.

"Look at this illustration." She pointed to a richly-detailed rendering of several Fae females dressed in white robes gathered around an obelisk carved with a familiar symbol—a circle bisected by a vertical line. "This young female, right here. Recognize her?"

Tristan bent over the book, squinting. "Is that—"

"Reena." Cassandra ran her fingers over her friend's face. "The caption says these are priestesses of Adelphinae. Did you know?"

"She's never mentioned it. Hard to imagine *Reena* as a priestess. Even harder than imagining you as a Sister." He traced a finger over her tattoo.

She snickered. "This was drawn during the early years of the war, before the Empire forced the priestesses to preach faith in the High Gods instead.

And that symbol on the obelisk? The Windrider who burned the ship down marked it on the wall. Any idea what it means?"

"No clue."

Cassandra flipped through the remaining pages in the book, but other than that single image, there was no more information on the symbol, the Fallen Goddess, her prophecy, or her priestesses. She expelled an annoyed grunt.

Tristan stroked her spine with his wing. "Guess we'll be paying a visit to the Fang and Claw when we get home."

*Home.* A complicated word for Cassandra these days. Where *was* her home?

The little house in Thalenn's southern suburbs that she'd shared with her parents as a child? The dilapidated apartment in the slums that she and Mama had lived in before her mother's obliviation? The Temple Cloisters?

None of those places felt like home in any real way. Merely random stops along her life's journey. She hadn't chosen a single one; they'd all been chosen for her. Even Tristan's comfortable bungalow, with its enticing scenery, was more of a last resort than a conscious choice. Shaking off the rising anxiety inspired by her untethered lifestyle, she closed the book.

"Well, if we're done with our research here, what should we do next? How much longer until the Artisan has an answer for us about the memory?"

"We've been in here for several hours," Tristan answered, rustling his wings. "I'm sure she'll contact me soon."

"So we're just going to sit here doing what? Twiddling our thumbs?"

Tristan aimed a saucy smile in her direction. "I can think of better ways to occupy our hands," he said loudly and with enough intent that their neighbor's head perked up. Tristan shot the man a hardened stare that could only be interpreted one way.

*Scram.*

To Cassandra's surprise, the man gave her an assessing glance, then offered Tristan a wink before he gathered up his books and abandoned his table.

"Come closer, playmate," Tristan murmured, inducing warm shivers throughout her body.

"Here in the library?" she whispered. "Anyone could turn that corner and see us."

He unfurled his wings. "Then it's a good thing I'm a Ghostwalker and can make us a hiding place."

"And what if someone hears?"

"What's the worst that could happen? We get kicked out? We've already learned everything we're going to learn here. Besides, I don't think anyone in Meridon would begrudge us an afternoon siesta. In fact, it's probably mandatory here."

Cassandra didn't think the frazzled librarian would agree. But the thought of performing a profane act on these sacred grounds was tempting, and stirred the recently roused wickedness within her.

They had time to kill. And at the moment, she couldn't think of a better way to slay it. She needed the distraction, now more so than ever after the ship, the Emperor's demands, the reappearing elemental magics. What a High-Gods-damned mess this all was. The unanswered questions wrapped around her throat, slowly choking off her breath.

The hungry gleam in Tristan's eyes loosened them ever so slightly.

Now that they'd resumed their arrangement to play together, she was finding it increasingly difficult to keep her hands off him.

Despite knowing it was a bad idea.

But there was something about this trip, about being away from Thalenn, that allowed her to believe the consequences didn't count here. Might as well take advantage of the pretense while she could.

She stood, nestling between his legs, and he pulled at her shirt—his shirt, actually, that she was still wearing from the night before. She stopped his hands as he folded his wings around them, puffing out his camouflaging feathers and cocooning them within.

"Oh no," she cooed. "If we are playing here, then *I* am in charge." His impish smile deepened. "We have a score to settle."

"Didn't I say we weren't keeping score?"

"I never agreed to that."

She settled his hands against his thighs, then leaned in and opened his jacket before dropping to her knees.

He licked his lips as his pupils dilated, his honey-brown irises diminishing to tiny rings.

She knew exactly what she wanted—to make him feel as good as he'd made her feel. The urge to taste his flesh was overwhelming.

"Cassandra, you—"

"Hush," she silenced him, lifting his shirt and exposing his deliciously ripped torso. She licked and kissed the golden-tan expanse above his waistband as she unbuttoned his pants and slid the zipper down.

Inch by agonizing inch.

Tristan's heart hammered in his chest, his excitement skyrocketing.

Cassandra wanted to suck him off. In public. Well, almost public since they were hidden inside his wings and the library was nearly empty.

He'd participated in his fair share of exhibitionism over the years, but had never been so keyed up with taboo anticipation. Was it because they were on the grounds of a sacred Temple? Was it because Cassandra herself had been off-limits mere weeks ago?

The thought of her lips and tongue on his cock had him instantly hard, begging to escape the increasingly restrictive cage of his pants.

And the fact that this was her idea? He was a goner. Knew this wouldn't last long.

She pulled him free then wrapped her delicate fingers around his shaft, stroking up and down as she spent a long minute admiring him.

The ravenous sparkle in her eyes had him desperate to yank her from her knees, strip off her pants, and settle her in his lap, burying himself to the hilt.

She stared up at him from underneath feathery lashes, her hand pumping his cock how she knew he liked it, squeezing harder as she reached the tip.

He tilted his head back, hissing through his teeth, trying to stall his climax and not end this glorious torture before it had even begun.

Latching her smoky blue eyes onto his, she unfurled her pink tongue and ran it from base to tip, flicking the sensitive spot just beneath his head. He bit down on his own tongue to keep from moaning and giving them away to any lingering patrons perusing the stacks.

How did she even know about that spot? Based on her history, he knew she'd never done this before.

He said a silent prayer to Letha, thanking the Goddess for supplying Cassandra with all those dirty memories. He nearly exploded at the thought of her viewing them, turning herself on by studying a scene exactly like the one she was now re-enacting.

She pursed her lips and dribbled a trail of saliva onto his burning skin, using her hand to coat and stroke his length. Smiling up at him, she laid his head against the flat of her tongue and then closed her lips. The sensation of his cock suctioned inside her warm, wet mouth made his hips buck.

"*Fuck*," he moaned before biting down on his lower lip hard enough to draw blood. He wrapped her long, silky ponytail around his wrist as her head bobbed in his lap. He desperately tried to keep his hips still, to not risk hurting her by slamming into the back of her throat.

She took him down so deep that her nose grazed his lower abdomen, and he couldn't help the loud groan that escaped him as the muscles of her throat fluttered around him.

"Quiet," she whispered, admonishing him, a prideful smirk gracing the lips he was dying to push his cock back through. "Are you trying to get us kicked out of here?"

He grunted softly, thrusting into her hand and choking out a ragged response. "I…*shit*…I don't know if I…*oh High Gods*," he nearly shouted as she swirled her tongue around his head. "You're torturing me on purpose, aren't you? For making you stay silent in the alley behind the Empress's Lap."

"Turnabout's fair play," she crooned, raising a coquettish eyebrow before dipping her head back down and sucking him harder, her hand stroking in tandem with her mouth. He was beyond words, beyond thought, nearly beyond consciousness.

She placed her hand on his thigh, squeezing in silent permission for him to be rougher, stop holding back. The gesture snapped the last lingering thread of his restraint.

Muffled groans seeped through his gritted teeth as he tightened his grip on her ponytail and plunged himself down her throat. "Fuck, I'm gonna come."

She moaned against him and the scent of her arousal, that sweet and spicy musk, surrounded him as he erupted. His feathers stirred as the last of his release leaked onto her tongue.

His chest heaved as he stared down at her, at this wanton goddess smiling wickedly from between his legs.

The tip of her tongue poked out to lick at a glistening drop at the corner of her mouth.

He had no control left, had just emptied it all into her, so he grabbed her arms and dragged her up his body. He needed to taste her swollen lips, suck her tongue, lick her teeth, pour as much of his gratitude into her as he possibly could.

"Cassandra," he whispered against her mouth, "that was…"

He kissed her again, relishing the feel of her soft body pressed against him. There were so many things he ached to say.

He wanted more of her.

Fuck, he wanted *all* of her.

He'd promised her patience, but it was becoming increasingly hard to come by.

He stroked his hand against her hair, smoothing it back before pressing another gentle kiss to her addicting lips. "You look thoroughly ravished," he said, relishing her soft giggle. "Everyone in here is going to know exactly what we've been up to."

She shrugged, pushing away from his chest to sit on her heels as she carefully tucked him back into his pants. "Like you said," she whispered, "I'm sure this kind of thing is mandatory in Meridon."

He was about to laugh when a gust of wind ruffled through his feathers and breathed a message from Cleo, the Artisan's Windrider lover, into his ear.

The name of a city. One he'd never visited, yet felt as familiar to him as Thalenn. One laced with painful, agonizing memories.

Cassandra perked up. "Was that news from the Artisan?"

"Yes," he grimaced, pulling his wings back and exposing them to the soft afternoon light spilling in through the library's high windows. "Let's go."

Cassandra stood, a puzzled expression on her face, though she didn't ask where they were going. She tucked her shirt into her pants and smoothed her hair, tightening her ponytail. A thrill shot through him that she appeared so undone because of him, but it wasn't enough to chase away his anxiety over their new destination.

As they made their way out of the library, they passed their pipe-wielding neighbor sitting at another table. He gave Tristan a knowing wink on their way out.

They strode into the small courtyard just inside the Temple gates and came upon a group of Sisters gathered around a stone bench, chattering in rushed whispers.

A name floated over, and Cassandra halted in her tracks, the color draining from her face.

"Did you say Sister Arelinn?" she asked, approaching the Sisters and addressing a woman with a long, dark brown braid nearly the same shade as Cassandra's own flowing locks.

"Yes," the Sister answered warily. "Who are you?"

Cassandra pushed up her sleeve, exposing her tattoo. "I'm a former Shrouded Sister. My partner and I," she gestured to Tristan, "came to the Temple today to do some, ah, research."

He swallowed a chuckle.

"Are you from the Temple at Primarvia then?" the Sister asked. "Do you know Sister Arelinn?"

"Perhaps," Cassandra answered carefully. "What did she look like?"

"Tall and thin," the Sister said. "Her hair was covered, but her eyes were the brightest green. Like emeralds. She arrived this morning to apprentice with us, then ran off. We haven't been able to find her. Do you know her?"

"No, I..." Cassandra paused, as if suddenly realizing she didn't want to reveal too much to this group of strangers. "Sorry, I thought...Sorry." She darted through the gates, Tristan following on her heels.

Once they were safely ensconced within the crowds on the bustling street, Tristan halted her with a gentle touch. "What was that all about?"

Cassandra's eyes were panicked, yet hopeful. "Arelinn," she said. "I've only ever heard that name once before. It's the name of a character in Xenia's favorite series of books. Tall, thin, green eyes. Xenia was here today." She whipped her head around, frantically searching the crowd for her friend. "She's alive. She was here, Tristan. In Meridon. What in the name of Stygios would she be doing here?"

Tristan could think of only one reason, but he was hesitant to share his thoughts, didn't want to crush Cassandra's blossoming hope. Maksym needed the blood of Shrouded Sisters to enact his plan. And it's not like he or his Deathstalker henchmen could just waltz into a Temple to abduct them. Richelle, a Sister, had captured Sister Kouris. Maksym had probably conscripted Xenia to do the same.

Cassandra bowed her head, massaging her temples, as if chasing away the rapid onset of a headache. "Do you think she's still here on the island?"

He didn't spare a thought before sweeping Cassandra into his arms. They spent the next half hour hovering over the streets, searching for messy blond curls. Curls he suspected they wouldn't find. But if Cassandra wanted to look, he'd do anything to keep her happy. She sagged further and further in his arms as their search proved fruitless.

"She's not here, Cass," Tristan whispered. "We need to go."

She sighed, settling her head against his shoulder and muttering, "I know. Where are we heading?"

He braced himself to say the name of the town he'd avoided for two centuries.

"Vaengya."

# CHAPTER FIFTEEN

Xenia sucked in a gasping breath. Her head pounded as she sat upright and her eyes adjusted to the quivering torchlight.

She was back in Maksym's dungeon.

*Fuck.*

She shuddered at the faint pink lines along her left wrist, reliving the searing pain of Alexei's venom thrashing through her body.

How long ago had that been?

And why did the scars—sticky to the touch—appear to be almost healed?

"You're awake." Cael's deep voice wrapped around her like a soft blanket.

She ground the heels of her palms into her eyes, trying to chase away the persistent throb that made her want to lay back down and bash her skull against the floor.

"Here," Cael said. Smooth leather nudged along her arm. "Drink some of this."

She leaned against the cool stone wall and cracked her eyes open. Cael knelt before her, pressing a round canteen into her hands. She tried to speak, but the words caught on her thick, dry tongue.

Cael screwed off the lid and wrapped his arm around her shoulders, then brought the canteen to her lips. She managed two swallows before he tipped the vessel back too far, and she choked on the stream of water.

She sputtered and coughed, shoving him away. "Are you trying to fucking drown me?"

"Just trying to get that nasty mouth of yours working again." He offered her the water, his eyebrows raised. Her stomach fluttered at the sight of the open tin of salve by his side—he'd healed her wounds. "Seems to have worked."

She snatched the canteen from his outstretched hand, then drained it dry in several long, audible gulps.

Cael tracked the tiny rivulets running down her bobbing throat and soaking her collar.

She pulled the canteen away with an overly dramatic smack of her lips, twisted the cap back on, and tossed it back to him.

"Where did you get that?" she asked.

"One of the Deathstalkers gave it to me this morning along with breakfast right after you left." He dipped his head, examining the canteen as he flipped it in his hands. "I was saving it for you, didn't know when you'd be back or if they'd given you anything to eat or drink."

"Thanks," she mumbled, touched by the gesture but unsure of what to do with the knowledge. She ran a hand through her hair, her fingers catching in her knotted curls. She hoped they'd let her clean herself up soon.

Cael fiddled with the canteen, and she swept an assessing eye over him. It was hard to get a clear picture in the patchy torchlight, but it looked like his face had completely healed.

"How do you feel?" she asked.

"Fan-fucking-tastic," he answered with a snort, then caught her narrowed eyes. "I'm fine, Blondie. My wing's better, but this is still a problem." He opened his hand and a small puff of wind kissed her cheeks, barely harder than the breath of a panting dog. "That's the extent of my magic at the moment. They gave me more healing suppressant while you were gone. I think it's the only reason they're still making me take it, to strangle my powers."

"How long ago?" she asked.

"A while ago. Right after Alexei snatched you away." He surveyed her with searching steel-gray eyes. "How do *you* feel?" He swallowed, dragging a hand down his face. Had he been that worried about her? "What happened?"

She told him about Meridon. Recounted the memory she'd pulled from that young woman showing Cassandra during the disaster on the ship. That she'd seen her friend and Tristan heading towards a colorful house on a hill behind the city, which Cael confirmed was the Artisan's home.

"What do you think they were doing there?" she asked.

"I don't know." He chewed the inside of his cheek and she shot him a confused look. "What?"

"How can you do that without cutting your mouth with your little fangs?"

He huffed, amused. "I can be very gentle with my *little* fangs when I need to be, Xenia."

She hoped the torchlight was dim enough that he couldn't see the blush creeping up her neck. "It's Zee, remember?"

"Oh, I am your friend again?" he asked with a smirk. "Thought I was an asshole."

"You can be both."

His low, deep laugh was as sultry as skin-warmed bedsheets.

High Gods, his voice made her want to do very bad things.

She quickly changed the subject. "I didn't complete the task Maksym assigned me. And as soon as I saw that memory, I escaped the Temple to find Cass. There are going to be repercussions, don't you think?"

"Maybe dosing you with Alexei's venom was punishment enough?"

"Maybe," she trailed off. "But not likely. And what if they punish *you* for my failure?"

He shrugged. Big, tough male with a foolish lack of concern about his own well-being.

"We need to be careful. I have an idea about the healing suppressant." She leaned forward, motioning for him to come closer, then whispered her plan in his ear.

Being this close, she could tell they'd let him bathe. He smelled like untamed lands after a thunderstorm, all wind-swept plains and rain-dampened rocks.

"We'll try it when they bring your next dose," she said. He nodded in agreement.

"I almost forgot," he said, unzipping his jacket and handing her a square of folded black fabric. "They let me bathe, so I washed and dried these for you. Figured you'd probably need them more than I do, in case they make you wear a dress again."

She unfolded the offering and laughed so hard tears rolled down her cheeks. Once she'd composed herself, she looked up into Cael's amused face. "Thanks, pterodactyl."

Then her face heated.

"But how did you know I needed underwear?"

The door to the dungeon creaked open and clacking footsteps echoed down the hall before Alexei appeared in front of the cell, two trays of food balanced in his pale hands.

"We see you are finally awake, little mouse. Do not think Maksym is ignoring that stunt you pulled in Meridon. He is busy thinking up creative ways to punish you." Alexei darted his vivid yellow eyes towards Cael, flicking his forked tongue along his scar.

The Deathstalker passed the trays to Cael, then motioned to the vial filled with shiny, eggplant-purple liquid. "Drink it."

Cael plucked up the vial, avoiding Xenia's gaze. Popping off the cork, Cael brought the vial to his lips and tipped his head back, making his throat pulse as if he were swallowing. Once he'd emptied the vial, Cael tossed it through the bars into Alexei's awaiting palm. "Satisfied?" Cael bit out, his tongue awkwardly stiff. Xenia hoped Alexei didn't notice.

"Very." Alexei's pupils dilated and his citrine eyes glittered with unspoken threats before he addressed Xenia. "Eat up, little mouse. Maksym would like a word after he's done entertaining his dinner guest. We'll be back to fetch you soon so you can clean yourself up."

Xenia stayed perfectly still as Alexei left the dungeon. She counted slowly to ten before scurrying over to Cael.

"Did it work? Were you able to keep it under your tongue?"

He nodded carefully, trying not to jostle the liquid.

"Good," she said.

Cael's brows furrowed. "Will it hurt you?" His words were rounded and muffled, his tongue held firmly in place to keep the suppressant from leaking out.

"No, I don't think so. As a Sister, I only have that small bit of magic, which is fading anyway. Besides, the princess in my books did this when her lover was poisoned and it worked out fine for them. Though she was immune to the poison." Cael's brows narrowed further. She dismissed his unease with a wave of her hand. "I'll be fine. We need you to get your power back. What other choice do we have?"

"Why can't I just spit it out?"

She rolled her eyes. "Where are you going to spit it? We need the canteen for water. And you can't spit it on the floor or onto our clothes—they'll see it. This is the best way to hide the evidence." She searched his gray eyes, touched by the concern she found. Concern not for himself, she knew, but for her.

He nodded before rising onto his knees and angling his torso so his face was directly above hers. He gripped her chin in his cool, roughly callused hand, and Xenia's heart rate spiked. He misinterpreted her reaction, assumed she was scared.

Which she was.

But not for the reasons he thought.

He tilted his head back, careful to not spill the liquid down his throat. "We don't have to do this, Zee. I'll just swallow it and we'll find another way to get out of here."

She grabbed his wrist. "I'm fine. Just do it. And hurry, before they come back to get me."

He stared down at her, his eyes darting back and forth between hers, soaking in her determination.

He gripped her chin tighter. "Open your mouth."

Even awkwardly delivered, the words set her entire lower body on fire.

She tipped her head back and parted her lips.

He tugged her chin down, forcing her to open wider, and lowered his face until their lips were almost touching. The rapid breaths sawing out of his nose coasted over her cheeks. As if he was just as affected by their proximity as she was.

Hints of silver flashed in his flinty gray eyes as he angled his head, slanting his mouth above hers. His pursed lips grazed hers, and she swallowed a moan.

He dribbled the liquid into her mouth and at the first splash of it against her tongue, already warmed by his body, she shuddered.

He closed his lips and tilted his head back. "Are you okay?" he asked, misunderstanding her quiver.

She nodded emphatically, keeping her mouth open, and squeezed his wrist, encouraging him to keep going.

He bent his head down, bringing his lips dangerously close again, and streamed the liquid into her mouth at a steadier pace. It poured over her tongue and down her throat, tasting sweet and tart, like blackberries, but with an aftertaste of spring-damp grass that was pure Cael.

Unable to look at him any longer, afraid she might lose control, close the distance between them, and sweep her tongue into his mouth, Xenia closed her eyes.

Thank the High Gods she'd closed her eyes.

Staring into those two shimmering depths of melted emeralds while surrounded by the musky scent of her arousal was testing the limits of Cael's restraint.

He cuffed her throat and tilted her face up, swore he heard her whimper. He pressed in closer, enough that every movement had his lips brushing hers as he drained the last of the liquid into her warm, waiting mouth.

Before he could reluctantly back away, she captured his tongue, sucking down the length in a long, hard pull that sent his cock straining against his zipper. She flicked the tip of her tongue around his lips before doing the same to her own.

He watched, mesmerized, as the soft pink tip gathered up the droplets of purple suppressant staining her bow-shaped lips, making them appear as flushed as if they'd actually been devouring each other and not performing some pale, yet kinky, imitation.

Her eyelids fluttered open and the heat in her eyes sent another jolt to his painfully hard cock. "Just making sure I got every last drop," she whispered.

"Very thorough," he exhaled. They hadn't broken apart, his hand still curled around her neck. He caressed the fragile skin, aching to lick at the vein thumping her pulse against his fingertips. Then lick other parts of her and feel those muscles deep inside of her grip his tongue.

He should move away, break this spell. The last thing she needed right now was some horny beast panting over her. Especially when she'd have to keep her wits to deal with whatever new horrors Maksym had in store.

But he was rooted in place, paralyzed by the warmth in her eyes and her shallow breaths.

And she wasn't moving away either.

Did she want this?

Did *he*?

His father's admonishments echoed in his mind.

*Keep your distance while you are in the colonies.*

*You are a* Zephyrus.

*Humans are not worthy of us.*

"Cael." The plea on her lips silenced his father's voice.

He bent his head down, prepared to taste her for real, when the dungeon door clattered open and they bolted to opposite sides of the cell.

Alexei appeared with another Deathstalker guard in tow, then pulled the iron key from his pocket and unlocked the cell door. "Let's go, little mouse. Maksym's almost ready for you."

A pool of dark blue fabric spilled over the other guard's forearm—Xenia's attire for the evening.

Rage swiftly overtook Cael's lingering desire. How dare they dress her up like a doll for that green-winged fuck?

She offered him a resigned grimace from across the cell, then unfolded the long legs he'd just imagined clenched around his temples. She strutted towards Alexei, her spirit intact and refusing to cower.

It took a special kind of bravery for someone like Xenia, who'd spent nearly her entire life cloistered behind the walls of that Temple, to face these terrors and remain unbroken. Bloody Stygios, he'd known Vestian Guards who would've succumbed to panic and helplessness by now. And Xenia thought *Cassandra* was the strong one? Just because Xenia couldn't throw a punch or wield a dagger, that didn't diminish her power. There were only a handful of people Cael would want by his side in these circumstances. And though he hadn't known her for very long, Xenia was certainly one of them.

Also didn't hurt that she was extremely pleasant to look at.

He felt like a cad for thinking such things at a time like this, but he was finding it harder and harder to suppress his attraction.

She strode straight past Alexei without giving the Deathstalker a second glance, knocking her shoulder into the asshole and padding out of view.

"What were you two doing in here?" Alexei whispered, his nostrils flaring as he twisted his neck to stare at Xenia's ass as she walked away.

Alexei's forked tongue darted between his lips, sucking in her scent. He closed the cell door, then slipped the key back into his pocket. "Maksym might not have a taste for mortal flesh, but we could probably convince him to let us sample her. Better go see if she needs help cleaning up." Alexei's fangs popped but before he could step away, his face slammed against the iron bars. Cael blinked as he looked down and saw his own hands fisted in Alexei's white jacket.

He barely even realized he'd moved.

Alexei was struggling to pull away, scratching at Cael's fists, the dagger at his hip clanking against the bars. The other guard took a step towards them, then backed off at whatever savagery he found on Cael's face.

"If you so much as breathe in her direction," Cael snarled, his voice a low rumble so guttural he hardly recognized it, "I will rip out your fangs and use them to put two more scars on that mutilated fucking wasteland you call a face."

Alexei ripped himself free, tearing his jacket in his desperation. As soon as he hit the opposite wall, he stood up straight, dusted himself off and plastered on an amused expression. But Cael had seen Alexei's genuine terror a moment ago. It was heartening that he could still inspire it in his weakened state.

Alexei flicked his head towards the end of the hallway, signaling the other guard to escort Xenia out of the dungeon. Alexei approached the cell again, staying well out of reach of Cael's long arms.

"You will pay for that," Alexei sneered.

Cael turned back into the cell, slid down the wall and propped his forearms on bent knees.

"Again," he crooned, "worth it."

# CHAPTER SIXTEEN

THE FLIGHT FROM MERIDON to Vaengya lasted about an hour, though it felt ten times longer to Cassandra, who spent the entire time anxiously ruminating on Xenia.

Her friend had used an alias with those Sisters. Why hadn't Xenia wanted to reveal her identity? Why wouldn't she have told them the truth, exposed Maksym's plans? Maksym must've threatened something truly terrible to ensure Xenia's cooperation.

And what had happened to Xenia after? Had Maksym or one of his goons returned to Meridon to recapture her? Cassandra prayed to every High God that Cael's father's forces would find them before something devastating occurred.

"We're almost there." Tristan's deep voice at Cassandra's ear shook her from her thoughts. She gazed out over the water towards a green and gray landmass framed by the fiery golden halo of the setting sun.

As they drew nearer, sheer, rocky cliff-faces came into focus, topped by flat stretches of flaxen fields and verdant meadows. White plaster houses with thatched roofs dotted the rolling farmlands, and at the bottom of the cliffs a stretch of black sand beach unfurled from a break in the rock face like a poisoned tongue. Tiny rowboats anchored to the seabed bobbed on the gentle waves. Between the boats and the beach, wooden posts poked above the water's edge in evenly spaced rows with mesh bags coated in slime and seaweed hung between them.

"What are those?" she asked.

"Oyster farms," Tristan answered. "All the pearls in Ethyrios come from Vaengya." There was a slight tremor in his voice, a low note of deep sadness that Cassandra almost inquired about before he tucked his wings in and pitched them into an exhilarating free fall.

As if to discourage further questioning.

He aimed for a small town perched on the cliff's edge.

"Have you been here before?" she asked as they touched down at the edge of the town's main thoroughfare.

"No."

She didn't realize it was possible for a single word to hold so much pain and regret.

Cassandra scanned the sleepy hamlet as Tristan settled her on her feet.

The white plaster buildings in the town square were reminiscent of the houses she'd seen along the cliffs, though none were more than two stories high. Tiny market shops lined the square, and crates full of fruits, vegetables, and fish spilled out from underneath sun-worn awnings in muted hues of ocher and saffron. A few humans dressed in the simple garb of farmers and fishermen milled about, with nary a Fae in sight besides the muscle-y one brooding next to her.

Then Cassandra's gaze caught on a pair of crimson wings attached to a hulking body inspecting oranges across the square.

"Hella!" Tristan shouted.

The female Windrider pivoted towards him, a broad smile lighting up her face and her golden eyes shimmering in the fading sunlight. Hella paid the shop owner for the fruit, then chomped into it whole as she stalked over to join them.

"You eat the skin?" Cassandra asked, her mouth pitched down in disgust.

"Yes, no waste," Hella answered around a mouthful of pulp and pith. "Is good for you. Make you big and strong."

Cassandra wasn't sure she believed that, though Hella's stature was undeniable evidence of the possibility.

"When did you get here?" Tristan asked. "I wasn't sure if you got my message since you never responded."

"I just arrive. And why waste wind?" Hella shrugged. "I see you when you get here." She finished devouring her orange, then rubbed her hands together, wafting a sharp aroma of citrus through the salty sea air and smoky scent of a grill fire burning in a nearby restaurant.

"So," Cassandra turned to Tristan. The bemused grin he typically wore had flattened into a tight line of...some wary emotion. Not concern or distaste. Edginess? Cassandra could understand that, given the stakes of their current mission here in Vaengya. But even in the most dire of circumstances, she'd rarely seen him look so troubled. "I don't suppose the Artisan told you exactly where we should be looking for this necklace, did she?"

"She did not," Tristan answered, surveying the square with distant eyes. He re-focused on Cassandra, noting her questioning stare, and attempted a faint smile. "This town was beloved by someone I once knew. Many lifetimes ago." Cassandra wanted to pry, dig deeper, but restrained herself. "Do you remember anything from Sister Aritia's memory? Any clue of where to start looking?"

A ghostly marble face floated into Cassandra's mind. "Is there a Church of the Forgotten here? I saw a flash of Nemosyna's statue that I assumed was from the Church in Thalenn. But it's possible it was from here in Vaengya."

"Let's find out." Tristan strode into the square towards an older man on a creaky bench, feeding bread to an unruly flock of seagulls. "Excuse me, sir!"

The man looked up from the attention-seeking birds, his snowy eyebrows jumping at the sight of Tristan and Hella.

"Second group of Fae visitors today," the man said in a time-worn rasp.

"Other Fae was here?" Hella demanded. "When? Where they go?"

The old man shook his head, scooping up a handful of bread cubes and scattering them at his feet, inspiring a renewed frenzy among his feathered beggars. "Didn't see 'em. Only heard about it. Folks said they were lookin' for some treasure, askin' around. Weren't very friendly 'bout it neither."

"Who saw them? Would they be willing to talk to my colleague here?" Tristan asked, clapping a hand on Hella's meaty shoulder.

The old man surveyed the group with narrowed eyes, then grunted, "Ask around the pub." He nodded towards the building behind him, the source of an enticing scent of grilled fish.

"I go," Hella said, perking up. She aimed for the pub. "No rush!"

"Is there a Church of the Forgotten here in Vaengya?" Tristan asked.

The man hooked a thumb over his shoulder towards the cliff's edge. "Down by the water. In the split between the cliffs on the black sand beach. Don't get much use though. Hard trip down there 'less you got wings." The man eyed Tristan's beauties enviously.

"Thank you," Tristan shouted as he scooped up Cassandra and pushed into the sky with a booming flap.

Fearing death by predator more than death by starvation, the gulls scattered and their benefactor squawked an amused chuckle.

Tristan landed on the black sand with a crunch, then set Cassandra down.

"Atmospheric," he quipped, gazing at a Church of the Forgotten unlike any he'd ever seen.

Nestled at the back of the crevice, the entire structure was carved into the gray rock. Waves of black sand poured from a wide square opening framed by two columns. Rectangular alcoves bracketed the columns, filled with unlit candles and a myriad of trinkets and mementos—oyster shells, pearl necklaces, dried bunches of flowers, even a few pieces of rotting fruit. Offerings to Nemosyna from the citizens of Vaengya, to guard them against obliviation. Lazy flies circled, the drone of their microscopic wings echoing off the cliffs.

As Tristan and Cassandra approached the Church's gaping maw, he turned back to the stretch of black beach. The sun was minutes away from slumber, a shimmering, golden pool on the horizon that melted into the surrounding waters. Though Tristan's Fae eyesight would allow him to see within the darkened

Church, Cassandra would be nearly blind; they'd need a light source.

He marched through the sand, the ground sloping slightly upwards, and plucked a fat candle from one of the alcoves. Striking the end of his dagger against the stone wall, he used the barest puff of wind to coax the spark into a flame before he handed the lit candle to Cassandra.

"You do come in quite handy now and then, Birdman." The dancing candlelight set her cheeks aglow.

Despite the teasing, he caught a sharp whiff of her fear. He clasped her hand, heartened that the scent dulled at his touch.

The alcoves lining the damp walls inside the Church were also filled with offerings to the Chronicler. Nemosyna's marble statue sat atop a dais at the far end of an expanse of bare stone floor. Cassandra and Tristan took opposite walls to see if the necklace was hidden among the haphazard knick-knacks, to no avail.

Cassandra circled Nemosyna, the candlelight swallowed by shadows as she rounded the statue. "Nothing," she shrugged. "Maybe I was wrong and this isn't where Cora hid the necklace after all?"

An echo of grim energy slithered up Tristan's spine. Something filled with torment and savagery.

Something *fresh*.

He joined Cassandra at the statue, unnerved by Nemosyna's placid eyes tracking his progress. The pristine, pearly white marble suggested someone maintained this shrine. The caretaker's absence increased his unease.

As he studied the statue, a cool breeze ruffled the underside of his feathers. He crouched down and ran his hand along the statue's base.

"Do you feel that?" he asked Cassandra, grabbing her hand and placing it along the seam.

Her eyebrows tipped up. "There's something underneath."

He stood, gesturing for Cassandra to back up a step. He placed his hands on the statue and pushed, but the stone didn't budge. He tried again from the front, the other side, and the back, with no luck.

Cassandra pressed on Nemosyna's various limbs and protrusions, then set the candle down and climbed into the Goddess's lap, scrutinizing Nemosyna's face for a button or trigger.

"Hang on," she murmured. "I have an idea." She trailed her hand down the statue's arm. "That frieze on the Artisan's door showed Nemosyna holding a candle in her right hand. Hand it to me."

Tristan picked it up, cursing softly when a rogue bead of wax burnt his hand. A soft push of his wind coaxed the excess wax onto the floor. He didn't want Cassandra to burn herself as well.

She offered him a grateful smile as she touched the candle's flame against the statue's right hand, then yelped as the thrumming grind of stone on stone broke the chamber's eerie silence.

Tristan helped her down as the statue slowly shifted to the left, then halted with a reverberating boom, revealing a set of stairs plummeting into a lightless abyss.

Cassandra gazed up at him with a self-satisfied smile. "Good thing you keep me around, Birdman."

"I don't know what I'd do without you, Daredevil." He wondered if she could sense the truth buried in his tease.

"You go first into the creepy death hole though."

"Good thing you keep *me* around," he shot back, before tucking his wings and brandishing the candle as he descended the stairs.

They arrived at a hexagonal chamber surrounded by three arched openings, each leading down a different dark path.

"Should we split up?" he asked, grinning.

"Absolutely fudging not." Cassandra pressed herself into him, and he wrapped an arm around her shoulders. "It's darker than Stygios's realm down here. If that candle goes out, I won't be able to see a thing. I may be brave, but I'm not suicidal."

"If that candle goes out, *I* won't be able to see a thing either." The faint trickle of light leaking in from the chamber above would fade soon. And he doubted the moonlight would be strong enough to travel down into these underground paths.

"Well," Cassandra whispered. "Which way?"

Tristan closed his eyes, trying to sense the remnants of pain and violence he'd felt in the upper chamber. They wafted from the center path.

"This way." He stepped through the archway, keeping Cassandra nestled in next to him.

A raw, meaty smell of violent death invaded his nostrils as they pressed onward, the candlelight bobbing with each step and throwing menacing shadows onto the damp stone walls. The tips of his feathers brushed against a rough ceiling that ducked ever closer. As if the rocky throat wanted to swallow them whole.

"Do you smell—" Cassandra whispered before Tristan shushed her. A faint wailing echoed from up ahead.

They glanced at each other then took off running down the claustrophobic hallway, finally met with the coppery aroma of blood mingled with pungent, acrid scents of fear and excrement. Tristan breathed through his mouth to keep from gagging. They careened through a bend in the path, then he stopped abruptly.

Cassandra slammed into his back, tangling in his wings and sending inappropriate shivers throughout his body as she attempted to free herself.

She pushed his feathers aside, then emitted a horrified yelp.

Splatters of thick, dark liquid dripped down the walls of the cramped crypt. Tristan didn't need to inspect them any closer to know they were blood.

The crypt contained two bodies, one face down on the floor, his arm outstretched above his head as if he were reaching for them. Or trying to crawl to freedom.

Along the back wall, another body—Fae by the smell of it—was prone on a stone altar. The male was stripped naked, his long, ash-blond hair streaked with green blood. His entire torso had been ripped open from groin to sternum, and glistening lumps of tissue encircled the altar.

The murderer had torn out his organs. Hastily and carelessly, by the looks of it.

A weak moan floated up from Tristan's feet. He crouched down and carefully flipped the man over. His chest was a criss-crossed map of blisters and charred flesh, his brown wool robe completely burned away.

Tristan passed the candle to Cassandra, then cradled the man's head in his lap. The man's face was deathly pale, his lips purple. He squinted at the candlelight and hissed in pain, as if even the faint light was too intense for his deteriorating senses.

"It's okay," Tristan said. "We're here to help you. What happened down here?"

"Took...." the man croaked, licking his split lip. "She took..." He stilled, overcome by the mere effort of speaking.

"Who is she?" Tristan asked.

"She asked me...to hide it," the man grunted, his terrified eyes scanning Tristan's. "The Sister...she..." He coughed up a glob of black blood that coated his chin. "The necklace..." He sputtered and choked, then stilled in Tristan's arms, his mangled chest ceasing its erratic rise and fall.

Tristan closed the man's eyelids and settled him on the floor. He stood, plucking the candle from Cass's limp fingers, and approached the altar.

She rubbed at the wound on her forearm as she crouched down and placed her fingers at the man's neck, feeling for a pulse.

"He's gone, Cass," Tristan whispered. "There's nothing we can do for him other than carry his body out of here."

"I know," she sighed. Just another disposable human caught up in the battles among his species. Guilt tightened his chest before he turned back to the gruesome sight on the altar.

"What the fuck?" he mumbled as he leaned in to inspect the body.

The smooth edges of the gaping hole in the male's chest suggested that this makeshift operation had been performed with a blade. The lungs and heart were intact behind the ribs, but the rest of his innards were scattered about the scene. His intestines tumbled into a pile on the floor, still attached to his body like a ghastly umbilical cord.

"Hey Cass," he asked, unable to tear his gaze from the Fae's open chest. "Does a subject need to be living for you to pull a memory?"

She padded over to him with nary a hitched breath at the gruesome scene; she'd likely seen all manner of atrocities over the years in sacrificed memories. Not to mention mere weeks ago she'd discovered the bloody pile of limbs that used to be the Broker. Pride swelled his chest at the sight of his iron-stomached partner taking in the ruined body with more curiosity than revulsion.

"I'm not sure," she whispered, her eyes darting towards the Deathstalker's face. "I've never tried it before. Do you think he was working for Maksym?"

"That's what I'd like to find out, if you can manage it," Tristan said.

"Even if I could pull the memory, I don't have anything to contain it in," Cassandra said. "We wouldn't be able to view it."

"What if I created a wind-shield around it?" he asked. "Would that work?"

"Worth a try?" Cassandra shrugged. She stepped behind the Deathstalker's head, placing her hands at the dead Fae's temples. She began the low, soft chant several times, but nothing happened. "I can feel something stirring, but it keeps sputtering out just as I'm grasping for the tendrils." She cocked her head. "What if there was a way to amplify my abilities? Could you share your magic with me somehow?"

"You'd have to ingest some of my blood."

"How much?"

He tried not to be insulted by how disgusted she looked at the prospect.

"You didn't have any problems ingesting my bodily fluids earlier today," he teased, pinching her nose.

She swatted him away. "You have a gift for making sexy things sound spectacularly unsexy."

"Let's start with a sip and see what happens." He dragged a canine across his wrist. A warm trickle flowed down his forearm and he held it out to Cassandra. A sacrifice he would willingly make for her, and her alone.

She gripped his wrist with gentle fingers, then wrapped her lips around the cut. His body tingled at the contact, never failing to react to her touch. He fought to control himself as the tempting sensation of her consuming his blood had his groin stirring. They had a serious task to accomplish. Plus, there were two dead bodies in this chamber. Not the most appropriate time or place to give in to his deepening arousal.

She pulled her mouth away, then licked a red drop from her lower lip.

"How do I taste?" he asked.

"Old." His responding laugh bounced around the small chamber. "But rich. With a hint of spice and…" She smacked her lips together. "Burnt oak. Similar to how you smell." He cocked a questioning eyebrow. "I love the way you smell, Tristan."

He grappled for his restraint. "Try to pull the memory again."

She glanced at her hands and arms. "I can feel your magic inside me." She giggled. "It tickles."

"How dare you. My magic doesn't *tickle*. I'm an all-powerful Ghostwalker," he mocked.

She stepped behind the Deathstalker's head again, placing her fingers at his temples, then closed her eyes and whispered the chant. Zapping, crackling green light twined up her fingers, and Tristan readied the wind to capture it.

She opened her eyes and guided the light towards him. "It's fainter than it should be," she warned, her curled fingers dancing as the green light sparkled through them. "I'm not sure we're going to be able to view anything helpful."

Tristan crafted a vessel around the light, spinning gentle gusts of wind into a ball to keep the memory from dissolving. He cradled the sphere between his hands as she angled her tattooed wrist above it.

"Ready?" she asked, touching his forearm with her other hand so that he could view the memory with her. He nodded.

She lowered her wrist, pushing through the vessel as she said the words and the memory overtook them both.

*He held the glittering diamond necklace in his pale hands, smiling like a fiend at visions of the rewards Maksym would bestow upon him for finding this integral treasure.*

*The mortal caretaker he'd forced to lead him down into this chamber was sniveling against the damp stone wall, muttering something about how he'd failed—*

*—a powerful blow of wind barreled into the chamber, throwing both him and the man into the side of the stone altar.*

*A familiar Windrider female stalked into the chamber, wings of pale pink flesh tucked behind her. He'd followed her here to the Church, and had found the caretaker while she was still wandering these labyrinthine halls.*

*He laid a hand on the altar and pulled himself upright, leaving his fangs out and readying himself for a brawl, knowing—*

*—the Windrider sent a scorching stream of flame towards the caretaker, and he crumpled to the ground in a wailing heap, slapping at his chest and trying, uselessly, to put out the flames devouring his robe.*

*The female lunged for him—*

*—clamped a burning hand onto his forearm. He hissed in pain as he tore himself away.*

*One bite. That was all he needed and she'd drop like a stone. It seemed as if she knew it as well, her radiant blue eyes darting from his own eyes to his fangs, then back again.*

*"Come out from behind that altar and face us, deserter," he sneered.*

*Her high-pitched cackle careened around the small space, tinged with a quiver of insanity that spiked his adrenaline.*

*"I'll be walking out of here with that necklace," she snarled, her words pouring out so quickly that he struggled to decipher them.*

*She curled her hand and he beat at his chest, feeling the air drain from his—*

*—Maksym would not be pleased to hear that the necklace had escaped his grasp once again. And especially not to her.*

*And he was suddenly grateful to be leaving this world rather than facing Maksym's wra—*

The memory dissolved from Tristan's mind, but before he could open his mouth to analyze what they'd just seen, a cold sting crept up his thighs.

The tiny stone crypt was filling with water.

# CHAPTER SEVENTEEN

"**F**UCK, FUCK, *FUCK!*"

Tristan's shouts bounced off the walls, and cold water lapped at Cassandra's waist as the dead Deathstalker's memory fragments leaked out of her mind.

Before she'd come back to this wet, horrifying new reality, she was thinking about how crystal clear those fragments had been, despite the *supplicant* being most assuredly dead. But perhaps only recently dead? Had embers of his life force still been burning within him? Or was it the boost of Tristan's magic in her bloodstream that had helped?

She didn't have much time to think on it as the frigid water crested her belly button.

Tristan pulled her into his arms. "We need to get out of here," he said as the candle snuffed out and darkness enveloped the crypt.

Cassandra clung to him, unable to help at all with her weak mortal eyesight.

"Can you see anything?" she shouted over the gushing roar.

Before he could answer, a booming thud shook the chamber.

"Well, there *was* the barest amount of light from the moon outside, but it was just shut out completely by the statue closing over us," Tristan grunted as he pushed through the torrent, struggling to keep Cassandra above the surface while dragging along his waterlogged feathers.

"I can swim, Tristan," she offered. "Put me in the water, but don't let go of my hand."

Though she couldn't see his face, she knew him well enough by now to imagine the struggle passing over his handsome features. Wanting to keep her safe within his arms, but knowing it would slow their progress. Grudgingly, he released her into the water, keeping a firm grip on her hand.

She paddled with her other arm, kicking her legs out and swimming through the rising tide, struggling to keep her chin above the surface as she choked on the salty liquid.

Tristan whispered a message into his palm and sent it gusting through the pitch-black corridor. Begging Hella for assistance, no doubt.

Tristan waded through the rushing waters, and Cassandra let out a high-pitched shriek as something brushed against her leg. She clung to Tristan's arm as he reached behind her, then exhaled a disgusted sigh.

"One of the bodies," he shuddered. "I'm not sure which one."

They pushed down the long, winding corridor, the water level rising at an alarming pace. It was already up to Tristan's shoulders, with barely a few feet before it reached the ceiling.

They reached the hexagonal chamber and Tristan turned frantically, struggling to identify the path they'd arrived from.

"Shit, fuck, *shit*!" He slapped at the surface of the water.

"Don't see how the swearing is helping," Cassandra muttered.

"Oh, it's fucking helping." He twisted his torso back and forth, scanning the openings.

Cassandra's feet left the ground as she struggled to keep her head above water, clinging to Tristan's hand. She trailed her other hand through the liquid, analyzing the flow.

"Straight ahead." She hoped Tristan could sense which way she was pointing. "The water is flowing in that direction."

Tristan squeezed her closer, then pulled them along in that direction. "Genius."

Cassandra's limbs were numbing, though she pushed alongside Tristan with every ounce of energy she could muster.

Her foot made contact with the staircase and she let out a cry of relief. Which swiftly curdled into terror as she knocked the crown of her head against the bottom of the statue.

"Tristan," she called out, her voice wavering. "What are we going to do?"

Water rushed up the steps, waves crashing against her feet and calves. Tristan's hands found her cheeks. "I will not let you die, Cassandra."

He pounded his fists against the statue, but it didn't budge. And though Tristan was supernaturally strong, he wasn't capable of beating through cubic tons of marble.

He roared in frustration. "Nestle into my wings," he growled, folding them around her in a makeshift cocoon against the stone wall. Even in the feathery space, the water was high enough to reach Cassandra's chest. They had seconds until it fully consumed them.

Cassandra covered her ears as gale-force winds buffeted the stone walls surrounding them—Tristan attempting to use his power to move the statue. When that didn't work, he turned and aimed it towards the water.

Cassandra knew he wouldn't be able to maintain this level of magic indefinitely. The stronger the force he used, the more quickly it would drain.

"I sensed a draft earlier coming from the path on the right," Tristan said through gritted teeth. "We may have to swim out of here. Take a deep breath."

Cassandra sucked in the deepest breath she could manage as Tristan let down his shield and the freezing water crashed around them.

Claustrophobic and panicked, she clung to him as he pushed off the stairs and swam down the hallway. His wings dragged, hindering their progress.

She lost all sense of time, clutching Tristan's chest as he propelled them through the rapids. Her lungs burned as she fought against the instinct to open her mouth and suck in air. Panic seized her and she clawed against Tristan's arm.

Tristan paused as a faint glow appeared up ahead, and the water rushing against them intensified.

Wrapping his wings around her and with one final, powerful push off the floor, Tristan shot them into the stream.

Tristan released her from the cocoon of his wings and they tumbled onto a rocky ledge. The Sea of Thetis rose next to them, flowing into the jagged hole they'd just escaped through. It looked as if some incredible force had blown through the cliff face.

Crouched on her hands and knees, Cassandra sucked in lungful after lungful of blissfully unrestricted air. Tristan lay prone on his back beside her.

Hella crashed down onto the wet rocks, then began rubbing and beating at Cassandra's back.

"Breathe, tiny human," Hella shouted. "You okay? What happen?"

Hella's attempts at first aid were making Cassandra feel worse, so she caught the Windrider's arm on her next downstroke. "I'm fine, Hella," she choked out. "Thank you. How did you find us?"

"Got message and rushed to Church, but water everywhere. Statue no budge, so I circle cliffs and find you like flopping fishes. We underneath town." Hella pointed her wing towards the top of the cliff.

Cassandra's gaze roamed up to the edge, then out over a jetty leading to a small island. Flat, crumbling gray stones poked up from the grass like broken, rotting teeth.

The town cemetery.

Perhaps the spirits of Vaengya's honored dead had somehow guided their path, helped them escape the watery labyrinth. A sudden urge to pay respects gripped her.

She stood on shaky legs and tip-toed a careful path down the jetty, stepping over slimy rocks as she wrung out her hair. Tristan and Hella followed, Tristan grilling the hulking female about what she'd learned in the pub. Not much more than Tristan and Cassandra had learned from the dead Deathstalker's memory.

"The Windrider that burned down the ship took the necklace," Tristan whispered to Hella. "The Deathstalker we found beneath the Church was working for Maksym. Based on the state she left him in, it's pretty clear that she's *not* working with them.

Were the Vestians in Meridon able to find any other clues about who she is, who she might be working for?"

Hella shook her head, her long, golden braids tapping against her leather uniform.

Cassandra stepped off the rocks onto an overgrown patch of grass. Offerings had been laid at a few of the gravestones.

Strong arms wrapped around her from behind, her blood stirring in her veins at Tristan's touch. Like her body, now filled with drops of his magic, thrilled even more intensely at his presence.

"Are you truly okay, Cass?" he whispered into her ear, resting his chin on her shoulder.

She reached up to stroke his cheek, improbably warm despite their chilly swim. "I'll be fine."

Cassandra's gaze caught on a headstone in the second row. She pulled herself from Tristan's grasp and rushed towards the familiar name.

He'd been acting strange since he'd learned that they were coming here. Had claimed that the town meant something to someone in his past.

And this headstone confirmed that his history was far more complicated than he'd yet shared with her.

She sank to her knees in the wet grass, and Tristan loosed a sharp breath.

"I think it's time you told me the rest of your story, Tristan." She traced her fingertips along the letters etched into the crumbling stone.

SAROS.

# CHAPTER EIGHTEEN

Cass's dagger beckoned, bobbing at Alexei's hip as he led Xenia through the breezeway.

Could she grab it? Slash Alexei's throat then fish that key out of his pocket and race down into the dungeon to rescue Cael?

The Deathstalkers wandering the halls chased away her escape fantasies.

Outside, a few spiny plants clacked against the stone walls. A soft yet menacing darkness blanketed the landscape beyond. Were there creatures lurking out there, peering hungrily through these open archways? It always made Xenia nervous, being so exposed here in the middle of nowhere. A rush of relief overtook her as they turned into the stark hallway with the two large doors.

Alexei paused, rapping on the second.

Maksym's craggy voice rumbled out. "Bring her in."

They'd taken her shoes again. She assumed it was to discourage escape and she snorted at the futility. But at least she wasn't without underwear this time.

There was something incredibly arousing about wearing Cael's underwear. As if he himself were cradling her most intimate areas.

She'd nearly let him access those intimate areas earlier.

She took a few deep breaths, trying to shake off the lingering sensations of their encounter. His hand gripping her neck with a gentle yet commanding pressure. The graze of his lips against hers. The taste of the warm liquid pouring out of his mouth and down her throat.

Sweet Amatu, she'd even surprised herself with that move she'd pulled, sucking down his long, muscular tongue and practically begging him to kiss her.

And for an instant before they'd been interrupted, that telltale nudge against her lower stomach had informed her that he was more than willing. Would he still be once he knew about—

A familiar, syrupy laugh drew Xenia's attention.

Richelle Pacha swirled sanguine liquid in a wide-bowled glass as she scraped her sneering turquoise gaze over Xenia.

"Honestly Maksym, I don't know why you'd waste such a fine dress on the livestock," Richelle said. Her jet-black curls gleamed in the golden light from the candelabras as she tipped her head back to sip her wine. Her tattoo had completely faded.

Xenia glanced down at the glittering, midnight-blue silk dress Maksym had insisted she wear this evening. It wasn't lost on her that it was the same color as a Shrouded Sister's dress robes.

The neckline—more demure than the green dress from the other night—tied into a halter and two long strings draped down her exposed back, tickling her bare skin with every step. The fabric hugged her hips and swirled around her legs like a liquid galaxy of stars. Under any other circumstances, she would've loved the dress, would've felt like a goddess of the night.

But here in this hall, with these monsters, the truth in Richelle's words stung. Xenia was nothing more than a prize sow on display.

So she decided to lean into the classification.

Staring directly at Richelle, Xenia crinkled her nose and snorted like a pig. Richelle's shocked face and the choked-up wine that dribbled down the bitch's chin were epically satisfying.

Even worth the pain from Maksym's sharp nails digging into her flesh as he dragged her to the table and threw her into a chair.

"Do not test my patience, *Sister*," Maksym sneered, his eyes blazing as he poured her a glass of wine. "Or I might start to question your usefulness. Drink."

"As I was saying, Maksym, our search has been quite challenging so far." Richelle leaned back in her chair. "We've reached out, discreetly, to Alcander. He would've been willing to offer us the necklace—for a steep price, no doubt—but he was understandably furious that we hadn't told him we'd acquired it in the first place. Even though it turned out to be a fake. His wife has abandoned him, which suggests she may have been in on the ruse. We have people searching for her as we speak, but so far she's proven rather elusive. Our sources have also informed us it was her obliviated sister who hid the necklace, though we can't access her either. She's being protected by that bitch bi-form inside the Temple. Even if we could get our hands on her, it's doubtful we'd get any useful information from her hollowed-out mind."

Xenia flinched at the callous description of her friend Cora, even as her mind whirled at all the new information. Pagonis's wife was Cora's sister? And was working *against* her husband? That suggested Cora must have been as well, surely?

Richelle fiddled with her cloth napkin, folding and refolding the edges.

"And?" Maksym barked out. "Surely that cannot be the entirety of your report. If so, you may find yourself sleeping downstairs with the *livestock*."

Green sparks snapped at the tips of Maksym's fingers, clenched so tightly around the stem of his wineglass that Xenia was surprised it didn't snap in half.

"You have been searching for that necklace for over a week with nothing at all to show for it," Maksym said. "I'm beginning to ask myself if you and your family are truly capable of the positions I've offered you, to rule over the humans in our new world."

Richelle pressed her shoulders back, sitting up straight and lifting her chin. "Apologies, Maksym," she sniveled. "We are doing our best, but our enemies appear to be a bit more clever than we'd anticipated. We have some other news as well." Her voice trailed off.

Maksym leaned back in his chair, flexing his fingers as the green sparks continued to pop and sizzle at his fingertips—a pointed demonstration of his power. "I'm listening."

Richelle swallowed. "Your former partner is stirring again."

Maksym's sparks hissed out and he splayed his palms onto the table. "Elaborate."

Richelle's eyes darted towards Xenia.

Maksym waved off Richelle's discomfort. "She is a meaningless pawn. A means to an end with little chance of escape. Say what you need to say."

"Roeki found a memory," Richelle continued in a low voice. "One that, though scrambled, revealed the location of the necklace. Our sources informed us that she stole it from a ship headed to Meridon. A ship which subsequently burned down and sank to the bottom of the ocean."

Xenia's ears perked up, but she didn't let anything show on her face. Sipped her wine and picked at her nails, trying to look bored and disinterested. Surely they were speaking of the ship Cassandra had been on.

"Interesting," Maksym said, sitting back in his chair and carving his fingers through his silvery tufts of hair. "Roeki does nothing without a purpose."

"Exactly," Richelle hissed, clenching her hands into fists. "Why join the playing field now? You two did not exactly part on the best of terms."

Maksym's joyless laugh made the hair on Xenia's arms rise. "I welcome her efforts. But it's best to never guess at her intentions. Even if you were right, she'll change tactics just to prove you wrong." His lips curved into an amused smile, full of reluctant admiration. "It's a shame our partnership had to end over a silly little dispute about her compensation."

"Regardless, we've been tracking her movements," Richelle said, blooming with pride. "We learned this morning that she was headed to Vaengya. We immediately sent Zakariah after her."

Maksym placed an index finger atop the back of Richelle's hand and summoned a small zap. She seized and let out a shaky whimper before drawing her hand back and sucking on the burn.

"Do not get ahead of yourself, Richelle," Maksym scolded. "If Zakariah fails, we are lost. The seam of Thalassium in the mountains is protected by the Empire and its allies. That necklace is our only hope of achieving our plans."

He rose from his chair to stand behind Xenia.

Xenia placed her wineglass on the table and squeezed her hands in her lap to calm herself, unsure of his intentions. Sure, he may still have a need of her to capture more Sisters, but there was plenty of harm he could inflict without rendering her useless.

He shoved a fist into her curls and yanked her head back so she was forced to look up at him. He grazed his sharp fingernails along her neck with enough pressure to scratch but not break skin. "You were very bad today. I question the sanity of anyone willing to betray me. But I'm not sure if you are insane or just monumentally stupid."

With his fist tangled in her hair, he brought his chin down upon her shoulder to whisper into her ear. A faint buzz emanated from his skin, as if those sparks she saw jumping from his fingertips were always there within him, resting just below the surface.

"Of course, there is another possibility." His lips brushed against her ear and she shuddered in disgust. "Perhaps the Windrider doesn't mean as much to you as I thought. Shall I test that theory?"

The tall door lumbered open, and Alexei and another Deathstalker guard hauled a shirtless Cael into the room, his wrists and ankles bound.

Cael's eyes cut straight to her, and he bared his teeth upon seeing her in Maksym's grip.

Xenia tried to leap from her chair, but Maksym held her still while Alexei and the guard strung Cael up in the corner, his arms and legs splayed and his magnificent wings on display. Xenia had to remind herself to breathe.

Watching someone else be punished for one's own failures was a special kind of torture. And just the kind of tactic she'd suspect from someone like Maksym.

She berated herself for trying to escape this morning. What had she been thinking? But she'd been caught between two wretched choices. In the end, someone was always going to get hurt. If she'd managed to lure a Sister, would she have felt better that a stranger was being tortured rather than someone she, grudgingly, cared about? Someone she was starting to care about more and more? Wrath of Vestan, she'd rather Maksym take his anger out on her.

"Don't hurt him," she whispered. "Today was my fault, my choice. He doesn't deserve to bear the consequences of my actions. Punish me instead."

"Xenia, shut the fuck up," Cael growled from the corner.

"Yes, I agree with your friend," Maksym said, yanking her out of the chair by her hair. Richelle snickered, and Xenia wanted to claw her eyes out.

But her fiery anger was swiftly replaced by the coldest fear at the unmistakable metallic hiss of a weapon being unsheathed.

Alexei brandished a massive Typhon-steel broadsword. The whorled pattern on the blade was both a testament to the bladesmith's craftsmanship and the most horrifying sight Xenia had ever seen. She knew how deadly these weapons were. They'd made countless appearances in the published histories of Ethyrios. The thought of that steel being applied to any part of Cael's beautiful body caused the wine she'd drank to rise up her throat, threatening to choke her.

A wound delivered to a Fae by Typhon steel would not heal quickly, if at all, and would leave permanent scars. The dragon fire that forged these weapons was just as effective a healing suppressant as that deep purple liquid they'd been forcing Cael to drink.

Maksym dragged Xenia to the corner of the room to witness up close whatever terrible punishment he had in store. "I warned you, little mouse, from the very first day. Behave, he gets rewarded. Disobey, he gets punished. Either you forgot those words or you care very little for him."

"Please, *please* don't do this," Xenia blubbered. "I'll do whatever you want. I won't try to run again, I swear."

Maksym nodded to the second Deathstalker guard, who stepped towards Cael and yanked his right wing out wide.

Alexei swung the sword up over his head, then arced it down through the air.

And sliced Cael's wing from his body.

# CHAPTER NINETEEN

IT WAS THE MOST excruciating pain Cael had ever felt in his centuries-long life.

But somehow, the sound of Xenia's anguished wail was worse. Like Maksym had shredded his chest open and dragged pointed fingernails over his pulsating heart.

His body compensated for the loss despite the chains supporting him, the quivering muscles in his back and legs releasing with the newly shed weight.

He loosed the breath he'd been holding, the one he'd used to brace himself against the blow. As soon as he'd seen that broadsword in Alexei's hands, he knew what was coming.

He'd never fly again.

Best not to give in to despair right now or he might just beg Maksym to lock him away in that dungeon for the entirety of his now-useless immortality. He'd worry about it later, once he'd gotten Xenia to safety.

He didn't dare try to fight, not yet. Didn't dare show that his power was returning thanks to his and Xenia's clever antics with the healing suppressant. By morning, he suspected it would be at full capacity.

A pile of loose limbs on the floor, Xenia clung to Maksym's legs, muttering *please* over and over. As if she refused to believe what she'd just seen.

As if she still had a chance to stop it.

"Zee," Cael muttered, and low moan seeped out of her. He was surprised he was able to speak, able to draw air into his lungs with the fiery pain lancing down his back. "Stop. It's done."

Alexei wiped Cael's blood off the sword with a cloth napkin, then re-sheathed the weapon and passed it to the other guard. Alexei strode towards Cael, all smug satisfaction, and loosened Cael's chains.

"We warned you. Now who is the mutilated wasteland?" Alexei's low laughter scraped Cael's bones, ratcheting his anger. Agony flared through his right side as his muscles tensed.

Alexei leaned in to whisper in Cael's ear. "She'll never want you now, cripple. Hope the taste you got earlier was enough."

Cael whipped his head sideways and sunk his *little* fangs into Alexei's nose, ripping through one of the

Deathstalker's nostrils. Alexei roared in pain and jerked his head away.

Cael grinned like a fiend though the garish green blood coating his lips.

Screaming a string of curses, Alexei covered his nose, doubled over in pain. He reared upright, his nostril knitting itself back together, and lunged towards Cael.

"Enough!" Maksym shouted, his booming voice rattling both his matte-green wings and Cael's chains. "Alexei, enough. Take them back downstairs." He yanked Xenia to her feet. "You will journey to the Temple in Primarvia tomorrow, *Sister*. If you fail again, I'll chop off his other wing."

Maksym shoved Xenia towards Alexei. His bloodstained hands left green streaks along her bare, golden shoulders as she twisted in his grasp.

His fangs popped down. "Keep struggling, little mouse, and we will dose you again."

Xenia stilled, but Cael scented the anger and anguish pulsating off her in smoky waves. Her emerald eyes shone through the tears flowing down her flushed cheeks. All for him.

She'd never looked more beautiful.

A bittersweet thought, since he was almost certain Alexei was right. He'd seen her admiring glances, not often, but enough for him to know that, despite all the shit she flung his way, she was attracted to him. He could certainly kiss that goodbye.

And the loss of something he wasn't even allowed to want in the first place was enough to trigger one of his episodes.

But he refused to give in to it. Sweet-talked it in his mind like a jealous, desperate lover. Asked it to hold off just a few more days. He'd fall into that dark embrace once he knew for sure she'd be safe.

He'd rescue her, then let the abyss take him.

"Cael," Xenia croaked, her throat raw and thick from sobbing. "Cael, are you there?"

Alexei and two Deathstalker guards had escorted her and Cael down to the dungeon, placed them in separate cells, and extinguished the torches.

A fitting punishment as the nothingness mirrored the atmosphere of her soul.

She would never, *ever* forgive herself for what they'd done to Cael. Because of her. She couldn't stand it. And maybe she was selfish and cruel, but she would have sacrificed a hundred Sisters to prevent the loss of Cael's wing.

She'd have the chance to prove that statement soon. Tomorrow, when they'd drag her to Primarvia and she'd be forced to help Maksym kidnap Shrouded Sisters again. Would she be able to do it this time? She'd have to. There was no *way* she would let that fucker take Cael's other wing.

"I'm so sorry," she whispered.

Something tapped against the iron bars of her cell.

"Come here." Cael's voice, soft and resigned, not angry, soothed some of her unease.

She crawled towards him, her knees scraping against the rough stone floor as she hitched her dress up.

Alexei hadn't returned to deliver her dress robes yet. She suspected he wouldn't tonight. They'd probably let her shiver in the cold until tomorrow as further punishment.

Not even the faintest hint of light leaked into the darkness, no glimmer for her eyes to adjust to and catch outlines or silhouettes. She had to rely on her other senses, her hearing and her touch.

She flailed out an invisible hand until it smacked against the stone wall, then followed that forward, reaching out with her other hand until it bumped against rough iron.

"Cael?" she whispered into the darkness.

"I'm here," he said softly. Close. As if he were right next to her.

She pressed her back against the wall, dragging her knees against her chest and resting her hand at her side through the bars. She heard a rustling noise, then cool, callused fingers brushed against hers.

She wrapped her index and middle fingers around Cael's, squeezing as hard as she could manage in a tactile apology. "I'm—"

"It wasn't your fault." His interruption was calm, measured. With no hint of reproach.

His tenderness cracked her open.

Her sobs poured out in choking, endless waves, violent and dry. The heaving, bodily earthquakes tightened her throat, and she couldn't breathe.

She tried to pull her hand away. How could he bear to touch her after the life-shattering devastation she'd just caused him?

But he refused to let go.

Gripped her fingers as tightly as if they were a lifeline tethering her in place.

Or was he trying to tether himself?

"I'm gonna give you ten more seconds to howl like that for me and then you need to put away your pity. Do you need a countdown?"

Xenia garbled out a phlegmy laugh, wiping at her nose with her free hand. "You are such an—"

"Asshole, I know. No loss of limb is going to change that, Blondie."

"If I had known this was the penalty, Cael, I would've shoved that tainted Delirium down the throats of every Sister in that Temple."

"No, you wouldn't have. And I wouldn't have wanted you to."

"What are we going to do? Even if we could get out of these cells, we don't even know where we are."

"I know where we are."

"You do?" she choked out. "How? I haven't seen pictures or read descriptions of landscapes like this anywhere."

"We're in the Desolation, the far southwest region of the continent and site of the final battle during the war, just before the Accord negotiations began."

"The Desolation? I've never heard of it."

"My father led the dragon of Typhon Mountain to the battlefield and it decimated everything in its path, both the opposing human army and the land beneath their feet."

Xenia shivered at the loss of human life on such a massive scale. "Odd that I wouldn't have read about it."

"Every single human who was there that day perished." Cael's voice betrayed not a hint of emotion.

Xenia had always found it difficult to discern his stance on humans. She had a feeling his opinion lay somewhere just above disdain for the species, maybe a tad more generous for specific individuals like herself.

"The Empire thought it best to suppress that knowledge, lest it lead to outrage among future generations of humans. This place is vast and extremely unforgiving."

"Who in the world would want to live here?"

Cael snorted. "A deranged zealot apparently. The question is, how far into the area are we? Maksym must be having supplies brought in, and he's been taking you out. We can't be too far from Rhamnos."

The port city at the mouth of the Dordenne, where the river flowed into the Sea of Thetis, was referred to as the cesspool of the continent—the place all the dregs and outcasts washed up. And despite its proximity to the colonies, it was said to be the most dangerous place in Ethyrios for mortals.

Cael continued. "If we can bust out of here and get to the city, there's plenty of ships that could take you south to the colonies. And high-speed trains that could take me north into the continent."

"Why would you want to do that?"

"Zee," Cael said, his voice drenched in weariness, "do you really think the Vestians will take me back like this? There's a reason you have to be a Windrider to join the ranks. The ability to fly is a non-negotiable skill."

Xenia swallowed, blinking back tears.

"My duty now is at home," he said. "My father will no doubt find *some* use for his crippled son."

Xenia's heart sank at the quiet bitterness in his tone, the hopelessness.

Technology on the continent was fucking *magic*. Surely someone could fashion him a prosthetic wing?

She wracked her brain for a memory of one, whether in real life or in a book, and came up empty. But that wasn't proof that such a solution didn't exist. Only that she didn't know about it or it hadn't been invented. Yet.

Xenia had always been an optimistic person. And even in the frankly hopeless situation in which she found herself, she refused to give up or wallow. She just needed a plan.

First step, escape the filthy sex dungeon.

Second step, survive the Desolation, the non-life-sustaining, dragon-fire-scorched wasteland outside the walls of Maksym's fortress.

Third step, don't get killed, eaten, or sold into slavery in Rhamnos, the dangerous shit-hole of a city they'd be passing through.

And the final step, once she'd slayed all of the above, was to help Cael heal. Both his wing—if possible—and his fractured spirit. It was the least she could do, since she'd gotten him into this mess in the first place. If he hadn't rushed into the bowels of Maksym's yacht to save her from Alexei, he could've gotten away. Wouldn't have been captured.

Would still have two wings.

"Are you in pain?" she asked, squeezing his fingers tighter.

"Less than I thought I'd be. Not that I've spent much time wondering what it would feel like to lose a wing."

Xenia's mouth dried up as she forced herself to ask her next question. "Are you sure it won't grow back?"

"I'm sure. The Typhon steel assured it." Cael's voice was as sharp and flat as the weapon he'd referenced as he unclasped her fingers. It felt like a punishment.

"So, how are we going to get out of here?" she asked, trying to hold her voice steady against a fresh wave of tears.

Cael sent a gust, the strongest Xenia had yet felt, careening into her cell and stirring her curls. "This will be ten times stronger by morning.

"I'm going to raze this fortress to the ground."

# CHAPTER TWENTY

CASSANDRA NURSED HER RED wine in Tristan's backyard, watching the ruby droplets trail down the glass.

They'd arrived home an hour ago after a long, limb-numbing, barely tolerable flight home from Vaengya that Cassandra had fortunately slept through, exhausted by the harrowing events of the past two days.

They'd both cleaned up and changed, then Tristan had prepared them a simple dinner of grilled fish and vegetables. And though her feelings about him were more confused than ever, she had to admit the male could cook. The magic he worked with a few simple, quality ingredients was even more impressive than the wind flowing through his veins.

Dinner was a quiet affair, and as soon as she'd taken her last, mouthwatering bite, she'd plucked up her glass and retired to the backyard. She needed some fresh air and a quiet moment alone with her thoughts.

She'd been out here less than five minutes before the double doors creaked open and an anxious presence loomed behind her. Iron scraped against the patio bricks as Tristan sank into the other chair, angling his wings over the back. He thunked his tumbler down a bit too forcefully and a slosh of amber liquor spilled onto the table.

"Oops," he mumbled with a brief grin, wiping the puddle with his hand and awkwardly rubbing it against his leather-clad thigh.

Why did he seem so nervous?

And why were *his* nerves making it harder for her to breathe?

He sat back and sipped at his drink. In the silence, Tristan's story stretched between them like a living thing, coiled and poised to attack before a thoughtless gesture or anxious breath scared it back into the shadows.

Tristan had not only Turned a human Fae—or at least attempted to—but Cassandra was certain he'd taken her last name. Those were human graves in Vaengya. The Fae didn't bury their dead; they burned them. Believed the fire would release their souls into whatever plane of existence their High Gods occupied. Better than keeping them trapped within Ethyrian soil for eternity.

It shouldn't bother her so much. She should be happy for her friend. Happy that he'd experienced a love so powerful he'd been willing to risk everything for it.

But despite knowing it was foolish and illogical and unwarranted, she was irrationally and insanely jealous.

Especially after everything that had transpired between them in Meridon.

She didn't know what to *do* with this seething envy. So she added it to the compost pile of festering emotions feeding her tortured soul and making her question every decision she'd made over the past few weeks. She'd never hated her own impulsiveness as much as she did at this moment.

She'd suspected that life outside the order would be messy. But she hadn't anticipated it being *this* messy. Or complicated. Or foreseen how helpless she'd feel trying to deal with everything on her own.

She ached to talk to Xenia. Her friend had as little experience with the outside world as Cassandra, but she'd certainly read more about it. Might have some helpful insights from her books about what to do when the most important person in your life was in terrible danger at the same time as you were falling for someone destined to break your heart. Even if Xenia didn't have any answers, just being in her sunny, optimistic presence always lifted Cassandra's spirits. High Gods, she missed her friend so badly.

Tristan cleared his throat, pulling her from her ruminations. A troubled expression tainted his devastatingly beautiful face.

Wrath of Vestan, why was his vulnerability so attractive?

It made it exceedingly difficult to stay angry with him. Especially at a time like this, when he truly deserved it.

He'd kept so many massive secrets from her, not divulging his heritage or the reason for his exile.

Even as the accusations churned, her righteousness banked. She herself had told him to take his time, that it was his story to tell. She'd given him permission to wait until he was ready, and she wouldn't renege on that promise.

Her features softened as she gazed into his golden-brown eyes, the small flecks of green at the edges of his irises illuminated by the retiring sunlight.

"What was her name?"

"Ione," Tristan whispered, his throat closing. "Her name was Ione Saros."

He swallowed, unsure if he'd be able get through this story. He hadn't recounted it in over a century and remembered only the big beats and the tiniest, most insignificant details.

Or were they the most significant?

The tiny scar on Ione's chin from a misguided childhood trek up a tall tree. The way her nose crinkled and her eyes squeezed shut in terror every time he took her flying. The caress of her warm fingertips along his feathers the first time he'd entered her.

Time, in its merciless procession, had worn away the skin, muscles, and beating heart of their relationship, leaving only picked-clean bones in its wake.

And what time hadn't ripped away, Letha had.

He closed his eyes, took a few deep breaths and a bolstering sip of his bourbon, then turned to face Cassandra.

To her credit, she displayed no judgment or accusation. Her striking features were carefully devoid of any emotion—a rarity for his feisty, passionate friend. He hoped he'd be able to call her that by the end of this story. Wanted to throw himself at her feet and beg for it. But he didn't want to manipulate her into excusing him due to guilt or pity. He would tell her the whole truth—everything he could remember, anyway—and leave the decision up to her.

"She was the daughter of a mortal chef at the palace in Delos. Her mother's culinary skills had impressed Empress Mila, my mother, on a visit to their restaurant in Vaengya several years before I was born. My mother *invited* Ione's parents to come work for our family, Ione's mother in the kitchens, her father in the gardens. The Empress had her own private collection of mortals whose talents she used for her own purposes. She'd compel them to take jobs at the palace, for which she paid them handsomely, but none truly had the option to decline the invitation."

He tilted his head up, greeted the moon shining through the ashen clouds. Strange to think it was the same moon that had witnessed this earlier era of his life.

"Ione was an only child, born at the palace two years after me to far less pomp and circumstance."

A small huff escaped Cassandra's nostrils.

"Not every day that a future emperor is born," Tristan continued, opening and closing his left palm, flexing his scar. "And my parents had been trying to conceive for decades. When I finally arrived, the entire continent shut down for a whole week to celebrate."

"That explains a lot," Cassandra said with a faint twinkle in her eye that tugged a smile from Tristan.

"My birth must've caused my mother's flood gates to open—"

"Gross."

Tristan chuckled softly. "—because my siblings were born in swift succession. Well, swift for the Fae. My brother Eamon, who you had the misfortune to meet, arrived five years after me, followed by our younger sister Belen eight years later."

"Your parents had a thing for names ending in *N*, didn't they?"

"My mother liked the way it flowed into Erabis.

"My childhood was suffocating. As soon as I was old enough to stand on two feet, every day was crammed with hours of lessons, some of which I enjoyed. Especially flying and combat training. And I found the history and language classes riveting.

"But as I grew into a young man, so much of my time was spent on classes that I couldn't have given less of a shit about: etiquette, diplomacy, court politics. My parents used to parade me around like a prize stallion, dangling me in front of their advisers and allies, merely a pawn to solidify their own power.

"Food was my only spark of joy during all those endlessly boring lunches, dinners, soirées, and balls. I was fascinated by the creativity, these mouth-watering creations pouring out of the kitchens.

"I started journeying there whenever I had a free minute, offering to help the chefs and kitchen staff with anything, no task too small, in exchange for their instruction. I wanted to learn how to do what they did, which I was shocked to find was not magic. Most of the chefs were mortals like Ione's mother.

"I was not very good help in those early years. I would've been about fourteen at the time, and my onion chopping skills were nearly as terrible as yours."

She shot him a sharp look but the left side of her gorgeous mouth twitched upwards.

"No one had the balls to correct the precious *heir*, so they just let me screw up their dishes for months.

"Then one day I'm slicing carrots, and a voice behind me, as haughty as the Empress herself, says 'You're doing that wrong. Your slices are uneven.'

"I think I fell in love with her before I even saw her face. No one had ever spoken to me like that and I was sick to death of being coddled and catered to.

"I whip around and there's this young girl glaring at me, utterly disgusted, not a hint of intimidation though she must've known I was the heir *and* she was easily half my size or less. I was a tall, gangly teenager— came into my height and wings early and it took the rest of my body a few more years to catch up.

"She had these sassy, blond pigtails that swung when she walked and I swore they were mocking me as she strutted over, knocked me out of the way with her hip, and proceeded to correct my mistakes."

"Meaning, she threw out your work and started over, did it herself?" Cassandra chimed in.

"Pretty much."

"My kinda girl." Cassandra's approving smirk nearly brought him to tears.

He'd barely spoken about Ione with anyone since he'd come to the colonies. Most of the Fae knew who he was, the title he'd lost. And some were even privy to the more sordid details of why he'd been exiled. But he'd only ever uttered Ione's name to Reena and Cael. He wanted to keep her to himself, a fragile treasure not meant for careless hands.

"Life as I had known it changed that day, as I watched her tiny fingers deftly wield that knife. I'd encountered a few mortals throughout the palace and on trips to Thalenn with my parents, but most of them were so deferent towards me that I never really noticed them. They were like decorations or background furniture."

Cassandra grunted and crossed her arms. He leaned forward, capturing her smoky blue eyes with his.

"Because that's what my parents, my tutors, every Fae individual in that palace had taught me. I didn't know any better." He hoped his words sunk in, that she'd understand why he'd defended the Windriders who'd abandoned the shipwreck. Because he himself had been one of them, once upon a time.

"Ione's skill in the kitchen, learned from her mother, opened my eyes. Here's this tiny creature besting *me,* a nearly immortal descendant of the High God Anaemos. I thought perhaps she'd have more to teach me than carrot slicing.

"After that, I came to the kitchens every day for cooking lessons with Ione and her mother. I'm still nowhere near as good a chef as either of them—I've yet to taste anything as divine as the food they served me in those years. There was more than herbs and spices flavoring those meals. They poured their heart and soul into their cooking, their love for their species and its history.

"Whenever Ione and I weren't in the kitchen together, I'd fly her all over the palace grounds. We'd go for walks in the gardens or take a boat out on the canals. And sometimes we'd sneak off into downtown Delos. She always knew where to find the best food in the city. Never at the fanciest establishments, usually just some hole in the wall in a questionable neighborhood that the future Emperor *really* shouldn't be wandering around in. But the kind folks who owned those places—Fae from across the continent—if they ever recognized me, they never said anything."

He paused to take a sip of his bourbon, let it burn down his throat and break apart the tightness taking hold. As he settled his tumbler down, soft fingers curled around his hand, giving him the strength to continue.

"Ione didn't know much about her species or her heritage, since she'd spent her entire life among the Fae, and as she grew older, so too did her curiosity. Ione would beg for stories of the colonies, of Vaengya, and her mother would regale us while we prepped the meals. The tales her mother told were so different from the carefully constructed lies in the books from my tutors that I started to challenge them during my lessons, asking questions they couldn't answer.

"If mortals were powerless, how had they managed to kill so many of us during the war? If the humans had left their lands willingly, why had so many of them rebelled and died during the emigration? If the colonies were such a wonderful, bountiful place to live, how were so many humans destitute, forced to sell memories? Why had so many been obliviated?

"And if humans were so different from the Fae, how was it possible for me to fall so deeply in love with one?

"Because I was. Recklessly, hopelessly, completely in love with her." He looked directly into Cassandra's silver-lined, blue-gray eyes. "The kind of love that hits you in the gut one day and you realize it's been there all along, waiting to catch you unaware and knock you off your feet. It took a very long time for me to gain the courage to tell her how I felt. I was terrified of what love from someone like me could mean for someone like her, how dangerous it could be. If my family ever found out...

"She never treated me like I was anyone other than myself. She wasn't interested in my magic or my wealth or my title. She didn't want anything from me but my company and my honesty. Being with her opened my eyes to what Ethyrios could be, if we could free the humans. I no longer held illusions that their circumstances were anything other than subjugation, despite the Accords and all the bullshit my people spouted about the good they'd done by *allowing* humans their lives in the colonies.

"For the first time in my life, I *wanted* the power my title granted me. I'd allow everyone, regardless of species, to have the same opportunities and access to resources that the Fae had hoarded for themselves for centuries. I wanted to create that world. For her."

He cleared his throat as he approached the sad, bitter end of his tale.

"The year I turned twenty-one, my parents decided it was time for me to choose a mate. My mother began planning a ball for my birthday, inviting the most prominent Fae families from across the continent, especially those with eligible daughters.

"But there was only one woman who could be my future Empress, and I was running out of time to confess my feelings for her. I refused to put that burden on Ione until I had a solid plan to protect her.

"Eamon and I were close in those years."

He clenched his hand into a fist at his brother's name, another unhealed loss that had scarred over.

"He was the only family member to whom I'd revealed my intentions as Emperor, my plans for a new Ethyrios. He was also the only person in the world who knew the depth of my feelings for Ione.

"Eamon himself brought me the plan to Turn her. He'd overheard a meeting in the throne room between the Emperor and Cleo's family—Psylbe's lover—where they'd come to beg my father to spare their daughter, despite her crime. Neither Eamon nor I had known such things were possible, but we found an ancient, forbidden text hidden in a locked chamber below the palace library that outlined the process, which was simpler than we'd expected: a slice across the palm to share blood, a few muttered vows, a...physical joining."

Tristan pressed his lips together before grabbing his tumbler and draining the last of his bourbon.

"I'd intended to do it the week before the ball, then make a grand entrance with Ione on my arm. She'd be Fae by then so no one could harm her and my parents couldn't object to our mating due to her species."

Cassandra reached out and squeezed his hand again.

"Believe me, I know how foolish this sounds now, but back then... I didn't consider how ruthless my parents were. How far they would go to maintain the status quo and our family's chokehold over Ethyrios.

"A little over a week before the ball, Ione joined me for a walk in the gardens and I finally confessed how I felt. How I'd loved her since the moment I'd met her. How I couldn't bear the thought of facing eternity without her. I explained the Turning ceremony, which I'd intended to perform the following night, and gave her a simple ring I'd swiped from my mother's overstocked jewelry box—a thin gold band with a solitary pearl in the center. From Vaengya. I wanted her to have a piece of the home she'd never seen.

"I slid the ring on her finger and she burst into tears, tears I couldn't help echoing. Then she kissed mine away. Told me she'd always felt the same and then shouted at me for waiting so long to say something."

Cassandra laughed, a wet, strangled sound. Tristan didn't dare look at her or he wouldn't be able to finish the rest.

"I made love to her right then and there, couldn't wait even another night until the Turning ceremony. It was the first time for both of us, so it was sweet and awkward and glorious and life-changing.

"And it's the final memory I have of her."

# CHAPTER
# TWENTY-ONE

CASSANDRA COULDN'T STAND IT, almost couldn't bear to listen to the rest of Tristan's heart-rending story.

She'd maintained the grip on his hand, but suspected that small bit of contact wouldn't be enough for him.

She didn't take the time to weigh the decision. Tristan's head shot up as the legs of her chair scraped across the bricks. His eyes trailed over her warily, but he didn't push her away as she crawled into his lap and settled her ear against his heart.

"Please tell me the rest," she whispered.

Tristan sucked in a shuddering breath as he encircled her in his arms, clasping his hands together and resting them at her hip.

"I'm not sure why Eamon did what he did. I assume he was jealous of me, jealous that I would be Emperor one day and he would not. Or maybe he was envious of what I had with Ione. Perhaps he was even jealous of *her*, that I'd spent so much of my time with this human and therefore had little to spare for my doting younger brother."

Tristan's derisive snort stirred Cassandra's hair.

"Whatever the reason, he told my father everything.

"I assume Ione and I were ambushed the next night. Once our plans had been thwarted, they sent me to the Temple in Thalenn and pulled my memory of the Turning. I have the scar, so we must've gotten at least part-way through it. But I don't know if she was fully Turned, or if we were interrupted before we finished the ceremony.

"After I returned from Thalenn to await my official public sentencing in the palace dungeons—a complete farce, since my parents had already decided what to do with me—Eamon paid me a visit. Didn't say a single word, just dropped the pearl ring, coated in dried blood, into my hand and walked away.

"That was the last time I saw *him* before last week.

"To this day, I have no idea what happened to Ione.

"After I'd been banished to the colonies, taking her last name as a final *fuck you* to my family, I spent a few fruitless years looking for her. But no one had any information and I was worried that, if by some miracle she were still alive, my search might endanger her.

"I gave up on the search, then spent a few more years wishing for death. Wondering why my father had decided to let me live in exile rather than ending me for my insolence. They'd made sure I was taken care of, even in my banishment, but I couldn't stomach the thought of spending a single *dracha* that had been earned by the pain and suffering of Ione's species. I wandered the colonies aimlessly, cursing the High Gods for not letting me die. For forcing me to live with the agony of knowing that not only had I failed Ione—"

His breath caught and she flattened a palm against his chest, rubbing in soothing circles as if she could will away the pain in his heart.

"But that I'd failed her people. Failed all of Ethyrios, really.

"Failed you," he whispered.

"Tristan," she choked out, overcome.

"Somehow, I ended up back in Thalenn, moping around the Fang and Claw until Reena had enough of my bullshit and told me I could either take a job at her place or get off her property." He chuckled at the memory.

"But I wanted to do something with *purpose*, something to help the humans after the disaster I'd caused. The Vicereine knew who I was, practically salivated at the chance to make me a member of her Vestian Guards after I refused to become a councilor in her sham government.

"And that's what I've been doing for the past two hundred years. Protecting the humans of the colonies, in whatever small way I can, to try to atone for my sins against them. For my family's sins against them."

Tristan rested his chin on her head and let out a long, slow exhale, so similar to a breath that signaled the end of a memory extraction. And perhaps he did feel like a supplicant, relieved to excise this story from his troubled brain and have no more secrets between them.

Except her own.

"Tristan?" she whispered.

"Mmm?" He'd unclasped his hands and was rubbing them along her hip and thigh.

"Do you remember that night at the Serpent's Den? When you said one day we could be brave together?"

"I didn't tell you all this to force you to share things you're not ready to share."

She pressed her palm against his and interlaced their fingers. "My mother is an obliviate."

Tristan squeezed her in closer. "Cassandra." His sigh was laden with guilt, as if he were the one who'd caused the tragedy. "I'm so fucking sorry."

"It happened the year after my father died, when I was thirteen. My mother was adrift in her grief and we had no support, no lifeline. We moved to the slums, not far from where Mistress Callas lives, and Mama started selling memories to keep me fed. I was with her at the Temple when it happened. Mother Superior took me in afterward. That's why I never left, even though there were times when freedom from the order was the most tempting prospect in the world. I couldn't abandon Mama, not after she'd sacrificed everything for me."

"I'm sure your mother wouldn't have wanted you to give up your life for her."

"I know that now. The day that I left the Temple, she…" Cassandra's eyes burned. But she'd shed enough tears tonight, couldn't possibly have any more to give. "She told me she didn't regret anything. Not leaving the order and certainly not her love for my father, despite all the pain his loss had caused. She said my father would've wanted me to live."

"Smart woman."

Tristan smiled against her hair. And though she really didn't want to know the answer, she knew she had to ask the question.

"Do you still love her?"

Tristan sighed. "I will always love her."

Cassandra closed her eyes and tried to ignore the ache stabbing through her chest.

She should have known. All the stories she'd heard about him and his conquests, all the women and females he'd had over the years. All nothing more than an attempt to distract from his one true love. Diversions—exactly what he'd promised her in Meridon.

His heart belonged to someone else.

As if sensing her discomfort, Tristan continued, "But it's hardened into something different over the years. Something less immediate, less fiery, less all-consuming. Honestly, I'm not even sure why she wanted *me* in the first place."

Cassandra scoffed. "As if it's possible for any female to not want you."

"Oh, yes, I'm such a catch. Behind this pretty face is a coward and a failure who prioritized his own desires above the needs of his people. Doomed an entire species to centuries of misery and servitude. If I had just done what my parents wanted, chosen a Fae mate and bided my time until I took over as Emperor, I could have fixed *all* of this. Your father might still be alive. Your mother might not be an obliviate. How can you even bear to be sitting here with me?"

She sat up in his lap and cupped his face. "Hey. Quit badmouthing my friend." He blinked and gave her a rueful smile. "You have no idea how things would've turned out. For all you know, you could've come into power, tried to change things, and then gotten yourself assassinated."

"Real comforting, Cass," he snorted.

"All I'm saying is, you can't change what's happened. The only path forward is forward."

"What even *is* that path anymore?" Tristan pondered. "We didn't get the necklace. It's fallen into the hands of an enemy we've yet to identify. I shudder to think what my brother will do once he finds out."

"Spin it," Cassandra shrugged.

"What do you mean?"

"It's actually positive news, when you think about it. We know Maksym didn't get the necklace. *And* we have clues about who did. Tell him that we're continuing to follow leads. I'm sure he'll be interested to hear about another Fae wielding resurrected elemental magic. And that symbol she was burning into the ship."

"You'd make a good politician," Tristan smirked, tucking a wayward strand of hair behind her ear.

She fought to suppress a shiver. "I'll head over to the Fang and Claw to talk to Reena tomorrow night, see what she might be able to tell us about the symbol."

Tristan opened his mouth to respond, but before he could get a word out, an errant wind stirred his feathers and he grimaced.

"What was that?" Cassandra asked.

"Windwhisper from my brother," he bit out through clenched teeth. "I've been summoned to the Vicereine's Palace to provide him with a report. Immediately."

Cassandra extracted herself from his lap as he pushed up out of his chair.

The moon had risen higher during their long chat, and his wings twinkled like stars in the silvery light. He speared a hand into her hair, cupping the back of her skull and tilting her face up. "Thank you. For listening. And for being kind."

He lowered his mouth to hers and her body melted, even as protests swarmed her mind. The moment his warm, soft lips made contact, a sob bubbled out of her.

He pulled back, then rested his forehead against hers. "What's the matter?"

"I can't…" A strangled whisper. *You're in love with someone else.* "I can't do this anymore."

She leaned back, surprised to see silver lining his own eyes.

"I'll always be grateful for our time in Meridon, but it wasn't real, Tristan. And the more we play, the less it feels pretend. I… it's starting to hurt."

"Cassandra, I would *never*—" Tristan sucked in his bottom lip, looked towards the sky before returning a pained gaze. "The last thing I would *ever* want to do is hurt you. Your friendship means too much to me."

And there it was.

The final blow against her bruised and battered heart.

*Friend.*

She'd never hated that word more.

But it was the very thing she needed to hear to strengthen her resolve.

"It's probably best if we give each other some space." She steeled her shoulders as she pulled out of his grip, his fingers lingering on her arms. Like he didn't want to let go. "I'll ask Mother Superior if I can come back to the Temple."

"No," he blurted. "No, you stay here. You'll be more comfortable. I'll return to the barracks and ask Hella to come stay with you."

"Tristan, I don't need—"

"A babysitter, yes, yes, I know. It's not for you, Daredevil, it's for me. After what happened on the ship, I won't be able to concentrate if I'm constantly worrying about your safety."

Cassandra nodded, scanning his honey-brown eyes. "You're a good person, Tristan. You don't deserve to shoulder the burden of your family's evils."

Tristan's brows furrowed and he turned towards the house. He looked back over his shoulder, his expression unreadable as he opened the double doors. "Goodnight, Cassandra."

"Night, Birdman," she replied with a small smile before he disappeared into the darkness.

By the time she awoke the next morning, he was already gone.

# CHAPTER
# TWENTY-TWO

CAEL WIGGLED HIS FINGERS, sending focused currents of wind that stirred the torches outside his cell.

Not strong enough to snuff them out, just enough to make them dance. Practicing his finesse for what he had planned as soon as Alexei arrived this morning to escort Xenia to the Temple in Primarvia.

With each sleepless minute last night, his growing power pressed its intentions against his skin. Begging to be unleashed. Stroking down his back and exploring the wound where his wing should've been.

He swore it wailed and raged at the absence.

Xenia's gentle, measured breathing floated over from the next cell. A comfort, since he wanted her well-rested for the trek ahead.

She'd woken in the middle of the night, screaming for her parents and terrified that she was alone in her cell again. He'd talked her down as best as he could from his side of the wall, but it had taken her hours to fall back asleep.

The dungeon door slammed open, whipping the torches into a frenzy, and Alexei's rushed footsteps echoed down the stone walls.

Cael stood, wing poised and hands raised, ready to suck the air from the fucker's lungs as soon as he stopped outside Xenia's cell.

But Alexei bypassed Xenia and came to a halt in front of Cael instead. His serpentine eyes glittered with amusement and a disdainful smirk twisted his scarred lips.

Cael curled his fingers, about to unleash his power, but was halted by the document clutched in Alexei's pale hands.

The sigil stamped onto the thick paper—two membranous wings bracketing a mountain peak on a field of verdant green—collapsed Cael's arms to his sides.

The sigil of Brachos.

Alexei's smirk widened into a crazed smile, his fangs popping.

"Your father is here."

One glance at those storm-cloud gray wings spread across an arched window, the pink undertones illuminated by the sunrise over red sand dunes, and Cael didn't even feel one-tenth of his one-hundred-and-ninety-two years.

He was a youngling again, desperate to win the approval and affection of the ancient Fae male before him. Beams of morning light glinted off the male's braided copper hair as his dark gray eyes bolted towards his son with the force of a crossbow.

Those eyes—Cael's eyes—betrayed no flicker of emotion as they swept across Cael's lone wing. Not a single question or word of comfort parted Arran Zephryus's lips as he tucked his own wings and stalked towards the long stone table. He pulled out a chair and took a seat across from Maksym, who was flanked by six Deathstalkers with popped fangs. An aggressive display, though Cael's father showed no hint of fear.

And he'd come alone.

Message sent.

Cael didn't dare display the return of his power. Not until he figured out what the fuck his father was doing here and why he hadn't already slaughtered Maksym and his tiny band of cronies.

"I told you," Maksym began, "that he was alive. And unharmed."

"Unharmed?" Arran asked, his bass-deep voice rattling Cael's bones. "He's missing a *wing*."

Maksym shrugged. "An unavoidable consequence."

Arran sniffed, stroking his long copper beard and blooming a shower of red dust onto the stone table as he grated his stormy gaze over Cael.

He flicked his eyes back to Maksym. "Tell me why I shouldn't just kill you now for what you've done to him."

Maksym raised his hand, green light sparking at his fingertips. "If there wasn't something else you wanted, you would have done so already. Wouldn't have agreed to this parlay when my scouts met your party out in the desert."

Arran crossed his arms over his broad chest and flared his wings. Sent a gust of wind across the table that extinguished Maksym's sparks. "Save your party tricks for someone else, Rosopa. One windwhisper from me and the Brachian warriors on-call less than a mile away will swoop in and tear this fortress, and you, to pieces. Your lightning magic will do nothing against our weapons."

Cael knew his father wasn't lying. All of Ethyrios's most powerful weapons were produced in Brachos. The peak represented on their sigil was Typhon Mountain, the origin of the very steel that had stolen Cael's wing. Not to mention many other killing devices—stun pistols, magic-seeking missiles, and a very deadly, portable bomb the size of a plum, crafted from wind magic and Deathstalker venom.

Cael often wondered why his father had invested so heavily in weapons manufacturing *after* the war. There had been little demand during these past five centuries of peace. The stun pistols and Typhon steel were occasionally purchased by law enforcement, both on the continent and in the colonies, but magic-seeking missiles? Tiny bombs that could level a building? What was the point of those?

Maksym placed his hands in his lap, patiently waiting for Arran to continue.

"The continent has been a powder keg since Eamon Erabis took the throne," Arran said. "You think you're the only player who's trying to hasten his downfall? He's a lazy leader, nothing like his father Leonin. Keeps himself holed up in that palace in Delos and has done nothing to set the tone for his reign. The ruling families in Cernodas and Akti have been begging him to help quash the rebel activity in their territories, to no avail. There is a power vacuum, and the vultures are swirling. Should your plan succeed, it might just be the very thing to set the entire continent alight."

"Should my plan succeed?" Maksym leaned forward. "Why, High Councilor Zephyrus, I thought you had come here to stop me?"

"I let the Emperor believe what he wants to believe. War would be a boon for my territory. Our weapons make us powerful. But a wartime marketplace? That will make us *rich*. We've been stockpiling for centuries, waiting for a moment like this. And I fully plan to cash out." He rose from his chair. "So lucky for you, I've only come here to collect my son. I'll leave you to your plans. If you succeed, come see me when you need the weapons to carry them out. But be warned, I'll be selling them to *your* enemies as well."

Maksym laughed, a swallowed, clicking sound, and shook his head. "You think your *Emperor* will allow that?"

A wicked smile curved Arran's lips. "My guess is he'll be too distracted to care."

"Very well," Maksym clapped his hands together. "I've no use for your son anyways, other than as leverage to keep his little human doing my bidding."

Arran's gaze snapped to Cael, a low snarl bubbling from his throat. "Human?"

Cael squared his shoulders and held his father's stare as the lie unspooled effortlessly. "She means nothing to me."

This exchange had not gone how Cael had expected, though he'd admit to being well removed from the goings-on on the continent for the past century and a half.

Before Cael had arrived in the colonies, Leonin Erabis had ruled the land not only with strength, but with the kind of respect that earned loyalty. And though Cael had never met Tristan's brother, he was aware of Eamon's treachery, of the betrayal that had led to Tristan's exile. Seems the male hadn't changed, losing more allies than he'd made during the two years of his rule.

Arran proffered a dusty hand, which Maksym stood and shook. "Best of luck in your *endeavors*, Rosopa."

"Pleasure, High Councilor," Maksym responded, ruffling his matte-green feathers. "Before you leave, please accept this token of my gratitude." He turned to the Deathstalker on his right, who handed him a black velvet sack emanating hints of rainbow light. "Should make your journey back to Brachos a bit shorter."

He handed the sack to Arran, who pried it open with two fingers, his copper beard bathed in a multi-colored glow as he smiled at the contents. "I haven't seen these in centuries. Where did you get them?"

"Same old friends who gave me this," Maksym said, shooting a crackling bolt of green lightning through the jagged hole in the ceiling. It careened off a broken piece of wood, exploding shards that dropped to the table in a smoldering pile.

Arran strode over to Cael, a disapproving frown showing through his beard. "Let's go."

He reached for Cael's arm, but Cael twisted away. He'd be damned if he let his father put his hands on him ever again.

He followed Arran out of the hall, his mind calculating a new type of plan.

A rescue mission.

"Cael?" Xenia whispered, pushing up off her straw mattress as the thin fog of shallow sleep released her. She cocked her head, listening for sounds in the next cell.

All night before she'd fallen asleep, she'd heard him moving around in there. A muffled grunt, the crack of a flexed wingbone, the creaking of his leather pants.

The silence squeezed her lungs, seizing her breath.

"Cael," she said, a bit louder.

Still no response.

Had he already used his newly restored wind magic to escape his cell? Was he upstairs, raining justice down upon Maksym and his slimy band of Deathstalker idiots?

Xenia chuckled at the vision, annoyed that he hadn't woken her to witness it.

She sat up and smoothed her glittering silk dress, untied and retied the straps which had loosened while she slept. If this was to be her escape uniform, so be it. Barefoot and begowned—what a way to travel through the desert.

She didn't fucking care, and was giddy at the thought of imminent escape.

Rising from the mattress, she padded to the front of her cell, curling her fingers around the bars and glancing down the hallway towards the scarred wooden door. Holding her breath, she strained to hear the expected sounds of struggle from the fortress above.

No shouting or scuffling drifted through the dungeon door.

Perhaps Cael had already dispatched their enemies? What time was it? How long had she been asleep?

A flutter of nerves erupted in her stomach.

Would Cael really not have woken her? Even if only to tell her to prepare herself before he wreaked his havoc upstairs?

Icy fear lodged in her heart.

Had Maksym defeated him?

Before speculation consumed her, the dungeon door groaned open and relief arrived, swift and soothing.

"Cael! Oh, thank the High Gods, I thought—"

Adrenaline burned a fiery, itching path through her veins at the sight of viper's eyes and that familiar silver scar.

Alexei shoved Xenia's breakfast tray underneath the bars, then turned to leave.

"Where is Cael?" she yelled after the Deathstalker. "What have you done to him?"

Alexei turned back, a serpentine smile pulling at his marred lips. "Your Windrider is gone. He's abandoned you. Practically leapt at the chance to save himself."

Shock tightened Xenia's chest. She didn't believe it.

"Our trip to Primarvia has been postponed," he said as he stalked out of the dungeon and slammed the door.

Xenia sank onto her mattress. Didn't touch her breakfast.

She remembered Cael's fingers slipping away from hers last night when she'd asked about his wing. As if he could no longer bear to touch her after the pain she'd caused him.

She hadn't thought he'd been angry enough to abandon her, but perhaps she'd been wrong. She berated herself for only ever seeing the good in people. Berated herself for her foolishness. For believing that Cael could ever care about a human.

She lay down and scratchy straw dug into her cheek as her tears began to flow.

# CHAPTER
# TWENTY-THREE

TRISTAN SLUNK INTO A white leather chair in the Vicereine's office, rubbing at his temples and trying to will away the pressure forming behind his eyeballs.

Fae healing abilities only worked at their fullest when the subject took care of himself. And last night, he most decidedly had not. Had instead drunk an entire bottle of bourbon to try to force himself to sleep.

It hadn't helped.

He hadn't gotten a wink last night, had tossed and turned trying not to think about Cassandra, about her reaction to his final confession. His pessimistic side—an admittedly small part of him, but the part that had been holding back his story in the first place—

knew that it would turn out this way. That she'd want nothing to do with him once she learned that he'd had the chance to save her species and had botched it. And though he knew telling her was the right thing to do, in the cold, harsh light of the morning in his lonely barracks room, he'd questioned that decision.

His brother sat behind the Vicereine's desk, the colonial leader herself standing beside him. Their black and gold wings tangled together in a wall of shimmering feathers, the only flashes of color in the stark white office.

Tristan was not in any kind of mood to be dealing with their bullshit this morning.

"Tell me again what you told me last night," Eamon said, leaning back in his chair with his hands resting on his stomach, a smug smile forming. "I want Varuna to hear it."

"You haven't already told her?" Tristan grumbled. "No pillow talk, huh?"

Eamon leaned forward and slammed his hands against the glass. "You are awfully flippant for someone whose mission was a complete and utter failure. Especially when I warned you of the consequences."

Tristan's stomach dropped. Eamon had threatened harm against Cassandra if they didn't bring him the necklace. He sat up straighter, needing to use every ounce of cunning to twist this meeting to his advantage.

"Would we call it a failure?" Tristan asked, glancing around the room as if seeking confirmation from an invisible audience. "Firstly, Maksym didn't get the necklace. Win." He listed their achievements, ticking them off on his fingers. "Secondly, we know Sister Cirillo is alive. *And* that no Sisters were abducted from the Temple in Meridon. Win, win. Thirdly, and thanks to Mistress Fortin's exceptional memory-pulling abilities, we have clues about the fire-wielding Windrider who managed to snatch the necklace. Win, win, win."

He sat back in his chair, folded his arms across his chest, and aimed a smug smile at his stone-faced brother. "All in all, I'd say it was a fairly successful trip."

Eamon dipped his chin, spearing Tristan with narrowed hazel eyes. "You and I have very different definitions of the word *successful*, brother."

He stood from his chair and rounded the desk, towering over Tristan in an effort to intimidate. Tristan merely gazed up at him, refusing to let the smile fall from his face.

"You failed to avert disaster on that ship, leading to the deaths of six of my citizens."

Tristan scoffed. Since when did his brother care about the deaths of *humans*?

Eamon sneered. "And you let an essential object slip through your fingers and into the hands of yet another enemy. You said you have clues about them. What are they?"

"We initially thought she might have been working with Maksym, since she also has re-awakened elemental powers. She destroyed that ship using fire magic." Eamon remained still, not a single flicker of emotion crossing his face. "She was burning a symbol into the wall—a circle bisected by a vertical line. Based on our research, it has some association with the Fallen Goddess. Any ideas?"

Eamon nodded, almost as if he'd been waiting for this confirmation. "There's an emerging rebel group on the continent using that symbol. We've been monitoring them for months. They've been stirring in a few cities in Cernodas and Akti, especially along the coast. Spreading lies about the restoration of the Fallen Goddess. Plus all the usual traitorous posturing; stolen artifacts, bombings of key Imperial buildings, terrorizing those loyal to the Empire. We were concerned that Maksym might be working with them. The only good news to come out of your trip is that he appears to be a rogue agent."

"Seems like something you should have warned me about beforehand," Tristan grunted.

"You had all of the information I deemed necessary at the time." Eamon pulled a hand through his short, black waves.

"You seem ruffled today, brother," Tristan jabbed, wanting to pierce through Eamon's defenses, get him to slip up and reveal something. His brother surely wasn't telling him everything.

Eamon clenched his teeth, a vein in his jaw jumping. "You have no idea the delicate balance it takes to sustain order among six continental territories and three different sub-species. While you've been off gallivanting in the colonies for the past two centuries,

I've been working with Father to maintain peace in Ethyrios."

"At any cost," Tristan muttered under his breath.

Eamon stood. "Your ridiculous idealism nearly cost our family *everything*. Did you ever consider the cost of Father's leniency? What he risked to take pity on you?"

"I never asked for his mercy!" Tristan roared. "I would've rather he ended me. And things worked out pretty well for you, in any case."

Eamon leaned forward, pointing a long finger at his brother. "Don't pretend it's a title you had any interest in. Your dreams were *foolish*, Tristan. I was trying to save you from yourself. I'm sorry you don't see it that way."

He would *never* see it that way. But this was dangerous territory. Territory that didn't need to be retrod today.

He changed the subject. "What about Officer Zephyrus and Sister Cirillo? Has there been any news of their rescue?"

"Arran Zephyrus contacted me this morning. Maksym has been dealt with and his son has been retrieved."

"What about Sister Cirillo?" Cassandra would *truly* never forgive him if anything had happened to her friend.

"Arran didn't mention her, but I have no reason to believe she wasn't rescued as well. Besides, it's time we turned our attention to more important local threats.

We have a new assignment for you." Eamon nodded to Varuna.

"These rebels seem far more numerous, and organized, than Maksym," the Vicereine said. "And their activities are leaking into the colonies. We believe they will try to make in-roads with disgruntled power players here among the elite."

"And who is the most disgruntled power player in all of the colonies?" Eamon asked.

"You have got to be fucking kidding." Tristan grimaced, leaning forward and resting his forearms on his knees.

"You have two choices, Tristan," Eamon whispered. "You can either help me destroy our family's enemies or you can sit back and watch this world tear itself apart. You may think me a monster but everything I am doing, every choice I have made, has been for our family. For Ethyrios. I am not your enemy, Tris."

Tristan's anger cooled at the childhood nickname. But was Eamon being genuine, or was this just another of the weapons he wielded? Tristan flopped back into his chair, bowing his head and running a hand over the back of his neck. "What do you want from me?"

Eamon sat back as well, the Vicereine sliding a comforting hand over his shoulders. "Help me avoid another war. Help me crush these rebels on behalf of the Empire."

"That is what you and Father never understood," Tristan said, shaking his head. "There will *always* be another Maksym, another group of rebels, if you insist on maintaining the status quo. These hierarchies between our sub-species, between Fae and humans, are bullshit. What are you going to do to change that? You're trying to fix the symptoms and not the cause."

"One problem at a time, brother," Eamon said. "Deal with this threat, and then we'll talk. But first, we need to understand which of the colony leaders are truly on our side. And which may be rebel sympathizers."

"Do you truly believe any of them are?" Tristan asked.

"Maksym opposed us from right under our noses," the Vicereine said. "How likely is it that he was the only one? The Fae who come to lead in the colonies are often seeking to prove themselves, prove their power. Some quickly become jaded, feeling like figureheads compared to their counterparts on the continent. It seems likely they'd be susceptible to other offers, to corruption and treason."

"Your disdain for me is well known throughout the colonies," Eamon said. "Start some conversations. Tease out their true motives. Mistress Fortin may yet come in handy again as well, given that the nature of your relationship has already been established. In fact, the colony elite have been buzzing about it for weeks."

"What are you talking about?" Tristan asked.

"August Lambros has been whining to anyone who'll listen about Ker, your new stunning, uppity mortal consort who had the gall to reject him at the Serpent's Den." Varuna regarded Tristan coolly. "She made quite an impression. The most powerful individuals in the colonies are salivating to meet her."

"Absolutely not," Tristan spat. "I refuse to put Mistress Fortin in that kind of danger."

"You would so easily dismiss the use of her memory-pulling skills?" Varuna asked, raising her eyebrows and pursing her blood-red lips. "You should take advantage of her while you can."

"I can ferret out the traitors without her. I don't want her exposed to that scene again," Tristan pleaded. "You know how those assholes treat their consorts. The expectations to...*share*."

"You never had a problem sharing before," Varuna's lips curled into a knowing smile as she leaned forward.

"That was your kink, Your Excellency, not mine," he growled.

"Careful, Tristan," Eamon said. "It's not your call to make. If we require her to do this work, she will do it. She wouldn't dare refuse."

Rage boiled Tristan's blood. The two monsters before him would use any pawns at their disposal, risk anyone's safety, to maintain a hold on their power. No sense arguing with them now.

"We done?" Tristan bit out.

"For now." Eamon said.

Tristan stood and turned to leave the room.

"Oh and brother?" Eamon piped up, dragging Varuna into his lap and arranging her wings over his shoulder. "There is *nothing* I would not do to protect our family's interests. I'm delivering a speech to my subjects in a little over a week. I expect a name by then—a rebel I can make an example of. If you dare betray me or fail to deliver, I'll have Mistress Fortin shipped to Tartarus as entertainment for the inmates. And will send you there in Nessite chains to watch."

Tristan's wings involuntarily shivered at the mentions of both the notorious continental prison and the elemental power-suppressing chains he remembered all too well from that night on Maksym's yacht.

He shot his brother a wicked grin. "I wouldn't dream of it, Your Imperial Majesty."

Eamon nodded as he turned to Varuna and whispered in her ear, running his hand up her thigh. She giggled like a schoolgirl before Tristan, barely able to hide his disgust, pulled the door shut.

# CHAPTER
# TWENTY-FOUR

Cassandra clung to Hella's broad shoulders, hanging on for dear life.

She normally relished moving through the clouds above her beloved jumble of a city. Loved watching the tiny people flow against each other like ants gathering food into their hill.

But she was normally doing so at a pace that didn't make her want to hurl.

Cassandra had quickly learned that Hella did nothing half-assed.

She'd nearly screamed when the red-winged giantess had barreled into her room this morning, crowing some nonsense about early worms and birds, then dragged her into the backyard for an invigorating workout session. Claimed they'd be doing it every morning while Hella was staying at the bungalow with her to keep her *spirits up.*

And the session *had* worked to keep Cassandra distracted from the reason her spirits were down in the first place—that heart-wrenching conversion she'd had with Tristan last night, the revelations on his history and his one true love.

Hella was a glorious training leader. At turns aggressive and encouraging, she'd pushed Cassandra to the brink of her capabilities and then nudged her just a bit further. It was the most empowering workout Cassandra had performed in years. It had allowed Cassandra to put her armor back on, refusing to mope around like some lovesick, heartbroken *fool.*

The update at breakfast had also helped bolster her mood. Hella had received a windwhisper from Tristan, informing them that Arran Zephyrus had taken down Maksym and rescued Cael and Xenia. Palpable relief had loosened some of the weight bearing down upon her. Though she knew it wouldn't fully lift until she saw her friend again in the flesh.

After breakfast, Cassandra had asked Hella if she would accompany her to the Temple. She wanted to check on how things were going since she'd been away, how the Temple and the supplicants had been faring since the Emperor had made weekly memory pullings mandatory. And after that, she planned to go to the

Fang and Claw to see if Reena could enlighten them on the meaning of that symbol.

"Hold on," Hella grunted as she tucked her wings and began a petrifying free fall towards the red-roofed Temple.

Cassandra closed her eyes and chomped down on her lip, caging in a scream as they fell out of the sky at maximum velocity.

Just when she was sure they were going to crash into the courtyard, Hella's wings snapped out like a clap of thunder. As the female settled gently onto the ground, Cassandra opened her eyes and took a deep breath, her faith in the High Gods spiking since they'd seen fit to save her from death by Windrider.

Cassandra grabbed Hella's arm to steady herself, to keep the world from spinning, and attempted to smooth her windblown hair.

"Wimp," Hella snickered.

"You're going to have to give me a few flights to get used to that," Cassandra grumbled before turning away and starting at the scene in the courtyard.

Several red-jacketed Empire soldiers brandishing stun pistols had lined up a group of twenty obliviates in front of the Temple. Their family members were gathered around, watching with pinched, horror-stricken faces. One woman in a dust-blue factory uniform was wailing on a stone bench, crying out for her husband.

Borea stood on the steps of the Temple, a mellow breeze stirring her platinum hair. Though the

Beastrunner appeared to be the portrait of preternatural calm, the claws curving down from her knuckles and the tense line of her lips suggested she was anything but.

Cassandra motioned for Hella to follow her as she slipped around the edge of the crowd and made her way towards Mother Superior.

Borea's eyes darted to Cassandra, bulged briefly at Hella, then snapped back to the courtyard. As if she didn't dare take her gaze off those Empire soldiers for a single second.

"What's going on?" Cassandra asked, fists clenched.

"A new Imperial decree," Borea answered in a low, guttural growl. As if her polar bear were about to take over. "Newly created obliviates are being shipped to the continent."

Nausea gripped Cassandra's stomach.

Obliviated humans had always been allowed to remain with their families. Or to find a place at one of the four Temples throughout the colonies if they had no family to return to.

"Why?" Cassandra asked.

"The decree lacked specifics," Borea answered tightly, her fiery gaze bouncing among the soldiers. "Though it did threaten my removal and the slaughter of my Sisters if we refuse to comply. Said that we could easily be *replaced*."

A soft snarl rippled from Hella's lips.

"How many days worth of obliviates is this?" Cassandra asked.

"Days?" Borea laughed, turning to Cassandra, sorrow dampening the cold fire in her pitch-black eyes. "These are just the obliviates from yesterday."

Cassandra swayed. At most, the Temple in Thalenn had experienced one, maybe two obliviations per month. To have twenty occur in a single day was unthinkable.

"What use could the Emperor possibly have for obliviated humans?"

"I don't know," Borea dipped her head into her hands.

A shriek burst through the crowd.

A Fae soldier aimed a stun pistol at a young girl who'd wrapped her arms around the legs of her obliviated mother.

"Don't take her!" the little girl wailed. "Please don't take her!"

Infuriated tears stung Cassandra's eyes.

The soldier yanked the little girl away from her mother and before she could think better of it, Cassandra's rage spurred her into action.

She swept down the stairs and shoved the Fae male—a Deathstalker with pistachio-green eyes—in the chest. "Leave her alone!"

He stumbled backwards, caught off-guard, and Cassandra cradled the little girl against her hip.

Hella ambled up behind her, flaring her wings, her hands drifting to her own stun pistol and dagger at her hips.

The little girl struggled out of Cassandra's grip and darted back to her mother.

The Deathstalker soldier straightened, the barrel of his stun pistol directed at Cassandra's chest. She refused to back down.

"She is interfering with official Imperial business," the male sneered. "Unless you'd like us to use this weapon against a child, we'd suggest you convince her to back away and let us do our jobs."

Cassandra crouched down next to the little girl, and Hella tucked in closer, her golden eyes holding the solider with such piercing intensity that the male's pistol wobbled.

The little girl sobbed quietly, squeezing her mother's legs.

"Hey," Cassandra cooed, placing a hand on her shoulder. "What's your name, sweetheart?"

"An-andrea," the little girl sniffled.

"Hi, Andrea. I'm Cass." She wiped a sweat-soaked strand of hair from Andrea's flushed face.

"Huh-hi."

"Do you have any other family here with you today?" Cassandra asked.

"No," Andrea howled. "She's…she's my only family. What's happened to her? Mommy, why won't you answer me?" Andrea clutched her mother's limp fingers.

A vision of gray-streaked dark hair and vacant espresso eyes stole through Cassandra's mind and it was all she could do to keep herself from collapsing on the ground and echoing the girl's anguished cries.

Cassandra glared up at the soldier, contemplated fighting him for the stun pistol and taking down the lot of them. She knew Hella would back her up. Borea likely would as well. Would shift into her polar bear and rip out the soldiers' throats.

But to defy the Empire so openly—and in front of so many witnesses—was unwise. She'd not only be risking her own future, but Hella's and Borea's as well.

She set her sights on saving this one little girl. She'd have plenty of time to plot and scheme later, as long as she escaped this situation with her life and her freedom.

She clasped Andrea's hand between her own. "Your Mommy has to go away for a little while. Can you be brave for me? Let's think of a happy memory before you say goodbye."

The little girl nodded, tears gathering in her lashes as she closed her eyes. Her eyelids fluttered as her lips curved into a small smile.

"What are you thinking of?" Cassandra whispered.

"We baked a cake yesterday." Andrea breathed a soft giggle. "Mommy was teasing me because I kept stealing licks of the frosting."

Wetness dampened Cassandra's own lashes. "That sounds like a very happy memory."

"Get on with it," the Fae soldier growled, crossing his arms and glancing quickly at Hella. As if to make sure his outburst hadn't angered her.

Cassandra ignored him. "Okay, Andrea, hold that memory in your mind and we're going to send it to your mother, so she has good things to remember on her journey. Are you ready?"

Andrea nodded, and Cassandra held the little girl's hand as she reached for her mother's with the other.

As soon as Cassandra's fingers curled around the woman's palm, sparkling heat surged through her veins. Her eyes slammed shut and her muscles stiffened as the little girl's memory flowed through her.

*The bittersweet taste of chocolate frosting.*

*Flour dust floating in a band of buttery light.*

*Bubbling laughter as a gentle hand swatted her fingers out of the bowl.*

"Andrea?" The woman's soft voice tugged Cassandra back into her own body and she opened her eyes.

The previously obliviated woman blinked, taking in the scene around her with a confused expression.

Cassandra's limbs tingled, and her tattoo shimmered as she passed a thumb over it. What in the name of Letha had just happened? She'd only been play-acting, a careful diversion to save the little girl, distract her from the pain of letting go of her mother.

"Oh, my darling, why are you crying?" The woman knelt down and swept her daughter into her arms, cradling her head against her neck.

Cassandra stood on shaky legs, and Hella placed a steadying hand on her shoulder.

"What did you do?" The Fae soldier grabbed Cassandra by the shirt and hauled her into his face, pulling her from Hella's grip.

Hella lurched forward, teeth bared, and was about to swipe her dagger from its sheath when Borea pushed between Cassandra and the soldier.

Borea placed a placating hand on the soldier's chest, encouraging him to back up a step. "Our mistake!" she crowed with false cheer. "These things happen sometimes."

The soldier tilted his head, a skeptical frown twisting his lips. "How did this obliviate regain consciousness?"

Borea shrugged. "It appears she wasn't obliviated after all. Merely stunned." Cassandra marveled at the swift smoothness of the lie. "We'll take her back inside."

The Fae soldier grunted, swiveling his head to observe the anxious, hopeful gazes of the other conscious humans and the angry impatience on the faces of his fellow soldiers. "Nothing to see here," he bellowed, then turned back to Borea. "Back away so we can get on with our business."

The woman scooped up her daughter, and Borea ushered them into the Temple, Cassandra and Hella following close on her heels. Hella held the door open and before Cassandra crossed the threshold, she glanced over her shoulder. Every cell in her body begged her to rush back into that courtyard to save the rest of the obliviated humans.

Hella, as if sensing the self-destructive direction of Cassandra's thoughts, placed a gentle, but firm, hand at the small of her back. "Too big risk," she whispered. Something vicious flared in Hella's eyes. "We save more soon."

The heavy wooden door thudded closed, cocooning Cassandra within the cool, quiet atmosphere of the Temple waiting room. She collapsed onto a stone bench as Mother Superior led Andrea and her mother into a private corner.

A few moments later, Borea glided over and crouched in front of Cassandra. "I've told them to stay here at the Temple for the night, to ensure that the woman's obliviated state doesn't return before morning. What happened out there?"

"I…I have no idea," Cassandra croaked, and Hella stroked a comforting wing down her arm. "As soon as I touched them both, it was like the little girl's memory flowed through me into her mother. It… I think the memory reawakened her."

"I assume this has never happened before?"

"No," Cassandra whispered.

"Have you noticed your abilities changing at all since you left the order?"

"No, I—"

The taste of charred wood and ancient spice rose on Cassandra's tongue, along with the feel of her lips on Tristan's warm skin, the sound of his soft grunts as she'd taken his blood.

"I think I know what caused this." She lifted her chin, glancing back and forth between Borea and Hella.

"And I think I know how we can help."

Cassandra shucked off her leather flats and tucked her feet underneath her on the Fang and Claw's rust-colored couch.

Reena ushered the tavern's few lingering patrons into the street's beckoning darkness before closing and locking the faded red door.

Cassandra ran a hand along a velvet-soft cushion, trying not to think about the last time she'd been sitting—or rather, sleeping—on this couch.

And who had been sleeping beneath her.

It was strange to have not seen Tristan in over twenty-four hours. Especially since they'd spent nearly every minute together for the past few weeks. She missed his teasing, missed his sly smirks and his thunderous laughter. Missed the way he'd always find ways to touch her—pinching her hip, tugging her braid, wrapping an arm around her shoulder.

But most of all, she missed his calming presence. He always knew what to do, in any situation. His jovial, unfaltering confidence kept her overactive mind in check.

And without him, it was running on overdrive. Especially after the events at the Temple this morning.

Though Cassandra was thankful for this unexpected new power, grateful that she had another method— besides larceny—to help humans avoid obliviation, bone-deep terror overrode her gratitude.

She couldn't shake those suspicious looks from the Empire soldier. He'd seen her face, had heard her say her name to that little girl.

Would he report the incident to the Emperor? Or had Borea's smoothly delivered lie been enough for him to dismiss the event as mere coincidence? There had been no outward sign of Cassandra's power, no glowing skin or bursts of light. No one watching would've known what had passed between Cassandra, Andrea, and her mother.

She stowed away her fears as Reena approached the couch and pulled up a wooden chair next to Borea, who sipped at a pint of frothy beer.

Borea smacked her lips in satisfaction, then downed a huge gulp and released a belch so loud it rattled the half-dimmed pendant lights.

"Excuse me." A sheepish grin formed as she wiped the foam off her mouth. "I forgot how good this was. I don't typically indulge. It wouldn't be fair to the Sisters."

Hella, sprawled next to Cassandra with a brawny arm draped over the cushions, snickered and saluted Borea with her own frosty mug. "Reena serves best beer in city."

Reena smoothed her auburn hair, her amber eyes shining with pride. "Come on now, you'll give a girl a complex." She turned to Cassandra. "You sure you don't want anything, sugar? I can't imagine why you begged me for this emergency meeting, but I'm guessing it's nothing good. Need some liquid courage?"

Cassandra shook her head. "Really, I'm fine, Reena, thank you."

"So, what crazy scheme have you all got cooking and why, exactly, do you think I'd want to be involved?"

Though she wanted her mind clear for this meeting, Cassandra second-guessed her decision to refuse a drink as she recounted what had happened at the Temple, how she'd reversed that woman's obliviation. Borea chimed in to inform Reena of the Emperor's decree, the order he'd given to have new obliviates shipped to the continent.

"Holy shit," Reena said. "I think *I* need a drink. What use would the Emperor have for obliviated humans on the continent?"

Borea drained the dregs of her pint, then waved off Reena when she offered a refill. "The few reasons I can imagine are all suitably horrifying."

"Fortunately, it seems we have the means to stop him." Cassandra held up her palms. "Me."

"Look at you, magic girl," Reena smirked. "Savior Sister."

"I'm not a Sister anymore."

Reena leaned forward, nostrils flaring as she sniffed at Cassandra's scent. "But haven't taken full advantage of that fact yet. What are you waiting for?"

Cassandra sent a panicked glance towards Borea, who chuckled. "You really think I didn't know what was going on between you and Officer Saros? I'm nearly seven centuries old, my dear. Do give me a *little* credit. And honestly, I don't blame you. A handsome, smitten, exiled Fae Prince? One could do worse."

Cassandra cheeks heated and a shudder ran through her at Tristan's title.

Hella yawned, covering her mouth with the back of her hand. "Too much chit-chat. Long day. What is point of this?"

Cassandra addressed Reena. "We want to use the Fang and Claw as a secret meeting place for me to un-obliviate Temple supplicants."

Reena chewed on her bottom lip. "Straight to the point. Why the Fang and Claw? Can't you do it at the Temple?"

"It's crawling with Empire soldiers throughout the day and night now," Borea answered, smoothing her platinum bob. "The only places they don't visit are the extraction rooms downstairs. Our plan is to hide any obliviated supplicants down there, then sneak them away for Cassandra to treat."

"Empire soldiers have been making random stops here too," Reena said, irritation twisting her features. "Harassing my customers, barking nonsense about *maintaining the separation of the species*. I'm lucky they haven't shut me down yet. Though they're probably too terrified to try. I usually chase 'em outta here with my tiger." She purred the last word, her substantial fangs lengthening and digging into her lower lip. "But so far, they haven't shown up after closing time. How would you get the obliviates here? You can't just parade them through the streets of Thalenn."

"Through the sewers," Cassandra answered. She and Borea had already discussed this part of the plan earlier. "There's an entrance beneath the Temple. I assume there's a grate here in the basement as well?"

"There is," Reena nodded. "And we should use the basement for this work anyway. Just in case we do get any after-hours visitors." She massaged her jaw, her tongue poking out to lick at a fang. "I like it," she declared with a nod. "I'm in."

Cassandra breathed a relieved laugh. "I thought you'd take more convincing."

"Fuck the Emperor," Reena shrugged. "And fuck his soldiers. What's the point of living for centuries if you can't indulge in a little criminal activity once in a while." Reena's eyes softened. "Does Tristan know about this? I can't imagine he'd be okay with you taking such a risk."

"I…I haven't told him yet," Cassandra confessed.

"He not be happy," Hella chimed in. "He want come and help. Protect you."

"His brother seems to be keeping him plenty busy," Cassandra said, an irrational flare of annoyance sparking through her at his absence.

*You asked him for space, you dolt.*

Borea leaned over the small table and placed a gentle hand on Cassandra's knee. "You're likely going to need him."

"What do you mean?"

"It was the infusion of his blood that allowed you this power in the first place. It's not like the magic you received when you were born—the effects won't be permanent. You'll need replenishments. Often. On our worst days, up to twenty human suppliants are obliviated. You won't be able to cure them all without him."

Cassandra dipped her head into her hands, expelling a long sigh.

"Why *wouldn't* you want him to help?" Reena asked. "Something happen between you two?"

"It's complicated," Cassandra grumbled. "Why does it have to be his blood? Couldn't one of you give it to me?"

Borea offered a sympathetic frown. "Tristan is descended from the oldest Fae bloodline in Ethyrios. His magic is some of the most powerful on the planet. How do you think his family ended up ruling the Empire? I don't think just any Fae blood will do."

"Just *any* Fae blood?" Reena cocked a groomed eyebrow. "Speak for your self."

Borea raised her chin. "No offense intended. But you suspect the same, do you not?"

"No, I agree with you," Reena said, her crimson lips pinched. "Just feel like you could have delivered that line differently."

"We settled?" Hella rose from the couch, pulling Cassandra up with her. "We have early start tomorrow. Tiny human need sleep."

Reena stood as well, stretching her long, golden-brown arms above her head before grabbing both Hella's mug and Borea's drained pint glass from the low table. "See you all tomorrow night," she called as she sashayed back to the bar to clean the glasses.

Cassandra stifled a yawn as Hella pressed a hand against her back, guiding her towards the tavern's faded red door. The black iron scrollwork was barely visible against the pitch-black night.

"Wait!" Cassandra yelped, running back to Reena at the bar. "I forgot that I wanted to talk to you about… something else." Cassandra wasn't sure if she should bring up Reena's history as a priestess of the Fallen Goddess in front of Hella and Borea. "Can I come back before the tavern closes tomorrow night?"

Reena tilted her head. "Of course, sugar. Everything okay?"

"I'll explain tomorrow." Cassandra grimaced. "And can you invite Tristan also? He should be a part of this conversation."

"Color me intrigued," Reena crooned as she began polishing pint glasses, then offered a saucy wink. "See you both then."

Cassandra ignored Reena's insinuations as she rejoined Borea and Hella on the street underneath the awning. "Borea…" she began, gathering her courage to ask the question she'd been pondering all day. Ever since Andrea's mother's had been revived. "Do you think… do you think my power would work on Mama?"

Borea's chin fell to her chest, her eyes laced with pity, and Cassandra's heart sank. "I fear she may be too far gone, my dear. Andrea's mother was obliviated only yesterday. I doubt your mother's condition is reversible after eight years."

Cassandra choked back a cresting sob. "Will you please let me try?"

Borea cupped Cassandra's face, stroking a finger across her cheek. "Are you sure you are prepared to weather the disappointment?"

Cassandra straightened her shoulders and sniffed back her tears. "I want to try."

Borea's features softened and her hand fell to Cassandra's upper arm. "Alright. I will bring her with one of the groups this week. Perhaps in a few nights, after you've had some practice?" Cassandra gave her a grateful nod, then clasped the hand on her arm. "Thank you for doing this, Cassandra. Reena was right. You are a savior. Even if you're not a Sister anymore."

Cassandra smiled, a wicked grin filled with the purpose she'd been missing since she'd left the Temple.

"Those sparks of rebellion are catching fire."

# CHAPTER
# TWENTY-FIVE

*A* SOUND AS PIERCING AS *a child's scream stole Xenia's attention from her book.*

*She perked her head up and peered out of the open window next to her cushioned seat.*

*Lucy, the family's black retriever, was sniffing something in the grass. The dog reared back, then bent down for another inspection and the screaming increased in frequency and volume.*

*Xenia threw her book down and rushed through the front door of the farmhouse.*

*"Shoo, SHOO," she hissed at Lucy. "What did you do?"*

*Lucy sat back on her haunches, her pink tongue lolling out of the side of her mouth, and cocked her head—a portrait of canine innocence.*

*Xenia pushed Lucy away, then crouched down to find a small puff of tawny fur nestled in the grass. A baby rabbit.*

*And the source of the screaming.*

*Why the neighborhood rabbits insisted on making their nests in a yard that clearly smelled of retriever was beyond Xenia.*

*"Oh, no," she choked out, reaching out her hands to pluck up the tiny baby.*

*Lucy approached, nosing at the injured animal, and Xenia swatted her. "Away, beast! You've done enough."*

*Xenia cradled the kit in her hands and though its high-pitched screaming had ceased, its furry body palpitated in her palms, breathing fast, its heart jumping frantically.*

*She tucked the rabbit against her chest and scurried back into the house.*

*"Mama. MAMA!"*

*She dashed into the kitchen to find her mother peeling potatoes in front of the hearth.*

*Mama dropped the peeler and crouched in front of her daughter, whose face was bathed in frustrated tears. "What's wrong, sweetheart?"*

*Xenia opened her palms. "Lucy got another one," she sniffled.*

*"Stupid rabbits," her mother grumbled, taking the ball of fluff from Xenia's hands. Its breathing had slowed considerably and Xenia wondered if it now felt safe. Or, if it felt death approaching.*

Death was a concept that Xenia, at eight years old, had learned of early. Chickens and pigs disappeared often. And then reappeared on the family dining table. Though it was a necessary part of life here on the farm, Xenia didn't like to think about it.

Her mother grabbed a dish towel and laid the rabbit upon it, stroking its fur and cooing soft noises.

"What should we do?" Xenia asked, wiping at her nose.

Xenia dreamt of becoming a healer one day. Animals or humans, she didn't yet have a preference. The thought of providing comfort, making living beings feel better, filled her with a sense of uncomplicated joy.

Her mother had already firmly, yet gently, quashed that dream. All of Ethyrios's healers were Fae, the possession of magic being the number one job requirement.

Mama brushed her fingers through Xenia's springy curls. "I'm sorry, my love. There's nothing to be done for it now."

Her mother returned to her dinner preparations and Xenia pulled out a chair, determined to watch over the dying baby in its final moments.

A helplessness gripped her as the baby rabbit's blood-stained fur slowed, then stilled completely.

She let out a sob and buried her head on folded arms atop the table.

Her mother ambled over, placing a gentle hand on her shoulder.

"Bless your tender heart, my Xenia. I pray this world will not steal it from you."

The dungeon door slammed open, waking Xenia from her nostalgic dream.

She glanced over her shoulder, not bothering to rise from her straw mattress as Alexei pushed her breakfast tray into the cell.

"I don't want it," she murmured.

Alexei said nothing, merely sniffed and then left the dungeon.

Leaving Xenia alone with nothing but her memories.

Her unflagging optimism had reached its limit, and despair like Xenia had never known had overtaken her mind—her soul—these past few days.

Even her cherished stories offered little comfort.

What was the point of eating, of breathing, even? She'd been left here to rot by everyone she'd ever thought she cared about. She honestly didn't even know why Maksym was keeping her alive. There'd been no talk of any trips to Primarvia, no talk of snatching more Sisters.

Though Xenia was grateful for that. She wouldn't have had the energy to perform even if Maksym had forced her to.

Her mother had said she had a tender heart, but she could feel it hardening.

She turned back to the wall, cold and numb and empty.

And wished for the predators of the world to end her.

Cael entered his father's office, his wing tucked and his hands clasped behind his back, buzzing with restrained anticipation. Through the two-story window, mist crept down the sloping meadow, spreading across the edge of the forest like a ghostly army—the front line of Brachos's ever-present dreariness.

It had been far too long since they'd left Maksym's fortress. Since he'd left Xenia. He prayed to any God who would listen that Maksym hadn't harmed her.

When Arran had refused to waste the opals Maksym had gifted him for their journey home, Cael had nearly blown his cover by protesting. What could have been a trip of mere hours instead took several days. While most of the party had flown back to Brachos, Cael had been forced to ride in the vehicles with the other non-winged Fae.

Cael had been beside himself with worry, but didn't dare slip away and risk his father coming after him again. He'd have to play this carefully, ensure he had his father's permission before leaving the territory again.

Permission he'd come to seek mere hours after his arrival in Diachre this morning. It was a bit ironic, really. How long he'd dreamed of returning to the continent, to Brachos, only to leave again immediately.

"What do you want?" Arran snapped, not bothering to lift his gaze from the dismantled stun pistol on his desk. He buffed the charcoal gray barrel with a tenderness Cael had rarely seen him use.

"I have a request," Cael said, anchoring his feet to the floor—a battle stance.

Arran paused his polishing, slashed his gray eyes towards his son and stood, spreading his wings. "A *request*? You think you're in any position to make a request of me after the risk I just took for you?"

Cael pulled his shoulders back and held his father's gaze. Cowering would only anger Arran further. "I have a few loose ends to tie up in the colonies. If you'll allow me back there for a week, once I return I'll do whatever you ask of me."

Arran huffed, sweeping a disgusted gaze across Cael's lone wing. "I've little use for damaged goods."

Cael clenched his jaw, refusing to show his father how much those words stung.

Arran cocked his head. "But I suppose you might make a good match for the daughter of one of my business partners. Laskaris, runs an ore mining outfit over in Cernodas. Beastrunner family—bear bi-forms. He and his wife have been inquiring about your brothers, but I've already got Windrider matches lined up for them. You don't need two wings to populate the world with a few more Zephyrus heirs. And who knows? Laskaris might even lower my costs to celebrate a shared grandchild."

Cael sniffed, cutting his gaze through the window. A hawk bobbed in the sky, sweeping over the spindly pine trees. "Whatever you want, Father."

Arran snapped his fingers. "Look at me. You heard what I told Rosopa, yes? The continent is about to explode. War is on the horizon and family, *alliances*, will be more important than ever. Our *weapons* will be more important than ever. I need you here, supporting our efforts."

"I understand," Cael bit out through gritted teeth.

"Do you?" Arran vented a savage chuckle. "What was that nonsense Maksym mentioned about the human you were captured with?"

Cael's chest seized. "I told you, she means nothing to me."

"I should hope not." Arran placed his hands on the desk, dangerously close to his pistol, the sharp talons at the peaks of his wings flashing a sinister glint. "You've always been too soft where humans are concerned. And she's clearly cost you *enough*. I'll allow you this final trip to the colonies, but if I hear any hint that you've gotten some foolish notion of going back to the Desolation, I will find her and personally end her myself."

Cael smoothed his features, not letting an ounce of emotion show on his face. "You don't need to worry about that."

"Good." Arran arced his wings over his chair and returned his attention to his cleaning project. "Take some *drachas* with you. In the top drawer behind you."

Cael nodded, turned on his heel and strode for the small table beside the door. He opened the drawer, and as he reached for a pouch of coins, a rainbow glow snagged his eye. Glancing sidelong over his shoulder to ensure he lacked his father's attention, he pried open the velvet sack and swiped a shimmering opal, hastily placing it in the pouch with the *drachas*.

"Cael," his father barked, and he nearly dropped the pouch. Gripping it closed, he turned back to Arran.

"Do not forget who you are." His father's sharp steel gaze sliced through him. "You are still a *Zephyrus*—" Arran banged his fist on the desk "—regardless of your…injuries. You represent this family, whether you like it or not. Whatever debasements you've gotten up to in the colonies *end* the moment you step foot back in Brachos."

"Of course, Father." Cael slipped out of the office and stalked down the shadowy, log-paneled hallways of Stoneridge, his mind swirling with plans.

He needed to get a windwhisper to Tristan, let him know that he'd escaped Maksym and was heading back for Xenia. Tristan would likely want to send aid, but Cael couldn't allow it. He'd need to keep this rescue mission as quiet and low-tech as possible. The opal he'd stolen would hasten his return to the fortress, and hopefully shorten their trek through the Desolation, depending on how long its power held. But he didn't dare ask for any additional support, lest word get back to his father.

He'd also need to inform Tristan of everything Arran had let slip about the mood on the continent: the impending conflict, the Emperor's slippery grasp on his control. If Tristan hadn't already been sucked into the fray, he surely would be soon. And once Cael had gotten Xenia to safety, once he'd returned to Brachos as he'd promised his father, he'd figure out how he could help his friend. Figure out what his own role would be in this battle for the soul of Ethyrios.

All that was too far in the future to worry about now though.

As he slipped into the misty morning, the hawk twisting through the pines let out a screeching cry.

Cael had one final stop to make before he began his journey back to the Desolation.

The armory.

# CHAPTER
# TWENTY-SIX

TRISTAN PROPPED HIS ELBOW atop the mahogany bar of the Fang and Claw, chin in hand as Reena worked her charm on the night's final customers.

Before he'd arrived at the tavern this evening, he'd had an interesting conversation with Cael. Though it had been reassuring to hear from him, if only via windwhisper, there was a new layer of tightness to Cael's voice. As if Cael wasn't sharing everything with him. What he had shared, though, was alarming. Arran Zephyrus had turned against the Emperor, had done nothing to thwart Maksym. And had left Xenia there. Cael had assured Tristan he'd deal with the situation, both Xenia's rescue and Maksym's lingering threats. He'd begged Tristan not to say or do anything until he heard from him again. The determination and desperation in Cael's voice had Tristan reluctantly agreeing to wait and see how this all played out before he said anything to his brother about the Brachian High Councilor's betrayal. If Tristan decided to inform Eamon at all.

He had to tell Cassandra, though. As much as he'd love to bear the burden of this worry alone, he didn't want to keep anything from her. Had already ruined his chances with her due to the *other* secrets he'd been harboring. He'd tell her tonight, after this cryptic *talk* that Reena had summoned him here for.

He wondered why Cass hadn't reached out herself. She hadn't said a word to him since he'd dumped his baggage in her lap and scared her away. He was trying very hard to keep his shit together.

The thought of seeing her tonight had his stomach in fluttering knots. A nervous excitement that not even the tumbler of bourbon pooling condensation onto the bar could tame.

She'd said she needed space, and he respected that.

But he had no idea how he was supposed to act around her tonight.

He knew how he *wanted* to act. The moment he saw her, he'd be fighting his instincts to wrap her in his arms and squeeze her close. Ask how she'd been feeling, what she'd been doing. Maybe sniff her hair like an obsessed freak.

And the fact that he no longer knew whether she would welcome or resent those gestures had him reaching for his drink and throwing it back in a single gulp.

He settled the glass onto the bar as Reena approached.

"What's this about, Reena? You were a bit vague in that message you sent me."

"I know as much as you do, big boy." She smiled slyly as she gestured to the front of the tavern. "But looks like we're both about to find out."

The red door opened, and Tristan's heart stuttered.

As Cassandra stepped into the tavern, her blue-gray eyes landed on him and he had to grab hold of the bar to physically restrain himself from running to her.

She ambled towards him, a shy, wary smile curving the gorgeous lips that he could still feel pressed against his stomach, his cock. As she approached the bar, her honey and rosewood scent invaded his nostrils and he almost wept with joy.

"Hi," she said.

"Hi." He bit back the tidal wave of questions flooding his mind.

*Have you been thinking of me as much as I've been thinking of you?*

*Do you still need space?*

*Are we still friends?*

"Reena said you wanted to talk to me?" That's what his brain decided to go with? Smooth.

Reena's feline gaze bounced between the two of them like a cat watching a mouse zigzag across the floorboards. Her crimson lips parted—about to pounce—but Cassandra cut in as she climbed onto the barstool next to him.

"Actually, I wanted to talk about Reena."

Reena reared back, the amusement falling from her face. "Me? I mean, I am a fascinating subject, but with everything you two have going on, why would you want to talk about me?"

Cassandra leaned across the bar and the delicate arch of her back had him itching to run his fingers down her spine.

"We need to talk to you about the Fallen Goddess," Cassandra whispered and Tristan released a disappointed breath. He should've known this conversation would be all work and no play. He berated himself for hoping otherwise.

Reena shot a glance at her fellow bartender, ensuring he hadn't overheard, then stepped over to ask him to cover for her.

She slid out from behind the bar and motioned for Tristan and Cassandra to follow her through a swinging door.

They traveled through the stock room, wooden crates of liquor bottles and silver kegs of beer lining the walls, to another door that opened upon a set of rickety wooden stairs. The steps groaned, barely holding Tristan's weight, as the trio descended into a damp, mud-walled space.

The basement was the same size and length as the bar upstairs, filled with cloth-draped furniture and piles of cardboard boxes. A single magically powered bulb hung in the center of the room, casting a circular glow upon the packed dirt floor. Shadows darkened the cob-webbed corners and spots of mold bloomed on the cloths. A rank dampness hung in the air.

Reena propped a hip against a liquor barrel, picking at her nails. "Why do you think I know anything about the Fallen Goddess?"

Cassandra snorted. "If you don't, why'd you lure us down into the basement?"

Reena's golden eyes flashed. A warning.

Cassandra raised her palms. "We saw a picture of you. In an old book in the Temple library in Meridon. You were a priestess of Adelphinae in the early years of the war, weren't you?"

Reena's tiger tail popped out, lazily waving behind her. Another warning.

"That was...a very long time ago. And very few people know about it. In fact, it seems that all three of them are now in this room." A low growl bubbled in Reena's throat.

Tristan stepped between the two females. He didn't really believe that Reena would do them any harm, but if they wanted to get any useful information out of her at all, he'd need to calm her down. Reassure her of their discretion.

"We haven't told a single soul," Tristan said, flashing his own sharp canines and puffing up his wings. An attempt to re-establish dominance. Not that it would do much good before these two. "Nor do we plan to.

We just need some information about a symbol. One that we encountered on a bad night on our way to Meridon. And one that's associated with a burgeoning rebel group on the continent."

"What symbol?" Reena asked, crossing her arms.

Tristan crouched down, then unsheathed his dagger, using the tip to trace a circle into the dirt. He swiped a single line through it.

Reena hissed, then dropped to her knees, flinging clouds of dust into the air as she frantically rubbed the symbol away. "Are you fucking insane? Don't put evidence of that symbol anywhere near me. If any Empire soldiers saw this, it would be a straight shot to Tartarus. Or worse."

"So you *do* know what it is, then?" Tristan grinned.

Reena sagged back against the barrel, holding her forehead in her hand. "Of course I do."

"Please, Reena," he begged. "If I don't start figuring out who the hell these rebels are, and who is in league with them, my brother will have my head." Cassandra's eyes flashed to him and filled with panic. "Well, maybe not literally."

Reena sighed, raking her matte-black fingernails through the silky strands of her auburn hair, her faraway gaze plastered to the wall above Cassandra's head. "In the decades before the war, around the time of my birth, my parents became enmeshed in a sect of Adelphinae's religion who adopted that symbol—Teles, it was called.

"Teles had been loosely used beforehand as a representation of the Creator herself, supposed to symbolize a mathematical ratio that was evidence of her influence over the natural world.

"The group co-opted the symbol, named themselves the Teles Chrysos. It means *ultimate balance.* They were obsessed with combining the species to create a race that would represent a true manifestation of Adelphinae's principles on Ethyrios. They believed that the combination of Fae and human bloodlines could eliminate the growing tribalism and cross-species clashes, and would result in the restoration of the dying elemental magics.

"They were led by a representative of Adelphinae called the Delphine, a female born once in a generation who possessed the precognitive abilities of the Goddess and interpreted the teachings of her sacred text, the Compendium of Creation."

"Ruled by a female," Cassandra smirked. "Wise people."

"You know it," Reena grinned.

"How did they hope to achieve their aims?" Cassandra asked.

"The Compendium, a transcription of the first Delphine's conversations with the Goddess, encouraged mating between Fae and humans. At least, according to the Teles Chrysos's translation. But human mothers weren't capable of giving birth to supernatural babies. As the child developed in utero, a fully human body couldn't sustain the magic and the baby would be born powerless, despite the father's Fae blood.

"They had much greater success when they tried it the other way, mating a human male with a Fae female. And some of the mixed-species females born from those unions were able to successfully birth magical babies. But the highest success rates occurred between Fae and Turned humans."

Cassandra stiffened and it was all Tristan could do to not run a wing down her arm. Given the direction their last conversation about Turning had gone, he wasn't certain his touch would be welcome.

"Turned humans often manifest greater levels of power than the Fae themselves even," Reena said. "It's why the Empire outlawed the practice, especially in Ethyrios's fragile state after the war.

"Some suspect that the Teles Chrysos themselves had invented the process, basing it off another disputed translation in the Compendium."

Cassandra cleared her throat, her fingers tangling together at her waist. Refusing to look at him. "How… how does it work?"

Reena darted a glance at Tristan, and he offered a subtle nod. "A mortal and a Fae would share blood, declare a vow to each other, and then consummate their union. If the Creator blessed their coupling, after a few days the human would be Turned."

Discomfort radiated from Cassandra as she shook her head and changed the subject. "What happened to them? The Teles Chrysos?"

"Once the Accords went into effect, they scattered, disappeared from recorded history. Along with Adelphinae. This was shortly after I posed for that painting with my fellow priestesses. My parents had sent me to one of Adelphinae's Temples as an acolyte. I was to commune with the Goddess until I reached maturity, then return to them to begin my work with the Teles Chrysos. Obviously, I never got that far. The Empire declared worship of the High Gods Anaemos, Faurana, and Stygios as the one true religion, and threatened imprisonment for anyone continuing to preach faith in the Creator. Empire soldiers destroyed Adelphinae's Temples, and I fled to the colonies with the humans. Been here ever since."

"What happened to your parents?" Tristan asked softly.

He read the answer in the anguish that tore through Reena's features before she smoothed them over, her eyes dead and glazed.

Cassandra piped up. "Do you remember hearing anything about a prophecy? One that describes the resurrection of the Goddess?"

Reena shook her head. "No. But if one exists, it's probably in the Compendium."

"Do any copies remain?" Cassandra whispered.

"Only one that I know of." Reena's eyes flicked towards Tristan again. "It's locked in a chamber beneath the palace in Delos. Property of the Imperial family."

Realization barreled through Tristan, chilling his blood more effectively than the basement's cool, damp air. "I've seen it. My brother showed it to me. It's how we learned about Turning, before I..." He held Reena's gaze, didn't dare look at Cass. Or finish his thought.

Cassandra pressed forward, her voice calm and steady. If she was affected by Tristan's confession, she wasn't letting it show. "And you're sure it's still there? It certainly appears as if the Teles Chrysos are stirring again—or at least a group that's using their symbol. Is there a chance that they've somehow gotten their hands on that copy?"

"I suppose it's possible," Reena answered. "But unlikely. The Imperial palace is the most heavily guarded building on the planet. I can't imagine anyone breaching it."

"Maybe there's another copy in existence," Tristan offered.

Cassandra finally turned to him, her beautiful face half shrouded in shadows in the dim basement light. Her guarded expression sliced at his heart. "Or some of the original members of the Teles Chrysos are involved in this new incarnation." She turned back to Reena. "Don't suppose you remember any of them, do you?"

Reena's brows dipped. "I never met any of the group members. I only know what my parents shared with me. Though before they were disbanded, there were rumblings of a meeting with Trophonios."

"Trophonios?" Tristan asked. "The inventor of Delirium? Why would they have wanted to meet with him?"

"The Teles Chrysos leadership at the time hoped to persuade him to join the cause, felt he might be amenable to it since he'd invented the elixir to save the humans from extinction. He's the most legendary scientific mind Ethyrios has ever known; they hoped to take advantage of his skills."

Tristan snorted. "Don't know why they'd think a snow leopard bi-form would join their group. They're not particularly prone to *community*."

Reena raised a shoulder. "Like I said, they were just rumors at the time. I'm not sure they ever even gathered the courage to approach him."

Cassandra blew out a long breath, then placed a hand on Reena's shoulder. "Thank you for telling us this, Reena. What you've shared stays between the three of us." She raised an eyebrow at Tristan.

"Yes, absolutely," he reassured the pale Beastrunner. He knew how she felt, reopening old wounds, dredging up a painful past. She looked as drained as he had felt the other night.

Reena pushed up off the liquor barrel. "I need to get back upstairs to close down the bar." She aimed a careful look at Cass. "You ready to tell him about the *other* surprise?"

Tristan stiffened, straightening his shoulders. "What other surprise?"

He'd barely gotten the words out before metal clanked behind him and he turned to see the sewer grate in the middle of floor sliding open.

His eyebrows flew to his forehead as Mother Superior climbed out of the hole, her platinum hair in disarray and splattered with mud.

Then he nearly leapt out of his skin as a group of thirty or so humans piled into the tiny basement, half of them clearly obliviates with their glazed eyes and slack features.

Hella climbed out of the hole at the end of the line, spreading her blood-red wings wide.

Cassandra burbled a nervous laugh.

"Surprise?"

# CHAPTER
# TWENTY-SEVEN

"WHAT'S GOING ON, CASS?" Tristan asked. "What is this?"

Reena strode to the stairs, calling back over her shoulder, "I'll leave you to it."

Cassandra aimed a careful glance at Mother Superior—Borea, Tristan remembered Cassandra had called her—who offered a subtle nod before gathering the obliviated humans and what Tristan assumed were their family members.

Cassandra took his hand, skyrocketing his pulse, and pulled him into a dark corner.

"Can you, uh, provide us with some privacy?" she asked, rocketing his pulse further.

He turned his back towards the room and spread his wings around them.

"Please don't freak out," she said.

As a conversation starter, it wasn't very comforting.

"Do I look like I'm freaking out?" he answered.

"I don't know, I can't really see your face."

The faint light from the single bulb in the middle of the room barely poked through his feathers and though he could see her face—her achingly beautiful face—clearly, she was struggling to see his.

Honestly, it was a comfort. He needn't control his features as carefully as he had been, could gaze upon her with all the longing in his heart and not be worried about the truths he might reveal.

"I'm not freaking out. Tell me what you need, Cassandra."

*I'll give it all to you and more*, he nearly followed with.

She toyed with the end of her braid as she regaled him with the incredible story of an obliviate restored. How, somehow, the blood he'd fed to her in Vaengya had deepened her power and allowed her to save a young mother from being shipped off to the continent by order of his heartless brother.

"Borea said it wasn't permanent though," she whispered, leaning closer, her face so close to his chest that he could hardly breathe. "I'll need to take a dose every night before I do this work."

He nearly bit into his wrist right then and there, ready to offer himself up to her, when the gravity of what she'd asked of him, of what she planned to do, crashed upon him.

"If Eamon or any of his soldiers catch you doing this…" He couldn't even finish the sentence.

"I know." She grasped his hand, running her thumb along the back of his palm, and goosebumps shivered across his limbs. She wasn't playing fair. "Tristan, I *know*. But I can't just sit back and do nothing. Not when whatever divine forces exist in this world have seen fit to provide me with this power."

"Thought you said *I* was the reason you've been given this power. Are you calling me a divine force?" He tugged her in closer.

She pressed her other hand against his chest, and her answering laugh warmed his insides, the effect far deeper and richer than the bourbon he'd tried to numb himself with earlier.

"You know you are," she murmured. She tilted her face up, her pleading gaze tearing through every reasonable part of his brain that knew this was a terrible risk, a terrible idea.

And yet.

Her compassion and selflessness were the very reasons he'd been drawn to her in the first place. To ask her to deny that part of herself was like asking a bird not to fly or a wolf not to hunt.

And he supposed that by helping her, at least being here and being present for the insanity, protecting her from her own destructive, though well-meaning, tendencies, made the whole thing a little easier to stomach.

"Okay," he breathed, and the tension melted from her body.

"What body part would you like to feed from?"

Cassandra snorted a laugh, Tristan's tease sending warm heat crawling through her.

He didn't play fair. Though she didn't know why she expected he would.

Seeing him again was torture. Self-imposed torture, she knew, but torture nonetheless.

She needed to focus on her task though. Reminded herself that he would never belong to her in the way he belonged to Ione.

"Your wrist will do just fine," she said.

She couldn't see his face, but thought she noticed his shoulders slump.

He lifted his wrist to his mouth, bit into it, and then held it out to her.

She gripped his forearm, swore she heard a soft sigh at the contact, then suctioned her lips onto the cut.

Her knees nearly buckled at the taste of him, the rich, spicy, oaky flavor of his blood. She took several long pulls, then removed her mouth with a pop.

Similar to the last time she'd drank from him, his

magic tingled through her limbs, sparkling and bubbly and heady. As intoxicating as champagne.

He drew his wings back and Cassandra stepped out of the shadows and into the awaiting group of obliviates.

"Okay," she nodded to Borea and Hella. "Let's get started."

The work was draining, and took nearly the entire night to complete.

But every one of the fifteen obliviates that had been brought to the basement of the Fang and Claw that night had been restored to clear consciousness.

Cassandra had never felt such a complete sense of pride in all her life.

Nearly every family member that had been brought along for the journey—a necessary part of the restoration, since they needed to focus on a memory they shared with the obliviate in order to complete the reversal—had burst into grateful tears upon getting their loved one back.

Many had thrown their arms around Cassandra, calling her the Savior Sister—she wondered if Borea had something to do with that title—and offering to pay her for the service. She waved every one of them off. She'd seen their memories, seen their modest dwellings and well-worn garments, felt the hunger in their bellies, and knew she'd never take a single *dracha* from any of them.

Once the work was complete, Borea accompanied the group back down into the sewers to return to the Temple.

As Cassandra watched the last of them disappear down the sewer grate, a ripple of uncertainty gripped her. She suspected she'd see many of them again. With the Emperor's demand for ten memories per week, there was no way that at least a handful of them wouldn't be re-obliviated.

The enormity of the task weighed upon her, but she'd do everything in her power to keep this up, keep mortal families from being separated.

Hella approached, settling a hand onto Cassandra's shoulder. "Time go, tiny human. Need rest."

Cassandra glanced to the side of the room, where Tristan was snoring softly, nestled onto his wings on top of a fabric-covered couch. She'd told him that he was welcome to leave at any time, but he'd refused. Said he'd be staying all night, every night, while she was doing this work. She'd argued that he'd need to stay sharp for what his brother had tasked him with, but he'd merely crossed his arms and refused to budge. Said Cassandra's own work was equally as important. Her chest had glowed at the compliment.

She crept over to him and brushed a lock of hair off his forehead.

He stirred, his eyelids fluttering open. "Is it dawn?"

"Almost," she smiled. "We're finished for the night."

He rose from the couch, stretching and spreading his glorious, iridescent wings. She never failed to feel awestruck at the sight of them.

She almost reached out to hug him, then thought better of it. "Thank you for doing this, Tristan."

He nodded, his lips pressed together in a tight line. "I…I've been meaning to tell you something all night. Figured I should wait until your work was finished."

The concern furrowing his brow had Cassandra bracing herself for the worst. "What?"

He placed his hands on her shoulders. "It's about Xenia."

That burdensome weight crashed back down onto her, crushing her more thoroughly than her bone-weary exhaustion. She brought her hand to her mouth, her vision clouding. "She's dead."

Tristan bent down and cupped her cheeks. "Oh High Gods, Cass. No. *No.* It's not that. It's… I was misinformed earlier this week. Arran Zephyrus didn't rescue her. He took Cael and left her there with Maksym."

A sob broke loose as fury and anguish collided in Cassandra's chest. "*Why?*"

He held her steady. "I don't know. But Cael is on his way back for her."

She gripped Tristan's arms, fighting the urge to fall to her knees as sweat slicked her palms. "We need to leave. Now. We need to go help them."

"We can't," he shook his head, looking as distraught as she felt. "Even if we could get to her before Cael, which is unlikely, my brother can't know about this. No one can. Cael is defying his father to return to her. And if Arran finds out, he'll kill her. We have to wait. We have to trust him." Tristan dipped his head. "I didn't want to tell you…didn't want you to worry."

"No," she whispered, her face and limbs going numb. "No, I'm glad you did."

Tristan lifted her chin with a finger. "Cassandra, I *swear* to you, Cael will find her. He'd tear himself apart before he'd let anyone harm her."

She dug her fingers into Tristan's muscled forearms. "One week. Cael gets *one week*. After that, even *you* won't be able to stop me from going after her myself."

Tristan smirked. "I'd be a fool to try."

"Yes, you would." She swiped a hand up her wet cheek. "A *dead* fool."

Tristan's booming laughter chipped away at her devastation. "There's my tiny, violent human." The smile fell from his handsome face, replaced by nervous hesitation. "Do you…should I come back to the bungalow with you?"

Her impulsive side wanted him to. Wanted to drown herself in his arms, his skin, his mouth. Wanted to forget about everything, if only for an hour or two.

But her cautious side knew that even a euphoric, limb-tangling play session wouldn't erase his words from the other night.

*I will always love her.*

"I'll be fine." She pushed out of his arms as he blew out a resigned sigh. "We both need to rest. It's been a long night."

He scrubbed a hand along the back of his neck. "Yes, it has." He opened his mouth, about to say more, then bit his lip. As if holding back a deluge of unspoken words.

His wings slumped as he turned to walk up the stairs and she couldn't help calling out to him, "See you here tomorrow night?"

His dimple appeared as he grinned over his shoulder.

"Count on it, Daredevil."

# CHAPTER
# TWENTY-EIGHT

ALEXEI YANKED OPEN THE door to the bathing chamber and shoved Xenia inside.

It had been a week since Cael had left, the dreadful days tracked by the number of barely touched food trays piled in her cell.

"Clean yourself up," he barked. "We leave for Primarvia within the hour."

Xenia glanced towards his empty hands. "Where are my dress robes?"

Alexei crowded her against the wall, so close she could smell rancid meat and bitter poison on his breath. His forked tongue darted out, caressing her jawline in featherlight strokes that were somehow more unbearable than hard ones. She clenched her teeth to corral a disgusted scream.

"You don't get dress robes this time." He brushed her matted curls from her neck and popped his fangs, dragging them across her jumping pulse, hard enough to scratch but not draw blood. "You think Maksym is going to make this task easy for you, after your disobedience?"

Alexei pushed off the wall and shoved her towards the tub. She flopped over the lip, her arms dunking into the cold water. They hadn't heated it for her this time. No surprise there.

"If I don't look like a Sister, how does he expect me to get into the Temple?" she asked, pushing upright.

"Not his fucking problem," Alexei snarled.

"And if I refuse?"

"Clean. Yourself. *Up*." Each word was punctuated with a dart of his tongue. "We'll be back to fetch you in ten minutes."

Alexei swiveled on his heels and slammed the stone door behind him, the boom echoing with a finality that sounded like the end of all Xenia's options.

She sunk down the side of the tub, and buried her face in her hands.

Cael had abandoned her.

Tristan and Cassandra weren't coming for her.

No one was going to save her and she was past the point of saving herself.

Despite her despair, she focused on the one thing she could control.

She would not help Maksym harm anyone else, refused to be a weapon wielded in someone else's war.

Even if it meant ending her own pathetically short life.

She stood and brushed away her tears, stony determination sweeping through her as she stared into in the tub.

What would it feel like? To sink beneath the water and wait for death?

She peeled off her filthy silk dress, then choked back a painful sob as she stripped off Cael's underwear.

She couldn't bring herself to be upset with him, with the choice he'd made. A part of her was grateful he'd found a way out, though she did wonder how he'd managed it. Maybe the answers would await her in the afterlife.

She crawled over the lip of the tub, the chilled water pebbling goosebumps along her skin.

Lowering beneath the surface, she closed her eyes and crossed her arms over her chest.

And waited for blissful oblivion to embrace her.

Xenia burst through the surface of the water, her lungs a conflagration of burning pain.

She couldn't fucking do it.

Couldn't even be brave enough to end her life rather than be used as Maksym's pawn.

Curse her useless survival instincts.

Her arms flopped over the side of the tub, her golden curls matted against her cheeks as heaving gulps of air razored down her throat.

As her breathing slowed, she scanned the small, circular chamber for anything she could use as a weapon. If she didn't have the willpower to end her own life, perhaps she could hasten her destruction by foolishly attacking her captors.

Her gaze caught on a corner of crumbling stone at the bottom of the wall.

She climbed out of the tub, searching for a towel.

Of course Alexei hadn't left her one.

She shook herself dry, then twisted her hair, squeezing out as much moisture as possible back into the water.

Cael's black underwear tugged against her wet skin, and the glittering midnight blue silk clung to her as she slipped her dress back on.

Crouching, she picked at the cracked stone, using a fingernail to pry off a small shard. It was thin and brittle, but the edge was sharp.

It would have to do.

She tucked the shard into the waistband of the underwear, hidden beneath the scoop of her backless dress, then leaned against the tub to await Alexei.

Ten minutes passed. Fifteen. Then surely twenty.

She strode to the chamber door and pulled on the rusted iron handle, but it didn't budge.

Pressing her ear against the door, she listened for sounds in the hallway, but the stone was too thick to hear anything through.

After what felt like an hour, the iron handle squeaked and the door groaned open.

Alexei poked his head in, his waist-length onyx hair falling over his shoulder, and grunted, "Out. Now."

Xenia pushed up off the floor and followed him into the breezeway, biting back questions about why she'd been left in the chamber for so long.

Cassandra's dagger bobbed at Alexei's hip, and Xenia folded her arm behind her, caressing the shard and buttressing her courage to use it.

Alexei led her into the fortress's great hall. Richelle and Maksym were in the midst of a heated conversation in front of the large map of Ethyrios, whispers hissing as flickers of lightning flashed down Maksym's wings. Color rose on Richelle's cheeks, her raven curls in disarray as if she'd been running nervous hands through them.

She slammed her finger onto a point on the map several times as Maksym flung his hands up in an exasperated gesture and turned away from her.

Several Deathstalker guards slumped in chairs around the long stone table, pointedly ignoring the argument taking place beside them.

One of them was missing. Zakariah. The ash-blond male who'd served her and Maksym's dinner.

The one Richelle had sent to retrieve the necklace.

"...*told* you not to underestimate her, Richelle," Maksym growled. "What were you thinking, sending Zakariah to deal with Roeki alone?"

Richelle's turquoise eyes dropped to the floor. "An honest mistake, Maksym," she murmured. "He assured me he could handle her."

Maksym rounded on her, cuffed her throat and slammed her against the map. Richelle didn't bother fighting back. She was a trembling fawn, caught in an angry predator's snare with none of her previous oily confidence on show. "I'm sorry, Maksym. I will do better."

Maksym barked a laugh so full of venom, it chilled Xenia's blood. He lowered his face to Richelle's, his grip tightening on her neck. "And what in the name of the Creator makes you think I will give you that chance?"

Richelle opened her mouth to respond but only a strangled sound came out as glowing green snakes of lighting twined up Maksym's forearm. Richelle's teeth clamped closed as tremors wracked her body, and her eyes rolled back, exposing white. Wisps of smoke floated off her skin.

The unmistakable scent of cooked flesh filled the room as Richelle's cheeks and exposed arms began to blister.

Xenia wanted to look away from the gruesome spectacle, but she was frozen in place, awestruck by Maksym's dreadful power.

Richelle's legs gave a final, jerking twitch, a dark spot blooming down the leg of her pants, and Maksym released her with a disgusted grunt.

Her body crumpled to the floor, small sparks still popping from her flesh, as her corpse spasmed with aftershocks.

Maksym turned on Xenia, his face a mask of unhinged rage. The face of a male who's carefully laid plans were all coming crashing down.

Xenia bit her lip to keep from smiling, but couldn't help a small snicker.

Maksym snapped. Stalked to her in three long strides and wrapped his hands around her throat, shoving her against the stone wall.

"You think this is funny?" he snarled, his fingers popping with sparks that coursed through her, seizing her muscles. She grabbed his wrist with one hand and snaked the other behind her back, trying to pry the stone shard from her waistband. Difficult as Maksym slammed her against the wall again.

Xenia gritted her teeth as another shockwave of Maksym's power blazed through her. "I think it's fucking hilarious," she bit out. "Your little fly-by-night operation is *done*, isn't it?"

Maksym squeezed her throat harder, and the lack of breath combined with her weakness from hunger made her head swim.

Still, she couldn't help taunting him.

She marveled that she'd ever been afraid of him at all. He was a small male with small plans. Just a petulant, powerless bully.

Uncontrollable laughter bubbled up her throat, forced past Maksym's vise-like grip, and burst from her parted lips.

"Stop fucking laughing!" he roared.

Her hilarity pitched higher, her body juddering as she felt his power building. He was about to strike, about to end her, but she couldn't help herself. Wouldn't give him the satisfaction of begging for a life she'd almost thrown away in that bathing chamber.

Her fingers finally pried the stone shard free of her waistband.

Maksym's eyes widened as she jammed it into the side of his throat, and he let out a burbling groan, but didn't release her neck.

Green blood streamed down her wrist, loosening her grip on the shard as she attempted to force it in deeper.

The shock of the blow shuttered Maskym's lightning. "You *bitch*," he snarled, low and wet.

Xenia glanced over his shoulder to see Alexei and the other Deathstalker guards rushing to help their master.

Before they could reach them, a seed of rainbow light bloomed behind Maksym, then expanded into a shimmering circle.

Relief, swift and euphoric, trembled through her as a single, storm-cloud wing angled through the portal.

Cael surged in like an avenging demon, risen from the fiery depths of Stygios's realm, wielding a Typhon-steel broadsword with a hammer-shaped pommel.

"Get your sparkly fucking hands *OFF* my human."

Maksym dropped Xenia and made to pivot, but Cael was too fast. The steel cut through Maksym's right wing like a hot knife through butter and the appendage crashed to the stone floor, matte-green feathers floating down upon it like a gruesome snowfall.

Maksym howled, falling face-first into the wall as Xenia darted beneath the table.

The world-ending rage twisting Cael's features rendered him barely Fae. A crazed, feral beast with only one goal in mind.

*Kill.*

Cael left Maksym writhing against the wall, then turned to Alexei and the Deathstalkers, curling his fingers and stealing the breath from their lungs. They collapsed to their knees, clutching at their throats, faces purpling.

Xenia had never seen Cael use such a massive amount of his power. As if it had been building while Maksym had been suppressing it.

His wind abruptly ceased, and Alexei and the guards sucked in gasping breaths, barely able to rise before Cael tore through them.

He whirled through the hall, piercing hearts and removing heads with meticulous precision—a breathtaking ballet of brutality that poured heat through Xenia's veins.

Cael returned his attention to Maksym, pulled the male up by the back of his blood-soaked jacket and slammed his face against the wall.

He snarled into Maksym's ear as the male groaned and grunted in pain, Xenia's stone shard still stuck in his neck.

"You are *finished*, Rosopa," Cael seethed. "Did you really think I wouldn't return for her?" His gray eyes darted towards her, and beneath the thundering fury, she swore she saw flashes of the deepest regret.

"Please, *please*," Maksym sniveled, his smug savagery and cool arrogance slithering away with the rivulets of green blood streaming down his neck and back.

Cael lifted the sword again and chopped off Maksym's other wing. A scream of utter agony and desperation escaped the male, and Xenia almost felt sorry for him.

She tucked her knees against her chest and laid her head between them, covering her ears to dampen the sounds of Maksym's messy, though deserved, end.

After several minutes, she slowly lowered her hands and raised her head. The only sound in the hall besides the rustling of her silk dress as she crawled from underneath the table was a faint panting noise.

Cael was slumped against the wall, the sword and Cassandra's dagger lying by his side, his face crumpled in tear-soaked anguish.

The desiccated Deathstalkers, Alexei included, lay surrounded by pools of green. Ended permanently.

Maksym, or what was left of him, was a limbless torso, his arms, legs, and wings scattered across the floor.

She approached Cael carefully, stepping over the oozing detritus of his wrath, and crouched down in front of him.

As soon as she touched his cheek, his eyes popped open, glistening with unshed tears.

"It's not enough," he whispered. "It wasn't enough."

She knew he was talking about his wing, about what Maksym had taken from him. No amount of violence or vengeance would bring it back.

She settled into his lap and he wrapped his arms around her, burying his wet face in the crook of her neck. "You came back for me."

He trailed a cool hand down her spine and she shivered at his touch.

He lifted his chin, bringing his lips to the shell of her ear as his arms tightened around her.

"We escape together or not at all."

# CHAPTER
# TWENTY-NINE

TRISTAN SIGNALED TO A tuxedo-clad waiter standing against the dark-wood wall of the Secretariat's small council chamber.

The mortal man rushed forward on quiet feet, then bent at the waist to whisper into Tristan's ear. "What can I get you?"

"Cup of coffee," Tristan said, stifling a yawn. All those late nights—or rather, early mornings—this past week at the Fang and Claw were taking a toll on his sleeping habits. "Cream, no sugar."

As the man bowed in recognition of the request, Tristan bit down on his impulse to thank him. Such pleasantries were not offered to the mortal help within this building. And to offer them would inspire gossip and speculation that Tristan had neither the time nor inclination to combat. He was acting a role at the moment. Better to have the waiter think him rude than expose himself. It was harder than he'd imagined.

He'd made little—alright, no—progress searching for rebel sympathizers among the colony elite. The few one-on-one meetings he'd been able to secure had been filled with platitudes and politicking. Their careful words and inscrutable smiles had signaled, outwardly at least, their unfaltering loyalty to his brother, to the Empire.

Tristan had even thrown in some leading questions about the Fallen Goddess, about the rumors regarding awakening fire, water, and lightning magic. Dropped Maksym's name when he got desperate, and still nothing. Not a misplaced frown or flicker of recognition from a single one of them. And nary a mention of the growing unrest rippling across on the continent.

Suspicions that this was just another fool's errand, another way for his brother to keep Tristan under his thumb, were beginning to take hold.

Luckily Eamon hadn't yet pressed him on the task. He'd been aloof and distracted at the one and only of these council meetings he'd attended this week.

Tristan had dashed out of that meeting as soon as the Vicereine had adjourned it, wanting to avoid Eamon's scrutiny. He worried his brother might be able to read something on his face about *another* group of rebels, those brave females who'd co-opted the Fang and Claw every night to defy his brother's orders.

Spending nearly every night with Cassandra again was exquisitely painful. And though they never exchanged more than a few dishearteningly shallow pleasantries, watching her work with the obliviates and their families, seeing her glow with pride at the end of every session… It was nearly as comforting to him as if he'd been able to hold her in his arms.

Nearly.

And holy High Gods, the after-effects of her consuming his blood…

He'd dreamt of her every night this week. Her lips suctioned to his wrist, her tongue flicking across his pulse, her soft hand gripping his forearm. The sensations transformed into something far more intimate in those few fitful hours of sleep in his sad, lonesome barracks room. Every morning, without fail, he'd wake with a stiff cock and an unrelenting ache in his chest.

An ache he, unfortunately, was all too familiar with.

And though it was happening far quicker than it had the last time, Tristan knew what it felt like to be falling in love. He almost wished Letha had taken *those* memories from him as well.

Then maybe he'd be able to ignore the punch to his gut every time Cassandra smiled. Or the way her laughter caused every cell in his body to light up. Or the way her stubborn independence inflamed his blood, made him ache to spar with her, force her to let him take care of her.

He tucked the feelings away, deep within that neglected corner of his heart that he kept cracked open for her despite the evidence that she wanted nothing more to do with him.

He'd content himself with feeding her his blood, his magic. And relish in his own quiet delight at just being in her presence night after night.

The waiter returned with Tristan's coffee, setting the dainty cup and saucer before him—the fanciest, most pretentious cup of coffee Tristan had ever been served. He pinched the tiny handle in his massive fingers before draining the entire thing in a single, slurping gulp.

A frosty glaze shivered along his skin.

The Vicereine glared at him from the head of the oval table. Over his boorish table manners or the dazed gleam in his eyes, he couldn't be sure. He'd missed the last fifteen minutes of the conversation as soon as he'd started thinking about Cassandra.

The Vicereine's crimson mouth curved into a disdainful frown. "Well, Officer Saros? Were you planning to bless us with your thoughts on the matter or did you intend to just sit there all day looking vapid and pretty?"

Tristan leaned back in his chair, threading his fingers together and cracking his knuckles, taking as much time as possible to answer the Vicereine's question. Let the curious gazes of the powerful Fae and mortals seated around the cherry table linger on him a bit longer.

"Sorry, Your Excellence," he drawled, dragging a hand through his hair. "Mind repeating the question?" He aimed a crooked grin at the Vicereine, who opened her mouth to reprimand him before the Fae to her left piped up.

"Why are you even here?" August Lambros sneered, flaring his sapphire wings in an unmistakable show of aggression. "Dogs aren't typically allowed a seat at this table, regardless of the palace they've crawled out of."

Tristan chuckled merrily. "What's the matter, Lambros? Still pissed my consort didn't want to fuck you?"

Lambros narrowed his espresso eyes at Tristan, sputtering for a comeback as Tristan logged the reactions around the table. Mostly shock, but he did note three councilors either biting their lips to suppress laughter or covering their mouths with their hands.

"Enough," the Vicereine bit out. "Save the dick measuring for my party tonight." Tristan kept his face carefully neutral. Party? This was the first he'd heard mention of it. "Though August, hate to tell you, you'd lose." She winked at Tristan and the three Fae that had been trying to suppress their laughter doubled over in audible guffaws.

One Fae, a massive beast of a male with glistening ice-blue tattoos swirling up his neck and across his exposed forearms, held Tristan's gaze as his laughter subsided. Amusement glinted in the male's single visible eye, a mottled blue and yellow marble. A black patch covered the other, and a gnarly scar spiderwebbed up through an ebony eyebrow, a stark contrast to the male's snow-white hair.

Tristan recognized him instantly—Ronin Matakos, the Butcher of Aethalia.

What the fuck was the ancient warrior doing in the colonies?

The Beastrunner—a white wolf bi-form—had slaughtered thousands of humans during the war. At the Battle of Aethalia in Cernodas, one of the bloodiest clashes, he'd been single-handedly responsible for the deaths of over two thousand human soldiers. A painting in the Imperial palace in Delos glorified the Fae victory, showcasing a colossal white wolf with blood-soaked muzzle and paws standing atop a pile of broken human bodies.

Some said the scar Ronin bore was from that battle; others claimed the male had given it to himself in an attempt to appear more intimidating. Given the crazed look in the male's single eye and the insouciant curve of his lips as he leaned back in his chair, Tristan was inclined to believe the latter.

An older mortal male with an ingrained air of authority spoke from across the table. "We were all wondering if there have been any breakthroughs in the search for my family's necklace," Alcander Pagonis said, flicking a speck of dust from the shoulder of his impeccably tailored navy suit. "Delirium sales are down eight percent this week in both the colonies and the continent. The populace is *spooked.*" The man's dark blue eyes flared as he pursed his lips, conveying the ridiculousness of the people's fears. "Afraid to drink a drop lest their minds get hijacked by a madman."

"Maksym has been dealt with, and the necklace has slipped from his grasp, thankfully," Tristan addressed Pagonis with the half-truth, wondering how Cael's expedition was faring, before turning to the larger group. "Though we suspect it may have fallen into the hands of even more powerful enemies: an emerging rebel organization who've been stirring here and on the continent. Their methods do not seem to be the same as Maksym's, though. In fact, we believe they may have taken the necklace solely to thwart him."

"Are you going to thank them for doing your job?" Pagonis crooned.

*Tough crowd,* Tristan thought as he surveyed the self-possessed man. He truly had no idea which side Pagonis was on.

The Vicereine turned her attention back to Lambros. "How's the mood in your district, August?" Varuna asked.

Lambros represented one of the suburban districts surrounding Thalenn, an area filled with the mortal class somewhere between the Heronswood ultra-rich and the tired and unwashed masses of the slums. Though, the population in his district was growing smaller and smaller by the decade as the Heronswood families and the Fae hoarded Ethyrios's wealth.

"Abysmal," August barked out, his sapphire wings rustling with the force of his outburst. Clearly this guy had one setting: aggressive asshole. "There have been several more attacks just this past week. And they've escalated from looting and petty vandalism. Last night, a bomb went off in the Imperial Capital Alliance on Front Street. Millions of *drachas* were destroyed. There are rumors spreading, people beginning to question my power."

Of course that's all he was worried about.

"Was anyone harmed in the explosion?" Tristan asked.

August shook his head. "Just a few low-level night clerks. No one important, thank the High Gods."

Tristan understood the subtext: only mortals had been killed. He smothered his rising anger. It was one thing to forgive the actions of those ignorant Windrider tourists who'd abandoned the ship disaster—they'd spent their entire lives on the continent and rarely visited the colonies. It was quite another to accept a brazen disregard for mortal life from a male who, in title, represented them.

"Did the culprits leave anything behind?" Tristan asked. "A note, a calling card?"

August ruffled his feathers, his eyes darting away from Tristan's piercing gaze. "There was a symbol painted onto the rubble at every scene. A circle slashed through with a vertical line."

Tristan clocked the reactions around the table, wondering if any of them would offer up the name of the symbol or the organization to which it belonged. But he was met with an unsurprising array of poker faces. Similar to the ones he'd seen in all his drudging meetings this week. These councilors had spent decades, centuries in some cases, playing these games.

"We'd do well to assign some additional protection to the districts," August said.

"Absolutely, August," Tristan said, plastering on a saccharine grin. "I'll have the Vestians assign patrols today."

"Wonderful," the Vicereine said. "Meeting adjourned. See you all at the palace tonight. Reminder that your consorts are very much welcome. Jealous spouses, of course, can stay home." She emitted a vicious chuckle as she rose, striding out of the room.

Tristan lingered at the table, noting the groups that naturally formed as the councilors strolled out of the chamber. Alcander sought out the two other mortals in the room, an older man and younger woman, representatives of smaller city districts. August stormed out alone, pushing through the remaining Fae councilors.

As Tristan left the table, Ronin lingered by the door. Tristan ambled over, and Ronin stretched out a hand. The phrase tattooed across the male's knuckles, *Inom Than*, translated to *become death* in Aramaelish.

Subtle.

"Nice to finally meet you, Ghostwalker," Ronin said, a hungry gleam in his eye as he crushed Tristan's hand. Tristan refused to flinch. "Your brother's told me so much about you. Been enjoying yourself, slumming it down here in the colonies for the past two centuries? Guess the access to all the easy mortal pussy's been a perk. August was telling me about your delicious new consort; she sounds like quite a treat. I'd love a taste at the party tonight."

Ronin squeezed Tristan's hand harder and Tristan squeezed back, refusing to cower at the male's domination tactics. What the hell was this party everyone was talking about? And why did Ronin think *Cassandra* would be there?

"I'm more than she can handle," Tristan smirked, before gnashing his sharp canines and fluttering his wings. "What are you doing in the colonies, Matakos? You been demoted?"

The white wolf bi-form smiled back, a wide, half-crazed grin exposing thick, sharp fangs. "Your brother asked me to come. Wanted me here for that speech he's making at the end of the week."

Eamon wanted the continent's most notorious human killer present for his speech? It would certainly set a tone.

Ronin tossed his head, flicking messy strands of white hair as he turned and exited the council chambers.

"See you and your tasty human tonight, Tristan."

"Why wasn't I informed about your party tonight?" The Vicereine flicked her eyes to Tristan before returning her attention to the document before her. The scratch of her pen across the thick paper made his teeth clench.

He cleared his throat and asked again. "Why wasn't I informed about your party tonight, Your Excellence?"

She pursed her scarlet lips. "I assumed your brother had already invited you."

"He hasn't said a word to me about it," Tristan huffed. "And what's this I hear about Mistress Fortin being there? I thought we agreed that she wasn't to be involved in any of this."

"Agreed?" Varuna expelled a breathy laugh. "You made a *request*. Which your brother and I have chosen to ignore."

She pushed out of her chair and rounded the desk, the mid-afternoon sun twinkling hints of butter and tangerine in her golden feathers.

She crossed her arms over her slim torso. "You do not get to decide how we choose to deploy our tools. If you'll recall, she *offered* to use her memory-pulling abilities to aid us in thwarting our enemies."

Tristan fought the urge to tear out the Vicereine's throat at the suggestion that Cassandra was her *tool*.

"She left the Temple weeks ago. Her abilities have fully faded," Tristan lied, desperate to keep Cassandra out of this. "She'll be of no use to us."

"Is that so?" Varuna cocked her head, her icy, predatory gaze stripping him bare. "Time's ticking, Tristan. You owe your brother a name. How have your meetings been going? Learning anything useful?"

Tristan clenched his fists at his side, his lack of answer an answer in itself.

Varuna's bone-rattle chuckle raised the hairs on his arms. "And there you have it. Mistress Fortin is a charming new trinket. Throw her at a few of the councilors and see what she's able to glean."

"If she's attending the party, she will do so posing as *my* consort. And *I* will be the one to escort her there," Tristan growled.

Varuna sank back into her chair. "I don't care how she gets there. Just that she *is* there. And that she's able to point us in *some* direction after your failure to do so." She returned to her document.

Tristan pinched the bridge of his nose. These political games made his head ache. He was a hammer, not a scalpel.

The Vicereine flicked her pen at him. "You're dismissed. See you and Mistress Fortin at the palace at eight o'clock sharp. Don't be late."

Tristan muttered a curse under his breath, turned on his heel, and left her office.

# CHAPTER THIRTY

Xenia's head pounded as she raced barefoot across the scorching red sand.

Ahead of her, Cael moved only slightly less gracefully, as if his body hadn't yet adjusted to the lack of counterweight on his right side. An almost imperceptible limp emerged whenever his right leg swung forward to connect with the ground, kicking up puffs of ruddy dust that clung to her sweat-soaked ankles. Skeletal plants reached out to tear at the skirt of her glittering silk dress; the most inappropriate attire imaginable for their trek through this wasteland.

They'd departed the fortress nearly an hour ago. Cael had left the Typhon sword behind—he wanted to travel light.

After gathering up Cassandra's dagger and filling a small sack with food and the canteen with water, Cael had shown her a small, egg-shaped rock, white and glittering with rainbow sparks, then whispered the word Rhamnos to the stone and gripped her hand.

An incredible force had speared through her chest, a divine arrow impaling her heart. She'd pitched forward, and her surroundings dissolved, blurry pinpricks of light extending into long strings as they hurtled through space and time. Her awareness narrowed to the piercing pain in her chest and Cael's frenzied grip on her hand.

The world had returned in a bone-shaking crash, and she and Cael toppled onto a red sand dune. He'd surveyed their surroundings with a disappointed grunt, then tugged her into their current jog.

Just when she thought she couldn't take it anymore, about to open her mouth and beseech Cael for a break, he paused, lifting her by the waist and setting her atop a smooth, white rock.

Cael offered her the canteen, and she took a small sip of water which was far from cool but quenched her thirst. She had to stop herself from gulping down the entire container.

He'd left his jacket at the fortress, donning only his leather pants—which must be absolute *torture* in this heat—and a loose, white cotton shirt. It was drenched in sweat, clinging to every ridge of muscle down his long, lean torso. The thick column of his throat worked as he took a long sip from the canteen, and Xenia was shocked it was possible for her to feel any hotter than she already did.

She wiped the sweat from her brow and temples, then gathered her springy curls and swept them on top of her head.

Cael's eyes dipped to her newly exposed skin before he tore his lips from the canteen. "You'll be dying for this heat once the sun goes down."

"Unlikely," she croaked, her lips dry and throat parched. "What was that stone you used to transport us here?"

"A fire opal, imbued with the power of the Fallen Goddess. Maksym gifted them to my father when he arrived to fetch me. I was hoping it would have transported us further, but I must have used up most of its power to return to you." He gazed down at her with an intensity that fluttered her pulse. "I would never have left you there to die, Xenia."

"How did you convince your father to let you come back?" she asked.

His eyes shuttered. "It's not important."

She wanted to press, but thought better of it. "Where are we heading? And how do you know we're going in the right direction?"

Cael scooted closer to her on the rock, close enough that she could smell the mossy green scent of his perspiration. How was it fair for someone that sweaty to smell so good? She wondered what she smelled like to him, scrutinized his face for a nostril flare or any other sign of displeasure. She found none.

He pointed off into the distance towards a rolling, shadowy mass on the horizon.

"Those are the foothills of the Icthian Mountains, the range that follows the Dordenne River. Should only be a few day's walk. We'll take them down into Rhamnos." A bead of sweat dripped from his sideburn and trailed along the sharp edge of his jaw. The unexpected urge to lick it brought to mind other, more pleasurable ways for them to sweat together.

High Gods, what was wrong with her?

Why was she thinking about sex after everything she'd just been through?

She guessed every individual's response to life-threatening situations was different; she never assumed hers would be uncontrollable lust. Though she'd never been in this kind of danger before, so it's not like she could've predicted how she'd respond. Plus, Cael had just freed her from a *literal* dungeon and laid waste to her captors—she'd forgive herself a bit of swooning.

He pressed the canteen into her hands, snapping her from her naughty thoughts. "Drink," he commanded. "You didn't take enough."

"I took plenty, it's fine," she countered. "We need to conserve it."

"Drink," he insisted, eyes narrowed. "I don't need you passing out and forcing me to carry your sweet ass over my shoulder all the way to the foothills."

Xenia expelled an outraged squeak, her anger rising but also stoking her desire. Why did she get off on arguing with him?

"You think I want to feel your rippling muscles digging into my stomach the whole time?"

And why were they incapable of arguing without complimenting each other?

"Don't make me force this water down your throat," he growled. "You know I'd do it."

She snatched the canteen from his hand and took a long pull, counting to three before she lowered it from her mouth and twisted the cap back on. She stood from the rock, but the minute the tender bottoms of her feet hit the sand, she yelped and collapsed back down.

Cael was instantly on his knees before her, grabbing her ankle to examine her foot.

"Bloody Stygios, Blondie! Why didn't you tell me you were in so much pain? Are you trying to burn the skin off your feet?" He ran a tentative finger down her insole and she clenched her jaw, hissing.

"I'll be fine," she bit out through gritted teeth. "I just need to get back on them again. I'll be okay once we start moving."

He gazed up at her with a tortured expression. As if her pain caused him physical harm. Her heart somersaulted.

"Besides," she said, aiming a careful look over his shoulder, "you must be worse off than I am and you're not complaining."

His face slackened and she knew it was the wrong thing to say.

He'd need to deal with the loss eventually, would need to talk to someone about what he was feeling.

And she desperately wanted to be the one he'd open up to. But she knew better than to push.

"If you continue walking on your burned feet, you're just going to make the blisters worse. You won't make it to the foothills, let alone survive the trek to Rhamnos." He pulled the tin of healing salve from his pocket.

Xenia's eyes widened. "Wow. I'm impressed you thought to bring that."

"Come on, Zee," he said with a cocky grin. "You think this is the first time I've had to make a daring escape into the Desolation from some crazy asshole's filthy sex dungeon?"

"Um, yes?"

He snickered. "I've been holding onto this tin since Alexei gave it to you. Figured it would come in handy eventually. And looks like I was right. Now hold still while I rub some on your feet, and try not to whine like a baby when it stings."

"Wait." She wrenched her foot from his grip. "I thought you said you didn't want to carry my ass all the way to the foothills?"

"Not what I said at all."

"It most certainly was!"

"No, I said I didn't want to carry your *sweet* ass all the way to the foothills. You missed the most important word in that sentence. Now quit fucking arguing and give me back your feet so I can heal your blisters."

Xenia bit her lip to keep from laughing and couldn't help the mushy feelings twisting her insides at his insistent description of her ass. She placed her feet back in his lap and tried not to groan with pleasure as he massaged the cool salve onto her hot, aching soles.

He pocketed the tin and slung the canteen over his shoulder. "Ready?"

"I— *eep!*"

He didn't give her a chance to respond as he ducked down and pressed his shoulder against her stomach, effortlessly lifting her. He banded an arm across her backside, his strong hand gripping her hip.

"Enjoy the ride, Blondie." Though she couldn't see his face, she could hear the wink in his words.

But the small smile tugging at her lips died as she looked down his back and saw the evidence of Maksym's cruelty. A vicious, jagged scar peeked out of the slat in his shirt where his wing should've been.

Her eyes stung.

Some wounds were not so easily healed.

# CHAPTER
# THIRTY-ONE

CASSANDRA BARELY RECOGNIZED THE temptress staring back at her from the floor-length mirror in her bedroom.

This morning after their workout, Hella had received a windwhisper from Tristan, informing them that Cassandra's presence had been requested at a party at the Vicereine's palace this evening. Where she was expected to pose as his mortal consort, sidle up to the councilors, and see if she could gather any hints about who might be working with the rebels.

Any calming effects from her session with Hella had immediately dissolved, her nerves swelling at the thought of being surrounded by the most powerful individuals in the colonies—not to mention the Emperor, who she was actively defying in her work with the obliviates—but also at the thought of posing as Tristan's consort again. And everything that would imply, if only for one evening.

In an attempt to shake off her buzzing energy, she'd walked the few blocks to the Fang and Claw to ask Reena if she could borrow something to wear. Reena had practically purred at the opportunity to play dress-up, then sent Cassandra back to the bungalow until she arrived an hour later with an armful of silky, colorful fabric and a case full of cosmetics.

They'd spent the afternoon prepping and primping Cassandra for the part she had to play: a woman sultry and confident enough to have caught the eye of an exiled Fae Prince. Not a meek, cowering Sister who'd been denying herself pleasure for years.

And staring at her reflection now, she had to admit Reena had done an excellent job transforming her. Maybe too good.

Her chocolate waves were gathered into an artfully-mussed side braid, her cheeks dusted with the barest hint of powder, just enough to even out her complexion without hiding her freckles—a playful contrast to her burgundy lips. Reena had also applied some kind of lengthening cream to thicken and darken Cassandra's eyelashes. She looked fresh-faced and naturally beautiful while her lips promised a hint of naughtiness.

Naughtiness echoed by her attire.

She and Reena had agreed that since she was posing as Tristan's consort, it would be appropriate to dress in black, the color that signified both the Empire and the Erabis family's wings.

A layer of iridescent chiffon covered the silk dress and, when she turned in the light, different colors shimmered across its surface, mimicking Tristan's feathers. Around each middle finger, a small loop of fabric ensured her sleeves stayed in place to hide her tattoo. A daring slit bared her right leg to the hip, and her back was exposed to her tailbone. She'd strapped a Typhon-steel dagger—borrowed from Hella—to her left thigh; she didn't dare attend this party unarmed.

"Cass?" Tristan's voice tripped into her room on shaky feet, followed by a soft knock at the door. "You ready?"

Was he nervous?

His nerves triggered her own, and a frenzy of bubbles churned in her stomach as she crossed the room and opened the door.

The dashing figure filling the frame struck her speechless.

He wore a modern black-on-black suit, no tie or vest, the cut of the fabric emphasizing his broad shoulders and muscular limbs. He'd left the top of his shirt unbuttoned, exposing a hint of tanned chest, and the black hair he normally wore tied back flowed in tousled waves to his shoulders.

Her mouth dried out, her lips parted, and she could've sworn his magic tingled through her blood as she gaped at him. A similar expression of awe reflected back at her as he took in her dress.

He leaned his forearm against the door frame, running his eyes from her black stilettos to her wine-red lips. "Cassandra, you look…"

"Fine?" she teased, arching her leg through the slit.

"Like my most mouthwatering dreams come true."

His burnt-honey eyes captured hers as he sucked his lower lip between his teeth, and she wished she'd worn something more substantial than thin, red lace panties. If he kept looking at her like that, they'd be soaked through before they even left the bungalow.

"You're going to set more tongues wagging tonight than any other consort. I'll be the envy of every male in the room."

"Flatterer." She swiped her hand, trying to dismiss the warmth dripping through her limbs.

"I have some news to share with you," he said with a delighted grin. "Which should hopefully make it easier for you to focus on our task tonight."

"What?"

"I heard from Cael. He has Xenia, and Maksym is dead. She's alive, Cass. She's safe."

Cassandra burst into tears and threw herself into Tristan's arms. He squeezed her tight then held her at arm's length, wiping her cheeks with his callused thumbs. "You're going to ruin your makeup," he chuckled.

Cassandra sniffled a laugh. "Where are they?"

"They're in the Desolation." She gave him a quizzical look. "It's a barren desert in the lower southwest corner of the continent. Cael's leading them to Rhamnos." He intertwined their fingers, stroking his thumb along the back of her palm. "They'll be home soon."

Cassandra exhaled a relieved breath. And though the crushing weight of her anxiety over Xenia's capture had abated, new worries swiftly took its place. Rhamnos could eat a mortal alive. She hoped that Xenia's brains combined with Cael's brawn would keep them both safe.

"Ready?" Tristan placed her hand in the crook of his elbow, then escorted her out to the sidewalk and their awaiting ride.

Two enormous Beastrunner stallions, their ebony hides glistening in the moonlight, scraped their hooves against the cobblestones. Behind the huffing beasts, a jet-black carriage with four spoked wheels blended into the night—a ride constructed for stealth. And since the gigantic creatures pulling the carriage were Fae, not animals, there was no driver.

"A carriage?" Cassandra gawked. "How positively *colonial*. Is everyone being picked up in one of these tonight?"

"All of the VIP guests, certainly," Tristan answered. "The Vicereine has a flair for the dramatic."

He opened the carriage door, placing his hand on her back to help her into the cab. She shivered as his fingers grazed her bare flesh.

She'd never ridden in a horse-drawn—Fae-drawn?—carriage before. In fact, the only *vehicle* she'd ever ridden in was Tristan's arms. Thalenn was a city made for walking and, until a few weeks ago, that had been her preferred mode of transportation. Sure there were a few magically powered cars in the colonies, but the cost to ride in one, let alone own one, was astronomical—an extravagance no mortal outside the Heronswood families could afford.

The brocade fabric of the bench chilled her bare leg, and she pulled at the slit of her dress, attempting to cover her crossed thighs.

Tristan snickered at her struggling, taking the seat opposite her. His tightly tucked wings smashed against the ceiling.

"Just like the Vicereine to make me as uncomfortable as possible on the ride over," Tristan grumbled.

"Worth it for the rather spectacular entrance, surely?" Cassandra smirked.

Tristan banged his fist on the ceiling, signaling to the Beastrunner stallions that they were ready to go, and as the carriage lurched into motion, Cassandra's nerves soared.

"So," she said, struggling to maintain the calm demeanor befitting a spy, "any suggestions of who my first mark should be this evening?"

Tristan grimaced. "As much as the thought boils my blood, see if you can get close to August Lambros. He was pretty cagey during the council meeting this morning when the topic of the bombings in his district came up. And there are reports of rebel activity in Akti, his sister's territory on the continent."

"August Lambros's sister is a High Councilor?" There was so much that Cassandra still didn't know about continental politics. It wasn't a topic deemed necessary for a Shrouded Sister's studies.

Tristan nodded. "Aurelie Lambros. There's bad blood between the siblings, too. Even though she's older, August believes *he* should've been given the position since he's the only son in the family." A disgusted scoff parted Cassandra's lips. "Perhaps the Teles Chrysos have lured him with promises of unseating her."

Cassandra hugged her arms around her chest. "Okay." She recalled the way Lambros had leered at her, that night when she and Tristan had encountered him at the Serpent's Den. And though his interest would likely make her task easier, it wouldn't make it any more palatable.

When Tristan was anxious, he often ran his tongue along his sharp canines or rustled his feathers. She tried not to be alarmed at the appearance of both gestures. "I hate that the Vicereine is using you like this."

"Something tells me she's not a female who should be refused. Don't worry," she patted the dagger at her thigh, "I can handle myself."

The corner of Tristan's lip tipped up. "I never worry about you handling yourself, Daredevil." Cassandra's heart skipped a beat—he'd barely used her nickname this past week. The reappearance loosened something in her chest.

"Then what are you worried about?"

Tristan ran a hand down his face. "There's a chance that some of the older, more powerful Beastrunner or Deathstalker Fae may scent my magic in your blood."

She jolted. "How?"

"Their sense of smell is far more attuned to subtle discrepancies than a Windrider's." He sat as still as a windless night, gripping the edge of the bench with white knuckles. "There may be a way to mask it though." He dragged his eyes up her exposed leg, across the tight fabric of her bodice, then lingered on her parted lips. "We'd have to hide it beneath another, more powerful scent."

"What kind of scent?"

His voice dropped to a low whisper. "I think you know."

She released a breathless sigh.

She'd suspected that posing as his consort would necessitate touching, maybe even a kiss or two in public to perpetuate the ruse. All of which she felt strong enough to weather for a single night.

But she hadn't considered that they'd need to do more than that. Didn't know if her gullible heart could withstand it.

"Tell me," she whispered.

"I'd rather show you. Do you trust me?"

*Did* she trust him? Of course she did. It was herself she didn't trust. Didn't trust that she wouldn't fall right back into the trap she'd been snared in during their trip to Meridon. The trap that allowed her to believe they could be something real despite his immortality, despite the laws of separation between their species.

And despite the fact that his heart didn't belong to her.

She was too much of a coward to bring any of that up now though. Couldn't bear to hear him confirm that this was an act of protection and nothing more.

She reminded herself that she had a part to play tonight. And if whatever was about to happen between them would help her sink deeper into character, give her some measure of safety among the dangerous beasts of the colony elite, she'd be even more a fool to refuse.

She squared her shoulders and raised her chin, meeting Tristan's molten gaze across the carriage. The blatant hunger in it swept away her hesitations.

"Yes," she exhaled.

He murmured something into his palm before opening the window and letting the windwhisper float out into the night. The carriage rumbled to a halt.

"Why are we stopping?" she asked.

"Because if this is the one and only time you're going to allow me to do this, I intend to savor it," he said as he removed his suit jacket. "And I don't want any interruptions."

He folded the jacket and laid it on the bench as he dropped to his knees before her.

She uncrossed her legs but kept them pressed together as he inched closer, never tearing his eyes from hers.

A dull, heated ache radiated through her lower belly as she realized what he intended. She'd seen couples perform the act in her dirty memory stash. They were her favorite scenes to watch, the ones she'd returned to the most often.

And she'd been desperate for him to do it since that first night they'd kissed. Could tell by the masterful strokes of his tongue that he would be very, *very* good at it.

He ran his hands up the back of her calves, warming and priming her skin. Her thighs shivered uncontrollably as he inched his fingers higher in light, teasing strokes.

"You want this as much as I do, don't you?" He grinned as he invaded her skirt, wedging his hands underneath her ass before lifting her hips from the bench. "Stay like that."

She shuddered at the quiet command, then hovered in place as he hooked his fingers through the straps of her panties and dragged them slowly—so, so slowly—down her legs and over her dagger, dropping the red lace at her feet.

She sat back down and he removed her heels, then grabbed the panties with his teeth, nipping her ankle as he tore them off completely. The bite of his sharp canine against her flesh inspired an exhilarating mixture of fear and arousal.

This ancient, savage, powerful creature could tear her apart with little effort. That knowledge, contrasted with his restraint, his gentleness, made her chest ache with destructive need.

This was a bad idea, one she knew she'd suffer for later. She was barreling towards the edge of a cliff, towards a broken and bloodied aftermath. But she couldn't slow herself.

He bunched her panties in his fist, then brought them to his nose. He closed his eyes as he inhaled deeply, a low growl reverberating from his chest. "I bet you taste as divine as you smell. Shall I find out?"

She couldn't get a word out, signaled her consent with a nod.

His lips curled into a sensuous smile as he placed her panties atop his jacket.

Then all traces of teasing fled his face.

"Spread your legs," he ordered in a rippling purr.

She obeyed, but couldn't resist the urge to taunt him. She held her skirt in place as she pulled her knees apart. Once her thighs were as wide as she could manage, she inched the skirt aside. Just for a moment before tugging it back.

He knocked her hand away, snarling. "*Mine.*"

Slickness bloomed beneath her silk skirt. High *Gods*, how that word thrilled her. And how she wished it were true.

He threw back her skirt, exposing her to the chill night air as he panted, a feral yet sharply focused beast. His warm breaths pulsed against her sex.

"Come closer." A guttural growl.

She shifted her hips until they were perched at the edge of the bench, and his deep, shuddering breath fluttered against her entrance. She was fragile enough to shatter at the first brush of his tongue.

He whimpered softly, appreciatively, as he braced his hands on her thighs and spread her open further. He leaned in at a glacial, torturous pace, extending his own sweet anticipation.

His lips met her slit in the softest, most tender, most reverent of grazes, and a low moan trespassed her parted lips.

"*Tristan*," she groaned as he pressed gentle kisses from base to tip.

He cupped his hands beneath her ass, massaging and squeezing, and began to lick. His soft murmurs of pleasure fluttered across her skin, and she undulated her hips, trying to drive his strokes where she wanted them.

She propped her hand against the carriage wall and lifted her head. His dark hair shimmered as he flipped it out of his eyes and caught her staring.

Holding her gaze, he dragged his tongue from base to apex, flicking the tip over her clit. Her inner muscles clenched, and she threw her head back with a ragged cry that mingled with his sinful chuckle.

The long, wide strokes of his tongue teased her open, building her climax. She wound tighter and tighter, her body begging for pressure to that one specific spot she knew would pitch her into oblivion.

He knew too.

His lips curved into a wry grin as he heightened her pleasure by keeping it at bay.

He dipped his tongue inside her—shallow at first then pushing in deeper. Thrusting. Swirling. Fucking her with it.

She moaned, grinding against his face and coating his chin with the evidence of her pleasure. He curved his tongue, lapping at the sensitive spot just inside her entrance, and her head fell back as a thigh-shaking wave of ecstasy crashed over her.

He slid his tongue out of her, then pressed two fingers inside, rubbing that same spot until she cried out, soaking his palm.

"Taste yourself," he commanded, his hand at her mouth. She wrapped her lips around his fingers, dragging her tongue along his rough calluses and delighting in her own sweet, salty flavor.

He popped his fingers from her mouth, then bowed his head, circling her clit with soft flicks of his tongue. She was seconds away from coming when he pulled away.

"Not yet," he teased, gazing into her eyes as he slid a finger inside her. Her head lolled back before his other hand was on her chin.

"You wanted to watch, right? Watch me make you come on my tongue."

The inherent possessiveness of his words intoxicated her. As if he was challenging her to find anyone else who could own her pleasure so completely.

He pumped his finger into her, a slow, sensuous rhythm as his tongue circled her clit. Her inner muscles clenched and released around him, leading her towards detonation. She quivered against the bench, exhaling one breathy gasp after another, each a higher pitch than the last.

And then, just when she thought she couldn't take another second, like her entire body was going to seize up, he circled the tip of his finger against that magical spot inside at the same time as he sucked her sizzling bundle of nerves into his mouth.

Her body fractured into dazzling pieces.

Her hips bucked frantically, slamming into his chin, and she threaded a hand into his hair to hold his face between her legs.

She screamed his name so loudly that one of the stallions outside whinnied and nickered in response.

He licked her through the throes of her orgasm, then kissed her inner thighs as she settled back against the bench, her ears ringing and her mind scattered among the stars.

He rested his cheek against her leg, one hand rubbing and squeezing her ass as the other trailed along the back of her calf.

Gawking at him with wide eyes and uneven breathing, she tried to remember where she was, where they were going, what High-Gods-darned planet she was on.

"Tristan," she croaked out.

366

He gifted her a smug smile, one of pure satisfaction and pride.

The way he'd just made her feel was beyond compare. She had no idea her body was capable of such a monumental release. And though Tristan was a master of the mechanics, some gentler part of her knew her pleasure had been heightened because it was *him* performing the act.

She bit back tears at the thought. She didn't have time for them tonight.

He rose onto his knees, the very clear evidence of his own enjoyment tenting his pants. He shoved a hand into them, and, with a pained grimace, tucked his length up under his waistband to mask the bulge.

She laughed, and he cocked an eyebrow. "Oh, so funny, is it? Just for that, I'm going to hold onto these for the rest of the night."

He slipped her red panties into his pocket, and she bolted upright with an indignant squeak.

"Protest all you want, but maybe next time you'll think twice before laughing at my pain. Which probably won't be going away anytime soon, since I'll spend all night knowing exactly what *isn't* beneath your dress. On second thought, this might be more of a punishment for me."

She laughed again, some of her uneasiness drifting away at his playful banter. She smoothed her skirt, the silk cooling her heated, swollen flesh.

"Plus, it will help with the scent. Every Fae in that room will be able to smell me on you." He swiped a hand across his chin. "And smell you on me." He winked as he shrugged his jacket back on, an awkward dance given the breadth of his wings in the cramped cab. He banged the ceiling to signal to the Beastrunners that they were ready to resume the journey.

The carriage rattled into motion, and Tristan affixed his majestic profile out the window while his hand futzed with her panties in his pocket.

Her body ached to cross the space between them. To tear off his pants, help him alleviate the impressive strain against his waistband. But her mind didn't dare. She was playing with fire and the burns were beginning to blister.

The carriage bounced to a stop, skidding in the curve of a gravel driveway before a sprawling stone palace.

Tristan turned his thoughtful, anxious gaze upon her.

"Show time."

# CHAPTER
# THIRTY-TWO

T**RISTAN** **STRETCHED** **HIS** **CRAMPED** wings as he
stepped out of the carriage, then turned back to
offer Cassandra a hand.

As he surveyed the grand stone facade, he couldn't
shake his underlying sense of dread. Couldn't help
feeling he hadn't done enough to protect Cassandra
from the sinister world she was about to plunge into.
Not that he didn't trust her to take care of herself. She
had shrewd instincts and an uncanny ability to read
people.

He had to admit some part of him *did* want to live
out this fantasy. One where Cassandra belonged to
him and him alone. He'd been dying to get his tongue

between her legs and the reality far surpassed his many fantasies.

He stroked the silky lace panties in his pocket, trying to calm the blood rushing for his groin. Though if he seemed a bit lust-addled tonight, all the better to perpetuate the ruse.

He placed his hand at the small of Cassandra's back, tucking his fingertips into the back of her dress and resting them against her tailbone. Might as well enjoy this while he could before Cassandra rebuilt her walls and went back to *all business* tomorrow.

The tart scent of her nervous energy tickled his nostrils. "Ready?" he asked as she shifted from foot to foot in the gravel.

"As I'll ever be." She blew out a shaky breath as her head tilted back to take in the massive fortress.

Tristan was immune to the grandiosity of the Vicereine's palace, having visited plenty of times for both professional and personal reasons. But he understood the awe it could inspire in a newcomer.

Three stories of arched windows peered between stone columns on an expanse traveling nearly two hundred feet in either direction. Three slate-tiled domes topped the structure, one on each end, the largest in the center. Magically powered spotlights hidden behind groomed hedges illuminated the facade, casting shadows that made the windows look like grinning skulls.

Appropriate.

"So much for our spectacular entrance," Cassandra snorted. Theirs was the only carriage in the driveway. Tristan had wanted to arrive fashionably late, but may have spent a bit too long delighting in his feast.

Cassandra shivered, then tore her gaze from the building, settling her features into a bored, blasé expression. "Let's get this over with, master."

And though the words were only for show, the sound of them dripping from her wine-red lips speared straight for his heart.

He chuckled, stroking his fingers against the base of her spine before guiding her through the arched entrance.

And into the lair of awaiting predators.

Tristan whisked Cassandra through the palace's imposing stone facade, then down one plushly carpeted hallway after another. Richly detailed frescoes lined the high, curved ceilings, scenes full of pomp and blood—a blustering visual chronicle of the Empire's power.

Cassandra wanted to linger, search for the iridescent, black wings of Tristan's family. But he didn't seem particularly interested in reliving the history, hurried her along with a gentle press.

After a long and winding trek, they arrived at a pair of gleaming white doors carved with the raven's wings and radiating lines of the Empire's seal.

Giving her a scant minute to compose herself, Tristan pushed the doors open and they stepped through onto a marble mezzanine. A thick red carpet cascaded down two matching curved staircases, ending at the ballroom's parquet wood floor.

To Cassandra's right, a row of arched windows climbed to the soaring ceiling, their view bracketed by red velvet curtains tied back with golden ropes. Through the windows, the geometrically-shaped topiaries and trimmed hedges of the palace's famous gardens stood at attention in military straight lines. Black-crystal chandeliers oozed from the ceiling, highlighting long tables overflowing with roasted meats, glistening fruit, frosted cakes—all untouched. Gathered around circular high-tops, the party-goers glittered, an extravagant blur of jewels, sequins, satin, and tulle.

In the center of the hall, several couples danced to the harmonious, lilting stylings of a string quartet. But Cassandra didn't see any musicians and couldn't imagine where the music was coming from.

A series of alcoves ran along the wall opposite the windows, each hidden behind curtains. Cassandra could easily guess *their* purpose.

Between each alcove, a pair of impassive Vasilikans—the Emperor's own legendarily lethal personal guards—monitored the room from beneath their raven-head helmets, their wings on proud display.

Wariness gnawed at Cassandra as she and Tristan glided down the staircase. The party was so *solemn*—conversations whispered, laughter swallowed, dancing subdued. This was certainly not the kind of warm, joyous occasion she'd seen in her supplicants' memories.

The spiritless atmosphere heightened her self-consciousness—there was not nearly enough revelry to distract from their entrance. Her skin crawled as every pair of eyes in the room grazed over her, poking, prodding, assessing.

Tristan traced soothing circles against her lower back.

"Deep breaths, Daredevil," he murmured into her ear. "Have the effects of our carriage ride really worn off that quickly? It's far too early in the night for me to have to pull you into one of those alcoves to calm you down."

Her curiosity sparked at the thought of performing such acts with nothing but a curtain separating them from the crowd. And she was a bit shocked by how tempted she was to try it.

But despite his teasing comments, his shoulders were tense and worry swirled through his hooded eyes. Worry she suspected was not for himself but for her.

She gathered her courage, determined to keep it together for him, to be his partner in this quest. She knew he would protect her at any cost—a thought that both thrilled and terrified her.

She wrapped her arm underneath his jacket and lightly stroked the hard muscles above his hip. He relaxed at the contact, her touch soothing him as much as his soothed her.

"Brother!" a booming voice called from the center of the dance floor.

Eamon peeled himself out of the Vicereine's arms and the party's whispered conversations petered out into deafening silence.

The Emperor stalked over to greet them. "The male of the hour. You're just in time."

Eamon snapped his fingers, and two Vasilikans abandoned their post, rushing for a couple tucked away at a high-top. The guards dragged the confused couple onto the dance floor, and the party-goers circled them.

Eamon wrapped an arm around Tristan's shoulder, pushing through the gathering crowd. Cassandra scurried to keep up.

The couple—a Beastrunner Fae male with golden eyes and long russet hair and a mortal female with a sharp black bob—didn't dare struggle against the Vasilikans, though their clenched fists and rapid breathing conveyed their fury and terror.

Eamon surveyed them with a sneer before turning to address the dead-silent party.

"It seems as though my absence from the colonies has inspired some of you to become rather lax with our laws." He shook his iridescent wings. "I blame Leonin Erabis—may he rest in peace in the realm of Anaemos. My father's leniency—" he glanced over at Tristan "—should never have been tolerated."

The party-goers pressed in closer.

"Many of you have taken humans as consorts, which is your right, of course. Feed from them, play with them, fuck them. That's what most of us are here to do tonight, right?" He smirked and the gathered crowd tittered, eying each other nervously.

"But I want to be extremely clear about where the boundaries lie." His cold hazel eyes once again darted towards Tristan, who wore a careful mask of neutrality. Cassandra didn't dare move closer, didn't dare touch him.

"You do not shelter them. You do not love them." He signaled one of the Vasilikans, who grasped the high neckline of the woman's dress and ripped it down. "And you certainly do not *mark* them."

The crowd gasped at the crescent-shaped scar on the woman's upper shoulder.

Eamon faced the golden-eyed Beastrunner, who was straining against the Vasilikan's hold. "What were you thinking, Hector?" His whisper sliced into the male, who collapsed against the guard like a puppet cut from its strings.

Eamon turned back to the crowd. "These laws are in place for a reason. The separation of our species must be maintained or we risk upending our fragile peace." His eyes cut back to Hector. "I do not share my father's laissez-faire attitude towards these crimes."

He signaled the Vasilikan again and the guard unsheathed a Typhon broadsword.

Though every cell in her body was screaming at her to look away, Cassandra watched as the Vasilikan pushed the quietly sobbing woman to her knees.

"Do you have anything to say?" Eamon asked Hector.

Hector gazed down at his consort, pure anguish contorting his features. "I'm so sorry. I love you, *ma'anyu*." His voice broke on the last word.

The woman beamed at him, mouthing *I love you* through tear-streaked lips.

The Vasilikan slashed the broadsword down, and the smile remained on the woman's face as her head toppled across the dance floor, coming to a stop at the foot of a Fae female who jumped back with a horrified squeak.

Hector roared—a howl of gut-wrenching despair—as the other Vasilikan dragged him out of the ballroom.

"Let this be a reminder to you all—" Eamon delivered the message directly to Tristan "—that while Fae and humans share this world, and intermingling in the colonies can't be avoided, there is a natural order that must be respected."

Several palace servants rushed in to gather the woman's body and mop the blood from the dance floor.

Eamon stepped over them while they worked, smirking. "Now that *that* nasty business is done, let's get on with our debauched evening!"

The lights dimmed and the anxious crowd welcomed the cue. More drinks appeared in hands, and sloppy laughter echoed as couples reclaimed the newly-gleaming dance floor. A different kind of music began to play—a slow, heady melody over a pounding beat.

Varuna, clad in a floor-length, sleeveless silk gown in a deep red that matched her signature lip color, slunk back into the Emperor's arms, giggling as he whispered in her ear before playfully biting the exposed neck beneath her tight chignon.

"I need a fucking drink," Tristan grumbled, ushering Cassandra towards a bar tended by a milky-skinned Deathstalker female.

Cassandra hung back as he ordered, attempting to calm her pounding heart and still her shaking hands.

Not a single one of the party-goers, not even the other mortal consorts, seemed bothered by what they'd just witnessed. Were brutal executions such a frequent occurrence at the Vicereine's gatherings?

Cassandra's eyes stung and she squeezed the skin between her thumb and forefinger to distract herself from the sorrow threatening to render her useless.

Someone stepped up behind her, and her stomach flipped as a deep, sinuous male voice cooed into her ear, "Hello, Ker."

She swiveled, nearly crashing her head into the chin of a massive, handsome Beastrunner holding a glowing silver bottle of Delirium.

Ice-blue tattoos glimmered across his forearms, and he wore a prurient smirk, somehow made all the more obscene by the scar snaking out from underneath his black eye patch—the nastiest scar Cassandra had yet seen on a Fae. His single visible eye, a swirl of blue and yellow, darted to the slit in her dress, and as he plucked up her hand, the word *Inom* danced across his knuckles. He pressed his full lips to the back of her palm. "Lambros wasn't exaggerating. You're exquisite."

"And spoken for," Tristan growled, handing her a champagne flute before he hauled her against his body and curled a hand around her hip. She melted against him, reveling in his temporary possessiveness.

"I can smell that," the male murmured, his nostrils pulsing as his eyes darted below her waist. "Though you might not want to appear so territorial after your brother's little show." He pinched her chin, examining her face. "This pretty head would be a shame to lose."

Cassandra wrenched herself from the male's grip and pressed back into Tristan, flicking her skirt aside to reveal the hilt of her dagger. "So would yours," she said with a wolfish grin.

The Beastrunner's eye glittered as his fingernails lengthened into claws and his canines thickened, sharpening into dangerous points. "Aren't you a wicked little delight?"

"What do you want, Ronin?" Tristan asked, taking a sip from his bourbon and running a hand up Cassandra's body. He stroked the side of her breast and she arched into the touch.

Ronin sipped his Delirium, his single eye following Tristan's finger as it rolled over Cassandra's nipple. The sharp peak poked at her silk bodice, and she swallowed a moan. "Well, since you don't want to share your toys, I was hoping for a word."

Tristan went still behind her. "About what?"

"In private." Ronin tipped his bottle towards the gardens beyond the windows.

Tristan knocked back his bourbon. "Give us a minute."

"Pleasure to meet you, Ker." Ronin's chin dipped in a slow perusal of Cassandra's exposed leg as the tip of his tongue caressed one of his thick fangs.

"The pleasure was all yours." She saluted him with her champagne flute.

"Wicked," he chuckled before running a hand through his snow-white hair, long on the top and shaved on the sides. "If you ever get bored of this exiled prick…" he tossed over his shoulder as he stalked away.

"Charming," Tristan snorted.

"Who was *that*?" Cassandra whispered.

"Ronin Matakos, the Butcher of Aethalia. A decrepit old war hero."

Cassandra would hardly have used the word *decrepit* to describe the male.

Tristan stepped away, and she almost whimpered at the loss of his hands on her body. He settled his empty tumbler among the discarded glassware on a nearby high-top. "I should probably go see what he wants. Will you be okay on your own?"

Her heartrate spiked, then slowed as she brushed her knuckles against the hilt of her dagger.

The creatures in this room weren't the only ones who could bite.

"Do your thing, Birdman. I've got my own work to do."

Tristan's brows dipped. "Be careful."

He wrapped a hand around her throat, tilting her chin up, then claimed her mouth in a fierce kiss. His tongue swept past her teeth, and her knees nearly buckled at the combined taste of smoky bourbon and her own earthy arousal.

He planted a gentle kiss on her lips before whispering in her ear, "Don't forget who you belong to tonight, *consort*."

Ripples of pleasure shivered down her spine before he disappeared into the crowd on the dance floor.

She crossed an arm over her chest and held her champagne flute at her waist, trying to ignore the many pairs of eyes and murmured conversations aimed her way.

"Enjoying the festivities, Ker?" A cool hand settled against her bare back and she fought the urge to flinch.

August Lambros leered down at her, fluttering his sapphire wings. "I see Matakos has already lured your master away. What did Ronin want?"

She took a sip of her champagne, the bubbles dancing on the back of her tongue, then licked her lips. "If I told you, Councilor Lambros, I'd have to kill you."

August released a hoot of laughter that stirred his cinnamon-blond waves and crinkled his blandly handsome face. "I do believe you could. Something tells me it would be a wonderful way to die."

He plucked the champagne flute from her hand and threw it onto the tray of a passing waiter. "A dance?"

He didn't wait for her reply as he hustled her onto the dance floor. She spied a familiar face in the crowd—a stunning one with unforgettable sea-foam eyes and spun-gold hair. Aneka, August's consort, was perched on the lap of a bruising, tawny-skinned Windrider, the male's hand working between her thighs as he fed on her lust.

August curled a hand around Cassandra's waist then grasped her palm as she placed the other on his shoulder, fully aware of the space she'd left between them. A space he attempted to breach with every step, every sway.

"Where in the world did he find you?" August whispered reverently.

She decided to tell the truth; a slightly embellished version of it at least. "He apprehended me in the midst of a crime. I offered him my body in exchange for his mercy. Afterwards, he decided to keep me."

August's espresso-brown eyes darkened. "Sinking your fangs in deep. Don't think I've forgotten how much they stung last time we met."

"Tastes change, Councilor," she purred, loosening him up and lowering his defenses. She didn't press her body against him, kept that inch of air between them. She'd use that tactic when it would be the most effective.

As he spun her around the dance floor, her mind whirled, trying to determine the most revealing line of questioning.

"How long have you known Tristan?"

August scoffed. "I was his father's right hand on the continent before Tristan was even a twinkle in his mother's eye."

"His right hand? Sounds like you were rather important. Why did His Imperial Majesty send you away?"

"He didn't…" A flash of indignation surfaced before August smoothed it over with a smug expression. "I was far too important to the Emperor to stay on the continent. He needed me here in the colonies, overseeing the transition of the humans after the Accords."

Recalling what Tristan had said in the carriage about the strained relationship between August and his sister, Cassandra went for the jugular. "Overseeing? Or being a lackey in service to a more powerful female?" She darted her eyes towards the Vicereine, curled against Eamon as his hands roved over her feathered wings.

August pulled Cassandra in tight, dipping his mouth to her ear. "Are you trying to get a rise out of me, little human? I assure you, it won't be the kind you're intending." He squeezed her ass and dug his fingernails into her flesh. "Or perhaps you prefer to fight before you fuck, get those passions stirring?"

She made to push out of his hold, but he clenched his arm around her waist. "Now, now, Councilor. I prefer males who aren't so easily riled. Surely you don't need to prove your power to a helpless mortal like me?"

He abruptly released her, only to grab her by the throat. "I've got more power in my little finger than your master and his brother could ever dream of. It would be unwise to test me. But perhaps I do need to prove it to you."

He dragged her off the dance floor towards the alcoves. Her pulse fluttered frantically as she scanned the room. Her panicked eyes landed on Aneka—still trapped in the lap of that Windrider—and a flash of concern passed over Aneka's face before she whispered into the male's ear, then rushed away.

August ripped open a red velvet curtain and tossed Cassandra onto the curved banquette. Tapered candles in a black-crystal candelabra dripped beads of wax onto a marble.

She held onto her dress, trying to keep the slit closed as August pushed her down against the banquette with his hand at her throat. His other hand worked at his waist, unbuttoning his pants.

His savage sneer revealed the true monster behind his carefully controlled facade, and fear stilled Cassandra's lungs. "Did you miss the point of the Emperor's speech earlier? You are nothing. Your kind is *nothing*. You're to be shared, used up, then tossed away as soon as your beauty fades. Do you know how many mortal women I've had over the centuries? How many your *master* has had? You're not clever, you're not special, and if I want to fuck you there's nothing you can do to stop me."

He crashed onto her, holding her down with his hips as his rough hands tore at her skirt. She bucked against his weight, snarling, and smacked a hand against his cheek to push his face away as his lips came dangerously close to her throat.

Her mind sharpened, traveling to that distant plane outside her body, and her panic ebbed away as she remembered she had claws of her own.

Her fingers fluttered under her dress and she unsheathed the dagger, whipping it up in a vicious swipe that landed just under August's chin. A quivering bead of blood bloomed where she'd nicked his jaw.

August backed off, his hands raised and his head tilted to avoid the razor-sharp edge of the blade. "Your fangs haven't retracted at all, I see," he bit out, heat blazing in his deep, dark eyes.

The curtains whipped open and Tristan rushed in, his face twisted in panic until he took in the scene. He closed the curtains behind him, snickering and shaking his head. "No means no means *no*, Lambros. Shall I ask Ker to carve it into your forehead?"

Cassandra's heart pounded, her chest heaving as she glared at August, keeping the dagger at his throat.

Tristan slipped an arm around her waist and curled his long fingers over her dagger-wielding wrist. His solid heat against her bare back slowed her agitation. As did the lips he dragged up her neck as he pushed her arm down.

"Come now, my beautiful blade," Tristan whispered against her skin. "He's not worth the spilled blood."

August refastened his pants. "You'd better keep this bitch under control." He smoothed his hair and shook out his feathers.

Tristan's answering chuckle rumbled through Cassandra's chest. "This *bitch* would've had you on your ass if I hadn't arrived. She's not named after the Goddess of Violence for nothing." Tristan brought his hand up to cup Cassandra's throat, tilting her head to the side and nipping at her earlobe. "Tell her you're sorry, then get the fuck out of here."

August huffed and pushed through the curtains. As soon as they were alone, Cassandra sagged back against Tristan, trembling. He sank onto the banquette, pulling her into his lap as angry yet relieved tears poured forth.

Tristan held her in his powerful arms as he whispered in her ear. "It's okay, Cass. You're safe. You're *safe*. I'll rip his wings off before he can lay another hand on you. That's if you don't slice his dick off first."

She choked out a laugh as he brushed away her tears. "What happened?" he asked. "Now you can see why I didn't want you involved in this."

"I'm fine," she insisted. "Honestly, the tears are more from shock than anything else. I should've known better than to bait him."

Tristan gripped her chin, forcing her to look at him. The candlelight illuminated the flecks of amber and chestnut dotting his irises. "Do *not* take responsibility for his actions. This was on him, not you."

"Actually, it might be on you." She snorted, and Tristan's eyes widened in shocked hurt. "Oh, Tristan, I didn't mean it that way." She brought a hand to his cheek. "What I mean is, he was ranting about how much more powerful he is than both you and Eamon before he…dragged me in here. I think conquering me was meant to be a strike at you somehow."

"How angry did he seem? Angry enough to be working with the rebels?"

"Perhaps? But if he was, why would he be so easily provoked?" She blew out a frustrated breath.

Tristan wrapped his arms around her tighter, staring into the candlelight and seeming far more exhausted than he had when his mood had dipped in the carriage.

Cassandra nestled in closer. "Are *you* okay?"

He scoffed. "I must look *really* off if you're asking me that after what just happened to you. You have no idea how much it means to me that you're risking your safety to help me."

"You've been risking your safety to help me this week, too, *master,*" she whispered. She loved the way his breath hitched every time she called him that. "How did your chat with Ronin go? What did he want?"

"I don't know. Aneka rushed out to get me before we had a chance to speak. He slipped this to me though."

Tristan reached into his pocket and pulled out a folded scrap of paper.

Cassandra's heart nearly lurched out of her chest as she opened the tiny note and read the elegantly scrawled message.

*Meet me at the Serpent's Den. Thursday night at 9. Room 702.*

In lieu of a signature, there was a single word at the bottom of the note.

Teles.

# CHAPTER
# THIRTY-THREE

XENIA AWOKE WITH A jolt and her teeth began chattering.

She had no idea when she'd fallen asleep.

Nor when she'd ended up cradled in Cael's arms rather than slung over his shoulder like a sack of potatoes.

Holy High Gods, the desert was *way* fucking colder at night than she'd expected.

"To be fair," Cael crooned, his lips brushing her temple, "I did warn you, Blondie. We'll stop here for the night."

Cael crunched through the sand towards a group of low rocks ringed by spiky plants. He set Xenia down upon a brick-red boulder, its surface blissfully warm after a day spent absorbing the sun's rays.

"B-bountif-ful F-faur-rana, that's div-v-vine." She hugged the rock, pressing her cheek against the rough surface, and the heat soaked into her skin.

Cael surveyed the prickly greenery, then used Ker to slice into the tallest plant. As clear liquid flowed into the canteen, Xenia became acutely aware of how dry her mouth was.

He handed her the canteen and she took a sip, nearly moaning at the deliciously sweet taste. She chugged half the container before remembering she should save some for him.

She wiped her mouth with the back of her wrist. "How did you know where to find water?"

He answered over his shoulder while he rummaged through the sack. "Survival training. Mandatory for the Vestians."

"Did you always want to be a Vestian?"

"In a way," he answered, sitting back against the rock, his knees pulled to his chest. He handed her an apple and her stomach growled.

She bit into the fresh fruit, then covered her mouth with her hand as she chewed. "You gonna elaborate, or are you gonna make me pry the answer from you? If you'll recall, my teeth are *deadly.*"

He snickered. "I want—well, wanted—to join the Vasilikans, the Emperor's personal guards. I was fascinated by them when I was younger. They'd accompany the Emperor on his visits to Brachos to meet with my father. They were terrifying, so still and calm. Everyone avoided them. But when they gave an order, there wasn't a single individual who wouldn't listen. Including my father *and* the Emperor. They had so much power. No one ever challenged them."

Cael bit into his own apple, its juices spilling down his chin.

"They were so in control," he continued. "Not only of their surroundings, but of themselves. Like nothing could rattle them. I…I envied them."

His tucked wing rested in the sand and he'd propped his wrists on his knees, his long-fingered hands dangling between them. He gazed out over the dunes, his straight nose jutting out above his flattened lips, the lower poking out almost petulantly. Wavy strands of ash-brown hair cascaded down his forehead, brushing his brow.

Xenia's chest squeezed as he stared off into the distance, grappling with his recently discarded dreams.

She'd never wanted to kiss someone so badly.

Xenia was fully aware of the concept of yearning, a frequent theme in the romantic adventure novels she loved so much. And she'd experienced yearning once before in real life. Or at least thought she had…

But nothing compared to the soul-deep ache she felt when she gazed upon her broad-shouldered, breathtakingly beautiful rescuer.

Cael turned towards her, and she chomped into her apple again, hoping he hadn't caught her ogling.

"What dreams did you have for yourself? Before you, ah, joined the order?"

Xenia rested her elbow on the rock and propped her cheek in her hand. "I hadn't really given it much thought, to be honest. Is there a job that allows you to read books for the rest of your life?"

"A librarian?" Cael offered sarcastically.

Xenia laughed. "Maybe. But I'm not that organized. I'd probably get too distracted reading while I was supposed to be re-shelving or something. I thought about becoming a healer when I was really young. Before I realized there were no humans in the profession."

Once she'd arrived at the Temple, Xenia had already given up on her naïve childhood dream. She'd resigned herself to her circumstances, determined to make the best of her situation.

And there had been plenty to be grateful for as a Sister. She was never without shelter, never without food. Not every human in the colonies was so lucky. And she'd had Cass to keep her company, a friend to laugh with, share her life with.

And she had her books. Life was never dull with a book in her hand.

"For what it's worth, I think you would've made a great healer," Cael said.

Xenia snorted. "Says the male who barely let me rub salve on his wounds."

*And won't talk to me about the loss of his wing.*

Xenia kept that remark to herself. She certainly wasn't done probing, but she was too tired and cold tonight to open that festering wound. But she did offer him some reciprocal encouragement.

"And I think *you* would've made a great Vasilikan. You've certainly got the whole *strong and brooding* thing mastered."

Cael snickered. "I don't brood."

"Are you kidding me? I think you may have invented brooding."

Cael shrugged. "I don't open up to many people. What's the point? When someone knows what you're feeling, they gain control over you. I'd rather be the one in control."

"Seems like a lonely way to live. Never making any kind of connection with another person."

Cael ran his tongue over his bottom lip and pushed a hand through his tawny waves, the motion bringing Xenia's attention to the bulging muscles straining against his cotton shirt.

"Oh I've made plenty of *connections*, Blondie. Don't you worry about that."

A montage of dirty images flooded Xenia's mind: Cael prowling up her naked body, stopping to suck on a tender nipple; Cael's lips on her neck as he settled between her thighs; Cael's tongue gliding into her mouth as he pushed his impressive length inside her.

High Gods, she didn't know whether to be grateful or ashamed of her overactive imagination.

Cael sniffed, then twisted around to face her. He was so close she could see the glowing flecks of silvery-blue in his flinty gray eyes.

"What are *you* thinking about?" Cael smirked.

*Your cock.*

"Nothing."

Cael's low, sexy grunt did nothing to stem the scent of Xenia's arousal.

Time to change the subject.

"Even if becoming a Vasilikan is out of the question, there's got to be something else you're good at. Some other talent besides brooding and fighting and—"

"Fucking?" Cael interrupted with a cocked eyebrow.

Xenia's face nearly melted off.

"I was going to say *surviving*, but sure, I'll take your word for it. What else though? Come on, pterodactyl," she mock-whined, "share one of your hidden talents with me."

Xenia could always tell when Cael's laughs were genuine. They crinkled the corners of his eyes and brought a joyful energy to his face that intoxicated her.

"Only if you promise to share one of yours. You go first."

"I can imitate any farm animal you can name," Xenia said proudly.

"Oh, I am immediately testing this." Cael turned to face Xenia, sitting cross-legged in the sand. "Duck."

"That's the first *farm* animal you thought of?"

"Humor me."

Xenia rounded her mouth and made a honking noise at the back of her throat.

Cael bit his quivering lip. "That's terrifying. Do a rooster."

Cael nearly doubled over with laughter as Xenia flawlessly imitated the sound of every animal he named: horse, pig, cow, dog, even a llama.

"How do you even know what a llama sounds like?" Cael sputtered, tears gleaming as he clutched his stomach. "And when did you realize you could do this? Do you *practice?*"

"High-Gods-given talent, I guess," Xenia answered, chuckling. "It's something I've always been able to do. I used to try to communicate with the animals on my parents' farm when I was younger. You'd be surprised by how many full-blown conversations I had."

Cael wiped at his eyes as his hilarity subsided. "Brilliant, Zee. You continue to surprise me."

Xenia's insides warmed. "Alright, your turn. What amazing talent do you have to share with me?"

"I don't know if I can follow *that*. Too much pressure."

"Oh come on. I just completely embarrassed myself in front of you! You need to return the favor."

"That wasn't embarrassing, that was genius."

Cael rubbed at his jaw, something inscrutable in his gaze. She'd never expected to woo him by making farm animal noises. She'd never expected to woo him at all. That's not what was happening here.

Was it?

"I do have one hidden talent I don't usually share with people," Cael said.

Xenia sprung up on the rock and clapped her hands together.

"But you can't look at me while I do it or I won't be able to perform."

"I'm shocked that's a problem for you," Xenia cooed with a smarmy smile.

"You're hilarious." Cael tugged Xenia off the rock, then nestled her in the sand next to him, wrapping his wing around her to keep her warm. "Close your eyes."

"Wrath of Vestan, you've got a lot of *requirements* for this performance," Xenia said, though she obeyed his request. "Diva."

"Hush before I lose my nerve."

Cael cleared his throat and his chest expanded as he took a deep breath, held it for several seconds, then blew it out slowly.

And began to sing.

Xenia had never heard such a beautiful, heart-breaking sound in her entire life.

Cael's voice was as sweet and rich as honey with a hint of raspiness at the end of the phrases. It invaded her body, shivered across her limbs, and seeded a dull throb in her lower belly.

She peered up at him through a cracked eye to see he'd closed his, completely lost in his serenade.

Xenia didn't recognize the song, but it had a plaintive melody and soul-weary lyrics. Something about a doomed affair, the pain of a forbidden love. The desperation for even one pretend moment, a memory to hold onto.

"*Just stay here in my arms, one night beneath the stars,*
*And if I must, I'll let you go tomorrow…or*
*tomorrow…or tomorrow.*"

Xenia reached up to rub at her cheek, surprised to find wetness there.

"Oh High Gods, was I that bad?" Cael asked as he gazed down at her.

Xenia shook her head, nestling in closer as fatigue tugged down her eyelids.

"Sing me another."

An hour later, Cael had nearly exhausted his repertoire and Xenia was definitely asleep. He left his wing around her as she breathed puffs of her sweet scent into his armpit.

He hadn't sung in front of anyone in decades, and huffed a laugh as he remembered the last time he'd done so in public: that disastrous live music night at the Fang and Claw when he and Tristan had made fools of themselves in front of those twins and the entire tavern. He chuckled at the memory and pulled Xenia closer.

He leaned his head back against the rock, listening to the eerie sounds of the Desolation at night—beastly growls, chilling yelps, the underlying drone of insects.

He kept a subtle wind-shield around the clearing, just enough of a breeze to deter investigating predators without completely draining his power.

Xenia stirred in her sleep, then threw an arm across his waist.

He didn't move her away, let himself get swept up in the fantasy.

The fantasy that she was his.

The fantasy that falling asleep in each other's arms was a normal, nightly occurrence.

The fantasy that she could fix him.

But that's all it was—a fantasy.

Even if she wanted to shackle herself to a broken male, he'd still have his father to contend with.

He knew he'd have to let Xenia go.

Maybe tomorrow.

Or tomorrow.

Or tomorrow.

# CHAPTER
# THIRTY-FOUR

HELLA'S INCESSANT SINGING DRIFTED through the walls of Cassandra's bedroom as she dressed for the night ahead, her lips quirking up at the sound.

Whenever Hella wasn't forced into silence for the sake of public decency, the red-winged Windrider croaked out tune after tune. Cassandra marveled that anyone could memorize that many song lyrics in so many different languages.

And what Hella lacked in pitch, she made up for in sheer volume.

The wall of sound had frayed Cassandra's nerves during those first few days of her stay, but by now,

Hella's off-key warbling had become something of a comfort.

Cassandra pulled on a pair of navy leggings and a flowy, peach-colored top—stylish pieces appropriate for live music night at the Fang and Claw, but still comfortable enough for her to work in after. She studied herself in the mirror, questioning her sartorial choices. She wasn't used to having options, her dress robes having been her uniform for so long. She wasn't sure if she wanted the privilege. Disliked having to worry that she wasn't dressed correctly, or hadn't chosen the appropriate outfit for the appropriate event.

She tugged at the open hem of her sleeve, grateful that she no longer had to hide her Letha tattoo.

Earlier today, Cassandra had decided it was time to get a cover-up, lest she start getting questions about why it hadn't faded. She'd dragged Hella to a tattoo parlor on the northern outskirts of Dienses Square. Pockets of darkness peppered her familiarity with the quaint, vibrant neighborhood filled with charming boutiques and artist's shops. She felt certain she'd been there before. Perhaps researching the potential value of treasures stolen during her previous life, any specific details torn from her mind by Xenia in their quest for caution.

Cassandra had paused at an ivy-covered art gallery, snared by the striking piece displayed in the window.

A gilded frame bordered a portrait of a female Windrider, her head thrown back, her ebony arms and butter-yellow wings reaching for the twilight sky.

Silvery, shining liquid clung to the female's shapely body, cresting just above her breasts. She stood atop a pile of human skulls that crumbled to ash beneath her feet. The female's sharp features were twisted into an expression that, viewed from one angle, could be interpreted as the height of ecstasy, and from another appeared to be gut-wrenching torment. Cassandra shivered at the title, etched in bleeding letters along with the artist's initials onto a gold plaque at the bottom of the frame.

*Delirium-SM.*

A bold, dangerous piece to be displayed so prominently.

Cassandra had searched the painting for hidden Teles symbols, but hadn't found any.

Shaking off the titillating, terrifying hope the painting had birthed in her heart, Cassandra crossed the square and entered the tattoo parlor. Hella had kept watch outside, her crimson wings blocking a majority of the view, while Cassandra approached the tattoo artist, a curvy Deathstalker female with purple-streaked hair and arms filled with colorful designs. Cassandra had gnawed at her lip, nervous to erase this central symbol of her identity.

As the first pricks of the needle had bitten into her wrist, Cassandra's anxiety transformed into excitement.

A few hours later, Cassandra was a Shrouded Sister no longer. Joyful tears had misted her cheeks as the tattooist rubbed a soothing balm across the fresh new ink.

Cassandra fingered the bandage wrapped around her wrist as she left her bedroom and crossed the hall to knock on Hella's door.

"I'm ready, Hella."

"Be down soon, tiny human," Hella sang back and Cassandra chuckled as she descended the stairs and plopped onto the couch to await her escort for the evening.

No sooner had she settled her head against the cushion than a knock sounded at the bungalow's door.

Cassandra's head perked up, instantly wary. She'd not received a single visitor this week. Was it someone looking for Tristan?

She padded to the door and peered through the peephole, startled by the shock of familiar flaxen hair poking out from underneath a dark hood.

She ripped the door open. "Aneka?"

The woman's head shot up. "Ker," Aneka said, her voice rich yet weightless, like the plucked string of a harp.

"What are you doing here?" Cassandra asked, jealousy ripping through her gut, hot and churning.

Had Aneka been here before?

She thought back to that night when she and Tristan had seen Aneka at the Serpent's Den. There'd been not a hint of familiarity on either of their faces. But perhaps they were just trying to hide it from August, Aneka's master?

She couldn't help the visions that slithered through her mind. The two of them entangled on the couch behind her, Tristan's head bobbing between Aneka's creamy thighs.

Curse Letha, Cassandra had watched too many dirty memories.

And based on her own recent experience with Tristan's tongue, she knew all too well that talent like that didn't miraculously appear without lots and *lots* of practice.

August's taunts echoed in her ear.

*Do you know how many mortal women I've had over the centuries? How many your master has had?*

It seemed so simple to ignore Tristan's history when they were together. But as soon as they were apart, the notches on his bedpost—not to mention the scar on his palm and the gaping wound in his heart—became all too apparent.

She stammered through the unwelcome vision. "How…how did you know where Tristan lives?"

"I didn't come to see him. I came to see you. I wanted to make sure you were okay after what happened at the Vicereine's party last night. I found Tristan's address in August's office after I visited the Temple this morning."

Her blood-boiling envy cooled, though confusion swiftly took its place. "The Temple?"

"I go there to have my memories pulled sometimes. It's…it's easier if I don't have to remember."

Aneka pulled back her hood and realization sank, sharp and heavy, into Cassandra's stomach.

A deep purple bruise surrounded Aneka's left eye, and only a sliver of striking, pale green shone through the swollen lid.

None of the woman's typical slinky confidence was on show. She seemed more like a broken doll, discarded without a second thought.

"Did August do this to you?" Cassandra asked.

Aneka hung her head, her pale golden hair spilling around her shoulders while she wrung her hands together. "I assume so. He...he was quite angry after we left the party. Only Letha now knows whatever happened between us once we returned to his townhouse."

Any jealousy or possessiveness Cassandra had felt over Aneka's obvious covetousness of Tristan hardened into righteous anger. No wonder Tristan had wanted no part of that scene.

Aneka tucked a strand of hair behind her ear, lowering her voice further. "I'm so envious of you. Tristan looks at you like you're someone to be cherished. Not a piece of property to be used and then—" Aneka's voice caught as she choked back a thick sob, and drops leaked from her swollen eye. "I want to get away from him, but I don't know where else to go, what else to do. What options does a mortal woman have in a place like this? I can't become a Sister. I'm...spoiled."

Cassandra weighed her options, her compassion, as always, overriding her good sense. No one deserved to be treated the way Aneka was being treated. Guilt twisted Cassandra's stomach that she herself was the catalyst for August's anger and therefore the cause of Aneka's garish bruise.

And she remembered the look of concern in Aneka's eyes at the party last night. How Aneka had seen August hauling Cassandra off the dance floor then darted away. Tristan had shown up moments later.

Perhaps she and Aneka could continue to help each other.

She only took a moment before deciding to share her secrets with the broken woman standing before her.

"Come inside," Cassandra said, stepping back and holding the door open. "And Aneka? My name isn't Ker."

"Well, do you have any idea when he might be back?"

Tristan placed his fingers on the desk of Ronin Matakos's assistant, a Windrider female with dark-brown skin and fleshy wings, who sat outside the male's temporary office on the second floor of the Secretariat.

He'd spent the afternoon placating his brother and the Vicereine, reassuring them that though Cassandra hadn't gained any specific evidence last night, she had been able to bait Councilor Lambros into admitting his disdain for the Emperor.

He hadn't told them about the note he'd gotten from Ronin. Not yet. He wanted to wait to see what the wolf bi-form had to share first.

He'd tried to find Ronin at the party last night after he'd rushed over to rescue Cassandra—who, unsurprisingly, had already rescued herself—but Ronin had disappeared. Tristan hadn't seen the Beastrunner since, and the few windwhispers he'd sent had gone unreturned.

Tristan didn't feel like waiting until Thursday to find out what the male intended to share with him. As far as Tristan could tell, Ronin was the only member of the colony elite who knew the circle symbol meant Teles. Or the only one who had yet admitted to such.

The Windrider female grinned up at Tristan. "I'm sorry, Officer, but he'll be away for the next few days. He's had me clear his schedule."

"Away where?" Tristan grunted.

"I'm not at liberty to share that information. My apologies."

"He's not answering his commstone. Do you know if he's received my messages?"

"I'm afraid I don't have the answer to that either." The female splayed her wings, the smile never leaving her face. A polite pillar of stone.

Tristan blew out a frustrated sigh and ran his hand down his face. "Nevermind. If you hear from him, just tell him I was looking for him. My name is—"

"Officer Tristan Saros." The woman lowered her voice, her head swiveling to survey the empty hallway. "Or should I say Prince Tristan Erabis."

Tristan flinched at his old title, frozen in place as his hands dropped to his sides. No one referred to him that way anymore. And he was shocked to hear the honorific uttered by this cheerful female. Did she understand how dangerous it was to say such things, especially in this building?

She crooked a finger, motioning him closer, and he leaned down so she could whisper into his ear.

"They still speak of you on the continent, you know. There are many who believe that you never should've been exiled. That you should've taken the throne after your father."

Her words sparked something inside of him—a dream he'd buried centuries ago that had been slowly reawakening ever since he'd met Cassandra.

He pulled back, staring into the woman's deep brown eyes. "Why are you telling me this?"

She shrugged, her lips still pulled into that interminable smile. "Just thought you might like to know. Have a pleasant day, Officer."

She continued to stare at him as he gave her a confused look. "I… Okay, thank you."

He turned away, nearly tripping over the chair as he stalked down the hall, the female's words echoing in his brain.

He recalled the similar sentiments of those Vestians in Meridon, though hadn't thought much of it at the time. Merely ramblings of Fae who were well-removed from both continental politics and the inner workings of the colonial capital here in Thalenn.

He'd just exited the Secretariat into the dusky glow of approaching twilight when a windwhisper fluttered into his ear from Hella, asking him to come to the bungalow. Something about Cassandra.

He shot into the sky without a moment's hesitation, trying to shake off the odd encounter with Ronin's assistant.

Tristan had no reason to be nervous.

He repeated it to himself, a mantra as he paced along the sidewalk a few houses down from his bungalow.

As soon as he'd landed, a paralyzing anxiety had gripped him.

It was stupid, really, to be this unsettled at the thought of seeing Cassandra again after what had transpired in that carriage.

Every taste of her only made him yearn for more. Playmates wasn't enough. Neither was pretend master and consort.

And the title of *friend* was becoming harder and harder to bear.

Fuck, he didn't want to be her *friend*.

He wanted to be her everything.

His desire for her clashed against his terror for her safety, spurred by echoes of Hector's anguished howl and barbed memories of a tarnished, bloody pearl ring—the cost Ione had paid for his love.

He was falling for an off-limits mortal woman again. People were calling him Prince again.

It was like the past two hundred years hadn't even happened.

A curtain pulled back in the house in front of him—his neighbor likely wondering who this crazy asshole was, wearing a path in the sidewalk.

Tristan took a deep breath, rustled his feathers, and stalked towards his bungalow, stirring the velvet-green leaves and serene white faces of the moonflowers along his route.

He swung open the wrought-iron gate and took the shallow steps two at a time. He crossed the porch swiftly, not bothering to knock before he entered.

Shrieking laughter bombarded him as he stepped through the foyer and wound around the staircase. A third voice that wasn't Hella's and certainly wasn't Cass's—he could pick her laugh blindfolded out of a cacophony of thousands—prickled his ears. He padded towards the kitchen at the back of the house, then stopped short as he approached the dining table.

What the fuck was August Lambros's consort doing here?

High Gods help him, his first instinct was to kick Aneka out. August would be livid if he knew his consort was in Tristan's house. He might retaliate by attacking Cassandra again.

"Hello?" he said tentatively, hesitant to interrupt their hysterics.

"Tristan!" A broad smile lit up Cass's face, obliterating the helpless organ in his chest.

She shot out of her chair and bounded towards him with open arms, then stopped herself. He guessed she was just as confused as he was by whatever this thing was between them.

She motioned him towards the table. "Come sit with us," she said.

Tristan held up his hand. "What are you doing here, Aneka?" He tried to sound neutral, but couldn't help the bite in his tone.

Aneka didn't miss it either. The smile fell from her face as she pushed her flaxen sheet of hair behind an ear, uncovering the nasty bruise swelling her eye shut.

He clenched his hands, his fingernails ripping into his palms as he pushed his fists against his thighs. This. This is exactly why he couldn't stomach these master-consort relationships. Fae males like Lambros, arrogantly drunk on their own inflated sense of importance, had little regard for mortals. Tristan wished he could just end them all and be done with it.

"I came over to check on Cassandra," Aneka said. Tristan raised an eyebrow at Cass, wondering why she'd shared her true identity with the woman. "She explained to me what you're trying to do, searching for members of this rebel organization within the colony elite. I want to help."

"Why? And how?" Tristan asked, taking in Hella for the first time since he'd walked in. Something very close to appreciation was radiating from her golden eyes as she stared at Aneka.

"August is involved in something," Aneka said. "His sister has cut him off and he's in a massive amount of debt trying to keep up his flashy lifestyle here in the colonies. He's been getting visits, always in the middle of the night. And always the same individual. I've never seen her, but I've heard her voice. It could be the rebels, but I'm not certain."

"What have they been discussing?" Tristan asked.

Aneka's hair slipped from behind her ear as she bowed her head. "I can never make out what they're saying. The female speaks so low and quickly." She whipped her head up, viciousness sparking in her sole open eye. "But I'll do whatever I can to take that bastard down. I can get you access to his house, his office. Whatever you need."

Cassandra reached out and squeezed Aneka's hand, wearing a matching expression of righteous violence.

Pride and fear battled through Tristan's chest. Though fear eventually won out.

"Can I speak with you privately for a moment?" Tristan asked Cassandra. He took her hand and ushered her into the backyard, shutting the double doors with a soft click.

He padded through the damp grass and into the shadowed corner of the fence, not wanting to be overheard by either Hella or Aneka. As an added precaution, he raised a wing around Cassandra, hiding them from view. "What's going on, Cass? Why didn't you talk to me before you pulled Aneka into this? How do you know you can trust her?"

Her pale blue-gray eyes flashed with indignant hurt. "Did you see her face, Tristan? Why would she have any loyalty towards August when he treats her like that? And what was I supposed to do? She arrived here completely broken, and I just...I had to let her in."

He cupped her cheek, stroking his thumb along her silken skin, and she released a soft breath at the contact. "How much did you tell her?"

"Everything," she shrugged, and his chin dropped to his chest. "I also may have promised that if she helps us, we'll get her somewhere safe—away from him. I'm sure Borea could find her a position at one of the other Temples. As staff, not a Sister. Maybe Meridon, since it's the furthest from Thalenn."

"And how are we going to guarantee he doesn't track her there?" Tristan asked. "You have no idea what these males are like. How territorial they are. Even though he shares her, she's still his property. His scent is all over her. I could smell it as soon as I entered the house. You may have promised her safety we can't guarantee."

"She helped me. When August attacked me last night, she went to fetch you, right? Told you what was happening?"

He couldn't deny it. Blinding white rage had overtaken his mind when Aneka had come rushing over in the midst of his conversion with Ronin. And he felt immensely grateful to Aneka for the warning, but couldn't help his wariness. What if this was some kind of trap?

"What exactly do you plan to do?" he asked.

"She and August will be at the Serpent's Den on Thursday night. She's going to give me her key to his townhouse so I can poke around, see what I might be able to find."

Tristan's lips twisted into a grimace. "No way. That's the same night that *I'm* supposed to be at the Serpent's Den with Ronin. No fucking way am I letting you do this alone."

"Birdman." She gave him a deadpan look but his heart leapt at his nickname. "I am *way* stealthier than you."

Tristan jostled his wings. "Ghostwalker, remember?"

She shook her head. "You need to talk to Ronin. I can do this, Tristan. I'll take Hella with me. You keep working your angles and let me work mine. We'll get the name you need faster this way."

He sighed, scrubbing a hand down his face. "Why can't I just ask Ronin if August is working with him? Pretty clear from that message Ronin gave me that he's either a member of the Teles Chrysos or he's got intel to share about them."

"And what if he doesn't? Then we're back to square one."

"I don't like it," Tristan grumbled. "But I know better than to try to stop you when you get these crazy ideas. You promise you'll take Hella with you?"

"I said I would. Overprotective babysitter," she smirked. He grabbed her hand and intertwined their fingers.

"Cass," he murmured.

She didn't look up at him, stalled by whatever emotions he'd just poured into her name.

He stepped in closer. "What are we doing?"

She kept her gaze glued to their interlocked fingers. But she didn't drop his hand, so he pressed forward.

"Are we okay?" he whispered.

"What do you mean?" She met his stare, her eyes bouncing back and forth between his own. Searching.

"After what happened on the way to the party last night?"

He swore he could see her rebuilding her walls, each brick sliding back into place. Blocking him out.

"We had to do that," she said flatly. "It was the only way to protect our secret. A duty between *friends*." The last word dripped disdainfully from her tongue.

She turned her face away, and he studied her profile. The upturned slope of her nose, her fluttering eyelashes and trembling lips. "Nothing like you and Ione."

He jolted. *This* is what she'd been worried about?

He was an utter, utter fool.

How did she still not understand everything she meant to him?

"Cass, she's gone. A cherished part of my past, but you…you're my future. And I…" A cracked whisper. "I feel like I'm losing you too."

Her eyes softened a fraction, and he inched towards her, intending to tug her against his chest, but she took a purposeful step backwards. "I can't do this right now, Tristan. I've got to focus on the work tonight."

She pushed back his wing and rushed towards the house.

"Cassandra," he called, following her.

Hella opened the patio door, her timing impeccable.

"Hey," the giantess grunted as Cassandra shoved past her. Hella narrowed her eyes at Tristan. "What do to her?"

Tristan tore a frustrated hand through his hair, pulling several strands from his knot.

"Nothing," he grumbled. "Let's go."

He wasn't sure *what* he was doing to her.

But she was carving out his heart.

# CHAPTER
# THIRTY-FIVE

Reena and Hella squealed, leaping from their seats as the band plucked out the first notes of a popular new song from the continent. Reena tugged on Cassandra's hand, beckoning her to join them on the rollicking dance floor at the Fang and Claw's weekly live music night.

But Cassandra didn't know the song. Nor was she feeling particularly joyful. Not after that awkward exchange with Tristan before they'd all come over to the tavern together to await Borea and the night's obliviates.

Tristan hadn't said another word to her, had sidled over to the bar as soon as they'd arrived. He was still sitting there, alone. Brushing off the many males and females who approached him.

Not that Cassandra was keeping tabs on him or anything.

She leaned against the wall, shrouded in shadows, and swigged her drink—a bubbly concoction with a spicy bite of ginger and plenty of liquor. Reena's pours were nothing if not generous.

Cassandra tapped her feet to the addictive beat, content to watch her new friends jump and twirl with the crowd, the bobbing pendant lights swaying like falling stars above them.

Cassandra rubbed at her new tattoo as Reena and Hella bounded back to the table, breathing calmly despite their boisterous dancing. Cassandra marveled at their glorious Fae stamina, knew she would've been a sweating, panting mess if she'd joined them.

Hella climbed onto the seat opposite Cassandra, carefully angling her wings over the back of the stool while Reena draped herself onto the seat between them. She signaled to one of her staff to refill their drinks.

"Another, sweetie?" Reena asked Cassandra. "Looks like you enjoyed it."

Cassandra drained the rest of the drink and licked her lips, her mind floaty and her limbs deliciously warm. "As long as it's not Aguaver."

Hella raised a golden eyebrow. "There is story here, yes?"

Reena flipped long, auburn locks over her shoulder, oozing one of her trademark sultry chuckles. "Cass here got shitfaced on the stuff a few weeks ago. That night when Tristan was poisoned by Opheron. As soon as I left them alone, she practically jumped his bones. Ended up sleeping on top of him the whole night."

Cassandra choked on her tongue. "How in the name of Stygios do you know that?" Her eyes darted to the black-winged male sulking at the bar and she lowered her voice. "Did Tristan tell you?"

Reena grazed her matte-black fingernails across Cassandra's cheek, encouraging her to look towards a sleek black box nestled in the upper corner of the room. "Is that," Cassandra sputtered, "an opticorder?"

Reena nodded. "I take security here very seriously, sugar. And my nosy, dirty little mind couldn't help but wonder what you two were up to."

Hella's snorting laughter drew an indignant glare from Cassandra. "I want see."

"I destroyed it already," Reena said. "Figured you wouldn't want any concrete evidence that you broke the rules of your order."

"Thank you," Cassandra responded primly.

"But now that you're no longer a member of that order..." Reena's breathy voice trailed off suggestively.

"And working with object of affection..." Hella added with a saucy wink.

"Oh, you two are worse than Xenia." Cassandra's giggle caught in her throat, sorrow squeezing her chest. She knew Xenia was out of any immediate danger. But until Cass could wrap her arms around her friend again, she would continue to worry.

"Seriously, sugar, what's going on between you two?" Reena asked, just as the bartender approached with their drinks. A tall glass filled with that fizzy, gingery concoction for Cassandra, a low tumbler of amber liquid for Reena, and a goblet brimming with pink and orange swirls for Hella.

Cassandra barked out a laugh. "What are you drinking, Hella?"

"Sex on Beach," Hella answered in a matter-of-fact voice, as if it were the most obvious drink order in the world.

"Oh no, nuh-uh," Reena scolded. "You're not glossing over the subject that easily. Spill it."

Cassandra took a sip of her drink, the bubbles bursting across her tongue. "I have no idea," she admitted with a sigh.

"Has he tried anything?" Reena asked.

A month ago, the question—and her answer— would have inspired some serious blushing, but Cassandra's cheeks remained cool. She internally patted herself on the back, celebrating her newfound maturity.

"We've…fooled around a few times," Cassandra admitted, the confession inspiring a montage of seductive sensations.

Tristan's warm, wet tongue gliding across her own. His fingers pumping between her legs. His ragged growl as he'd spilled himself down her throat. The purr of his filthy words: *How badly do you want to fuck me right now, Daredevil?*

And here came the blushing.

Not to mention a pulsing in her veins, sharper and more urgent than any she'd yet felt. As if the drops of his magic in her blood ached to reacquaint themselves with their source.

"Smells like you enjoyed it," Reena cooed, taking a slow sip from her tumbler. "I assume you want to do it again."

"No," Cassandra answered, far too quickly to be anything but a lie.

"Why?" Hella asked, taking a loud, obnoxious slurp of her fruity drink.

"What's the point?" Cassandra said, dejected. "He's Fae and I'm mortal. It's literally illegal for us to be together as anything other than master and consort. And I've never even been with anyone before. We could never be anything serious. Plus he's…I don't think he thinks of me as anything more than a friend. And occasional diversion. He told me about the woman he tried to Turn. He said he's still in love with her."

Reena cocked a groomed eyebrow. "Were those the exact words he used?"

Cassandra thought back to that heart-wrenching night at the bungalow, trying to recall Tristan's precise statement.

"No, not exactly," she admitted. "I asked him if he loved her and he said he would always love her."

Reena knocked back the contents of her tumbler, then wiggled it at the bartender for a refill. "Okay. I'm gonna give you the benefit of the doubt because you've been sheltered behind the walls of that Temple for most of your life. Allow me to offer a new perspective.

"First, who cares if you're a virgin? The best assets a female can offer in the bedroom are an enthusiastic attitude, a lack of judgment, and a curious willingness to try new things. *None* of that requires an ounce of experience.

"Second, sex is a blessing. No, fuck that. It's a High-Gods-damned *right*. Now that you've left the order, you owe it to yourself to explore. Have some fun! You've earned it. And I don't think I need to tell you that you can't ask for a better male than Tristan to explore with. He's gorgeous, skilled, respectful...and just the right amount of dirty." Reena winked. "You know I'm right.

"Third, Tristan couldn't give less of a shit about the laws against relationships between Fae and humans. He's damn near the reason they're in place.

"And lastly, everyone holds a special place in their heart for their first love. Regardless of whether they ended up together or not. Just because he was in love once and it ended tragically, doesn't mean he'll never love again. Or that he's still holding a candle for her. Have you talked to him about it since?"

"Well, no, but—"

"Don't you think you should?"

Cassandra leaned back in her chair, bringing her glass to her lips and taking a long, thoughtful sip. The seeds of hope in her heart bloomed to life, nourished by Reena's proclamations.

"What do you think, Hella?" she asked.

"I with Reena," Hella declared, before regaling her tablemates with some very long, very descriptive stories of the many, many, *many* lovers she'd taken over her four centuries of life. Mortal and Fae. Male, female, and every gender in between. And in numerous arrangements often including more than two individuals. In Hella's opinion, love, and the act of making it, was a joy to be shared with as many people as possible and without an ounce of shame or guilt or jealousy.

"But what if he doesn't feel the same way I do?" Cassandra asked Reena, then gazed across the room at Tristan.

Her partner.

Her protector.

Her *friend.*

The word was losing its sting.

"Oh, sweetie," Reena said, her honey-gold eyes softening. "There's only one person who can tell you that. But don't you think it's worth asking the question? Don't let fear hold you back from experiencing something great."

The band had descended into a slower song, one with a sultry beat topped by syrupy, indolent strings. On the dance floor, a male Windrider with multi-colored wings pressed up against another male. In the low, smoky light, Cassandra couldn't tell if the second male was mortal or Fae.

She was overcome with an overwhelming urge to talk to Tristan. To stop being a coward and just *talk* to him. Find out how he was feeling. They'd never had an issue talking through things when her chastity vow had so clearly defined the boundaries of their relationship. Now *she* had the power to define those boundaries. And she ached to know where his own lay.

"I'll do it," she said.

Hella gathered Cassandra into a rib-crunching hug and hooted with joy. "Yes, tiny human! Get your male!"

Cassandra attempted a laugh, strangled by Hella's vise-tight arms. "After we finish our work tonight," she told the two Fae, then polished off the rest of her drink.

"Just keep a few more of these on hand, Reena. In case I lose my nerve."

Tristan seemed to be making up for avoiding Cassandra upstairs, his amber gaze anchored to her as she bathed the obliviates with her restorative magic.

*Their* restorative magic, she supposed.

That thought, combined with the wonder and longing in his stare, dripped a languid, radiant heat throughout her limbs.

She tried to concentrate as she grasped the papery hand of the sixth, and final, obliviate for the evening: an older gentleman with rheumy, unfocused blue eyes and wisps of silvery hair clinging to a shiny, peeling red pate.

Cassandra reached for the man's wife, whose hand shook as she regarded Cassandra through filmy glasses.

"Savior Sister," the woman whispered with hushed adulation.

Cassandra shrugged off the title. "*Your* memories will restore him. I'm merely the conduit. Do you have one ready?"

A peaceful smile bent the old woman's wrinkled lips. "Ever since Mother Superior told me that I'd have to pick a memory to restore my Shefton, I've been thinking back on our life. It's not the big events that I remember the most clearly. Not the day we met, nor the day we were married. Or even the day our son was born. It's the in-between moments. The quiet times. Sitting in front of a fire together at the end of the day, me reading a book and Shef working on his carvings."

The backs of Cassandra's eyes stung. The life the woman described sounded so different from the tumultuous, dangerous one she'd been living.

And seemed so unattainable.

Though she couldn't deny that she yearned for such a peaceful existence with someone.

Maybe even the black-winged male drinking her in from across the room.

"You'll have him back," Cassandra vowed. "I promise. Hold the memory in your mind."

The old woman closed her eyes, her trembling fingers closing around Cassandra's, and a surge of sparkling heat blazed through Cassandra's veins.

*The crackle and pop of a fire.*

*A sweet, honeyed scent of baked apples tucked behind the smoke.*

*The cool, pebbled leather of a book spine and the smooth swish of a turned page.*

*The snick of a knife carving into a small wooden sculpture, shavings showering the floor.*

The old man's grip crushed Cassandra's fingers, stronger than she'd anticipated, and he looked over at his wife. "Mona," he breathed. "My sweet Mona."

Cassandra wrapped the couples' hands together, then stepped away to give them privacy.

Shefton swept his wife into his arms, running a hand over her hair as they held each other, shaking with grateful sobs.

Cassandra sidled up to Borea, who'd nearly fallen asleep against a chair. Reena and Hella had gone back upstairs to keep watch. "Why were there so few obliviates tonight?"

"It's the strangest thing," Borea yawned, rubbing at the corners of her eyes. "Several of the obliviates that you've restored have returned to the Temple for extractions, but they don't forget anything."

Cassandra cocked her head. "What do you mean?"

"You've somehow made them immune to memory pulling," Borea answered. "The memories come out, but without any loss of remembrance on their part. And not a single one of them has been re-obliviated."

Cassandra marveled at her limbs, warm and tingly after the six restorations she'd just performed.

"How… do you think it has something to do with Tristan's magic?"

Upon hearing his name, Tristan ambled over. "What about my magic?"

"It seems as though our combined power makes humans immune to obliviation. Offers them protection against it."

Awe—and something deeper—flashed across Tristan's face. "You're incredible," he breathed, the exhalation nearly a prayer.

Borea's gaze volleyed between them, and she stepped away to tend to the couple.

Cassandra pressed a hand against Tristan's solid chest. "Only because you've made me that way."

Tristan settled a hand over hers. "We're better together."

"Tristan, I—"

The metal grate clanked open to reveal a woman with gray-streaked dark hair, and any intentions Cassandra had for starting this heart-pounding conversation with Tristan snuffed out like a candle in a chill wind.

Mama's slow feet dragged across the dirt floor, leaving a trail of dust as a young woman—likely a member of the Temple kitchen staff—guided her over.

"I thought it was time to try," Borea said as she rejoined them.

Cassandra's throat thickened and her sinuses burned. "What if…what if it doesn't work?"

Tristan cradled her face. "You have to try, Cass. Don't let the fear win. Not over something this important."

He sounded like Reena. Though she could've sworn he was talking about something else.

She blew out a quivering breath. "Okay."

The certainty in Tristan's gaze strengthened her.

It always had.

"Okay," she said, more firmly, calling up scraps of confidence.

Tristan released her, and she approached her mother. Dark, vacant eyes stared through her, past her. Seeing nothing at all.

"I'll give you some privacy," Tristan said, turning away, but Cassandra stilled him.

"No, please," she whispered. "Stay with me."

A small smile graced his lips. "Always."

He tucked in behind her, a solid, reassuring wall of warmth and strength at her back.

Borea stepped off to the side with the young woman who'd escorted Mama, observing with tense stillness.

Cassandra had so few memories of her mother before the obliviation, the clearest of which was Mama wailing by the front door on the night her father died.

Too cruel a vision to use for a restoration.

Cassandra closed her eyes, pitching herself back in time to the small, cozy house she'd shared with her parents, scrolling through half-remembered scenes and snippets.

Before the obliviation, before her father's death, her mother had loved music. Her father had taken a second job working as night-shift security at a Fae bank for months to afford a well-worn upright piano. Cassandra could still recall the pure, undiluted joy on her mother's face the day it had been delivered. Mama had played for hours that night, and Cassandra had fallen asleep listening to the wobbly tinkling of the untuned instrument.

Her mother had spent the next months teaching Cassandra to play, showing her how to rest her thumb on middle C and curl her fingers just so, poised above the stained ivory keys.

In-between moments.

Cassandra reached for her mother's hands.

# CHAPTER
# THIRTY-SIX

*T*HE PIANO BENCH CREAKED *as Cassandra swung her legs, her feet not quite reaching the floor nor the pedals.*

*She scooted closer to Mama, pressing into her hip, and her mother's lilac and cinnamon scent wrapped around her like a lingering hug.*

*Mama took hold of Cassandra's wrists. "Not there, my darling." Her soft voice mingled with the birdsong and children's laughter floating in through an open window. She moved Cassandra's fingers down several keys. "This is middle C, remember?"*

*"I always forget," Cassandra giggled, resting her head against her mother's shoulder.*

*Mama trailed her fingers through Cassandra's hair, examining the strands. "It's okay. I forget sometimes too." Something wistful and forlorn tinted her mother's words.*

*A breath of wind rippled the sheet music spread across the piano, caressing Cassandra's fingers, and her mother looked out the window.*

*Mama stiffened.*

*Cassandra followed her mother's gaze, welcomed by nothing more than the ordinary view: a sprawl of cozy brick houses fronted by fluffy shrubs. Flowering trees shed white petals that twirled like dance partners in the wind.*

*"Play," her mother said. A swallowed whisper.*

*Cassandra looked at the sheet music, but could no longer read the notes. The dots and lines melted down the page, as if the sheet had been dipped in water and the ink was running.*

*She pressed a key, but the sound that came out wasn't the expected plunk of a note.*

*It was a low, wavering wail. A human voice.*

*She snatched her hand back, horror frosting her veins.*

*Her mother's face was still angled towards the window, her mouth a thin line and her eyes blown wide.*

*"Play, Cassandra," she begged. "You've got to play."*

*A swirling vortex of black spread across the horizon. Something pulsing and moving quickly, deeper and darker than any storm cloud Cassandra had ever seen. The jagged edges of thousands upon thousands of feathered wings beat at the sky.*

*"Cassandra." Her mother gripped her chin, turning her away from the looming terror. "Do it now. Play!"*

Frustrated tears coated Cassandra's heated cheeks and fear paralyzed her fingers. "I don't know how, Mama!"

The black mass swallowed half the sky and the neighborhood outside went deathly silent. Turbulent winds ripped at the trees, then whipped through the room, billowing the curtains and knocking over a vase of flowers. The glass shattered, spilling water and white lilies across the pocked floorboards.

Mama laid her fingers atop Cassandra's. "We'll do it together." Her shaking hands escalated Cassandra's already galloping heartbeat.

Her mother pressed down on Cassandra's fingers, forcing them onto the keys, and a symphony of screams burst from the instrument, layer upon layer of agonized wails dragged from the pits of Stygios's realm itself.

Every chord they struck increased the screams' volume, until Cassandra could scarcely bear it, her eardrums near to bursting.

The dark cloud outside now blanketed the entire sky and one by one, the houses across the street disappeared, crumbling into an undulating, obsidian abyss.

Sweat coated Cassandra's palms, her fingers slipping off the keys.

"Mama," she sobbed. "Please stop. I'm scared."

A bone-jarring crack sounded as the front of the house splintered, plaster and brick tumbling into the encroaching black hole.

Mama leapt off the bench, sweeping Cassandra into her arms and backing away, her hand tangled in Cassandra's hair as she pressed Cassandra's face against her chest.

*"Don't look," she whispered. "Don't look."*

Cassandra pinched her eyes shut and clapped her hands over her ears, but it wasn't enough to drown out the sounds of the house falling to pieces around her.

The floor beneath them trembled violently and disjointed screams from the piano tumbled away, echoing as the instrument was swallowed by the pulsing darkness.

Cassandra opened her eyes, could barely breathe as tendrils of black oozed up the splintered walls.

The ground beneath them cracked, and Mama threw Cassandra onto the intact portion of the floor as she plummeted into the pit, reaching out with a hand to grab a cracked floorboard. It barely held her weight, bending as she struggled to pull herself out.

*"Mama!"* Cassandra screamed, laying flat on the floor and gripping her mother's wrist, trying to pull her to safety.

She pulled, grunting and gritting her teeth with the effort but Mama was too heavy and Cassandra was too little, too weak.

The floorboard cracked further, her mother slipping from her grip.

Frantic, she gazed down at Mama, but her mother's expression had changed.

*"Find her,"* she said, her voice coated in steel.

*"Find who?"* Cassandra wailed.

Her mother's dark eyes shifted to an opaque white and the voice that parted her lips was not one voice, but thousands. Millions. Every voice that had ever existed and would ever exist in the whole of time, yet it held a hint of feminine softness in its terrible echo.

*"I see without seeing. I know without knowing. I live without living. I am the beginning and the end of eternity."*

*"Mama,"* Cassandra whimpered, scrabbling for her mother's slipping fingers.

*Mama's dark eyes returned and her voice was her own once again.*

*"Don't cry, my bravest girl in Ethyrios."* A smile of pure peace and contentment bloomed on her mother's lovely face.

*Mama's fingers slipped away with a pop and Cassandra screamed as her mother fell away, her words fading as the darkness consumed them both.*

*"I'll be waiting for you."*

*A needle of sunlight pierced her eyelids as she reached across the bed—empty, yet still warm from his body.*

*Satin sheets slid from her naked form as she sat upright and surveyed her surroundings, a room crafted entirely of white rock glistening like milky ice in the morning light. Throughout the floor and walls, rainbow-colored sparks shimmered like distant galaxies.*

*Beyond the bed, an arched double door opened onto a balcony crafted of the same glowing rock.*

*She plucked up her black silk robe, a spill of ink against the pale floor, and a heaviness at her back strained against the fabric before slipping through. The unfamiliar weight dragged as she stepped onto the warm floor, the rock heated by some inner fire.*

*Through the doors, monumental, snow-topped peaks speared for the sky like a row of fangs.*

*She strode onto the balcony, the weight at her back lifting, spreading, soaking in the sun's rays.*

*A rumbling roar rose from a sea of people stretched across a plain of lilies, white bell-shaped petals cupping yellow spikes nestled in a field of green.*

*The roar morphed into a word, chanted relentlessly with a reverence that caused the weight at her back to climb higher.*

*The word tickled her ears, sent shivers through her soul.*

*She approached the edge of the balcony and the chant soared to a fever-pitch. The sea of bodies rippled, pushing forward, cresting closer.*

*She closed her eyes and stretched her arms towards her worshipers.*

*The word was her destiny. The reason for their worship. The source of her power.*

*Her role in this world.*

*In every world—*

Cool dirt pressed into Cassandra's back and strong hands gripped her cheeks.

"Wake up, Cass. Wake *up*."

She blinked her eyes open, Tristan's terrified face forming before her unfocused gaze.

Her muscles protested as she attempted to lift her heavy limbs. She opened her mouth to speak, her tongue a dry, hefty lump.

Tristan sat down beside her, pulling her head and torso into his lap.

"Did it work?" she croaked out, though based on those visions, she feared she already knew the answer.

"No, sweetheart." He brushed sweaty strands of hair off her forehead. "I'm so sorry."

A hot tear dripped from the corner of her eye as she turned her head to gaze over at her mother, crumpled on the floor, panting heavily, her eyes swimming behind her lids and her limbs twitching and jerking as if she were having the most horrible nightmare. Borea was crouched beside her, holding her hand and trying to soothe her.

"What...what happened?" Cassandra asked, closing her eyes and just letting go, her spent body draped across Tristan's powerful thighs.

"You disappeared," he said, his shaking voice etched with terror. "As soon as you touched your mother's hands. There was a flash of rainbow light and it was like you both just winked out of existence."

"H-how long were we gone for?"

"Not more than a few minutes, thank the High Gods."

Cassandra exhaled a weak chuckle at his relief. "Were you worried about me, Birdman?"

She gazed up at him, but he wasn't laughing. Fierce resolve hardened his features, and he gripped her hand so tightly, she worried he might break her brittle fingers.

His eyes blazed bronze, pinning her in place and stealing the breath from her lungs.

"I would have traveled infinite worlds, shredded the cosmos, to find you."

That wall around her heart shattered, and everything she felt for him, all those vast, terrifying emotions, rushed through her body, his magic following with a scintillating tingle.

She reached a quivering hand up to cup his cheek and he nuzzled into her touch. She didn't have the strength to respond. Not yet. Not after everything she'd just experienced.

But she would. Soon.

He seemed to understand. Stood, and helped her to her feet.

He supported her as she made her way over to her mother, then crouched down on creaking limbs next to Borea.

Cassandra reached out to touch her mother, but stopped herself.

Borea grabbed her hand and clasped it with Mama's. "It's safe. You're not concentrating on a memory, so you can touch her without worrying about the consequences."

Borea's own features were drawn tight.

"Will she be okay?" Cassandra asked, gripping her mother's hand, frightening echoes of both visions pounding through her ears.

"I believe so, yes. She will need to rest for a few days." Borea slowly shook her head. "I've... I've never seen anything like that before. Where did you go?"

"I don't know," Cassandra answered honestly. "At first, it just felt like a normal memory viewing, but...it twisted somehow. Turned into a nightmare."

She told Borea and Tristan about the visions she'd seen, that terrible, boundless voice her mother had spoken in, her cryptic words.

*Find her.*

"What do you think they mean?" Cassandra asked.

Borea tilted her head with a sympathetic frown. "Likely nothing, my dear. You're exhausted. You've been working too hard, researching the Fallen Goddess, restoring obliviates and filtering their memories. And the High Gods know what else you've been up to with this one." She cocked a thumb at Tristan, who raised his palms, proclaiming his innocence. "It's probably best if we pause the restorations for a bit. Besides, I fear the Empire soldiers are growing suspicious about the lack of freshly obliviated supplicants."

Cassandra rose to protest, and a wave of dizziness nearly toppled her off her feet.

Tristan was there in an instant, scooping her into his arms. "Okay, Savior Sister," he said with a crooked grin. She shot him a slitted glare. "That's quite enough excitement for one night."

Borea nodded, picking up Cassandra's mother and motioning for the young woman from the Temple. "We'd better get back."

Tristan trudged towards the stairs. "And I'm taking you home," he whispered into her ear.

Cradled in Tristan's strong arms, Cassandra tried to answer as fatigue more draining than she'd ever known shuttered her lids and stilled her tongue.

*I'm already there.*

# CHAPTER
# THIRTY-SEVEN

T HE DESERT WAS PLAYING tricks on Xenia's dehydrated mind.

She limped along behind Cael, her skin burnt and itchy from two days bared beneath the scorching sun. Though the healing salve might have offered some relief, they'd agreed to conserve it.

There were far worse terrors stalking through this apocalyptic wasteland.

The endless red dunes were suspiciously quiet during the day. But at night, a symphony of clattering claws, rumbling growls, and other-worldly wails sang of death in a hundred different ways. The monsters who slumbered in the daylight were lured by the moon's cool kiss, emerging to fight and fill their bellies. Xenia hadn't yet seen any of the nocturnal creatures, only heard their savage howls. She couldn't decide if that was better or worse.

The hot winds whipping the red sands into a dusty frenzy burned differently at night. A burn so cold it froze the sweat on Xenia's skin. She wasn't too proud— or prude—to shelter within Cael's sole remaining wing for warmth as he serenaded her to sleep each night.

As the sun climbed to its midday peak, the taunting winds worsened. Shimmering at the edges of the world, they crafted visions of pools and swaying trees. Mirages that refused to grow closer, stubbornly fading with Xenia's every crunching step.

She and Cael *did* seem to be nearing the foothills of the Icthian mountains. Each day, the shadowy summits crept higher into the sapphire sky.

The pair had barely spoken these past two days since their shared talent show. But despite Cael's silence, Xenia was immensely grateful for his presence. When they'd drained their canteen yesterday, he once again used Cass's dagger to stab into a spiky plant and fill the vessel with water.

Though the life-giving plants were growing sparse. She hadn't spied a single one today, so they'd been conserving what little water they had left. They took the barest sips from the canteen and only when absolutely necessary—when the beating sun and burning winds threatened to extinguish them.

Xenia closed her eyes, sick to death of seeing salvation shimmer away into nothingness on the horizon. She followed the sounds of Cael's uneven footfalls as he stalked through the sand ahead of her.

When she re-opened her eyes, she was shocked to find the illusion hadn't disappeared this time. If anything, it appeared closer—an indigo slash surrounded by puffs of blessed greenery.

Cael paused, his sole wing kicking up like a dog's ear. Waiting and listening. Assessing the danger.

Xenia stopped behind him, grateful for a moment's rest. She studied the thick muscles of his back.

During their long daily treks, he'd strip off his shirt and pants and drape the garments around his neck. Only his unlaced boots and skin-tight black underwear remained. Xenia was still wearing a matching pair of the latter.

The tight shorts stopped at mid-thigh and left *very* little to the imagination—from any angle. Xenia stole glimpses of the impressive bulge between his legs every time they stopped for a rest or a drink.

Sometimes she felt as if it were the only thing keeping her sane, the sight of him glistening in the sun like the painstakingly carved statue of some prehistoric god.

Well, that and her niggling curiosity about what, exactly, he had hidden under the form-fitting black cotton. Much more fun to play *that* guessing game than focus on her hunger, her thirst, her desperate need to be anywhere but this High-Gods-damned fucking desert.

Xenia had always tried to find the silver lining in any situation. And the tantalizing view of Cael's nearly naked body was one of the best silver linings she'd ever found.

"It's real," he croaked.

His words snapped her sanity and she took off as fast as her weary legs could manage, her feet pounding through the sand as she shot past him.

"Blondie, wait!" he shouted, snatching her around the waist. "I need to make sure it's safe first."

"How will you be able to tell?" she asked.

"Predators can smell other predators," he whispered in her ear, resting his chin on her sticky shoulder. She could hear the smirk in his voice as he held her against his sweaty chest. Her own chest heaved from her ill-advised sprint. "Let me check the water before you go plunging to your death."

She should've been grateful when he let her go, not needing an ounce of the additional body heat provided by their proximity. But as he walked away, she leaned forward, lured into his gravity.

"Stay behind me," he grumbled over his shoulder. "And don't dip a fucking toe into that water until I give you the all-clear."

She grunted her acceptance as she stomped along behind him, then nearly groaned with envy when he waded into the water. Watching the spray around his long legs spiked her thirst to unbearable levels.

He dipped beneath the surface, then pushed off the bottom, tucking his wing against his back and arrowing through the water as fast as a sea serpent.

He made several turns around the pool before the sun dipped behind an accommodating cloud and the water deepened to an opaque midnight blue.

Xenia moaned with relief at the absence of the sun on her skin.

The water simmered, stirred by the wind, but there was no sign of Cael. Her relief edged into panic as she realized he'd been under too long.

The feathery fringe of tall grasses tickled her bare arms as she tip-toed towards the edge of the pool, searching for any sign of disruption—a glimpse of a gray wing poking above the surface like a shark fin, perhaps.

She didn't dare call out his name. It might draw the attention of the invented creature beneath the surface whom she was sure had eaten her companion.

She leaned out over the water, peering at her reflection, and was greeted by windswept curls, dust-stained cheeks, and splotchy, sunburned skin.

The portrait of the savage little desert creature staring back at her dissolved in a churn of bubbles as Cael shot through the surface and pulled her into the blissfully cool water.

She sputtered, laughing, and dragged her hand down her dripping face, her toes digging into the silky, sucking sand at the pool's floor.

"Asshole," she chuckled, pushing her sodden curls off her face. She cupped some water, but paused before taking a sip. "Is it safe to drink?"

Cael nodded. "There's a hole in the depths. The water's much colder down there. Probably run-off from the Dordenne. We must be nearing the foothills."

She barely heard him as she began sucking down gulps of the sweetest water she'd ever tasted. Even sweeter than the liquid from those tall, spiky plants.

Once she'd slaked her thirst, she rubbed at her arms and legs, attempting to clean the caked grime from her skin.

"We'll stay here until dusk," Cael said, splashing water onto his bare torso and running his hands along the muscled dips and grooves. Xenia tried not to stare at the sparkling droplets trailing down his perfect form as the hidden sun escaped the rare pocket of clouds.

"Why only until dusk?" she asked.

"This is the only source of water we've seen for miles. As soon as night falls, we'll be an easy meal for the creatures who'll no doubt congregate here."

Xenia shuddered, but a gnawing pain gripped her gut at the mention of a meal. They'd consumed all the food in the sack, hadn't eaten anything other than a wedge of hard cheese and the last slices of bread this morning.

Cael's nostrils flared, scenting her hunger, and he paused his hand shower. "We'll stay a bit after dusk then. Make a meal out of one of those creatures ourselves."

Xenia pulled at her filthy silk dress.

She cleared her throat, snagging Cael's attention. "Can you, uh, turn around please? I want to clean my dress."

Cael nodded stiffly, then obeyed, turning in the water and exposing his ruined back. She hadn't seen it this close since their first day in the desert when he'd carried her over his shoulder.

She reached out a tentative hand to caress the scar, prove to him that it didn't disgust her, but lost her nerve halfway. Instead, she pulled off the dress and swished it around, then scrambled out of the water to hang it on a scraggly tree before returning to the pool.

Her body was hidden below the water's dark surface, but she didn't want to take any chances. She crossed her arms over her breasts, tucking her hands into her armpits.

"Okay," she said. "You can turn around now."

Cael swiveled, his wing sending a small wave of water crashing over her. The left side of his mouth kicked up. "Why are you hiding yourself, Blondie? You know I've already seen you partially naked."

"Right! I forgot you were a total creep while I was changing in the cell."

He shrugged, his powerful shoulders glistening. "You wouldn't begrudge a wounded male a peek now and then, right?"

"You're not wounded anymore," she arched an eyebrow.

"Still a creep though," he said, aiming a pointed look beneath the surface. "I'll show you mine if you show me yours."

She splashed him, and he chuckled, shaking off his wet hair.

"You barely speak to me for two days, and *this* is the first conversation we're having?" She shook her head incredulously. "We need to talk about what happened back at that fortress."

His face shuttered and he turned, his dead eyes aimed across the dunes. "No," he bit out. "We don't."

"Cael," she said softly, reaching for him.

He evaded her grasp and stalked out of the pool, shaking his wing and sending water droplets flying. He stopped at a low, wide rock at the other end, then laid face down upon it, fanning out his wing to dry in the sun.

She blew out an exasperated breath and uncrossed her arms, leaning back to float in the cool water, alone again with her thoughts.

Helping this stubborn male heal was going to be much harder than she'd anticipated.

# CHAPTER
# THIRTY-EIGHT

"There." Cael spied movement at the edge of the horizon, just beneath the molten sunset. "Do you see it?"

Xenia shifted on the branch, the only one thick enough to hold their weight. Cael had wrapped them both in his wing, a makeshift camouflage as they awaited their first fresh meat in days.

"I can't see anything but a blur of orange light," Xenia said, squinting beneath the delicate hand shielding her eyes.

The small, furry lump—some kind of hare, no doubt—shuffled through the sand. Cael's Fae eyesight worked just fine, unlike his flying abilities.

He didn't understand why she kept trying to get him to *talk* about it. What the fuck did it matter now? His wing was gone. He'd never fly again. End of story.

Burdening her, or anyone really, with how he *felt* about it wasn't going to make his wing grow back. And sure as fuck wasn't going to make him feel any better either.

He shoved the festering thoughts down, deep down, letting them rest at the bottom of that pit inside him—the one that was sure to swallow him as soon as his mission to get her to safety was complete and he returned to his father.

But first, they needed to survive this last night in the Desolation.

The Icthian foothills were about half a day's trek. And if this oasis were any sign, they'd be at the Dordenne River another half day after. From there, they'd follow the river down into Rhamnos and safety.

Well, relative safety. Different monsters than the ones prowling this desert roamed there. More savage, sentient ones.

The ruddy brown hare continued its hop towards the pool, pausing every few seconds to sniff the air for predators.

If the hare felt safe enough to approach the pool, Cael could suck the air from its lungs. He'd have to be quick though. One brush of his wind against the hare's fur and the little thing would scurry away faster than he could catch it.

Which wouldn't be a problem if he could fly to chase it down. He buried *that* thought in the pit with the others.

"I see it!" Xenia cried, then slapped her hand over her mouth when the animal paused, perking up its ears. "Sorry," she whispered. "Didn't mean to scare it."

He held a finger to his lips as the hare reached the grasses at the edge of the pool, then stood on its hind legs, its twitchy nose poked into the air. Creeping to the water's edge, it sniffed again, then lowered its head and began to drink.

Cael shot Xenia a wicked grin. "Now comes the fun part."

He unfurled his wing, then stretched his arm out, mingling a few gentle kisses of wind with the soft breeze. Masking his power so as not to startle the creature.

The hare kept drinking as the gusts stirred its tawny fur.

Cael curled his fingers and the hare seized, toppling onto the bank, squeaking and gasping for the air he was stealing from its lungs. The whole attack took less than fifteen seconds.

After a final, desperate twitch, the hare's hind leg stilled.

"Dinner is served," Cael smiled at Xenia, whose emerald eyes dampened. "Oh, come on, Blondie. Do you not know where meat comes from?"

"Of course I do," she sniffled. "But knowing it and seeing it happen are two very different things."

Cael cocked his head. "Never pegged you for squeamish."

"I don't like seeing any living thing in pain." She aimed a pointed look over his shoulder.

"Right," he mumbled, not taking the bait. He leapt from the branch, his boots crunching in the gravel. He turned back to help her down, trying to ignore the way her pulse increased when he gripped her slim waist.

He leaned down to pick up the hare carcass, but it had disappeared.

What the fuck?

Ripples radiated along the water's surface and a shadowy mass appeared beneath.

"What happe—" Xenia's words were lost as a massive, reptilian beast burst from the placid pool and snapped its long snout onto her leg.

Her anguished scream sparked a murderous rage within him.

The water churned around the beast's crocodilian head and dripped off the mottled green and brown scales covering its serpentine body as it dragged Xenia down the bank.

She batted her tiny fists against its pebbled nose and blood ran down her leg as she kicked at the beast's thick teeth. She shot a panicked look at Cael—a heart-stopping sight he'd never forget as long as he lived—before the creature rolled, attempting to drown her in the shallows.

Cael attempted to draw the breath from the beast's lungs, but he couldn't get a grip on it under the water.

"Fuck!" The tossed curse kicked him into gear.

He dashed for the tree, then ripped off one of the branches to use as a makeshift weapon. He thought about using Ker, but the dagger didn't seem capable of doing enough damage against the massive monster. As he clambered to the treetop, he scolded himself for leaving that Typhon sword behind.

Rage incinerated all rational thought as he cast a draft of wind, then grasped his sole wing to awkwardly glide down to the pool and perch on the beast's back.

The creature paused its roll, but didn't release Xenia's leg. She sputtered and choked in the shallow water, gulping in deep breaths.

Cael rammed the branch into the soft flesh between the scales on the creature's back.

It let out an ear-splitting roar and released Xenia, then craned its head back to snap at him.

Xenia scrambled out of the pool, her splashing luring the creature's attention right back to her.

"Oh, no you fucking don't," Cael grunted through gritted teeth, yanking the branch free and plunging it into the monster's hide again.

The creature rolled, the branch buried in its flesh, and flung Cael aside.

He plunged into the water, then broke through the surface, treading as the beast darted for the depths and circled the black hole at the bottom.

The water grew eerily still, rippling softly from Cael's swirling limbs and Xenia's urgent splashing as she pulled herself to shore. She grunted in pain, dragging her ruined leg behind her.

Her limb was still intact, praise Anaemos. He'd never want her to suffer the same fate as him. But the deep gash in her calf bled furiously, coating the dry grasses.

"Move back farther!" Cael shouted.

Xenia lifted her head, her eyes glassy. But she nodded, gritting her teeth as she pushed up onto her elbows and crawled to the tree. She grabbed Ker and braced it in front of her, prepared for further attacks. His chest glowed with pride at her fierceness, her bravery.

The water quivered, and an open maw of sharp, white teeth appeared beneath him, aimed right for his legs.

Without a second's hesitation, he gripped the edge of his wing and shot a blast of wind into it. The wing snapped taut and he lurched upwards.

The beast's jaws crested the surface, its teeth slamming shut mere inches from Cael's dangling foot.

Using carefully aimed blasts of wind into the wing-sail above his head, Cael managed to swoop down upon the creature's back and wrench the branch free, tearing out a few scales before bobbing back into the sky.

The beast roared in pain, blood gushing from the gaping hole and staining the water a deep red.

Cael hovered above the pool, branch angled in his hand like a spear.

He had one shot.

He tucked his wing and plummeted towards the creature's amber eye, then shoved the branch in deep with a squelching crunch.

The beast threw Cael onto the shore as it reared and bucked, sending angry waves drowning the surrounding grasses. With a final, bone-rattling growl, the creature slunk beneath the surface.

Cael stood on the bank, chest heaving, hands resting on his thighs as he watched the shadow disappear into the abyss.

A tortured moan had him rushing for Xenia. He dropped to his knees before her to examine the wound.

Her curls snagged in the trunk's rough bark, her eyes squeezed shut. She sucked in hissing breaths through clenched teeth as her leg oozed deep claret puddles that mixed with the dusty gravel.

Cael wrapped a hand around her ankle, gently lifting her calf, and she screeched, her eyes popping open, darting and panicky.

"You'll be okay," he panted. "You're going to be okay."

Any other option was inconceivable.

He pressed his hand against the torn, gaping gash and blood bubbled through his fingers.

"Don't suppose that salve will work on a cut this deep?" she choked out.

"No. You're going to need something more powerful." He used one of his fangs to tear into a vein at his wrist. "Drink," he ordered, pressing his wrist to her mouth.

She pressed her lips shut, angling her head away. "It's illegal."

"And who is going to arrest you out here?" He made a show of looking around, eyebrows raised. What a time for her Sister-ly propriety to rear its prim head.

She pushed limply against his wrist.

"Just fucking drink, Xenia! It will help you heal!"

She glared at him, her emerald eyes blazing. But thank the High Gods, she obeyed.

Grabbing his wrist with an increasingly pale hand, she held him against her mouth and lapped at his blood.

"Suck *harder*. You need to get at least three full swallows."

She did as he asked, suctioning her lips over the cut.

He tried to ignore the warmth flooding his groin at the feel of her soft lips on his skin, the heady sensation of his blood flowing into her mouth.

She leaned forward, gripping him harder and sucking deeply. A jolt of excitement shot down his spine, and he drew in a sharp breath, swallowing a moan. He didn't think she'd appreciate his ill-timed arousal.

Then her eyes locked on his and her scent shifted, bathing him in a sweet, musky perfume.

She gulped down a final swallow, then pushed his wrist away. Blood smeared her lips and teeth, her breathing ragged.

She poked her tongue out to lick at the red stain on her teeth and lower lip, never once tearing her heated gaze from him.

He was paralyzed, afraid to move. The minute he released control of his muscles, he'd pounce on her.

A line of his blood coated her upper lip.

"You still have…" He pointed at her mouth.

"You get it for me," she begged in a low, throaty voice he'd never heard her use. She squirmed against the gravel, pressing her thighs together.

*Fucking* Stygios.

He glanced at the wound on her leg, heartened to see the torn flesh threading back together.

He cupped her cheek, then ran his thumb along her lip to wipe away the blood.

She wasn't drunk on his blood. Fae blood didn't have any drugging effects on mortals.

No, something else entirely inspired the heat in her eyes and the scent of her arousal. Something he *very* much wanted to explore.

What was the harm in allowing himself a taste after everything he'd suffered, the harrowing encounter they'd just barely survived?

He brushed his blood-smeared thumb along her lower lip, and her tongue darted out to lick it as she nodded slowly. As if to encourage his rapidly deteriorating self-control, acknowledge his tortured desires.

He leaned in closer, a magnetic throb pulsing in the diminished space between their lips.

"Yes," she whispered.

"Just a taste," he answered, unsure which one of them he was addressing.

Then lowered his mouth to hers.

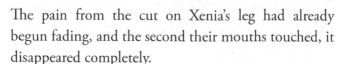

The pain from the cut on Xenia's leg had already begun fading, and the second their mouths touched, it disappeared completely.

She pushed up onto her knees, fisting Cael's shirt and yanking him closer. He wrapped an arm around her lower back and cradled the nape of her neck, pressing his lips to hers in featherlight grazes.

It wasn't enough.

"Fucking *kiss* me, Cael," she growled against his mouth. "I'm not going to break. Neither are you."

He chuckled softly. "Just trying to ease you into your first kiss."

She popped her eyes open, capturing his warm, gray gaze. "This isn't my first kiss," she whispered.

His eyes widened, but she didn't detect any judgment as his pupils danced back and forth along her own.

A wicked smile formed on his gorgeous mouth, exposing his fangs. He gripped her hair and tugged her head back, slanting his mouth over hers.

"Tempting little sinner."

He had no idea.

He crashed down onto her in a devouring kiss, and his tongue parted her lips. They both groaned as she matched his strokes, tangling her hands in his soft, ash-brown waves.

Leaving one hand gripped in her hair, he slid the other down her back, squeezing her ass and pressing their lower bodies together. She gasped into his mouth as she felt that delicious, enormous bulge poking her stomach, hot and hard and ready.

He made a low, rumbling sound as she wiggled against it, marveling at the size of him.

She sucked on his tongue, nipped at his lips, licked his fangs, delighting in his rain-drenched taste.

He broke the kiss to trail open-mouth pecks down her throat as he cupped and massaged her breast over her dress. Her nipples sharpened into aching peaks, her body throbbing a voracious chant.

*Want. Want. Want.*

Just as he was about to push the silky material aside, expose her eager flesh to his roving fingers, a howl rent the night.

They broke apart, both panting heavily.

"We need to get out of here." He touched his forehead to hers. "It's not safe."

She nodded, acknowledging the wisdom. Though at the moment, she'd rather risk death by a thousand desert creatures than stop kissing him.

A crescent moon gilded the dunes as dusk's lavender light slunk below the horizon. Shadows crept closer, drawn by either the pool or the scent of her blood.

"Sit back down," he said, easing her into a sitting position. "Let me spread some healing balm onto your leg and wrap it."

He lifted her ankle into his lap, shifting the hem of her dress up her thighs. His eyes followed it briefly before he refocused on her calf.

He rummaged through the sack and pulled out the tin, then massaged the balm onto her wound. She moaned as it cooled her heated, achy skin, and he shuddered at the sound before tearing a sleeve off his shirt and wrapping it around her calf.

He stood, offering her a hand up, and she was amazed at how normal her leg felt. Other than a dull ache, she was able to stand and walk perfectly. If humans were offering the Fae their memories, why were the Fae not returning the favor and offering humans their blood? She knew the answer to that question, but couldn't help thinking the world would be so much better with a little reciprocity.

A burbling growl, closer than the howl, drifted over as Cael filled the canteen from the pool.

"Sorry we lost dinner," he said. "If we walk through the night, we should be able to reach the foothills by morning where we can hopefully find food and some shelter."

She nodded, flattening her hands across her grumbling stomach.

Cael placed Ker in the sack, his expression so disappointingly guarded after that explosive kiss. He didn't even look at Xenia as he swept her into his arms.

And so began their final, silent trek through the Desolation.

# CHAPTER
# THIRTY-NINE

Cassandra woke in an unfamiliar bed, shrouded in darkness as comforting scents washed over her.

Clean, crisp sheets.

The ashy tinge of an extinguished candle.

The burnt vanilla aroma of bourbon.

And beneath them all, her favorite scent in the world—the one she treasured even more than her own.

Charred wood and ancient spice.

*Tristan.*

His hulking shape occupied the chair next to a bed that was twice the size of her own, covered in smoky gray linens with four wooden posts spiking towards the ceiling. Moonlight speared through the gauzy curtains and she wondered how many hours, how many days, she'd been out.

She shook off her sleep-addled confusion and scooted towards the edge of the mattress. Studied the beautiful male sleeping less than an arm's length away.

His hair spilled in a thick tangle across his forehead, the strands stirred by his rhythmic breaths. Sculpted arms crossed over his broad, bare chest and his long legs kicked out straight, one ankle crossed over the other. His magnificent, iridescent wings drooped over the back of the chair, his feathers twinkling.

She wanted to stay here, in this in-between moment, forever. Watching him sleep peacefully, no sign of trouble or worry marring his handsome face.

She was certain he'd been in that chair the whole time. Watching over her. Making sure she was safe.

*I'm taking you home.*

He'd pronounced it like a vow, a promise leaving his lips and piercing her heart.

She crept from the bed and stole a glance through the neckline of the sleep shirt Tristan had no doubt put her in. She giggled at the panties he'd chosen—the sparkling black pair, the color that matched his wings. Staking his claim in his choice of her undergarments.

He didn't stir as she approached and stripped off her night-shirt, standing before him utterly naked except for the panties. She took a quiet moment to drink him in. This male that had somehow become more essential to her survival than food, water, breathing.

Her home across infinite worlds.

She straddled his lap and brushed his hair from his forehead.

As his eyelids fluttered open, the haze of sleep fell from his toasted honey eyes and his pupils dilated. "What are you—"

She stopped his words with her lips, kissing him deeply as she wrapped her arms around his powerful shoulders. She pushed her bare breasts against his chest, dragging her tight nipples along his flesh. Zaps of electricity zinged through her, settling between her thighs.

"Am I dreaming?" he murmured, coasting his hands down her back and massaging the swells of her ass as he rocked her hips against his growing hardness.

She poked her tongue at his lips and he opened for her, allowing her to lick his teeth, his tongue, the roof of his mouth. She wanted to crawl inside of him and never come back out.

"I want you, Tristan," she breathed. "Not for distraction." She kissed his neck. "Not for duty." Ran her tongue along his jaw, relishing his tortured, rumbling groan. "Not as a ruse." Nipped at his bottom lip. "Just *you*."

"Now I *know* I'm dreaming," he shuddered, leaning in to press tender kisses to her chin, her throat, the swell of her breast. He swirled his tongue around an aching nipple and she moaned, wet heat slicking her panties.

"I'm ready," she whispered. "*Please.*" She ground herself along his rock-hard erection, the friction of the fabric torture against her increasingly sensitive flesh.

"I love it when you beg, Daredevil," he said, thrusting up against her and rocking her with a shockwave of need so sharp that she whimpered. She tore at her panties, needing them gone, needing him inside of her this very second before she burst into flames and burned herself out of existence.

He wrapped a hand around her wrists and held them behind her back, forcing her to arch her breasts towards his awaiting mouth.

"I put those on, I'll take them off," he said before dragging his tongue along the underside of her breast and tucking his fingers into her panties, caressing her weeping entrance.

She angled her hips, trying to drive his fingertips inside of her, but he tightened his grip on her wrists and pulled her back. A frustrated whine escaped her lips.

"So impatient," he snickered, grabbing her ribs and tossing her onto the bed.

He rose from the chair, his cock tenting his loose black pants, his exquisite wings a glimmering wall behind him.

A wild, powerful beast poised to conquer his prey.

She propped herself on her elbows, panting with overwhelming desire as she ogled his sculpted chest and arms, all those smooth, sleek, golden-brown muscles. All for her.

He hooked two fingers into her panties, then dragged them off slowly and tossed them over his shoulder. Placing his strong hands on the insides of her thighs, he spread her open, baring her sex.

"Stay open for me," he commanded as he pushed his pants down and his cock sprang free. She writhed against the cool, crisp sheets, mad with anticipatory pleasure as he stroked himself hard and slow. He trailed his other hand along her inner thighs, passing over her center in tauntingly short swipes.

She laid back, basking in his ministrations and the glorious sight of his hand moving over his proud length. Their eyes met as he dipped a single finger inside of her and she pulsed around him, crying out in a keening wail. This was sheer torture. But she trusted him to reward her for her patience.

He teased his thumb along her clit as he pumped his finger into her, and she felt her orgasm building faster than ever before.

She was seconds away from coming when he pulled his hand away. That wicked thing deep inside of her clawed its way to the surface, as it often did whenever he was around. And it did not appreciate being denied.

He ignored her answering snarl, throwing his head back in a low, dark laugh, his wings shivering.

His heated gaze caressed her naked body, his lips parted and sharp canines gleaming. "You want my fingers or my tongue first?"

"Both."

"Ravenous, exquisite little human," he chuckled, squeezing his cock.

"*Tristan,*" she nearly screamed.

He laid back on his wings on the bed and tugged at her arm, guiding her to hover over his face.

Her eyes went wide as she stared down at him, his silky feathers tickling her knees.

Curving his hands around her ass, he pulled her down and a strangled moan forced her head back at the deliciously soft glide of his wet tongue against her swollen flesh.

He pushed two long, dexterous fingers inside her while flicking and sucking her sensitized clit, and she clenched around him as that glorious tension built again.

Abandoning any self-consciousness, she rode his face, drowning in the heady sensations of his warm mouth, his skilled fingers, his sexy grunts of appreciation rumbling up through her. She trailed her hands up her body to cup her breasts, pinch her nipples, and he pulled his mouth away to admire the view.

"Holy High Gods," he groaned, splaying a hand across her stomach. "You look so fucking gorgeous when you're about to come."

He licked her again, pumping his hand between her legs, and her entire body bunched in on itself, then pushed out in a glorious, thigh-shaking explosion.

She crashed down onto him, panting, each breath crushing her breasts against his chest. He nuzzled her neck and wrapped his arms around her, his hips gently rocking his cock against her thigh and slicking it with moisture.

He ran his fingers through her hair, rubbing at her scalp as she traced her fingertips along his collarbone. "I intend to make that happen many, *many* more times tonight. Think you can handle it?"

She'd never wanted to be ruined so badly. Wanted him to turn her into a mindless, senseless pile of quivering flesh and bones. Wanted to know nothing except his taste, his touch, his body. She was done worrying about the consequences. Well, except for one.

"Wait," she pressed a hand against his chest. "I'm not... I've never... I'm not taking anything to prevent pregnancy."

He tucked a strand of hair behind her ear, his palm lingering on her cheek. "I'm under an infertility spell. Stipulation of my exile."

She exhaled a relieved breath, even as her heart clenched for everything his brother, his family, had taken from him. Though he didn't look the least bit upset about it at the moment.

"Okay," she breathed. "Destroy me."

He flipped her onto her back, then knelt before her and draped her legs around his waist.

"Never," he whispered as he pushed into her, resting in her shallows, giving her body time to adjust to the sheer size of him.

He slid in agonizingly slowly, then retreated, filling her up in increments. His eyes glistened with something akin to worship. He was shaking, holding his breath, restraining himself from the frenzy she could tell he so desperately wanted to unleash.

His tenderness tore through her, ripping apart her insides more forcefully than his brutality ever could.

He reached a point where she wasn't sure he could go any further, his progress halted by some barrier inside of her. She felt a tiny pinch and held her breath.

He leaned down, his wings rising behind him, and pressed his glorious weight on top of her. He cupped his hands against the crown of her head, tangling his fingers in her hair.

"*Fuck*, you feel incredible," he breathed against her mouth. "You have no idea how long I've wanted you like this." He gazed into her eyes. "Are you okay?"

She nodded, and bit his lower lip. Permission. His magic sparkled through her veins, stealing the pain as he thrust forward and seated himself fully.

Then began to move.

Every part of her narrowed to the place between her thighs where they were joined and a sense of fullness, a completeness she'd never known, consumed her. As if a missing piece of her soul suddenly sighed into place.

She wrapped her legs around his waist, resting her ankles on the backs of his hard thighs, feeling as though she were dying and being reborn with each one of his powerful thrusts.

Her inner muscles quaked, pulling him in further with every rock of his hips, and delicious warmth spread from her core, radiating out along her limbs. She cupped his cheeks and stared into his beautiful face as his breathy grunts pulsed against her lips. He pushed, and pushed, and pushed, hitting that magical spot inside of her that had her opening wider for him.

She glanced down between their bodies, nearly climaxing at the sight of his glistening cock plunging into her, pillaging her, stealing that last shred of her interminable innocence.

But it was no theft.

It was a gift.

One she'd ached to give him since the moment they'd met.

Another climax built, her body coasting along tiny waves of tension that crested and crashed, tumbling her towards euphoria.

"*Oh High Gods,*" she moaned, and he sat back, kneeling between her thighs again. He gripped her hip with one hand as he pulled out, then eased back in slowly, setting a languid pace and gently circling his thumb against her clit.

"I can't..." she croaked. "I need..."

"What do you need?" he crooned, continuing his feathery assault on her taut bundle of nerves as he dragged his cock in and out of her slowly. Too slowly. "Tell me. I want to hear you say it."

The words ripped out of her, clawing past her shredded throat.

Raw and rough and *real.*

"*Fucking harder, Tristan.*"

She didn't need to ask him twice. He pounded into her, gripping her hips with both hands, his fingers digging into the soft curves of her ass. Glorious gusts of his wind licked across her clit.

Her second climax obliterated her.

She became a bucking, writhing mass of need, sucking in his thrusts and screaming so loudly that Tristan covered her mouth.

"Shhhhh." He chuckled softly. "Hella's still here."

Her mind returned to her body, her limbs loose and floaty. Something about Hella hearing them, knowing exactly what they were up to, ratcheted Cassandra's desire up another notch and she nipped at his fingers as he pulled his hand away.

"I don't fucking care," she ground out, needing *more* of him. Needing to annihilate him as deliciously as he'd just annihilated her.

"Where did that filthy mouth come from, Daredevil?" he smirked, pulling her up from the bed and settling her into his lap.

She straddled him, angling herself on top of his engorged head and placing her hands on his shoulders, his feathers kissing her knuckles.

As she lowered down, he slid into her with ease, sinking deeper than she'd ever thought possible.

He groaned as she rode him, pushing her down onto his cock with one hand as he cupped her neck with the other. She dragged her teeth along his hammering pulse and his head kicked back with a strangled growl.

"You're killing me," she moaned. "I could die from this. From wanting you."

His gaze returned to hers and they fell into each other, the room silent save for their ragged breaths and the juicy, sucking sounds of their joining.

"Then we'll die together."

Tristan was in ecstasy.

And agony.

He'd been holding back, didn't want to hurt her. Didn't want to scare her away with the full, consuming, brutal force of his need for her.

But his Daredevil had always defied his expectations.

And if anything, this first world-shattering connection between them had proved that the force of her own need was just as strong as his.

She was still moving on him, grinding her sweet little ass against his balls. Her rosy nipples dragged across his chest, and her trembling sighs coasted over his overly sensitive skin.

And the feel of her tight, wet, warmth wrapped around his cock?

Amatu fucking *spare* him.

Her walls rippled and shuddered around him with every stroke, fraying the ever-weakening threads of his self-control.

The beast within him, his baser Fae nature, began snarling a mantra. Louder and louder with every plunge, matching the drumbeat of his savage heart.

Claim.

Claim.

*Claim.*

He gripped her hips, stilling her, and she whimpered. Insatiable little thing.

He pulled out, his cock hovering at her slippery apex, and held her neck. Her wide eyes glowed bright with lust and affection.

"I'm yours, Tristan," she whispered, blowing his mind apart and tearing a hole straight through his chest. "For as little or as long as you want me. I'm *yours*."

He wanted to promise her forever, though he knew it was reckless. Her forever would be much shorter than his.

But she'd turned him into a greedy bastard.

He'd take all of her forever, could no longer deny himself. And when she was gone from this world, her brittle, mortal body mere dust upon the soil, he'd belong to her still.

"For eternity." He pushed up with a mighty, powerful thrust, wringing a pleasure-soaked scream from her gorgeous lips.

He cradled her against his chest, baring his teeth against the soft mound of skin where her shoulder met her neck.

And as he drove into her, relishing the sensation of her shuddering around his cock as he wrested yet another climax from her perfect, pliable body, he sunk his teeth in.

Deep.

Hard enough to break skin.

Marking her.

Her blood, light and sweet and earthy with that honey and rosewood taste that was pure Cassandra, flowed into his mouth.

He erupted, slamming into her. Emptying every piece of his tarnished existence into her.

As he came down from the high, descended back into himself through space and time, he lapped at the blood spilling down her neck and coating her heaving breasts.

"I'm yours too, Cassandra," he whispered, pushing her silky hair off her face. "I've been yours since the moment I forgot you."

She opened her mouth to respond but he stopped her with a soft kiss.

The mark he'd just placed upon her was a promise. A warning to other Fae to stay away. And a danger to them both.

He didn't care. He'd never fucking cared. And he'd do everything in his power to make sure she didn't suffer the consequences of his selfishness.

He crashed back onto his wings, draping her along his body as he pulled out, their combined releases oozing down his thigh.

He rubbed her back, her scalp, as she panted against his chest, tickling him with her slowing breaths.

"That was fucking amazing," she sighed.

He laughed. "I don't know if I can handle your scandalous new mouth."

"Imagine how shocked Xenia will be," she chuckled before her voice faded to a whisper. "I miss her so much."

He hated the pain and longing in those words. "She and Cael are on the outskirts of Rhamnos. He sent me a windwhisper earlier this evening. They'll be back in the colonies in a few days."

She flew upright, robbing him of her soft warmth, and he reached for her, but she batted his hands away.

"Why didn't you tell me?"

He bit his lip, both to stifle his laughter and to distract from the urge to bury himself back inside her, insanely aroused by the sight of her fire. "I was planning to, but got a bit distracted by you riding my co—"

"Bastard," she huffed, smacking his chest. He snatched her hand and kissed her fingertips. "A few days!" Her eyes sparkled with relieved joy and she leapt back into his lap, pressing sloppy kisses all over his face and neck.

And he wished to have good news to share with her every second of every day, if only to inspire such a reaction.

She nestled down onto him, laying her head against his chest once more and trailing light fingers along his jaw—a lover's intimate touch. His feathers rattled at the contact and she snorted a laugh. "Have I found your spot?"

"You've found *all* my spots, beautiful." He noticed her new ink for the first time. "You got your cover-up." He pulled her wrist towards his face, admiring the artistry of the Typhon steel dagger. The tip of the patterned blade kissed the dip at the base of her palm.

"Blade up, fear down," she said with a wink.

"Murderous." He ran his tongue along the tattoo, loving the quiver of pleasure that cascaded through her body.

She rubbed at the wound on her upper shoulder, already closed thanks to the blood he'd been sharing with her. "You marked me."

He sat upright, scooting back and pressing his wings against the headboard, and Cassandra straddled him, wrapping her folded legs around his hips.

He cupped her cheeks, drowning in her inquisitive gaze as fear prickled down his spine. He struggled to find words to express what had happened to him in that moment. "I just… being inside you was… it felt too good. And when you said you were mine, I had this overwhelming urge to… Should I not have?"

She captured his lips, scattering his worries, then shifted in his lap. She was still completely naked. And very wet. His cock thickened, begging for round two.

"I'm honored to bear your mark, Tristan," she said. Her smoky eyes blazed so fiercely that the beast inside of him released a victorious howl.

"You're going to need to hide it, *ma'anyu*," he admitted.

"*Ma'anyu*," she pondered, her eyebrows furrowed. "That's what Hector called his consort."

"It's what marked partners call each other," he said, running his thumb along the mark. "It means *unbreakable* in Aramaelish."

"That's very beautiful," she whispered, rubbing her cheek along his hand.

"The mark means far more than the mingling of our scents. If anyone were to see it—"

She kissed him, then shrugged. "I'm used to wearing high necklines."

He chuckled at her irreverence, remembering the high-necked robes she'd worn as a Shrouded Sister. "And I've just conveniently guaranteed that I'm the only one who'll be allowed to see you naked."

"All my other Fae lovers will be terribly disappointed," she pouted.

He flipped her back onto the bed, settling himself between her soft thighs.

He gripped her chin and thrust his tongue into her mouth. Giving her a taste of what was to come. "Don't test me, Cass," he growled, inching into her.

She moaned, a sound he'd never tire of hearing, then encircled him in her arms, stroking his feathers as she angled her hips, taking him deeper.

"I kinda like you all growly and possessive," she giggled. "*Ma'anyu.*" He thrust into her again. Hard. She cried out, giggles abruptly severed.

"Only for you," he whispered, kissing his mark and relishing the shiver that coursed through her body the moment his lips made contact.

He lost track of how many times he took her that night.

How many times he thought those three little words, terrified to say them despite how deeply he felt them.

The last time he'd uttered them, his world had blown apart. He didn't want to tempt fate.

But a part of him, the part connected to her via the blood they'd shared, could've sworn he heard her saying them back.

# CHAPTER FORTY

"HELLA, THERE'S NO WAY I can eat all this."

An elaborate array of breakfast foods spread out before Cassandra: plump sausages, crispy bacon, cured meats and cheeses, a bowl of plump grapes, and a steaming heap of cinnamon buns dripping with white icing.

Hella approached the bungalow's dining table, beams of sunlight caressing her crimson feathers, and set down yet another dish—brown toast squares piled with scrambled eggs, each topped with a peach-colored slice of smoked fish.

"Eat what can," Hella ordered, untying her apron and taking a seat. "Need energy, tiny human. You had dramatic few days."

Cassandra wondered which activities had inspired Hella to serve her such a replenishing meal: the draining, disastrous attempt at her mother's restoration or the very loud exertions that had occurred in Tristan's bedroom last night?

Cassandra yawned. "I'm fine, really Hella. All things considered, I feel pretty incredible this morning. Tristan took good care of me."

As if saying his name had summoned him, Tristan shuffled into the kitchen with sleep-mussed hair and a lazy grin, rubbing at his bare chest. The sight of his hip-baring pants made Cassandra instantly ravenous. And not for the spread laid out before her.

She tugged at the collar of her sleep shirt, ensuring his mark was covered. Not that she worried about Hella ratting them out, but better not take any chances.

"Oh, I took care of her all right," Tristan crooned as he stepped into the kitchen and filled a mug with coffee before joining the two females at the dining table. "Cass and I fucked like bunnies last night."

Hella hooted a laugh, slapping Cassandra on the shoulder and nearly knocking her face into the cinnamon buns. Then Hella's eyebrows knit together. "I not understand saying, fuck like bunnies. Bunnies fuck fast. Is bad thing. Why want fuck like bunny?"

Tristan blew a tendril of steam from his coffee before taking a thoughtful sip. "Good point, Hella. Never thought about it that way. What creature in the animal kingdom fucks the longest and leaves its partner the most satisfied? That's what we fucked like."

Cassandra groaned, placing her face in her hands. "It's far too early and I haven't had nearly enough coffee for this conversation."

Tristan shot to his feet, then dashed to the kitchen to grab her a cup of the life-giving liquid.

He clunked a piping mug before her, along with a small carafe of cream and a ceramic cup filled with sugar. He pressed a kiss to her cheek before retaking his seat, then settled his warm hand on her bare thigh. Sipping his coffee, he stroked her leg, trailing his fingers under her shorts.

Her body tingled as she prepared her own coffee, fighting the urge to tell Hella to bugger off so she could tackle Tristan to the floor for round five? Six?

"What plan tonight?" Hella asked, grabbing a bun and shoving the entire thing in her mouth. She licked the sticky icing from her thick fingers.

"You and Cass will head to August Lambros's house while I have my meeting with Ronin at the Serpent's Den," Tristan answered, plucking up a glistening, fatty strip of meat. He dangled it above his face before lowering it into his open mouth. "By the end of the night we should finally have some answers about the Teles Chrysos, and hopefully a name to give to my brother."

Cassandra picked up a bunch of grapes and popped them in her mouth one by one. An itch suddenly flared to life between her shoulder blades. She squirmed, unable to reach it, subtly scratching her back against her chair.

"What will you be doing for the rest of the day?" she asked Tristan.

He squeezed her thigh. "As much as I would love to spend it with you, I have more meetings to attend at the Secretariat. There was another attack in August's district yesterday, this one on the offices of a prominent Fae trade organization. He's fuming. Forced the Vicereine to call a special session to deal with it."

Cassandra perked up. "You're not going to reveal the name of the organization, are you?"

"Not yet," Tristan said. "We'll see how the meeting goes. I don't want to scare off Ronin, cause him to rescind my invite to the pleasure house tonight."

She smacked his chest. "You'd better behave yourself, Birdman. No sampling the merchandise while you're there."

Tristan grabbed her hand, tracing the letter M across her palm.

*Ma'anyu.*

Cassandra's insides glowed at the secret message.

"You wound me, Cass. When have I ever taken advantage of such a situation?"

Cassandra snorted a laugh, then leaned over to whisper in his ear. "I'll be your reward at home later."

"Proper motivation," he murmured, before gripping her chin and leaning in for a kiss. He pushed his tongue into her mouth, overwhelming her senses with the tastes of coffee and cured meat.

Her back tingled again, and his magic stirred through her veins, settling in her chest.

"I leave you two," Hella piped up, rising from her seat.

Tristan broke their kiss, leaving Cassandra aching for more despite the slight soreness between her legs.

He stood, shaking Hella's hand across the table. "Thank you, Hella. For watching over her and keeping her safe this week."

Hella waved him off. "Is no trouble. I pack things and head back to barracks. We meet later, yes?"

"See you then," Cassandra nodded as Hella left the kitchen and clomped up the stairs.

As soon as she was gone, Tristan grabbed Cassandra by the waist and hoisted her onto the table. He carelessly pushed plates of food away, spilling the remnants of breakfast.

"One more time," he begged, pushing his hand up under her shirt to caress her breast as he tugged down her shorts and panties. "I'll be quick like a bunny."

She laughed, pulling down his waistband and freeing his cock. She gripped his hard, silken length and settled him between her thighs, then bit her lip to stifle her groan as he sank into her.

"Sweet Amatu, I can't get enough of you," he grunted as he fisted her hair, pulling her head back and exposing her throat to his hungry mouth.

She wrapped her legs around his waist and ran her hands along the shifting muscles of his back as he pushed into her again and again. The breakfast dishes clattered against the table with the force of his thrusts.

"The feeling is most definitely mutual," she gasped as he splayed his broad hand across her lower belly and stroked her tender nub with his thumb.

She ran her fingers along the downy feathers where his wings met his shoulder blades and his thrusts became harder, frenzied. She clamped around him, dazzled by the number of orgasms he'd coaxed from her body over the past few hours.

"Fuck, fuck, *fuck,*" she moaned in a series of breathy hiccups as she toppled over the edge.

Tristan chased behind her with his own shuddering grunt of pleasure, then laughed against her neck. "Filthy mouth."

They stayed like that for a moment, Tristan's head burrowed into her shoulder, his arms braced against the table as she clung to him.

"Nice ass, bunny," Hella sang from the hallway on her way out the door.

"It's the nicest!" Tristan shouted, and Cassandra broke apart into a fit of giggles beneath him.

She wholeheartedly agreed.

# CHAPTER
# FORTY-ONE

"T HAT'S RHAMNOS?"
The pictures didn't do it justice. If this was the cesspool of the continent, Xenia couldn't imagine how grand and beautiful the other cities must be.

The glittering metropolis unfurled before them in strokes of gold and cream, gleaming towers bracketing the Dordenne and kissing the cloudless sky. Flashing glares of midday sun bounced off rows upon rows of windows, bathing the orderly grid of streets below in an otherworldly sheen.

Sandstone bridges lined with ornate pillars crisscrossed the meandering path of the mighty ink-blue river, her waters mingling with the Sea of Thetis in a crescent-shaped bay capped by a massive concrete dock. It speared into the sea like the pointed tip of a fish hook, with cargo ships and smaller vessels cramming both sides.

The gilded port city, capital of the territory of Akti that spanned the continent's southern coast, seemed built for commerce, not corruption. Though Xenia supposed the two often went hand-in-hand.

"Don't let her hide fool you," Cael warned, clomping down the dusty path spilling them from the foothills' dense forest. "The bitch has a wicked bite."

The unremarkable village they'd stayed in last night certainly hadn't prepared Xenia for the city's twinkling opulence. The crumbling inn with its tiny rooms and hearty fare had called to mind several establishments in Thalenn, the only differences being a near absence of humans and a growing concentration of magic. The thrumming buzz had zapped at Xenia's skin, heightened by the drops of Cael's own magic pulsing through her veins.

They'd wolfed down their dinner—seafood stew in a peppery red broth so deliciously spicy that Xenia ordered seconds—then gotten a few fitful hours of sleep in separate beds. They hadn't spoken a word about Xenia taking Cael's blood, nor the aftermath.

That *kiss*.

In the moment, she'd expected the toe-curling encounter to alter the fabric of their relationship. And was half-disappointed to find the seams stubbornly intact, not a frayed string or dropped stitch in sight.

Cael hadn't even probed about her confession that he wasn't her first kiss, that secret she'd been guarding for years. She'd never told a soul, not even Cass.

Xenia was only mildly bothered by their communication's giant leap backwards, her bone-weary exhaustion overriding any discomfort she might've felt around him.

The path they now walked ran parallel to a smooth, double-lane roadway, and curvy vehicles in an eclectic rainbow of colors zoomed past them, rushing into and out of the city. So different from the lumbering, boxy vehicles in the colonies.

Windriders zipped overhead, speedier than the vehicles, and a few Beastrunners in their mammal forms—horses, camels, lions, a zebra, even an elephant—ambled along the path. Other than a few wary side-eyes, no one spared Cael and Xenia a second glance.

She tugged at the high collar of the formless, sky-blue dress Cael had purchased for her yesterday, baking in the heat but grateful for the long sleeves that hid her arms from the blistering sun.

"You remember our story?" Cael asked, his boots kicking up clouds of dust that clung to his leather pants.

"We came up with it last night," Xenia scoffed. "You think I would've forgotten already?"

"Indulge me."

Xenia sighed, then recited the story they'd invented together. "I've been purchased by a family in Akti to serve as a housemaid. They hired you to escort me to protect their investment. You lost your wing to a band of traffickers that attempted to steal me."

"Good. The fewer details, the better. And keep your tattoo covered."

"I *know*," she seethed. "It's almost fully faded anyway."

"Rhamnos is crowded, but you *will* draw attention. The only humans who pass through these streets are legally purchased workers or those being sold off for much more nefarious purposes."

"Didn't the Accords make trafficking humans illegal?"

Cael shook his head, a bitter laugh piercing his lips. "The traffickers pay a cut to the Empire to look the other way."

"Of course they do," she murmured.

"We only need to stay out of trouble long enough for me to make contact with Ohan Stolia. He's a yak biform from Brachos, an old acquaintance of my father's. He owns one of Ethyrios's largest shipping companies. He'll be able to arrange safe passage for you back to the colonies."

"And what if…what if I don't want to go back?"

"Zee," he said, his tone softening. "You can't stay here. If what my father said is true, war is about to erupt across the continent. I won't be able to protect you."

"What will *you* do?" Xenia asked, her eyes glued to the dirt path, her heart lodged in her throat.

"I already told you. I'm going back home to Brachos. My duty is to my father now. To our allies and business partners. He's…he's arranged a match for me."

A riotous storm brewed in Xenia's stomach at the mention of war. And at the thought of Cael marrying someone else. "Is that what you want?"

"What I want doesn't matter anymore," he said, hanging his head and kicking at the rocks littering the path. "It's what he's always wanted for me. Fought me tooth and nail when I told him I wanted to be a Vasilikan. I'm lucky he even allowed me go to the colonies and prove myself as a Vestian. He was sure I'd either grow tired of it or fail. He was right."

"Cael, you haven't…" She was too exhausted to argue with him.

They walked in silence for the next twenty minutes as Rhamnos's gleaming skyscrapers gobbled up the view.

Xenia craned her head, gawking like a tourist. She'd never in her life seen buildings this tall. Her head spun with vertigo as she imagined what it would be like to stand at the top of one. Wondered how far she'd be able to see from up there.

All the way to the colonies?

All the way to Cass?

As they crossed into the city, the cracks in Rhamnos's lustrous facade began to show: fissures in the sidewalks, broken windows, alleys filled with piles of garbage and rotten smells.

The streets teemed with Fae, many well-dressed in sleek, boldly-colored fashions that had not yet trended to the colonies and likely never would—the fabrics were far too expensive.

But there were plenty of others donning tattered rags and weary faces, shuffling through the streets and begging for spare *drachas*. Wings of every color on the spectrum brushed past her and she cringed every time she saw the serpentine eyes of a Deathstalker. Many Beastrunners remained half-shifted, with claws, tails, horns and fangs on proud display. So different from the bi-forms in the colonies who preferred to blend in with the humans.

That thrumming, suffocating energy, the concentrated magic of so many Fae crammed together, pressed against her skin, making her feel keyed up and jittery. Like a spark hissing at the end of a very short fuse. She didn't know how long she could endure the feeling, certain it would drive her mad.

They approached the corner of an intersection of two bustling avenues. A group of Fae gathered around a Deathstalker standing atop a wooden box.

"Open your eyes!" The Deathstalker's amplified voice washed over the half-skeptical, half-curious crowd through a cone-shaped device. There was an odd symbol painted onto the back of his white trenchcoat—a circle slashed through with a line. "The evidence of her influence is all around us. She is coming to deliver us from the shackles of the Empire. Join the movement while you can." Snickers erupted from the gathered

Fae. "Before you will be forced to choose. Before the cleansing chaos restores our world's balance."

The Deathstalker raised his hand and a flame burst to life in his open palm. Half the crowd gasped and turned away from the spectacle, while the remaining onlookers surged towards the male, volleying questions about the appearance of the long-dead fire magic.

Xenia paused, transfixed.

The whine of a stun pistol cut through the din and a line of Empire soldiers in red jackets and golden helmets ringed the crowd. The lingering gawkers scattered, but the Deathstalker remained, eying the soldiers with mad, placid defiance.

"Show's over, everyone! Move along," one of the soldiers shouted before two others grabbed the Deathstalker and began hauling him away.

"You're too late." The Deathstalker hissed a laugh. "She will not be so easily overtaken this time."

"Yeah, yeah," the head soldier said. "That's what your crackpot friends keep telling us. You can discuss it over tea from a cell in Tartarus."

As the soldiers dragged the Deathstalker down the teeming avenue, one turned back and his eyes flew right to Xenia. "Hey," he began, taking a step towards her.

Panic seized Xenia's lungs as she barreled away from the soldier, pushing through the press of supernatural bodies, wondering where in the name of Stygios Cael had disappeared to.

She careened around a corner and crashed into a tall Beastrunner with ruddy skin and closely-cropped platinum hair.

"Hey, watch it," the sleek-suited male snarled, tapping at the commstone beneath his left ear. His annoyance melted into a lascivious grin as his eyes trailed down Xenia's body.

"Hang on a minute," the male said, pressing the violet-colored stone again. "What do we have here? A tasty, frightened little human? Must be my lucky day."

He yanked Xenia into a shadowy alley, then shoved her against a wall, caging her between his arms.

"Give us a sample, love, yeah?" His nose and jaw elongated into a fox's muzzle with razor sharp teeth beneath glowing amber eyes. Whiskers tickled Xenia's cheeks as he sucked down gulping breaths, heightening her fear.

Tortured screams overtook her mind and uncontrollable tremors wracked her body. She'd never been fed from before, didn't know how to make him stop. She was paralyzed, shouting internally at her legs, her mouth to *move*. A futile effort, as tortuous as trying to wake from a nightmare.

A booming voice echoed from the alley's entrance.

"Let her *go*."

The Beastrunner whipped his head over his shoulder as Cael stalked into the shadows, blasting wind into the fox bi-form's chest that caused him to stagger back.

The fear leaked from Xenia's limbs, and she rushed to Cael, who clapped a possessive arm around her shoulder.

The Beastrunner's muzzle shortened as he chuckled, straightening the black lapels of his suit jacket. "No offense intended. Didn't realize she already had a master. How much you want for her?"

"She's not for sale," Cael growled, placing Xenia in front of him and wrapping his arms around her waist, stealing her breath.

The Beastrunner cocked his head. "I'm sure I can make it very worth your while, mate. I've got a client up in the Northern Territories who's been begging me to procure him a pretty little blonde pet. How does two-hundred and fifty thousand sound?"

Xenia blanched at the astronomic sum.

"Not even close," Cael scoffed, his breath tickling the back of her neck. "Her new owner has already paid double that. Fuck off."

The Beastrunner sniffed, then reached into his pocket and passed Cael a small black card. "Call me if you change your mind. Or if you come across any other delicious specimens like this one. Blondes are so rare, my clients are willing to pay a premium."

Cael didn't bother answering as he dragged Xenia out of the alley and down the sidewalk.

They were propositioned four more times on the way to their hotel.

The cesspool of the continent, indeed.

# CHAPTER FORTY-TWO

XENIA WRAPPED HERSELF IN a fluffy, white towel as she stepped out of the enormous marble shower.

After days of barely washing at all, and with water only, it was bliss to scrub away both the grime and her lingering nerves from the harrowing encounters on the streets. And the toiletries provided in this fancy hotel smelled wonderful—a sweet, citrusy mix with hints of lemon and verbena.

Seems Rhamnos did indeed have a few bastions of luxury.

She didn't have any sleep clothes, but had found a plush robe and pair of slippers tucked away in a closet.

She slipped into both before brushing her teeth at the sink.

Nighttime ablutions finished, she opened the door to their suite, a luxurious room decorated in pale tones of daffodil and lavender. The steam from her blessedly hot shower snaked out behind her.

The flickering glow of neon signs seeped through the wall of windows, blanketing the space with manufactured brightness despite the late hour.

Cael lounged on his bed, his damp waves curling across his forehead.

Xenia indulged herself while he wasn't looking, let her gaze linger on the thigh-clenching sight of him sprawled atop the covers in nothing but his tight black underwear.

He stared up at the ceiling with his hands tucked behind his head, his lone wing draped beside him and his brow scrunched as he chewed the inside of his cheek. Completely unaware of Xenia's gawking.

She crossed to her own bed, a spacious double with a pile of pillows and thick, puffy linens. She did an awkward little dance, attempting to pull on her underwear without throwing open her robe and exposing her intimate bits to Cael. Once completed, she tucked herself under the covers, shucked off the robe, and tossed it to the floor.

She laid her head upon a decadently squishy pillow, feeling safe and relaxed for the first time in weeks. This far above the city streets, the press of the continent's magic wasn't as jarring, and had faded to the occasional faint tickle. She turned to face Cael, his arresting profile limned in the sleepless city's harsh light.

"Didn't think you were ever going to come out," he said.

"I almost didn't," she responded.

He sighed, flopping onto his side and tucking a hand under his cheek. His thundercloud eyes pinned her in place. "We'll meet with Stolia tomorrow morning, down on the dock. One of his ships leaves for the colonies at dawn."

A caustic rush of adrenaline scorched through her veins at the thought of leaving him.

"Do you trust him?" Xenia asked. The only safe question. She bit back the thousand others perched on the tip of her tongue.

"I would *never* risk your safety, Xenia," he said, blinking slowly. "At least, not more than I already have."

"How many times do I have to tell you that it wasn't your fault? Anyway, I'm the one coming out of this scenario unharmed. The High Gods have already exacted their price from you."

He didn't scoff or thin his lips or turn away—a small bit of progress. So she pressed onward.

"You *flew*, Cael. When you were fighting that monster. It may not have been the most graceful flight, but you managed it. Surely that's got to count for something?"

He shrugged, rubbing at his cheek. "I guess. But I'm not sure I could do it again if I tried. I was completely focused on getting you out of harm's way. Every other thought left my mind."

His words sparked warm tingles throughout her body. Thank Amatu they'd gotten a room with separate beds.

Or curse Amatu?

Xenia's feelings towards Cael were so conflicted, she didn't know how to react. But she embraced the confusion. Fighting it would only make it worse.

"Didn't the Vestians teach you warriors any meditation techniques? Battle preparations? That kind of thing?" she asked.

"They tried, but I've never been capable of it. My mind has two modes: constant assessment of every surrounding piece of sensory information or deep, dark pit of numbness. When that happens, I'm lucky if I can get out of bed in the morning."

"Too bad you're not coming back to the colonies. Cass is a master at battle meditation. She might be able to teach you a thing or two."

"I have no doubt she could." He stared at Xenia from across the short yet seemingly insurmountable expanse between their beds, his eyes churning. Like he wanted to say something else, but was hesitant to spit it out.

She didn't know where this shy, vulnerable Cael had come from. But wished he'd show up more often.

"Xenia, I...I'm sorry for kissing you at the oasis. It was...I never should've taken advantage of you like that."

His apology landed like a fist to her gut, and she choked back the hurt and shock. Taken *advantage* of her? She'd practically begged him to kiss her.

"I was overcome after I gave you my blood," he continued, slicing the palpitating organ in her chest to ribbons. "It never would've happened if I'd been in my right state of mind."

Something about the cadence of his voice, the way he wouldn't, or couldn't, meet her eyes hinted his words were far from the truth. But it didn't make her feel any less skewered.

If this is what he wanted, then fine. She'd play his game. A lie for a lie.

"Don't worry about it," she said, pulling the covers around her tighter and covering her naked shoulders. She didn't want to expose any more of herself than she already had.

"I was feeling the effects too." Lie.

"I never would've asked you to do it otherwise." Lie.

"Probably best if it never happens again." Huge lie.

She could've sworn a flash of disappointment skittered across his face as he turned away from her, his gaze cemented to the ceiling once again.

"So you gonna tell me the full story of how in Ethyrios that *wasn't* a Shrouded Sister's first kiss?" he asked, his lips curving to expose a pointed canine.

"Only if you agree to tell me one of your own secrets after," Xenia smirked.

"Deal," he said. "Spill it, Blondie."

Xenia shuddered a shallow breath, then pivoted onto her back, unable to look at him as she confessed her deepest, most shameful secret.

"He was a scholar from the university in Delos," she began. "Beastrunner. A stallion bi-form from the steppes surrounding the capital."

"So I wasn't even your first *Fae* kiss?" Cael mock-whined. "I don't know if my ego can handle this story."

She laughed softly, then continued. "He'd come to the Temple library to research some of the older texts. He was studying the ancient human and Fae civilizations of Ethyrios, cataloging the first interactions between the two species. Trying to determine if any cross-breeding had occurred during those early days."

"When was this?"

"A little over two years ago," Xenia said. "I'd see him in the reading hall, bent over his books every afternoon. His eyes were constantly darting towards me while I was curled up in an armchair with one of my romantic adventure stories. My choice of reading material likely inspired me to assign far too much weight to his glances."

Xenia had long ago made peace with herself over her fling with Jaz, the scholar. But that didn't make recounting it any less painful. Didn't make her feel any less foolish.

"One day, he mustered the courage to approach me. Made some ridiculous claim about needing a human's perspective on the passage he was studying.

I was terribly flattered, of course. Played right into his hand."

Xenia dared a glance at Cael. His features were tight, unreadable, his sensuous lips pulled down at the corners. A few weeks ago, she would have dismissed it as his resting face. But she'd studied him enough by now to know there was more behind it. Jealousy, perhaps? She didn't dare hope.

"He lured me between the stacks. To *look for more source material*, he claimed. But the instant we were alone together, he plied me with compliments. Told me how beautiful I was, how he'd been watching me for days, how he couldn't stop thinking about me each night when he left the library."

Xenia still vividly recalled how she'd felt in those stolen moments: exhilarated and terrified. Not only by Jaz's words, but by the thought of getting caught. Cass had been a year into her robberies by that point, and Xenia was envious of her friend's rebellions. Pining for a bit of danger and intrigue to pierce the veil of her own mundane existence. Jaz had come along at the perfect time.

"We spent an entire week meeting in quiet, dark corners of the library every afternoon after my Temple shifts, each encounter more heated than the one before. I thought…" Xenia paused, ashamed of how naïve she'd been. "I thought he was falling in love with me."

A low grunt escaped Cael's throat, but he kept his eyes aimed upwards.

"He claimed he was desperate for me. That he'd die if he couldn't have me. Told me he'd find a way to take me with him, bring me back to Delos. He had a potion capable of masking his scent so we could take that final step without risking Mother Superior's punishment. He promised to return for me in a month, after he'd made arrangements on the continent. Claimed there was a ball at the university that he wanted me to accompany him to."

Xenia fought the prickling behind her eyes. She'd wasted enough tears on that manipulative scumbag.

"Of course, I gave in. Believed every single one of his seductive lies. The only thing he *wasn't* lying about was the potion. After he had me—a quick, painful coupling against the stacks and not at all the romantic encounter I'd envisioned—Mother Superior never found out. He left for the continent the very next day. And I pranced around the order like a lovestruck fool for an entire month, practicing my dance steps, imagining the beautiful gown I would wear to the ball. I didn't even consider how any of it would be possible. And of course, I never saw him again."

Cael turned towards her, his cloudy gaze swirling with sympathy and rage.

"I wasn't even angry with him after," Xenia said. "I was furious with myself. How could I have been so *stupid?* And the worst part was he nearly ruined that library for me. The one place in the entire world I'd always felt safe and wholly myself. He'd poisoned it along with all the romantic stories I'd cherished."

"But you're not a cynical person, Zee. How'd you move past it?" He asked, a dose of desperation tinting his question. Like he needed the answer as much as he needed air to breathe.

"I realized he was the cynical one. He'd twisted my freely offered love and affection into something tainted and temporary. And that was his problem, not mine. Love isn't a limited resource. There's a boundless capacity for it within us all. Just because someone takes yours and is careless with it doesn't mean you should stop offering."

Cael regarded her as if she were a puzzle he was dying to solve. After several charged seconds, he gently shook his head. "I think you may be the most guileless person I've ever met. Why didn't you ever tell Cassandra?"

"I didn't want her to worry about me. She had enough she was dealing with at the time. Plus I thought she might try to track him down and maim him to defend my honor."

Cael's hearty laugh crinkled the corners of his eyes, lighting up his handsome face.

Xenia wanted to cross the space between their beds, taste his lips again, feel his hands on her body. Chase away the depressing memory of her first, and only, sexual encounter.

His features softened into a thoughtful sincerity. "I'm sorry that happened to you."

"I'm not. What are we but the sum total of our experiences? I like to think it makes me a bit more interesting."

"You were interesting to me before you told that story," he whispered. "And your scholar didn't lie about everything."

"Oh, no?"

"Xenia, you are beautiful. And far from stupid. I want to splinter a few of his limbs for ever making you question that."

Xenia swallowed and held her breath, feeling like she'd burst into tears the second she pulled air back into her lungs. She took a moment to compose herself. "So, that's my one deep, dark secret. You promised me one. Better make it good. Any hidden, long-lost loves tumbling around in that stone heart of yours?"

He chuckled. "Just one," he said, shocking her with his answer. She couldn't imagine this grumpy, closed-off individual capable of the kind of intimacy necessary to form and sustain a love connection. "His name was Killian. We grew up together in Brachos."

Xenia raised her eyebrows, questioning, and Cael responded, "I fall in love with the person. Their parts are irrelevant."

"What happened to him?" she asked.

"Nothing epic or tragic," Cael said, shrugging. "I wanted to come to the colonies and he didn't. End of story."

"But surely that didn't need to be the end of your relationship? You couldn't have visited each other on weekends or something? Made the long-distance thing work?"

Cael snorted. "The Vestians don't work like that. It's a full-time commitment. Doesn't leave much room for romantic entanglements. At least not the long-term kind. And Killian didn't want to wait for me, not that I would've asked him to. I heard he'd married a few decades ago. He and his husband adopted an orphaned pair of Windrider twins. I'm sure he's much happier now than he ever would've been shackled to someone like me."

"What does that mean? Someone like you?"

He turned away from her again, running a hand through his waves. "I have...episodes. That pit of numbness I mentioned earlier? Sometimes it overtakes me and I just disappear for weeks at a time. I have nothing to give myself, let alone a partner. No one needs to be subjected to that."

"How did Killian feel about it?"

"The first few times, he was convinced he could *fix* me. Like if he could just love me harder, the pit would go away and I'd snap out of it. What he never realized is that only made it worse. The guilt I felt for not being able to pull out of it, reward him for his efforts... After a while, he stopped trying. And even though I knew it was easier on him that way, it made me feel even worse. It's part of what destroyed us, in the end. And made my decision to leave for the colonies easier. I used to tell myself that if he truly loved me, he never would've stopped trying. But he was a good person. It wasn't his fault he fell in love with someone irrevocably broken."

Cael laughed bitterly. "And now my outsides match my insides. Very fitting."

"Now who's believing lies about themselves," Xenia countered.

Cael turned his back to her. "Don't waste your good heart on me, Xenia. There's nothing waiting for you here but pain and regret. And I'm not nearly selfish enough to subject you to it."

Xenia opened her mouth to protest, but couldn't think of anything else to say. Nothing that would convince Cael of his own worth. He'd had centuries to reinforce these misguided beliefs about himself. And also happened to be the most stubborn person she'd ever met. What could she do to break through to him?

She mulled it over as she drifted off into a shallow, restless slumber.

# CHAPTER
# FORTY-THREE

S LEEP WAS AN ELUSIVE mistress.

The sheets irritated Cael's scar and the glowing neon lights outside the curtainless windows pulsated behind his eyelids.

He'd spent the last several hours wrestling with what he wanted versus what was right.

A war-torn continent was no place for a human. And even if he were able to sneak Xenia into Brachos, he shivered at the thought of what Arran would do if he found her. If his father ever realized how much she meant to him…

Cael knew Xenia needed to return to the colonies. But being around her, soaking in her positive energy, made him feel better about his own miserable circumstances.

And he couldn't stop thinking about that kiss. He'd told her it was a mistake. Which it probably was.

Still, it haunted him.

The sweetness of her lips, the softness of her body, the urgency in her embrace.

As if she wanted him just as desperately as he wanted her.

How was it possible to be torn apart and put back together in the span of twenty seconds?

Dawn was approaching far too quickly. And with it, their final hours together.

Music began to float into the room—a slow, melancholy melody. A street musician warming up for a day of busking, perhaps.

He flopped onto his side to study the woman in the bed across from him. The hand tucked up under her chin, the wild curls spread across her pillow, the bare shoulder peeking out of her duvet.

Xenia's story about the scholar hadn't necessarily shocked him. What male could resist her? And he knew she shared a streak of rebelliousness with her friend Cassandra, though Xenia's had softer edges.

No, the part of the story he couldn't stomach was that the scholar had stolen something from her. And hadn't exposed himself as a thief until it was too late for

Xenia to protect herself. The bastard hadn't even made it enjoyable for her.

Even if Cael couldn't fix himself, he *could* fix this. Provide her with the pleasure she'd so cruelly been denied.

He wouldn't take her, as much as he longed for it. Especially since they'd be parting ways later this morning. That would make him no better than the scholar.

But he could give her *something* to hold onto.

A memory for them both to hold onto.

Xenia woke to gentle music and her blankets slipping away.

Cael stood at the foot of her bed, sheets clutched in his hands, and sucked in a sharp breath as the fabric slipped below her breasts.

She made no attempt to cover herself as she whispered, "What are you doing?"

"Righting a wrong." He tossed the linens aside, devouring her nearly naked body in his storm-cloud gaze, then held out a hand. "Dance with me."

She pushed upright and took his hand, afraid to ask another question. Convinced her tortured heart would tumble out the moment she opened her mouth.

Cael wrapped an arm around her waist and cradled the back of her head, tucking her against him.

She released a contented sigh at the skin-on-skin contact she'd been craving for so long. She snaked her arms underneath his armpits, clutching his powerful shoulders, and goosebumps pebbled her limbs as her breasts crushed against his hard, naked chest.

He shuddered, dipping his mouth to the base of her neck, and pressed his cool lips to her overheated skin.

The music ebbed and flowed as they swayed together, clinging to each other, both utterly exposed in a mournful goodbye.

As he pulled back to look at her, a lock of hair tumbled down his forehead. He brushed his mouth across hers—a plush, whisper-soft graze.

Her knees buckled and the arm around her lower back tightened, supporting her, as he deepened the kiss and swallowed her answering whimper.

She poured all of her reckless need for him into this last kiss. If this was the final taste she'd be allowed, she intended to take *everything*.

He groaned into her mouth as she stroked her tongue along his, his frenzied hands memorizing her body.

Turning and pushing her against the wall, he gripped her wrists and raised her arms above her head. Radiant heat flooded her veins as he licked her collarbone, kissed down her torso, rolled a tender nipple across his tongue. He nipped at her neck, his breath warm on her throat as he whispered, "Do you touch yourself, Xenia?"

He ground his hips into her aching center, pressing his hardness into her, and she shuddered out her answer. "S-sometimes."

"Show me." He stepped back, then dipped his hand below his waistband, stroking himself under his tight black shorts as his ravenous gaze blazed a trail along her ignited flesh. As if he were starved for her, wanted to devour her whole and suck the juices from her very bones.

She trailed a hand down her body, never tearing her eyes from him, and tucked her fingers into her underwear.

"No. Take off your panties. Let me see you."

His command echoed through her, pulsing a deep throb between her legs. "You first," she begged.

He angled an eyebrow, the side of his lip rising into a crooked smirk as he pushed his shorts down.

All of the air whooshed out of Xenia's lungs as she beheld the most breathtaking cock she'd ever seen. Not that she'd seen many.

But Holy High *Gods*.

It strained towards her, long and thick and heavy and *perfect*. He stroked himself again, squeezing out a glistening bead of moisture that she ached to taste. "Your turn."

Finding her breath again, she lowered her panties to the floor, then stepped out of them and leaned her shoulders back against the cool cloth wallpaper.

His searing gaze followed the finger she traced down her stomach, and his wing shuddered as she dipped into her growing wetness before slowly circling her clit. With her other hand, she cupped and massaged her breast, and a jolt of pleasure-soaked pain shot to her core as she pinched her nipple, imagining her fingers were Cael's fangs.

Fangs that gleamed between his parted lips, his chest heaving. The veins on his muscled forearm bulged as he tugged his cock, and he expelled a whimpered curse as she plunged two fingers inside herself, pressing her clit with the base of her palm and rocking her hips as she chased that delectable friction.

She anchored her hooded gaze to his savage, beautiful face, and the sight of him coming undone as he touched himself, watching her, was enough to bring her to the edge.

It was the hottest fucking thing she'd ever witnessed.

Until he lowered himself to his hands and knees, his wing splayed above him, and *crawled* to her.

She stared down past her breasts as he lifted her leg and arranged it over his shoulder.

"Promise me you'll never settle for less than you deserve again, Xenia."

A breathless whisper sighed out of her as she braced her palms against the wall. "What do I deserve?"

"A male who will worship your body." A long, slow lick up her inner thigh. "A male whose greatest pleasure is delivering yours." A reverent kiss to her glossy, swollen lips.

"A male who would beg to drop to his knees before you."

She could barely speak. "Are you that male?"

"I hope you'll allow me the delusion. Just for tonight." He breathed her in, whispering against her quivering sex. "I'll never deserve you, Xenia. I'm—"

"If you say what I think you're about to say right now, Cael, I swear to fucking Amatu, I will smother you between my thighs."

His low, dark chuckle tickled her inner walls. "A death I'd gladly welcome."

Bracing her thigh open, he licked straight up her center and she screamed, clutching his hair and knocking her head against the wall.

He fucked her with his tongue, slowly, ardently, and she rocked her hips against his face, that coiling tension rising again.

His thrusts matched the rhythm of the hand at his waist, and she clenched around his invading tongue, imagining he was filling her with that gorgeous, enormous cock. An appreciative rumble buzzed her sensitive flesh.

He replaced his tongue with two fingers, spreading her open, massaging a spot within that had her rising onto her tiptoes. "*Fuck*, Cael."

He sucked her clit into his mouth, steadily flicking the engorged bud as he continued to plunge his fingers into her. Waves of scintillating heat concentrated low in her belly, her thighs trembling.

Cael stroked himself faster, his ragged breaths coating her insides, and the sight and sensations were too much to bear.

"That's it," he sighed against her. "Take your pleasure from me, Xenia. Fucking *own* me."

She gripped his rock-hard shoulder for leverage, undulating her hips to the push of his fingers and rolling her clit against his tongue. "Shit, *I'm coming*."

His steel gray eyes shot to hers as molten streams of ecstasy exploded from her center. Staccato moans pulsed out of her throat as her entire body convulsed, blown apart by the most intense orgasm she'd ever experienced.

Cael's fangs grazed her throbbing lips as he roared his climax up into her, spurting glistening white ropes onto his fist and abdomen.

She slid down the wall, her exhausted, sated muscles no longer capable of holding her upright, and he gathered her into his lap, arranging her legs around him, and buried his face in the crook of her neck.

They held each other for long minutes, fully entwined as their breaths slowed. Content to ignore the fate that stalked them behind the encroaching sunrise.

Xenia snaked her hand up Cael's back towards his scar.

He stiffened, but didn't push her away as she traced her fingers along the puckered skin.

"You're not broken, Cael," she whispered.

He pulled her closer.

"You make me want to believe it."

# CHAPTER
# FORTY-FOUR

ROOM 702 OCCUPIED HALF of the Serpent's Den's top floor. And it was far larger and more ornate than the room Tristan and Cassandra had visited last month when they'd sought information from Yulia, the courtesan who'd ultimately led them to Cora and Sister Kouris.

An intricately twisted chandelier coiled down from the vaulted ceiling, its flickering candles suffusing the room in an amber glow. Rectangular squares of white trim lined the matte-black walls and fluffy black rugs decorated the marble floor. At the back of the room stood an enormous, circular bed with ivory satin sheets, large enough to accommodate several winged individuals at once. The romantic, elegant space was reserved for the establishment's most important clientèle.

Tristan lounged on a white leather settee across from the bed, sipping at the drink he'd poured himself while waiting for Ronin to finish his...activities.

The Beastrunner sat cross-legged on the bed, leaned over a chessboard across from a pretty, red-headed courtesan who was running a white rook along her strawberry lips.

Elbows propped on his knees, Ronin clasped his hands beneath a scowl. "I think you may have bested me again, Rosana." He slowly moved his queen across the board and even from Tristan's vantage point, he could tell he'd left his king unprotected.

"Checkmate!" Rosana crowed as she moved her own queen into position.

Ronin flopped back onto the bed, flinging an arm over his eyes and groaning. "Third time tonight."

Rosana giggled as she straddled his waist, kicking the board over. The black and white pieces clacked together as they tumbled across the bedspread. "Can I claim my prize now?" she cooed as she rolled her hips.

Ronin squeezed her ass, his massive hand covering an entire cheek as he stilled her. She let out a disappointed whimper. "Not yet, love." His eyes darted to Tristan. "I've got some business to attend to first. Come back in an hour."

She pouted as Ronin lifted her off the bed and ushered her to the door.

"Warm yourself up for me," he winked as he nudged her out of the room, then waltzed over to the credenza to grab a bottle of Delirium. Plopping down on the settee, he clinked his glowing drink against Tristan's glass.

"To the Erabis family," he said, not without a hint of sarcasm. "Long may they reign."

He tipped his head back and drained the contents. The pupil in his single eye dilated and he released a satisfied exhale as the euphoric effects of the drink took hold.

"Respectfully, Matakos," Tristan asked, "what the fuck am I doing here?"

"Please," he set the empty bottle onto a low table with a tinkling thud, "call me Ronin. I'm hoping we'll leave this conversation as friends. Partners, even."

"That entirely depends on what you have to share." Tristan's savage smile exposed his sharp canines.

Ronin's smarmy arrogance slid from his severe face. "They've asked me to recruit you."

"Who is *they*?" Tristan asked, leaning in closer.

"Don't play dumb, Your Exiled Highness." Tristan snarled at the honorific. "You were coy during that farce of a meeting at the Secretariat today, but I suspect you already know who we are. The Teles Chrysos. We've been working in the shadows since the Accords went into effect, biding our time and waiting for the moment when your family was at its weakest to strike. We didn't dare do anything other than surreptitiously build our ranks while Leonin Erabis held power. But as soon as your weak-minded brother took the throne—"

"The Butcher of Aethalia is a member of the Teles Chrysos?"

Ronan flinched at the title, then shrugged. "People change."

Tristan scoffed. "Is chess with mortal courtesans part of your rehabilitation plan?"

"Women *love* to play games with dangerous Fae males." Ronin's sly smile melted away. "And you're not the only one who's been acting a role lately."

Tristan sipped his drink, savoring the biting spice that burned down his throat and bloomed warmth in his belly. "How much support do you all have?"

"Enough," Ronin chuckled, popping his tattooed knuckles. "I'm sure this will be hard for you to believe, but your brother is not very popular on the continent. Other than this trip to the colonies, he hasn't set foot outside Delos since he took the throne. The Windrider families who rule the territories have been begging him for support that he refuses to supply. They're barely clinging to power, especially in Cernodas and Akti where the majority of the population are Beastrunners and Deathstalkers. One tiny push and the continent will go up in flames.

"Needless to say, our recruiting efforts have been rather successful. The growing unrest is likely one of the reasons Maksym believed his ridiculous plan to distribute tainted Delirium would work to incite a rebellion. Too bad we've already beaten him to the cause."

"And what exactly *is* your cause?" Tristan asked.

"The emergence of a New Ethyrios. Balance between the species and sub-species. An end to the hierarchies and interspecies anti-propagation laws."

"Not an unworthy endgame," Tristan said.

"Ethyrios's magic has been dwindling for centuries. And the Empire, in suppressing Adelphinae's influence, is exacerbating the deterioration. As we've been restoring her faith, she's been restoring the other elemental powers. Blessing our ranks with magic capable of wonders, healing more powerful than any Fae has ever known."

"How? By cross-breeding Fae and humans?"

Ronin ran a thumb along his lips. "Though I'm not personally opposed to it, no. Those were the methods of our predecessors. Ours are a bit more…scientific. Modern times and all."

"Was Maksym one of you then?" Tristan asked.

"At one time, yes. But he and the leaders of our movement had a falling out several years ago. We do not believe in the subjugation of humans. Maksym disagreed, so they kicked him out. But not before he benefited from our practices."

"Which are what, exactly?"

Ronin spread his muscled arms across the back of the settee. "Join us and you'll find out."

Tristan grunted. "So what, you're a supporter of humans now? After all the harm you've done them?"

Ronin remained calm, didn't take the bait. "Someone important convinced me of the error of my ways." He rubbed at his black eye patch.

"How do I know I can trust you?"

"You must trust me already, if you're drinking my liquor."

Tristan's eyes went wide as he sniffed at the tumbler in his hand.

Ronin laughed, a throaty bark. "Relax, Your Highness."

"Stop calling me that," Tristan snapped, his hackles raising. Barely anyone had referred to him that way in centuries. And it was happening far too frequently lately. If his brother heard anyone calling him that...

"The Emperor wants me to expose the group," Tristan said. "Has insisted I provide him the name of a rebel before his speech this weekend."

"Odd that he'd ask you to do that," Ronin said. "I would've thought he'd want you to stay as far away from us as possible."

Tristan cocked an eyebrow. "Why?"

"You are at the core of our most sacred prophecy."

Ronin closed his eye, his pale eyelid fluttering. When he finally opened his mouth, the words pouring out chilled Tristan to the core.

"*Two futures sown, one future known. Born from phantom wings and mortal bones, a new Delphine will rise to...*" Ronin trailed off.

"Will rise to what?" Tristan asked.

"That part of the prophecy remains a mystery. The lines are buried within the only remaining copy of the Fallen Goddess's Compendium."

Tristan tucked his chin. "The one at the palace in Delos?"

Ronin nodded. "The Teles Chrysos are desperate to retrieve it. Yet another reason they want you to join us."

"I haven't been back there in centuries. Nor do I expect they'd welcome me back willingly."

"Perhaps they could be persuaded if you had an army of elemental-magic-possessing rebels at your back?" Ronin smirked.

Tristan snorted, then uncrossed and recrossed his legs, shifting uncomfortably at the conversation's unexpected turn. "Why do they believe the prophecy refers to me? *Phantom wings* could easily refer to one of my siblings."

"The Teles Chrysos leadership claim the prophecy has already been fulfilled."

"I've been saddled with an infertility spell since I was exiled," Tristan mumbled. "Pretty sure I don't have any children knocking around Ethyrios."

"Not for a lack of trying, I've heard." Ronin pushed up off the settee, crossing back to the credenza to grab another bottle of Delirium. "Anyway, the original prophecy was written in an obsolete dialect. There are multiple ways to translate the word born. Bred. Created. *Turned*." Ronin gazed at him sidelong over a muscled shoulder. "What do *you* want, Tristan?"

"Peace," he answered without a moment's hesitation. "And opportunity. For *everyone* in this world."

Ronin stirred his drink before returning to the settee. "The Teles Chrysos want nothing more than that."

"More than what? For me to become the leader of a rebellion against my family?"

"Why not?" Ronin asked, his lips curling into a sneer. "Your family exiled you. Left you to rot in the colonies for centuries while they clung to a power they reserve solely for themselves and their lackies. Nothing will ever change as long as your brother rules Ethyrios. You know this. You've *known* this. Who better than you to do something about it?"

"He will not go down easily," Tristan replied. "And certainly not without a fight. Many lives could be lost along the way. Innocent lives."

"True change is always painful," Ronin uttered, his eye glazed with long-buried pain. "And rarely bloodless. Are you willing to make the sacrifice?"

"Are you?"

"I wouldn't have approached you otherwise."

Tristan twirled his glass, watching the amber liquid swirl and coat the sides. "If I don't provide my brother with a name by tomorrow, he's threatened harm against...someone I care for very deeply. He's convinced that there are other members of your organization within the colonies' councilors."

"There very well could be."

"You don't know?"

"I don't have any contacts in the colonies. And most of the membership on the continent keep themselves hidden, including the leadership. We've been communicating through coded messages. It's possible that there are other Fae working for them here, but you'll have to smoke them out yourself."

Tristan rustled his wings, sat back against the settee and crossed an ankle over his legs. "I could give him your name."

Ronin shrugged. "Maybe I want you to."

Tristan's head was spinning, tired of Ronin's enigmatic riddles. "What are you talking about?"

"My twin sister is a prisoner of the Empire, locked away in Tartarus. She was a member of the movement as well. Not a fighter—an artist. Captured while distributing propaganda for the Teles Chrysos ten years ago. The leadership have plied me with empty promises for *years* that we would travel to the prison to rescue her, but never followed through. Another mission always came along that was somehow more important. I'm sick of waiting. You need a name to deliver to your brother to make him believe you are working against us? Use me. With any luck, he'll send me to Tartarus and I can rescue my sister myself."

Tristan snorted. "That's a foolish plan. In the seven centuries of its existence, no one has *ever* escaped Tartarus."

"Well, I've never tried, have I?" Ronin said with a sly smile.

Tristan pinched the bridge of his nose, trying to chase away the headache forming behind his eyes. This was certainly not the meeting he'd expected. "You can save your daring rescue plans for another time. I've got another name in my sights. One I'd relish giving up." He held his tumbler on his knee. "August Lambros. Has he ever approached you?"

Ronin shook his head, his tongue darting out to lick at a fang. "Never. But again, he'd likely have no idea that I'm working with the Teles Chrysos either."

Tristan scrubbed a hand down his face, hoping that Cassandra's journey to Lambros's house tonight was going smoothly. And productive.

"I've got to hand it to you, Matakos. You've got bigger balls than most. What made you so confident to approach me?"

Ronin snickered. "I can see it in your eyes, in your very bones. You're ready to leave these miserable islands and reclaim what your brother stole from you. We've been waiting for you."

Ronin's words prodded at that slumbering ache in Tristan's chest.

Could he really stay in the colonies, cocooned in a false peace while others took up his mantle on the continent?

Or could the Teles Chrysos help him achieve the ends he'd dreamt about as a boy?

There was a part of him, a very large part, that wanted to try.

For himself. For his people. For Ethyrios.

For Cassandra.

"Well, Ronin," he said, raising his glass. "To a new partnership."

Ronin's lips parted into a predatory smile as he saluted Tristan with his bottle.

"To a New Ethyrios," he answered.

A frantic knock sounded at the door and the two Fae males eyed each other warily.

"Expecting more company?" Tristan growled, rising from the settee and following Ronin to the door.

"I was going to summon Rosana for another round of chess after you left," Ronin said over his shoulder. "Winning makes her so wet, I always lose on purpose. But she knows better than to interrupt me during meetings."

He whipped the door open and Aneka spilled into the room, her cheeks flushed, but her flaxen hair pin-straight. Not a strand out of place.

Untouched.

Hands braced on her knees, she gulped frantic breaths as if she'd taken the stairs two at a time.

"August never showed up."

# CHAPTER
# FORTY-FIVE

Lambros's ornate, five-story townhouse a few blocks away from the Secretariat was dark and quiet when Cassandra and Hella arrived. Just as Aneka had assured them it would be.

A heady thrill rushed through Cassandra as she scaled the wooden fence ringing August's backyard, prowling through the shadows in the thieving uniform of her previous life: the dark cloak and black training attire. A familiar skin of thievery and rebellion.

Cassandra entered using the key Aneka had provided, then crept up to August's second-floor office while Hella kept watch out front.

Messy piles of documents spilled across August's desk, and tall shelves lined the walls, chock-full of overflowing filing boxes, empty bottles of Delirium, and rows of books arranged in random patterns, spines facing both in *and* out.

As unnerving as the haphazard organizational system was, the board on the wall behind August's desk was a thousand times worse.

Cassandra crept closer to examine it, and acidic bile crawled up her throat.

Pinned to the board were dozens upon dozens of pictures of human women, their bodies in various states of undress and covered with seeping wounds and purple bruises. None of the pictures showed any faces, and Cassandra couldn't decide if that was better or worse. As if the women were nothing more than lumps of flesh in August's eyes.

Shuddering as she turned away from his sickening trophy wall, Cassandra pulled back the hood of her cloak and sunk into a leather chair behind a sculpted cherry desk.

Beams of moonlight spotlighted the veritable mountain of evidence laid out before her. Enough to suggest that not only was Lambros working with the Teles Chrysos, but that he'd been the one orchestrating those attacks.

She plucked up a map of August's district, tracing her fingers across the hastily scrawled circles around the buildings that had been bombed.

Underneath that was a diagram of a spherical device with a pin through the top, plus instructions on how to activate and deactivate the weapon. A black-and-white sigil underneath the diagram showcased a mountain peak bracketed by two leathery wings. Cassandra didn't recognize it, but assumed it signified one of the continental territories.

As she rolled up the map and diagram, her gaze caught on a note written in swooping letters she didn't recognize, its edges blackened. As if it had been singed.

At the bottom of the note was a Teles symbol.

She carefully folded the burned note and placed it in her satchel with the other documents, then stood from the chair.

A creak sounded in the hallway.

Her stomach tumbled to her feet as she tiptoed to the door, then pressed her ear against it, listening for any additional signs of movement.

Silence.

She didn't dare call out for Hella as she crept back to the window. The backyard was still and silent, no lights suddenly ablaze to chase away the lingering shadows.

As quietly as possible, she slunk back to the door and wrapped her hand around the knob.

Before she could pull it open, it was yanked from her grip and an icy flare of adrenaline scorched through her veins.

August Lambros spread his sapphire wings, his bland face contorted with delighted rage.

She bent to duck around him, but he seized her throat, his cold fingers boring into her skin and crushing her windpipe.

"Oh Ker," he chuckled, shooting tendrils of wind down her torso. He pulled the air from her lungs with terrible gentleness, savoring the sight of her consciousness slowly slipping away.

"We're going to have such fun together."

# CHAPTER
# FORTY-SIX

FETID WATER DRIPPED ONTO Cassandra's temple,
luring her towards groggy awareness.

She attempted to brush the drops aside, but her
hands lurched to a stop with an echo of clanking metal.

Iron cuffs bit into her bare wrists and ankles,
connected by a chain woven through a metal loop on
the wet stone floor. She dragged herself to a seated
position, her feet planted and knees bent, arms cradled
in her lap. She shivered, exposed to the cold damp
in only a lemon yellow bra and panties. August had
stripped her of her clothing, her shoes, and her satchel,
piled them along a curved wall behind her.

Faint shafts of moonlight trickled in from a grate high above, providing just enough illumination for her to study her surroundings.

The circular chamber, made entirely of slime-slick stones, had no windows. And based on the smell, Thalenn's sewers were on the other side of the rusted door to her right.

To her left loomed a long, silver table with a wide trough beneath. A cart stood next to the table, but she was too low to see what it held. She probably didn't want to know.

Panic shuddered through her as she began to yank at her cuffs, trying to pry them over her folded hands.

She whipped her head over her shoulder at the whine of the circular door handle. It came to an ominous, clanging stop, and as the door groaned open, two cobalt wings angled into the room.

August approached calmly with a broad, horrifying grin, then bent down to unlatch her chains. He dug his fingers into her scalp and pulled her to her feet by her hair.

She swallowed her terror, refusing to give him an ounce of it.

August sniffed at the air, groaning. "Your fear has such a lovely bouquet. My favorite appetizer."

He dragged her to the metal table as she pulled at the chains, digging her bare toes against the stone floor in a futile attempt to gain traction. Her feet slipped out from underneath her and she crashed to her knees.

August chuckled as he yanked her up, then slammed her onto the table, attaching her wrist and ankle cuffs to the edges.

Disgust, rank and oily, slithered through her as he trailed his cold hands over her arms, her stomach, and she writhed, desperate to escape his clammy touch. "Such a pristine surface. Pity I'm going to ruin it."

His gaze caught on the crescent-shaped mark on the top of her shoulder and he traced it with a soft finger. No calluses. Lazy bastard had probably never done a minute of manual labor his whole life.

"He didn't..." August laughed, a low, menacing rumble. "Tristan's always been such a fool when it comes to you mortals." He twisted towards the cart, returning with a scalpel that glinted in the moonlight. She flinched as he ran its blunt edge down her cheek.

"You took a drop of my blood at that party the other night. I think it's only fair that I take some of yours in return." He snarled, bringing his fangs so close to her cheek that she could feel them prick against her skin. "I don't know what you saw back there in my office, but I guarantee it's not what you think." He angled his face directly above hers, his espresso eyes shimmering with manic glee. "It's so much worse. I'll bleed you dry, feed on your terror, then cut you apart and send the pieces to your *master*."

A howl of impotent fury shredded Cassandra's throat.

August breathed in her scent and she wished she wasn't at eye level with the bulge tenting his pants. "Fear peppered with anger. *There's* the meal."

She bucked off the table as August pushed the scalpel into the supple skin of her stomach, dragged it in a curving line just below her belly button.

She panted through gritted teeth as he pulled away to examine his work, then tensed her stomach muscles as he brought the scalpel down for another pass.

He paused, his brows furrowed as he watched the wound scab over. Not a full healing, as it would've been if she were Fae, but certainly quicker than any mortal was capable of. An effect of Tristan's lingering magic in her blood.

A blazing sear of pain followed the second line he carved underneath the first. Warm trickles of her blood flowed onto the table, soaking through her panties. She chomped down on her tongue to keep from crying out.

August trailed a finger through the stream, then brought the red tip to his mouth and his eyes flew wide. "Tristan's not only a fool, he's a criminal," he guffawed, with not a trace of irony.

Though Cassandra supposed, in the eyes of the Empire—and Eamon especially—what August was doing to her was far more forgivable than Tristan sharing his magic with a human.

A tear tickled the hair at her temple.

"Don't waste your tears now, Ker," he crooned as he switched out the scalpel for a sharp tool with a flat, blunt edge. "There'll be plenty to cry about as our night progresses."

He plunged it into her side.

And her tears began to flow in earnest.

Throbbing pain radiated through Cassandra's body, the loss of blood dulling her senses and fuzzing her brain.

Every time she was on the brink of passing out, a tempting surrender to blissful darkness, August stabbed or sliced again, yanking her back into this waking nightmare.

She tucked her chin to examine her torso, a red-smeared canvas of half-healed slashes and scabbed holes oozing coagulated crimson. Blood drenched the table, soaking through her once-yellow bra and panties as her life slowly dripped away into the trough beneath her.

Tink.

Tink.

*Tink.*

She'd lost all sense of time. Had no idea how long August had spent carving her up, letting her heal, and then starting again.

He'd stopped talking to her, ceased taunting her. His silence was worse. As if he'd excised the last of her humanity, transformed her into nothing more than a ritual sacrifice to his feverish bloodlust.

August leaned in with the scalpel, and Cassandra clenched her jaw in delirious anticipation as the cool metal pressed against her skin. But the sharp bite didn't follow.

He paused, cocking his head.

"Don't move," he growled.

She almost laughed. Where did he think she was going to go?

He stalked for the door, ruffling his feathers.

Despite her weakened state, she pulled at her cuffs, unwilling to let him crush her lingering defiance. Her blood-drenched wrists and ankles provided enough lubrication to inch the cuffs back, but not enough to slip free. She strained against them, her frustration boiling over, and she bit her lip to muffle a howl.

August placed his ear against the door before it flew inward. The whining metal crumpled, crushed by some massive force, and August skidded across the floor into the curved stone wall.

The air in the room rippled as something—or someone—pushed in, and Cassandra swore she could feel a combustible rage radiating from the invisible mass.

August cowered against the wall, rubbing at a gash on his temple. He sensed the presence as well, and wind erupted from his outstretched fingers.

It was deflected by a stronger gust that shot from the rippling air. August scrambled to grab the scalpel that he'd dropped on the floor before a large hand burst from the mass, hauled August up by the throat and slammed him into the stones. Wind churned around him, stirring his dirty blond waves and ruffling his feathers, sucking the breath from his lungs.

August choked, then stabbed the scalpel into the hand. A yelp, and the hand released August before disappearing into the swirling morass.

August tried to duck, but a fist slammed into his face, sending his head ricocheting off the wall with a fleshy thud. Crumpling to the floor, August pressed a hand to the back of his skull, then roared as he examined his blood-soaked fingers.

He attempted to rise, but booted feet burst forth, stomping his wings and pinning him to the ground as more gusts attempted to tear the breath from his lungs.

Gasping like a dying fish, August clawed at his throat. He shot out with another gust, a powerful blow that sent the mass slamming into the opposite wall.

Iridescent, black feathers parted to reveal Tristan, his chest heaving and his face twisted in tempestuous fury.

A sob built in Cassandra's throat, along with a bubble of blood as she tried to scream his name. She pulled at her cuffs, desperate to break free and help take down this winged asshole. Her eyes met Tristan's, and his wrath and anguish cracked her open.

He'd become a mindless killing machine. All because she'd been threatened.

Tristan rose, spearing a typhoon of concentrated wind towards August. The powerful gusts shredded August's feathers and he screamed, unable to lift his hands, unable to move at all as the torrent crushed him against the wall.

Tristan increased his power as he stalked forward, the force of his wind ripping through August's clothes and peeling away his skin.

Tristan towered over his rapidly deteriorating enemy, a bellowing war cry pouring from his mouth—the world-ending roar of a furious, vengeful god.

Cassandra raised her head in gleeful anticipation of witnessing August's messy end, but couldn't see anything other than spurts of blood and feathers swirling through the torrent.

The veins in Tristan's neck bulged as he drained the last of his power.

As soon as the last breeze evaporated, revealing what had become of August, a horrified cry tore from Cassandra's throat.

A ghastly, grinning skull bobbled atop cream-white bones draped in strings of chunky flesh, and a corona of crimson stained the stones behind the corpse—what was left of it.

Tristan panted in the middle of the room, his arms at his sides, his eyes darting around like a caged animal. As if he were trying to calm himself, soothe his rage, before he approached her.

"*Tristan,*" she croaked out, and his trance snapped.

He rushed to her side, scanning her cut-up torso. "I'll fucking melt him to blood and bones all over again."

She tried to reach up, needing to touch him, but her cuffs clanked against the table. He cradled her wrists in one hand while he ripped through the chains with the other. He did the same at her ankles and she curled in on herself, yowling as the most recent cuts re-opened, leaking fresh flows of claret.

"Don't move, Cass," he said. His gentle tone belied the fury crawling across his beautiful, savage features. He unzipped his leather jacket and pulled out a silver tin of healing balm.

She tried to grip his hand, but even that subtle movement set the world around her spinning violently.

"Stay still," he whispered. "I'm going to rub this over your wounds to stop the bleeding. Then you need to take some of my blood. It will help you heal faster."

"How did you find me?" she asked, closing her eyes. The fear and panic leached from her body now that she knew she was safe.

"Aneka found me at the Serpent's Den. August never showed up. We ran into Hella on our way to the townhouse." Tristan ground out Hella's name through clenched teeth. "Aneka assumed that this is where August would've taken you. She's... she's been to his torture chamber before." Grief churned Cassandra's gut, and her heart broke that Aneka had ever been forced to endure such a monster.

Tristan worked quickly, using featherlight strokes to paint her torso with the cool, tingling balm.

He bit into his wrist, then pressed it to her lips. "Drink, Cass," he whispered, cradling her head.

She sucked down mouthfuls of his rich blood, and scintillating warmth spread throughout her body as drops of his magic refilled her, healing her final few cuts. That incessant itch at her back flared to life again.

He pulled his wrist away, his wound already closing.

"You're going to feel light-headed for a bit," Tristan said, scooping her up.

Her head lolled against his shoulder and the last of her fear dissolved, chased away by his strong arms before the darkness swallowed her.

# CHAPTER
# FORTY-SEVEN

THE GROUP GATHERED AT the bungalow, Tristan and Aneka flanking Cassandra on the couch, Reena draped in an armchair, and Hella standing at attention behind her.

Cassandra had awoken on the flight back to the bungalow, insisted that Tristan call everyone here so they could review the materials she'd found in August's office. See if Reena could interpret that note. Plus, she wanted to hear how his meeting with Ronin had gone.

He'd protested, fiercely, claiming she needed to rest after her ordeal, but she'd insisted. Physically, she was only a little woozy from the blood loss. Tristan's infusion had done plenty to restore her. She felt better than she expected.

Mentally, however... Every time she closed her eyes, August leered over her, scalpel in hand, his black-brown eyes glinting with feral glee, and nausea roiled her gut. She needed the distraction of the work, the distraction of plotting their next move.

"Can we get this moving, please?" Reena piped up, examining her long, matte-black nails. "I've got a bar to close and a gorgeous hunk of white-winged male waiting to warm my bed. No offense, Cass."

Cassandra grinned, appreciating Reena's priorities.

"You're welcome to leave at any time, Reena." Tristan flashed her a wicked smile.

"Fuck that," Reena answered, sitting upright. "I wanna see what you all found. Curiosity kindles the cat."

"I not sure that is right phrase," Hella said, crossing her arms over her chest and aiming not-so-subtle glances at Aneka.

"It's my phrase, sugar," Reena winked. "Come on, Cass. Let's see what you got."

"I don't want to see it," Aneka croaked out, cowering beside Tristan. "The less I know about all of this, the better."

"He's gone, Aneka," Cassandra said. "You're free. We've arranged for you to travel to the Temple in Meridon. You'll be safe there. The Sisters will watch over you."

"I take you now, if want," Hella stated. Perhaps in need of an escape herself. Tristan hadn't said two words to her since she'd arrived at the bungalow. He was likely still upset about her security failure. Though Cassandra didn't blame Hella; they'd *both* mistakenly assumed the townhouse was empty.

Aneka cast a watery glance around the room, then pitched herself over Tristan and gripped Cassandra in a fierce hug. "Thank you," she whispered.

"Thank *you*," Cassandra responded, squeezing Aneka briefly before releasing her. "We couldn't have done this without you."

Aneka stood, glancing down at the short hem of her champagne silk nightgown. "Do you have any clothes I could borrow? The Sisters might turn me away if I show up like this."

"They would never," Cassandra assured her. "But please, raid my closet. Up the stairs, second door on your left. Take anything you want."

"I wait out front, golden beauty," Hella said with a sincere nod. Aneka blushed, then scurried up the stairs.

"Ready?" Cassandra turned to Tristan, who nodded, trailing a comforting hand down her spine, nestling his fingertips underneath the lace camisole she'd changed into as soon as they'd arrived.

Reena rose from the armchair, lithe as a wisp of smoke, then perched herself next to Cassandra on the couch.

Cassandra grabbed her satchel from the floor—Tristan had retrieved it before they'd left

August's chamber—and pulled out the documents she'd collected.

She spread them across the table and Tristan let out a low whistle as he examined the map and the diagram of the strange weapon.

Reena plucked up the singed note, holding it to her face.

"Can you interpret those symbols?" Cassandra asked. "Do you know what it says?"

"It's been a very long time," Reena said softly, scrutinizing the strange markings. "This is a cipher that the Teles Chrysos used. My parents used it to send me letters while I was an acolyte of Adelphinae." She turned to Tristan. "Got something to write with?"

Tristan pushed off the couch, then rummaged through a drawer in the side table and handed her a pencil.

She spread the note onto the table, and Cassandra watched her furious scratches with rapt attention. She seemed to be merging the top half of the first symbol with the bottom half of the last symbol, performing the same combination as she moved towards the center of each word.

What she wrote out was still indecipherable to Cassandra, but she did at least recognize the Aramaelish letters that graced glowing street signs all over Thalenn.

Tristan leaned over Reena's shoulder to read the decoded message, then cut a wide-eyed glance at Cassandra.

"What?" she asked. "What does it say?"

Tristan traced his fingers over Reena's pencil strokes. "*The necklace has been delivered. Prepare for the next attack.*"

"Necklace?" Cassandra breathed out. "But that means—"

"August was working with the fire-wielding Windrider who burned down our ship," he answered.

"So they're *both* members of the Teles Chrysos?" she asked.

"It would seem so," Tristan answered. "Ronin told me this evening that Maksym was a member of the organization at one time as well."

"Who *isn't* a fucking member of this group?" Reena snarled.

Tristan shook his head. "Maksym was kicked out years ago. They didn't approve of his attitude towards humans. His plans were wholly his own."

"But they approved of *August's* attitude towards humans?" Cassandra barked, incredulous.

"Maybe they weren't aware of his extracurricular activities," Tristan answered softly and Cassandra shuddered, clamping down on the memories that slithered through her mind. He ran a gentle wing down her back.

"Did Ronin know that August was working for the organization?" Cassandra asked.

"He didn't. Their membership is still cloaked in secrecy. He said he hasn't even met the leaders. Though he claims their numbers on the continent are vast, maybe even more numerous than my brother is aware of. He asked me to join them."

Cassandra gasped and Reena let out a small snarl of protest.

"You can't seriously be considering it," Reena barked. "Are you?"

"He did make it sound rather tempting. Claims that they're after peace between the species. An end to the hierarchies, and the promise of a more equitable world."

"And you believe him?" Cassandra asked.

"Reena, can you give us a minute?" Tristan said.

"I'm out," the tiger bi-form answered. "Need to get back to my boy toy anyways." She placed a hand on Tristan's shoulder. "Be careful, old friend. I'm not sure this is a game you can win."

"Gotta keep immortality interesting somehow, right?" Tristan answered with a strained smile before Reena left the bungalow.

Cassandra pulled a knee onto the couch, removing the silk scarf she'd put on to hide his mark. The fabric tickled over her shoulders.

"I don't like this, Tristan. Your brother wouldn't hesitate to execute you if he suspected you were actually *helping* the Teles Chrysos."

"He'd have to catch me first," Tristan smirked, leaning over to press a kiss against his mark.

"Not amusing," she answered, smacking him lightly. "Are you going to tell him that you killed August?"

"I've got all the evidence I need to prove that August was a traitor, so why not? Eamon would likely see it as an act of loyalty on my part."

"And then what? You're just… you're just going to feed August's name to Eamon and join the rebellion against him in secret?"

He grasped her hands. "This could be our chance, Cass. Everything I've wanted for two centuries. This movement can help me achieve it. Eamon claims he's working for the good of Ethyrios, but he's pitted the entire world against our family, holding everyone beneath his boot. He will never change unless I force him to. And I can't do that alone. I need *allies*. And now there's a continent full of them waiting for me."

"Are you sure they're allies you can trust?" she asked.

"We won't know until we join, will we?"

"We?"

"I can't do this without you," he said, his honeyed eyes filled with yearning. "You dream of it too, don't you? What Ethyrios could be if our species were able to live as equals, without the divide of the continent and the colonies, these arbitrary lines drawn between us? Without humans forced to sacrifice memories and risk obliviation just to survive?"

Cassandra recalled those nights at the Fang and Claw, the camaraderie and affection she'd seen there among Fae and humans. Like a daydream from a different, better world.

He placed his hand at her waist, his gaze beseeching yet shining with determination. "My destiny, since the moment I was born, was to rule Ethyrios. Though it's a fate I hardly wanted, even before I was forced to forsake it. Now I think maybe I wasn't meant to rule Ethyrios, but to free it. Turn it into something better. Will you help me, Cass?"

She scoffed. "How could I possibly help? I'm nothing. Just a human with tiny scraps of nearly useless magic."

Even as the dismissal left her mouth, that cosmic voice from her vision pelted her brain.

*Find her.*

Something shivered across her shoulder blades as she recalled the rapturous masses sweeping across a field of lilies.

Recalled the word they'd been chanting.

"You are far more than that," Tristan said, as if he could sense the turn of her thoughts. "You're a legend among mortals in the colonies. Just as much of a symbol as I am. Imagine what we could accomplish together, the Exiled Prince and the Savior Sister."

It was a tempting, though daunting, request. One that led down a long and treacherous path.

"Don't you want to change the world with me, Daredevil?" He traced the scar above her collarbone. "I didn't place this mark on you lightly. You are mine and I am yours. For your lifetime and beyond."

He leaned in to cup her cheek, stroking her cheekbone with his thumb.

"I want to make this world better for you." He leaned in and pressed his mouth to hers, a gentle touch of their lips.

She pulled back, her throat closing with welling emotions. "For everyone. I think... I think this is my purpose too, Tristan. I'm with you."

He swept her into his lap, capturing her mouth in a desperate, claiming kiss and circling his arms around her.

"I will never let *anything* happen to you, Cass," he said, pushing a strand of hair behind her ear. "You will always be safe with me. If the Teles Chrysos ever threaten that, we'll leave immediately. I swear it."

"And go find a deserted island somewhere to live out our in-between moments in solitary peace?" she teased.

"Actually, that sounds incredible," he chuckled. "Should we just do that instead?"

She kicked her head back with a throaty laugh. "Neither of us is wired that way. You'd never get over the guilt if you had an opportunity to make real change and you didn't seize it."

"Speaking of seizing..." Laying her down on the cushions, he lifted the hem of her camisole and pressed whisper-light kisses to her exposed skin.

She threw her arms behind her, gripping the armrest. "Careful, Birdman. A woman could get spoiled."

He stroked his tongue into her belly button and pulled at the waistband of her loose, silk pants, looking up with a questioning gaze.

Asking for permission after the terrifying encounter she'd endured earlier.

She nodded. His touch was exactly what she needed to chase away that darkness.

"I'd happily spend the rest of your life spoiling you rotten," he whispered.

Her heart clenched briefly at the thought that his lifetime would be so much longer than hers.

But she dismissed the anxiety. She was done worrying about his past and their future. She'd take as much of him as she could get and be grateful for it.

Tristan moved his mouth lower, showing her how much he wanted her in licks and strokes.

The tingling at her back grew more intense.

She ignored it as best she could and focused on her *ma'anyu*.

No matter what the Emperor or the Teles Chrysos had in store for them, that's what they were.

Unbreakable.

# CHAPTER
# FORTY-EIGHT

CAEL PACED ALONG THE concrete dock, a cool breeze ruffling his tawny waves and prickling the fine hairs coating his wing.

"He should've been here by now," he grumbled.

"Will you relax, pterodactyl?" Xenia said, hugging her chest and rubbing at her upper arms to chase away the chill. "Maybe his alarm didn't go off?"

Cael shot her an annoyed look. Now wasn't the time for flippancy.

Whatever spell they'd been under during that glorious fever dream this morning had broken as soon as they'd disentangled and Xenia had darted into the bathroom to dress.

Stolia had agreed to meet them here at the dock fifteen minutes ago. A large cargo ship loomed next to them, *Eurybia* printed in white block letters on the black hull.

The dock teemed with Fae workers unloading cargo, untying lines, and running checks on the ship as gulls cawed overhead, seeking breakfast in the awakening seas.

Footsteps clomped down the metal staircase, and a hulking figure in a wide-brimmed white hat and oatmeal-colored linen suit waved at them. The Fae's bushy silver beard and flowing hair whipped against his broad torso in the briny air.

"Cael, my boy!" Ohan Stolia boomed as he approached. He crushed Cael in a bruising hug, clapping a hand against the scar on Cael's back and making him wince.

Ohan pulled back and his jollity faded into concern. "What happened to your wing, son?"

"We encountered some difficulties on our journey. It's not important."

Stolia didn't need to know all the sordid details.

Ohan nodded carefully, then turned his attention to Xenia. "And this must be your precious cargo, I assume?" He grasped Xenia's hand and pressed a gentlemanly kiss to her knuckles. "Charmed, Mistress. He didn't mention how beautiful you are, but I can see why he's so eager to get you to safety."

Xenia blushed and pulled her hand from the Fae's grip. "It's nice to meet you, Master Stolia."

"Please. I'm only Master Stolia to people I don't like very much. Call me Ohan."

Xenia laughed, already falling prey to the legendary charm that allowed the yak bi-form to successfully steer one of Ethyrios's largest enterprises. "Okay, Ohan. And you can call me Zee, since we're going to be friends."

Cael swung an arm across Xenia's shoulder, and Ohan snickered.

"Follow me, dear friends!" Ohan cried as he took the bobbing aluminum plank into the ship. "I'll show you to your berth, Zee."

Cael guided Xenia into the hull, tucking his wing as Ohan led them through a cramped maze of low-ceilinged hallways and staircases. They arrived at a tiny room lined with narrow bunks.

"Normally, a few of the crew would be sleeping in here, but they've agreed to stay up on deck to give you some privacy, my dear," Ohan said.

"Oh, that wasn't necessary. I don't want to put anyone out."

"It'll do, Ohan," Cael said. "And thank you for the privacy. Trust me, Zee, you're going to want it. Even though the trip is only three days, you don't want to be shacked up with a bunch of randy, smelly Fae sailors."

"Wouldn't be any different than the past few days," she quipped, smirking. Though the smile didn't quite meet her eyes.

"Right," Stolia said, clapping Cael on the shoulder. "I'll leave you two to say your goodbyes. Ship launches in thirty minutes. I've let Captain Krieger know you're on board, my dear. He'll make sure his crew leaves you alone, but will send meals down for you. Head's back there." He motioned towards a small door at the back of the room.

"I trust that we can keep this quiet?" Cael said. "My father can never know about her."

"Of course, of course. Bon voyage!" The hulking Beastrunner ducked through the door, shutting it with a metallic thunk.

Cael turned to Xenia, pulling Ker from the sheath at his hip. "Here. Take this with you. For protection, and also to return it to Cassandra when you see her. And tell Tristan—" his voice wavered on his friend's name "—that I'm sorry I lied to him about returning to the colonies."

A war waged across Xenia's face. She was clearly ecstatic at the thought of being re-united with her friend, but something was holding her back.

She'd grown too attached to him. He couldn't bear it. He'd brought her nothing but danger and misery. And even if, by some miracle, he could find a way to keep her, all that likely awaited them was an ending exactly like the one he'd had with Killian—a rift that had grown wider and wider with each of Cael's subsequent episodes. He'd battle Vestan the Warrior God himself before he'd put anyone through that misery again. He would not be Xenia's emotional vampire.

She reached for him, then halted when he took a large step backwards.

The hurt darkening her emerald eyes gouged his heart.

He bit the inside of his cheek to stop his own startling tears, kept his expression as cold as possible.

"There was never anything between us, Xenia," he ground out, the lie hammering through his chest. "Real life doesn't have as many happy endings as your ridiculous stories. It's dark and cold and cruel. And the sooner you realize that, the better off you'll be."

Her gaze guttered, her beautiful, bow-shaped lips pinched tight as she wrapped her arms around her chest. Closing herself off to him. Thank the High Gods.

This was the right thing to do.

Right?

So why did it hurt so fucking bad?

She stared at him, as if she could read every emotion churning beneath his granite surface. She opened her mouth for a retort, then closed it, shaking her head and turning away to sit on a squeaky bunk.

A beam of sunlight broke through the porthole, lighting her up like an angel and nearly shattering his resolve.

"I hope you find what you're looking for, Cael."

He stormed out of the suddenly claustrophobic berth, needing to get off this ship before he did something incredibly stupid.

Like rushing back into that tiny room and sweeping the gorgeous, sunny, sassy woman there into his arms.

And confessing that he'd already found it.

# CHAPTER
# FORTY-NINE

CAEL'S CLANGING FOOTSTEPS FADED to a ringing echo. Though his harsh words stung, Xenia didn't believe he meant them.

She was sure they'd been some misguided attempt to *save* her. Keep her from getting too close. Still believing himself broken despite all the good he'd done, all the good he was capable of doing.

And she'd be damned if she let him give up on himself that easily.

Thirty minutes. That's all the time she had to make the most important decision of her life.

Stay on this boat and return to safety, to her friends, to the only life she'd ever known?

Or chase down the tortured male who'd just tried, and failed, to rip her heart out?

He'd dismissed her stories as overly optimistic, useless trifles. But there was more to glean from romance novels than happy endings. And Cael's unfeeling dismissal fell squarely into the *hero makes the ultimate sacrifice* trope.

She didn't dare yet imagine it was for love.

But she knew he was lying when he said there was *nothing* between them.

Was that seed of hope, no matter how starved, worth risking everything for? Finding a new path and abandoning the order? Gambling her safety in a city about to be plunged into a war?

She glanced down at her wrist, at Letha's tattoo now almost entirely faded.

If she returned to the order, would she be able to perform the ritual? And even if she could, did she want to?

This little adventure had opened her eyes to the wider world. All the thrills and dangers it had to offer. It might be terrifying, but at least it was *real*.

"Forgive me, Cass," she whispered, rubbing at her wrist.

She couldn't go back. Not with so much unfinished business between her and Cael.

The plan she'd made back in Maksym's dungeon remained incomplete. She'd throw herself upon the mercy of Rhamnos to achieve that final, and most critical, item.

Help Cael heal.

And not just his wing, but his fractured spirit.

Xenia *never* left a to-do list unchecked.

A soft knock sounded at the open door of the berth and a ripple of panic shuddered through her at Captain Krieger's serpentine eyes. But his genuinely warm smile chased it away.

She scolded herself. Not all Deathstalkers were as terrible as those she'd met these past weeks.

"Hello, Mistress Cirillo," the Captain bowed slightly as he stepped into the room. "Welcome to the *Eurybia*. Master Stolia has informed us, in no uncertain terms, that we're to make your trip with us as safe and comfortable as possible. We're getting ready to disembark. Is there anything we can get you?"

The gold buttons on his red jacket glinted in the rays streaming in through the porthole. He tucked his hands behind his back, tilting his head expectantly.

"Actually," she said, rising from the bunk, "there is."

The ominous bleat of the *Eurybia's* foghorn rattled Xenia's bones as the massive ship pulled away from the dock.

Alone on the empty concrete, surrounded by white-capped waves and circling gulls, she could almost convince herself she was the only person left in the world. Adrift on an open sea with nothing but miles and miles of water leading all the way to the colonies.

To her old life.

To Cass.

But that was not the path she'd chosen.

Xenia hoped her friend would forgive her someday. If she ever saw her again.

She crunched the torn piece of paper in her hand, glancing down at the hastily scrawled address—her sole request of Captain Krieger.

As she turned, the towers of the glittering metropolis winked menacingly in the sunlight like flashy lures on a baited string.

She had absolutely nothing on her person. No food, no water, no *drachas*. Nothing but a Typhon-steel dagger as she marched into the city where she had not a single friend.

Other than the one she'd made this morning.

As she began her trek to Ohan Stolia's headquarters, the wind off the Sea of Thetis pushed at her back.

As if the High Gods themselves were urging her on to her next chapter.

Cael was wrong. Sometimes, life was *exactly* like her stories.

She held her head high, a fierce princess embarking on an adventure into an unknown land to rescue her scarred prince.

# CHAPTER FIFTY

THE CROWD SWARMING THE expansive plain in front of the Vicereine's palace grew restless.

Cassandra couldn't blame them. There'd been little excitement over the past hour as they awaited the Emperor and the speech he'd called the entire city of Thalenn here to witness.

Well, little excitement other than the spectacle of several red-jacketed, gold-helmeted Empire soldiers brandishing stun pistols to eject a band of human protesters. The shouts had since quieted to a hushed murmur.

Cassandra fidgeted in her seat. Behind her, a metal fence lined with soldiers held the crowd at bay. Tristan had secured her seat so that she didn't have to brave the mob. He'd wanted her up on stage with him, but Eamon had refused. Said it wouldn't jive with the theme of his speech to have mortals joining him on stage.

The comment had set Cassandra on edge.

She tried not to think on it as she surveyed her seatmates, Thalenn's mortal councilors. A bland, forgettable party outside of Alcander Pagonis, from whom she'd purposefully sat as far as possible.

A podium bearing the Empire's sigil awaited Eamon's presence at center stage, Tristan to its right while Vicereine Lykan and Ronin Matakos occupied the two seats to the left.

At the back of the stage, three Vasilikans perched sedate and statuesque in their carved-feather uniforms.

Black and gold banners bearing the Empire's sigil sliced through the white palace walls, unmoving in the stagnant air. There was no hint of a breeze beneath the woolly gray clouds, as if the entire city were holding its breath in anticipation of their first official visit from the new Emperor.

Yesterday, Tristan had confessed to killing August, had given Eamon the documents that revealed the name of the rebel organization and proved that Lambros had been a traitor all along. Tristan hadn't, however, told his brother of Cassandra's involvement, nor that they'd sent August's consort to safety.

Eamon had then personally invited both Cassandra and Tristan to attend today's event, which Cassandra supposed would be a denouncement of both August and the Teles Chrysos.

She wrestled with an uneasy sense of foreboding, comforting herself with glances towards her fierce, powerful *ma'anyu* and the reassuring presence of the Typhon dagger tucked into her boot. She'd dressed head to toe in the color of the Empire today—black on black on black. Playing the part of a loyal Imperial servant.

Excited whispers fluttered through the crowd as the arched doors to the palace creaked open, and footsteps crunched through the gravel.

Emperor Erabis marched up the steps to the stage, his magnificent, iridescent black wings flared and a circlet of onyx stone feathers nestled in his jet-black waves.

Tristan and the Vicereine tucked their wings tightly against their backs, genuflecting to his Imperial Majesty and his power.

A hush fell over the crowd, the only sound the Emperor's echoing footfalls as he speared across the stage and paused behind the podium.

He spent a long minute surveying the still, silent plain, a princely portrait of cool arrogance. Completely assured of his own dominance over the masses before him.

"Citizens of Ethyrios," he boomed, his voice amplified by the magical metallic stem jutting from the podium, "it's an honor to stand before you today. I've come to discuss a topic that's been weighing on my mind lately. Peace. Our peace. And the measures we need to take moving forward to maintain it."

Cassandra dared a peek at Varuna, whose blood-red lips curled into a sinister smile.

"As many of you well know, there have been a series of cowardly attacks plaguing your city," Eamon uttered, his brows dipping in feigned sympathy. "The group behind them, the Teles Chrysos, are spreading dangerous lies about our two species, openly flaunting their vile practices in defiance of the High Gods. They seek to smudge the very clear boundaries between our species which have cradled us in serenity for the past five centuries."

Cassandra peered over her shoulder, cataloging the crowd's expressions in the wake of Eamon's carefully twisted words. She was shocked by several nods of agreement. How could anyone be buying this?

"The Empire will not abide such practices, cannot stand back and watch these inflammatory ideas take hold and tear us apart. I come before you today to proclaim that if any individual in Ethyrios, whether on the continent or in the colonies, mortal or Fae, is seen harboring or assisting these rebels, he or she will be declared an enemy of the Empire."

Half the crowd roared their agreement, boiling at Eamon's declaration. The rest tittered, tentatively joining in.

Cassandra kept her face carefully neutral, ashamed that so many of her fellow mortals had gleefully accepted this yoke of subjugation cloaked as freedom, as protection. Lapping at the hand that barely fed them.

"Which turns my attention to the enemies among us." Eamon stepped back from the podium, surveying the Fae seated to the left and right of him. "Unfortunately, not even your trusted colonial leadership is immune to these traitorous ideals. One of them has been working to undermine our peace, a member of the very organization sowing discord and destruction within your cherished city."

Cassandra braced herself to hear the name of the male who had tortured her, pinching the skin between her thumb and forefinger to distract from the terrifying memories threatening to overtake her sanity.

"In fact," Eamon said, "he sits among us even now."

Shock, raw and tingling, blazed down Cassandra's limbs and she speared a glance towards Tristan, who avoided her gaze with calculated stoicism.

Eamon aimed a curt nod at one of the Vasilikan guards who flashed to Ronin in a supernatural blur of black, then yanked the Beastrunner from his chair and dragged him to the center of the stage.

Ronin didn't fight them. Why wasn't he fighting them?

"Councilor Matakos," Eamon began, "or should I say *former* Councilor Matakos. You have been accused of conspiring with the Teles Chrysos, in defiance of your Empire and the High Gods. Do you deny these charges?"

"Never," Ronin declared, determination gracing his lupine features.

The crowd surrounding the stage gasped, followed by a buzz of angry whispers.

"The Teles Chrysos will restore the Creator to glory and see your palace of lies crumble to the ground," Ronin roared. "A New Ethyrios will be born from your ashes!"

Something flared in Cassandra's chest at Ronin's defiant proclamation, as if a second heartbeat thumped behind her own. The prickling at her shoulder blades transformed into a fiery blaze. It was all she could do to stay seated, sweat beading at her temples from the control she exerted over her body.

"Enough!" Eamon roared, a billow of wind blasting from the podium and rushing across the plain. "You will be delivered to Tartarus to await sentencing from the Imperial Council in Delos. Though considering I am the head of that Council, I don't like your odds."

Ronin smirked as the vicious mob rattled the fences, and the Vasilikan marched him from the stage.

Tristan caught Cassandra's eye and traced the letter M along his thigh, an attempt to calm her with their secret message.

Eamon regained his composure, tugging at the cuffs of his elegant black and gold brocade jacket and straightening his circlet. He raised his hands to the crowd, quieting their fury.

"Friends, as much as it pains me to say this, Councilor Matakos is not the only enemy hiding within our midst. While our dear Vicereine Lykan has been doing everything in her power to maintain peace in your precious colonies, there are a number of my own species here working in opposition to her. Operating dens of sedition where the lines between human and Fae blur. Giving rise to mutinous philosophies like those of the Teles Chrysos."

A line of Empire soldiers burst from the palace, dragging several beaten and bloody Fae up onto the stage.

Cassandra nearly burst out of her chair at the familiar, auburn hair among the line-up.

Reena.

No no *no.*

The Beastrunner female radiated a murderous rage despite her swollen black eye and bleeding split lip. Two Empire soldiers propped her up, facing her towards the snarling crowd. Her one good eye was dull and glazed, likely the result of a suppressant to stop her from calling upon her tiger and cutting the soldiers to ribbons.

Reena's fingertips were coated in blood and black bits of gore. They'd torn out her fingernails.

Cassandra's gorge rose, and she made to stand from her chair, but Tristan shot her a hard look.

They could do nothing to help Ronin or Reena right now. Not with all these eyes upon them. And though Tristan's face was carefully neutral, the vein ticking in his jaw warned that whatever fight Eamon had just started would not be ending today.

"The traitorous Fae you see before you will be joining Ronin Matakos in Tartarus. And my sincerest apologies for allowing them to lure your species into a false sense of camaraderie. Our peace can only thrive when the strict boundaries between our species are maintained."

Cassandra had never felt so aware of her own mortal blood, tinged though it was with drops of Fae magic. Every molecule in her body was screaming at her to run.

The Empire soldiers marched Reena and the other battered Fae off the stage and into the palace.

As Eamon pivoted to the crowd, his hateful eyes snagged Cassandra's, coating her insides with shards of ice.

"Thank you for being patient, my friends," Eamon crooned. "I know this is not a pleasant business, but it's one we must endure. For your safety and the safety of all Ethyrios."

"*Long live Emperor Erabis!*" a voice called out from the crowd. It swelled into a fierce chant.

How far would Cassandra and Tristan get if she rushed the stage and jumped into his arms right now, convinced him to fly them away from here?

Not far, she figured, her stomach plummeting as she inspected the many pairs of tucked wings cresting over the Empire soldiers' shoulders. Not to mention the matte-black monstrosities spearing up behind the Vasilikans.

Her heart pounded in her chest as Eamon flashed the crowd a beaming smile that didn't warm his eyes. He patted his hands against the air, once again encouraging silence.

"There is one final enemy to reveal. This one, I'm afraid, comes from your own species," Eamon whispered.

The crowd booed and hissed.

How were these Cassandra's people? What had happened to them? She'd never known the humans of Thalenn to be so cruel.

More Empire soldiers exited through the palace doors, and Cassandra's heart dropped to her feet.

A line of Shrouded Sisters was paraded onto the stage, their dress robes torn and bloodied, their faces covered in weeping cuts and ugly bruises.

At the end of the queue, two soldiers propped up Borea, her platinum bob stained red and hanging in limp, disheveled strands across her placid face. Her gaze was as dull as Reena's had been.

The Sisters' eyes spiraled, unfocused, and many pairs of lips were moving, no doubt muttering soft prayers to Letha.

"There have been rumors," Eamon began in a cryptic tone that had the crowd straining forward, "of a Savior in your midst."

*Run, run, RUN,* the voice in Cassandra's head screamed, but she was paralyzed with fear, her catatonic limbs burning with useless adrenaline.

On stage, Tristan tensed into a terrifying stillness. Tiny eddies of wind stirred the tendrils of hair draped across his forehead.

"A Savior who has taken it upon herself to decide which of you is worthy of salvation and which of you should be sacrificed to rot in oblivion."

Cassandra didn't dare turn her head to look back at the crowd. She could tell by the slithery sounds of their hisses that they were eating up Eamon's words.

What was wrong with them? Did they not realize the *Empire* had put them in the position to rot in the first place?

"A wolf in a Shrouded Sister's robes!"

The crowd roared its disapproval and Cassandra scanned the faces of her Sisters, though none returned her anguished stare.

Eamon stepped from behind the podium, and stalked over to the line of Sisters, snatching a Typhon broadsword from one of the Vasilikans.

He yanked Borea out of line and pushed her to her knees before him, then yanked her head back and exposed her throat.

"Which one?" he snarled into the Fae female's ear.

"I'm sure I have no idea what you're talking about," Borea answered calmly.

Eamon pressed the edge of the sword to Borea's neck, hard enough that blood beaded and trickled down the steel. "Who is the Savior Sister?"

Borea remained the portrait of pacified stillness. "A myth, your Imperial Majesty."

Eamon snapped his fingers and a row of Empire soldiers crested the stage to line up behind the Sisters, pushing them to their knees. The soldiers drew their swords, a coordinated metallic hiss, then rested them in the crooks of the women's necks. Several Sisters blubbered, tears and snot mingling on their lips.

Cassandra's heart slammed a violent drumbeat against her ribs as she observed her beloved Sisters kneeling broken upon on the stage, about to take a punishment that she herself had earned.

She cut her eyes towards Tristan, found him staring at her, trembling with silent pleas, *begging* her to stay seated, not reveal herself.

Eamon leaned down and whispered into Borea's ear, though Cassandra heard every word. "Then I suppose I'll just have to kill you all."

He nodded to the soldiers and they raised their swords as a synchronized, keening wail burst from the mouths of the Sisters.

Cassandra was pulled from her feet, enveloped inside a pair of powerful arms and a cocoon of black feathers, torrents of wind a deafening rush around her.

"Don't." Tristan released a shuddering sob against her neck, his fingers curling against her back as muddled shouts and the whine of stun pistols echoed through his shield. "Don't you fucking *dare*, Cassandra."

"Tristan," she whispered, pulling back to cup his cheek. "I can't let them die for me."

"*I* will die if I lose you," he croaked, crushing her palms against his thrashing heart. "I'm already dying."

"You're not." She shook her head. "You *won't*."

"Don't let him take my life away from me a second time," he pleaded, his voice fracturing. "Not after I just found it again."

"Listen to me." She poured everything she felt for him into her fierce gaze. "I was trapped before I met you, using my vows as an excuse to cage myself. You *freed* me, Tristan. Broke me out and showed me all the messy, imperfect joy this life has to offer. Showed me what I want to fight for. *You. Us.* We are unbreakable, remember?"

His face crumpled as his shoulders carved forwards. "Cassandra, I lo—"

She stopped his words with her fingertips. "Don't say it now, or I won't be able to…" Her voice broke as she gripped the back of his neck and pressed their foreheads together. "Say it when we find each other again."

She lowered her hand and claimed his mouth, salty tears mingling on their tongues as he crushed her body against his. He dug his fingers into her ribs as if he wanted to scoop out her heart and keep it for himself.

"You have to let me go," she whispered against his lips and his agonized growl blew back her hair. "Let me go, *ma'anyu.*"

The shield dissolved with a pop as Tristan sank to his knees.

"*STOP!*" she bellowed, pushing past his wings.

Several of the soldiers on the stage aimed pistols towards her and Tristan, while a few maintained their upraised swords above the Sisters' heads. They all glanced towards Eamon, who stilled them with a hand and a victorious smile.

Cassandra had barely stepped away from Tristan before two more soldiers seized her, their hands iron vises around her arms as they marched her towards the Emperor.

Tristan's wind exploded from behind her, rattling the Vicereine's feathers and nearly tipping the podium. He rushed for his brother, a piercing arrow of black wings and fury, arms outstretched and aimed for Eamon's throat.

One of the two remaining Vasilikans whipped a length of Nessite chains from behind his back, holding it in a leather gauntlet and flicking it towards Tristan. The glowing, olive metal wrapped around Tristan's neck and as soon as it touched his bare skin, he seized and crashed to the stage.

The Vasilikan hauled Tristan to his feet and his eyes darted madly, a prisoner in his own body.

The Sisters blubbered and Borea's head sagged as Cassandra kicked and flailed at the two soldiers dragging her onto the stage. A useless struggle against their superior strength, but she'd be damned if she went down without putting up at least some semblance of a fight.

"Here she is, Thalenn!" Eamon boomed to the crowd. "Your Savior Sister!" He spat the words as if they singed his tongue.

Tears pricked Cassandra's eyes as she scanned the frothing crowd, shocked and disheartened by the furious animosity reflected back at her.

She'd been trying to save them.

Why couldn't they see that?

All her efforts had been for *nothing*. All the robberies, all the reversed obliviations, and she'd still ended up here. Not a blazing icon of defiance, but an ineffectual gnat crushed beneath the Empire's boot.

Her gaze caught on an older couple within the crowd. Two of the few faces not twisted in hatred or anger.

Shefton looked solemn, pained, as he gathered his wife in his arms. Unwilling to join in the jeers but helpless to stop them.

Mona's tear-streaked face pressed against her husband's shoulder, unable to watch.

Cassandra broke, dipping her head. Waiting for Eamon to pronounce her fate.

"Mistress Fortin will be sent to Tartarus with the other traitors to the Empire to await the judgment of the Council," Eamon proclaimed. "Do you have anything you wish to say? An apology, perhaps, to the many fine citizens you have betrayed with your bold actions against me?"

That fire continued to lick at her back, the second entity within her distending her skin. Begging to be unleashed.

She looked to Tristan, mouthed the word *unbreakable*, then turned to Eamon. "This is far from over," she promised, only half-believing it but unwilling to admit defeat. "The mortal citizens of Ethyrios will remember who their true enemy is. And I swear to you, I will live to see the day when they rise up against you to claim their freedom."

The crowd surged forward, hurtling ruthless slurs.

"Doesn't seem they agree," Eamon smirked with a curt nod to the soldier on her left.

The soldier lifted his stun pistol, aimed it at her stomach, and pulled the trigger.

And Cassandra's world evaporated into a dark swirl of searing pain.

# CHAPTER
# FIFTY-ONE

"I DID WARN YOU WHAT would happen if you dared to betray me, brother."

Eamon's voice floated down the hallway beyond Tristan's cell beneath the Vicereine's palace, his clipped footsteps echoing.

He paused in front of the warded bars, his hands behind his back, and Tristan's wind battered his skin with barely contained vehemence. If his power weren't being held back by those wards, he'd whip a spearing gust through his brother's neck and sever his head from his body.

Eamon's cool hazel eyes swept across Tristan, slumped against the wall with his wings tucked and his arms resting on bent knees.

Despite the fantasies of his brother's violent demise, there was no fight left in Tristan's body. It had fled along with the beautiful, defiant woman who was no doubt being transported to Tartarus at this very moment.

"How did you find out?" A low, defeated mumble.

Eamon licked his lips, then winked. "Ronin's not the only one who visits Rosana at the Serpent's Den. Mortal women *are* a rather amusing pastime after all. And so willing to play spy for a little coin and a bit of Fae cock. She overheard a very *enlightening* conversation." Eamon chuckled. "You are so predictably *noble*, Tristan. It's always been your greatest fault. Though you and I have been doing this dance for far longer than you suspected."

Eamon brought his hands from behind his back, revealing a familiar object.

And if Tristan were capable of feeling anything besides molten fury at the moment, he might have laughed at the sparkling diamond and Thalassium necklace now dripping from his brother's palm.

"Where did you get that?" he asked.

Eamon shrugged. "Roeki gave it to me."

"Who?"

"The fire-wielding Windrider I sent to assassinate you on that ship. She was supposed to make it look like an accident. Make it look like you had been killed by her former associates in the Teles Chrysos," Eamon sighed. "Obviously, she failed. Both times, since you didn't drown at the Church in Vaengya either."

Eamon crouched before the bars, his face eye-level with Tristan's. "I should thank her, probably. And August as well. The plan we came up with after those failed attempts has played out beautifully. If I couldn't make it appear as though the Teles Chrysos had killed you, I figured I could put you on a collision course to join them. I've long had my suspicions about Ronin. And August was more than willing to play his part, though the price he paid was a bit steeper than what I offered him for his cooperation. Destitution is an excellent motivator. And now that I have proof of your treachery, I can finally silence your supporters in Delos."

"What are you talking about?"

Envy, slithery and sharp, snaked through his brother's eyes, his calm control abandoned. "You think I haven't heard the whispers? From multiple corners of not only the colonies, but that fucking Imperial Court? From High Councilors who've pledged fealty to our family? I am the *second* son. The weak-minded spare. Your shadow stretched over me all the way across the sea, despite your crime. They may have dreamed of installing you in my place, but they won't abide outright treason against the throne."

Tristan dipped his forehead against his arms and laughter *did* overtake him. "You've been playing me this entire time. You know, some part of me suspected. I should've known better than to question my instincts where you're concerned. What was the point of those attacks throughout the city?"

Eamon swished a palm. "Theatrics and confusion. Even when you're gone, I'll still have the *real* Teles Chrysos to deal with. Any humans who might have considered supporting them will think twice when they remember the destruction the group has wrought throughout their precious *colonies*." Eamon stood, tucking the necklace into his pocket. "And the delightful cherry atop this particular sundae was learning that your precious little human is the Savior Sister who's been restoring my obliviates. Did you know?"

Tristan clenched his jaw, fisted his hands at his sides. Eamon cocked his head, reading the answer in Tristan's defiant silence.

"What do you mean, *your* obliviates?" Tristan growled.

Eamon snickered and shook his head. "You'll see. Depending on how long I let you live." His hazel eyes blazed with renewed menace. "I did consider killing her, you know. Right in front of you on that stage. But where would be the fun in that? Tartarus will tear her apart. And there's not a fucking *thing* that you can do about it."

Tristan's rage bucked as Eamon's cruel laughter pelted him. His brother sauntered away, leaving Tristan alone with his thoughts. His regrets.

He'd been so incredibly foolish to think he could outmaneuver his twisted brother. He hung his head between his knees.

And now Eamon had ripped away Tristan's *ma'anyu*. Tristan hadn't even told her that he loved her. Why hadn't he just said the fucking words?

History repeating itself.

Cassandra was right though. This wasn't over. Not by a long shot.

Tristan would find a way out of this.

And when he did, he would bathe Ethyrios in his brother's blood.

Tristan didn't know how he'd managed to fall asleep. Perhaps the weight of his crushing desire for vengeance had dragged him into a restorative slumber.

Though he felt anything *but* restored when he was awakened by a strange prickle of energy.

Something electric that made his feathers stand on end.

He shot from the floor and surveyed the empty cell, then stepped towards the bars and angled his head to gaze down the dark, silent hallway.

He turned away from the warded iron, about to retake his slumped position against the back wall when a glow pierced the edges of his vision.

A seed of multi-colored light appeared before him, floating in the still air, then widened into a hazy circle.

A pair of blinding white wings with iridescent rainbow feathers pushed through, and Tristan fell to his knees, his fragile heart splitting in two.

She was even more devastating than she'd been as a human, lit with an inner glow that haloed her honeyed hair and shone from her indigo eyes. Her simple white trench coat didn't seem to fit her new ethereal countenance.

Tristan croaked out a choked whisper. "How did you… What are you…"

"Hello again, Rebel Prince," Ione said with a beatific smile. The faded red scar bisecting her palm whipped his pulse into a galloping frenzy as she reached for him, pulling him on shaky feet towards the rapidly fading portal.

"I am the Delphine.

"Welcome to the Teles Chrysos."

# CHAPTER
# FIFTY-TWO

A HARSH, ORANGE GLOW BLOOMED behind Cassandra's swollen eyelids.

She cracked an eye open, assaulted by a slash of blindingly bright light. She snapped the eye shut and groaned as her head, her entire body, throbbed in endless waves of dull, nagging pain.

She managed to tuck her arms and push her broken body from the hard floor, and her torso swayed as she peeled back her lids.

Blinking at the jarring red light, she leaned against a slab of ebony stone topped with a thin mattress and twisted white blankets.

Had she been sleeping in this bed? And had she somehow fallen out of it?

She placed a hand against the flimsy mattress and pushed herself upright. She tried to stand, but her protesting head forced her back down onto the bed.

After several minutes, the relentless pounding subsided enough for her to survey her surroundings. Not that there were many of them.

The small cell was barely larger than a broom closet, an alcove carved from black stone threaded with veins of glowing red crystal. The only furniture in the room, other than the bed, was a thin ledge against one wall with a metal chair beneath.

Bracing a hand against the wall as her head swam, the rushing pound of blood through her ears triggered a flashback.

A crowd snarling, roaring at her.

Tristan's wild eyes darting madly in his paralyzed face.

The word *Tartarus* falling from the Emperor's cold, cruel mouth.

She flopped onto the bed as the name of her new home reverberated in her rattling brain.

She was briefly thankful she was alone, before remembering Reena and Ronin had been brought to the prison as well.

She padded over to the thin slice of window at the top of her cell door, too small to see anything other than what was directly across from her cell—a smooth expanse of black wall.

A crashing sob wracked her mangled body, and she slumped back onto the bed, curling in on herself and noting her inmate number—161803—inked in blocky letters above the right breast pocket of her gray shirt. She rubbed at Tristan's mark, grasping for any comfort, wondering if the soldiers who'd dressed her had seen it.

She couldn't decide which was worse; the soul-rending separation from her *ma'anyu* or that she'd been dumped to rot with the most dangerous, deranged criminals in Ethyrios. How long until she'd meet her fellow inmates? A wail broke from her chest.

She dragged her hands through her blankets, wanting to curl up and sleep forever, when a glimmer caught her eye. An iridescent white feather kicked up from the blanket and floated through the air in lazy swipes before settling onto the floor.

She plucked it up, running her finger along its soft edge, her heart constricting. It felt exactly like running her fingers along Tristan's feathers, the night they'd—

A torrent of fire ripped down her back. As if someone were dragging a blazing poker along her shoulder blades and melting her skin apart.

She arched, screaming, and folded her arm behind herself. Her scream dissolved when her fingers brushed against tickling, downy feathers.

What in the name of Stygios?

She pulled at one of the feathers and the pain was so intense, she broke out in a cold sweat, trying to catch breaths that suddenly seemed far too shallow.

The magic in her veins pulsed and sparkled, easing her pain into another sensation entirely.

Transformation.

Her eyes squeezed shut as a heavy pounding assaulted her head, as if all the blood in her body was attempting escape through her eggshell skull.

The pounding stopped abruptly, replaced by whispers, moans, echoes of shouting.

Where was that coming from?

When she opened her eyes, the room snapped into sharp focus, a stunning clarity she'd never experienced.

She peered through the rectangular window and was shocked that she could plainly see the texture of every glimmering red seam in the stone across from her cell, even from her vantage point on the bed.

She hyperventilated as she realized the sounds were prisoners in the surrounding cells. How was she able to hear them so clearly?

A new power coursed through her veins, wind tickling her insides. Curious to break free of its new master. But it sputtered out as quickly as it had stirred to life. Stifled, no doubt, by the elemental magic suppressant that flowed through the very air of the prison.

She pitched forward onto the bed as crawling, poking swipes rippled down her back. Something pushing against her skin.

She screamed again, but not at the pain. There was no pain. Her entire body had gone numb and tingly.

Like when an arm she'd slept on all night rioted against its wake-up call.

No, she was screaming at the squelching sounds of her skin ripping apart.

Two supremely heavy weights burst from her back, shredding her shirt to ribbons and pitching her forward onto the bed, heaving and topless. Wet warmth trickled down her ribs, and red spots stained the white blankets.

She groaned as she tucked her arms beneath her, struggling to sit upright as the oppressive weight on her back tugged at her broken skin. As if it were trying to help her up.

A flash of rainbow colors twinkled in her peripheral vision as she coaxed her uncooperative body into a seated position, then glanced over her shoulders.

Two beautiful, iridescent white wings unfurled from her back.

The sparkling feathers rustled, whispering secrets. Repeating the vows she and Tristan had made to each other the night they'd consummated their relationship. After they'd shared each other's blood.

*I'm yours, Tristan.*

*I'm yours too, Cassandra.*

*Ma'anyu.*

Unbreakable.

Tristan had Turned Cassandra Fae.

# ACKNOWLEDGEMENTS

The Dunning-Kruger Effect: a psychological phenomenon in which people who have low levels of knowledge or ability in a specific area tend to overestimate their knowledge or ability in that area.

That was me writing the first book in The Memory Puller Series.

And that was most decidedly *not* me writing this second book, which seemed infinitely more difficult. The only thing that made the task feel a little less daunting is the village of supporters I must thank below.

Of course, I'll always begin with Mark—my supportive, unflappable husband. I apologize for all the nights and weekends I ignored you. I promise those sacrifices will be worth it. I love you, I love you, *I love you.*

To Susan, for your incomparable editorial feedback and insight. You asked all the right, tough questions and I'm so thankful for the push. The end result is a thousand times better than I ever imagined.

To Noah, for your keen eye with prose and for all those helpful cuts you made "for the sake of the sexy."

To Rena, I didn't think it was possible for me to love a book cover more than I loved the one for *The Memory Puller*, but you proved me wrong. The magic you work with a few simple prompts never ceases to amaze me and I'm forever in awe of your artistry.

To Sally and Austen Marie, thank you for bringing my characters to such vivid, stunning life! I stan you both SO HARD and cannot wait to work with you again.

And of course, I would be nowhere with you, my cherished reader. In the acknowledgments for *The Memory Puller*, I promised you more adventures with these characters and I hope I've delivered on that promise! And please know, there is so much more to come. I can't wait to go back to Ethyrios with you.